OCT 16

SHOOT 'EM UP

Maisie McGrane Mysteries by Janey Mack

Time's Up

Choked Up

Shoot 'em Up

SHOOT 'EM UP

Janey Mack

KENSINGTON BOOKS
www.kensingtonbooks.com

KENSINGTON BOOKS are published by

Kensington Publishing Corp.
119 West 40th Street
New York, NY 10018

All Kensington titles, imprints, and distributed lines are available at special quantity discounts for bulk purchases for sales promotion, premiums, fund-raising, educational, or institutional use.

Special book excerpts or customized printings can also be created to fit specific needs. For details, write or phone the office of the Kensington Sales Manager: Kensington Publishing Corp., 119 West 40th Street, New York, NY 10018. Attn. Sales Department. Phone: 1-800-221-2647.

Kensington and the K logo Reg. U.S. Pat. & TM Off.

eISBN-13: 978-1-61773-695-7
eISBN-10: 1-61773-695-3
First Kensington Electronic Edition: October 2016

ISBN-13: 978-1-61773-694-0
ISBN-10: 1-61773-694-5
First Kensington Trade Paperback Printing: October 2016

10 9 8 7 6 5 4 3 2 1

Printed in the United States of America

For Dad,
who carries my heart in his

Acknowledgments

Mom, David, Jameson, Hud, and Grayson—for every big and little thing.

Dori, my brave and true friend.

The Home Team: Bob and Nicole, James, Polly Ringdahl, Barb Pearse, Georgann Shiely, Cristin Clark, Bob and Char, Beau Stadum.

A heartfelt thanks to the clever and canny Chris Keck.

Deepest gratitude to: Michael Fritz, Walker Hester, Dr. Greg Purchase, Mike Riche, and as always, Glen Schiffer.

And cheers to the crew who keep me going when I think I'm tapped out: Richard Avirett, Maegan Beaumont, Katherine Bohn, Will Champagne, James H. Carroll, Carl Dickey, Les Edgerton, Lincoln Farish, Connie Flynn, Mark Giarrusso, Jesse Gomez, Carlos Grieco, David Gryniewicz, Joe Hyne, Kathy Jund, James Kennedy, Christopher Ledoux, Emersen Lee, Marilyn Lichtenthal, Leo Louchios, Peter Brian MacDonald, Jon Mack, Mark Morrison, Leon O'Dell, Steve Ozbolt, Derek Park, Robert Pugh, Paul and Lori Renick, Michael Ring, AJ Rodriguez, Jeff Schoonover, Mark Siciliano, John Snyder, John Souerbry, Jennifer Steager, Dave Sutton.

Agent Laura Bradford, Editor Martin Biro, Production Editor Paula Reedy, Copy Editor Christy Phillippe, and Publicity Director Karen Auerbach.

Chapter 1

The siren bawled as Lee Sharpe, eyes flashing, grinning like a demon, loomed over my gurney. "Who stabbed you, Maisie?"

Sweat trickled down the hard planes of his face. He was in full SWAT battle rattle—balaclava down around his neck, Pro-Tech Tac 6 full-coverage vest, combat shirt, tactical pants, and a Sig Sauer .45. Delta helmet and rifle handed off before he got in the ambulance.

I tried to look as pathetic as possible from beneath the oxygen non-rebreather strapped on my face. Which wasn't too tough. The hilt of a five-inch SOG Seal Strike knife stuck out of my thigh, wrapped and packed courtesy of the newbie paramedic whom Lee had kicked to the front of the bus with the driver.

"Don't . . . know," I lied.

He looked away and ran a hand through his hair. "Christ."

The heavy plastic gear cases and oxygen tanks clattered and shook as the ambulance took a tire-squealing turn. Even though I was strapped down, I slid beneath the canvas belts, sucking in a breath through my teeth. The blade in my leg seared like molten steel.

Hank's Law Number Thirteen: Anyone can endure expected pain.

Frowning, Lee leaned in close. "Maisie?" He snapped his fingers in front of me. "Maisie? Can you hear me?"

"Yeah." *What's wrong?*

The heart monitor beeps started pinging double-time.

"Maisie?" He eased the mask off my face and bent low, eyes searching mine.

I swallowed. "Lee?"

He kissed me.

What the . . .

Not hard, not soft. Just bizarrely familiar.

Jaysus Criminey.

Before I could move my head away, he left me with a flick of his tongue across my upper lip.

Cinnamon.

"You kissed me!"

He replaced the oxygen mask over my nose and mouth. "You're delirious, babe. You don't even know who stabbed you."

You opportunistic sonuva—

He leaned back on the squad bench. "Don't remember, my ass."

A metallic roar ripped through the ambulance. Lee went airborne, slamming into the front partition. Canisters of oxygen snapped from their moorings, clanging into the gurney and the doors. Tools and boxes shot out of the cabinets. A heavy plastic case jumped the security rail and landed, crushing my legs and smashing the knife.

The ambulance convulsed and stopped dead. The siren kept wailing. I ran out of breath and quit shrieking.

Warm wet spread across my thigh.

Oh Jaysus.

My arms and legs were strapped down. I couldn't get the case off. "Lee!" I twisted my head frantically, trying to get a look at him.

He was slumped on the floor, equipment littered around him. "Lee!"

He blinked awake, eyes unfocused.

I shivered. "Help me."

He rolled onto all fours and used the wall to pull himself upright. He staggered over.

"Move it." My voice was a whisper to my own ears.

Trying to keep his feet, he lifted the heavy plastic case off my leg. The knife had gone sideways, the packing around it soaked bright red with blood.

My body was ice cold. I panted from the chill.

Lee squinted and shook his head. Hand over hand, he applied pressure at my groin and yelled at the front of the 'bus. "Medic! Get back here!" He stared at me, pupils dilated with concussion. "Talk to me, Maisie."

I opened my mouth but no sound came out. I felt floaty and light.

He swayed and yelled at the EMTs again.

A steady stream of blood trickled down Lee's ear onto his shoulder.

I smiled.

Funny, really, him trying to stop my bleeding when he has his own to worry ab—

"Suffering Christ!" My brother Cash's voice jackhammered my eardrums. "T-boned. What kind of asswipe EMT takes a live intersection at forty miles per hour?"

"Shhh," Mom said.

"How's Lee?" Da asked.

"Concussion, handful of stitches," Cash said. "Nothin'."

My eyes were glued shut. I raised my hand and set off a series of electronic beeps.

"Maisie?" Mom pressed my left arm down. I raised my right. "You're okay, baby. You're in the ICU at Rush University Medical Center. You were stabbed in the leg. The ambulance was in an accident. You're out of surgery, and you're going to be fine."

"I know," I croaked, rubbing my eyes. My throat hurt.

Da put his hand on the back of Cash's neck. "Tell the lads she's awake."

Mom waited until the door closed behind my brother. She laid a hand on my cheek and leaned close, her voice low and serious. "You're in a significant amount of legal trouble, darling. Do you understand what I'm saying to you?"

"Yes." My mind was furry and my mouth tasted of chemicals and unspoken lies.

"I've called in a fixer. We'll get you out of this."

Da leaned over and stared me right in the eyes. Deep grooves of worry were etched at his eyes and mouth. "Keep your yap shut. Eh, *a ghrá?*"

Aww, shite.

I nodded.

He kissed my forehead. I turned my head toward Mom, but before I could tell her I was cold, I fell asleep again.

A hospital room is never completely dark. Maybe that's so you don't panic and think that you've died. I knew I wasn't dead.

Yet.

My large private room—which felt more like a sterile Scandinavian hotel room—was filled to the gills with my family. Hospital rules were irrelevant to the McGranes. Cops and lawyers were above the laws of mere mortals.

The only man I wanted to see wasn't there. Still, I couldn't help but smile.

Da sat in the bedside chair, reading a case file. My brothers Flynn and Rory were at the built-in bureau, sifting through cards and flowers from my assumed "get well" wishers. Wedged together on the couch, Mom and the twins—Declan and Daicen—argued in hushed voices. Cash, on the other side of my bed, was setting up a portable electronic station complete with power strip and chargers.

My five older brothers were carbon copies of Da: dark-haired, dark-eyed, hard-muscled men imbued with the treacherous black-Irish combination of charm, piss, and vinegar and the blasphemously un-Irish ability to tan.

"Not while your sister's in the middle of this," Mom said. "Talk about an obvious conflict of interest."

"Yeah? But for how long?" Declan put his hands behind his head. "Who's the fixer?"

Daicen adjusted his wristwatch. "Let it lie, Dec."

"Like hell. We're taking the case."

"Silly me," Mom said. "I thought you aspired to make partner one—"

For a Few Dollars More flashed on the hospital's flat screen, theme blaring. "Got it," Cash said loudly, turning the volume down. "She's set up. I need a chair. And a beer."

"Get me one while you're up," I rasped.

"About time you're awake," Flynn said.

Mom came over and held a plastic cup and straw to my mouth. "How are you, honey?"

Kitten weak and toy-scissors sharp.

"A-okay," I said, taking the cup from her hand.

Funny, it didn't look like it weighed six pounds.

I took a sip. Flat 7UP never tasted so good. I drank half, then set it on the tray table with nary a tremor.

Flynn put his hands on the Formica footboard of my hospital bed. "So, Ginger Snap, what I want to know is, how in hell did you manage to get stabbed during a Class X Armed Robbery?"

"Not me," Cash said. "I just want to know how you hooked up with a Serbian crime lord in the first place."

Neat-o. Interrogation by torture committee.

The twins knew better than to ask a question without knowing the answer, and instead eyed me for tells like hawkish gamblers. Rory kept his back to me, messing with the flowers.

"I . . ."

"Leave her alone," Rory said. "She's safe as sleeved aces, now. That's what matters."

A rap sounded on the door.

"The fixer," Cash said and answered it.

A lightly tanned man with flaxen hair in his early fifties wearing a slim-cut Kiton suit strode into the room. Walt Sawyer. The Bureau of Organized Crime's Special Unit commander. He also ran an elite and secret squad of undercover police officers.

Mom's fixer.

My boss.

Ah, the irony. Painfully delicious.

All my life I wanted to be a cop, like my da, like my brothers. And now that I was one, I couldn't say a thing.

My father believed I was too reckless to be on the job. So much so, he'd had me expelled from the Police Academy on a technicality. For my own safety as well as my potential partner's, of course. *He might have had a small, though insignificant point.*

Walt Sawyer, however, saw me as a perfect recruit for deep-cover work—one with all the training and none of the acquired "tells" of a police officer. Stannislav Renko and his chop-shop operation had been my first assignment.

And my clan would never know. Could never know.

Da stood. Mom went to Sawyer, hands extended, and kissed him on both cheeks. "Thank you so much for coming, Walt."

I could fairly hear Flynn, Rory, and Da's teeth grinding together. Not much got homicide cops hotter under the collar than working cases only to have them yanked away at resolution. One of Sawyer's specialties.

"You were right to call me, July." Sawyer crossed the room to shake hands with Da over my bed. "Conn."

Rory's eyes flickered over Sawyer in disgust. He plucked the card from a vase of a dozen sun-gold roses. "Who's Paul Renick?" he asked me.

Who?

"The news director at the *Chicago Sentinel*," Sawyer answered. "Your sister's freelance employer."

My hastily assembled cover.

It's coming back to me now.

I wasn't up for this. Not by a long shot.

And Walt knew it, bless his deceptive heart. "As you know," he said, "Maisie was injured in the midst of a Class X Armed Robbery. While Renick had assigned her to write a story on chop shops, he was ignorant of the relationship Maisie had cultivated with Serbian enforcer Stannislav 'The Bull' aka 'The Butcher' Renko." Sawyer smiled winningly at Mom. "I've spoken with the state's attorney. As long as Maisie voluntarily complies with a suppression order, he will forgo all interest in her as a witness, accessory, or accomplice."

Da and the boys looked at me as though I'd turned scarlet and sprouted Hellboy horns.

"Seriously? You're working at that goddamn rag?" Flynn said.

"Jaysus feck." Rory shook his head.

Lovely, really, how they're not bothered with the whole Serbian killer bit.

"As policeman and attorneys, you are not unfamiliar with those who bear grudges." Sawyer passed a measured look over each McGrane before continuing. "Maisie cannot afford the faintest hint of impropriety, and frankly, neither can I. There will be no interference or reexamination. You are all going to let this sleeping dog lie. Agreed?"

Like that's going to happen.

My five brothers reluctantly nodded. "Agreed."

"May I speak with Maisie alone for a moment?" Sawyer asked.

"Yeah." Da started toward the door, the rest of them following in his wake.

Mom paused to give Sawyer a squeeze on the forearm. "Thank you."

"No trouble, July." He smiled. "Truly."

Mom's lashes fanned her cheeks. I watched him watch her leave, still smiling.

Sawyer took Da's chair next to the bed and put his hand over mine. "Congratulations are in order. Stannislav Renko's chop-shop organization has been effectively dismantled, and we have four solved murders in the prosecution loop, as well as numerous arrests."

"Stannis escaped," I said.

"No matter." Sawyer sat back in the chair. "This is Chicago. Renko's illicit connection to the mayor would've trumped any charges. Not to mention, not a single worm has turned. His barbarous brutality seems to have left an indelible impression."

"I failed, sir."

"Hardly. Overall Operation Steal-Tow was a success. Your work garnered new insight for the Bureau of Organized Crime into both the New York syndicate as well as Chicago's own mafioso Veteratti family. Special Unit now has a line into the Grieco cartel. A strong showing for a veteran, much less a rookie." He tipped his foxy, clever head to one side. "Did Renko stab you?"

No sir. Hank Bannon, the love of my life, did.

Walt pressed his fingertips together. "The two of you were emotionally intimate."

"Yes." Stannis was charismatic, handsome, and charming. *Until he put a gun to my head.*

"Stannis wanted to take me back to Serbia." I swallowed hard. "One of his . . . er . . . men disagreed and threw the knife in my leg."

"Forcing Renko to leave you behind."

Yes, thank God, Hank, and the baby Jesus.

I nodded.

A small smile played at the corner of his lips. "A providential and beneficent escape. The BOC would have been hard-pressed to get you back on American soil."

Yeah, I've got more good fortune than a pack of Lucky Strikes.

"Any news of Renko, sir?" *Or Hank?* I raised the cup of 7UP to my lips. My hand shook.

"Gone to ground, I'm afraid. Don't expect to see hide nor hair of him or his team for a month or two." He smiled. "Your family would be proud of you, if they knew, Maisie."

"Thank you, sir, but I think you've mistaken proud with punitive."

Sawyer chuckled. "Take your time recovering. I prefer a formidable hundred percent to a lagging seventy-five." He stood. "Special Unit's erased all traces of your presence at Renko's penthouse. Your clothes and incidentals were boxed and placed in the trunk of your car in his parking garage. *Chicago Sentinel* credentials in the glove box."

He removed a black velvet bag from his suit coat pocket and placed it on the tray table. "Spoils of war."

He opened the door, stepped into the mob of my brothers, and shut it behind him.

I shook the bag out into my lap. The Cartier diamond earrings and Tank wedding band Stannis had given me as well as all my own jewelry I'd brought to the penthouse. At the bottom of the bag were Stannislav's stainless Aquanaut Patek Philippe watch, his thick John Hardy necklace, and a pair of platinum and diamond cuff links.

Spoils of war, indeed. A bit of a shocker they're letting me keep the earrings and wedding band, but Stannis's leftover loot?

I put the jewelry back in the bag and slipped it under my pillow. Stashing it was going to be another issue altogether, as I hadn't yet gotten out of bed.

Cash came back in, Flynn behind him. They set up on either side of me.

"We've got first shift." Flynn laid a hand on my head and mussed my hair. "No questions."

Cash turned the spaghetti western on and up. "Until after you get outta here, maybe."

"Knock it off," Flynn said.

I closed my eyes. Bullets and bad thoughts swarmed in my head like cranked-up yellow jackets.

A nurse came in with a paper cup of pain pills and the world became a quiet and pleasant place again.

Chapter 2

Day four. I couldn't bear to lie around, but it hurt like a bitch to get up. The ten feet to the bathroom had me whistle-breathing through my teeth.

Mom took the rare vacation day from Corrigan, Douglas, and Pruitt and spent it with me, steering clear of any dangerous conversation by enlisting traveling-spa services, adhering to Grandma Pruitt's adage: When in doubt, pretty it out.

In other words—fix yourself up so you don't feel so damn pathetic.

By the time she left, I'd suffered through an awkward shower, blow-out, mani-pedi, and makeup application. And yes, I actually did feel better.

Talk about all dressed up and no place to go.

I'd be suffering the night with my most torturous of brothers, Cash.

He sat next to me, knees bouncing, knuckles cracking, chewing gum. Irritatingly mobile as we watched Fox News. He hit Mute. "You gotta tell me."

"No questions."

"It's not about that. It's about Hank."

I closed my eyes. "Fire away."

"Didja guys break up over Renko?"

"No."

"Then where is he? No flowers, no visits, no calls?"

I felt an ever-expanding bubble the size of a yoga ball in my chest.

I wanted to spill. Everything. To tell Cash I'd played Stannislav Renko's beard to hide his sexual relationship with the mayor of Chicago from the NY syndicate, the Veteratti mob, and his Serbian crime lord uncle, Goran Slajic.

That Hank worked for Slajic as Stannis's protector. And mine.

He'd installed his own men in Stannis's operation to watch over me. He'd saved my life and my cover before smuggling Stannis back to Serbia.

Instead, I sighed. "He's out of the country."

"Hanging with The Butcher." Cash shook his head. "Feck. If you had balls, Snap, they'd be titanium-plated."

If you only knew.

His phone gave a series of sonar pings. "Cripes! Is it really six thirty?" He clicked it off, shoved it in his pocket, and stood up. "Okay. Peace out."

"Really?" I said, trying to keep the hope out of my voice.

Oh, happy day! Alone time.

"Well, it's not like you're gonna die or anything. Check you." And with a parting slug to the shoulder, he was gone. Leaving the door, naturally, wide open.

Didn't matter. Some nurse would be in to bother me in thirty minutes or less. Sooner if I fell asleep. As if that would happen. I swiped through my phone and the two different message sites Hank had set up to contact me if things were dire.

Zip.

"Maisie?" Lee Sharpe knocked on the open door holding two paper bags. He was wearing blue jeans, black T-shirt, and a leather jacket. Clean-cut, clean-shaven, there was still something about him that screamed one hundred percent badass. "You decent?"

"Er . . . Rarely," I said. "What are you doing here?"

"Thanks, I'd love to come in." He closed the door, walked over to the bed, and took a good long look at my face.

Which made me love my mother even more. Just because I was in love with Hank didn't mean I wanted to look like dog hurl in front of anyone.

"Funny seeing you here, Mr. Sharpe. I thought you were waiting until . . . Hmm. How did you put it a week ago?" I tapped my finger against my cheek. "Oh yeah. Until I came to the realization that you're the sexiest MF I'd ever met and called you."

Lee shrugged. "I figured with your leg and all, you couldn't reach the phone."

I tucked my forearm tight to my chest T. rex–style and waved my fingers in mock futility at the iPhone less than a foot away from me on the wheeled table. "If only I could call Lee. . . ."

He gave a growly chuckle that would have made plenty of women weak in the knees.

"Thanks for saving my life, by the way."

"Anytime." He let his eyes drift down to stare at my raised leg. "What's the prognosis?"

"Dr. Williams said I'm one of the unlucky-luckies."

"Oh?"

"The stab wound was a gimme. It was the artery puncture from the ambulance accident that was the sonuvagun. Light duty for two weeks. Whatever I can stand after that."

Lee dropped into the chair next to the bed. "Pretty painless lesson, when you think about it."

"Tell that to the OxyContin."

He reached into one of the paper bags and pulled out a couple of Coors. "I know you're on painkillers and all, but it didn't seem to hurt Amy Winehouse . . . Oh wait . . ."

I reached for it and he jerked it away in tease, then popped the top and handed it over.

"Saint Sharpe." The bottle was still ice cold. "Mmm. Why is the first sip of beer so good?"

"Anticipation gratified." Out of the other bag came two cardboard cartons from The Scout restaurant. Grilled cheese sandwiches and tomato basil dipping sauce.

"Wow. Talk about feeling comforted."

Lee grinned at me and took a bite.

I held out through the beer, half the sandwich, and preseason football small talk before cracking. "What's my lesson learned?"

He crumpled up his wrappers and opened another Coors before answering, "That you're out of your league in Special Unit."

I laughed. "I think I came out all right."

"Renko's not going to leave any loose ends hanging around." Lee leaned forward, elbows on his knees, and casually tossed a brick of Black Cat firecrackers on the campfire. "Put in for an immediate and permanent transition to desk duty."

"Or?"

Lee's cheek twitched. His eyes went flat. "I'll have your family do it for you."

What the . . .

"Purposefully revealing an undercover field agent? A career-ending lawsuit will be the least of your worries." I scoffed. "I'll take you down so hard you'll bounce."

"Give it your best shot, Bae."

Holy cat. He's serious.

"Hold up, cowboy. Who are you to tell me what to do?"

"A goddamn Marine and a CPD SWAT squad leader."

Well, that explains the chest-bursting, swinging-dick attitude.

I broke eye contact before I broke his nose with my beer bottle and glanced up at the TV. Right into the face of the only human being I truly loathed.

Talbott Cottle Coles, the mayor of Chicago. Six feet tall, he weighed in at a smoker-slim 165 pounds, with a Zoom! white smile, Botoxed forehead, and salt-and-pepper hair that seemed to grow darker at each appearance.

He was playing to a full house today on an outdoor stage set up in front of City Hall. The street, cordoned off, was packed with supporters. Blue nylon AFL-CIO jackets out in full force.

I don't know if it was Lee throwing his weight around, the Oxy, the beer, or just the sight of that self-righteous bastard that kicked my ire up and disconnected my mouth from my brain. "I'm a hell of a lot harder than you think, Lee."

He smirked. "Sure, Bae."

Come a lil' closer and let me wipe that smug smile off your face.

"Six days ago, I cut off Coles's little finger with a cleaver while Stannislav Renko held him down."

Lee squinted, trying to find the punch line. Only there wasn't one. Amazing, really, what you're capable of when your life and someone else's were on the line. If I hadn't done it, Coles wouldn't be alive today.

But Lee didn't get to know that.

I tipped my head toward the television. Coles's bandaged left hand hung at his side while he waved to the crowd from behind the podium.

Lee turned to me, eyes narrowed. "Bullshit."

"Ask Coles. Or Sawyer."

"Bullshit," he said, less certain.

"Heck, ask him." I pointed at a massive black man in the center of the crowd in front of the stage. He was wearing, as always, the Coles-mandated, ridiculous 1920s-style chauffeur attire. "Poppa Dozen. Coles's driver."

Ignoring my confession, Lee got up and stepped to the TV. "That's a class-A fuckup right there. His driver's blocking the point bodyguard's line of sight." He outlined Coles's protection detail in diamond formation from amidst the sea of citizens. Obvious from their black-suited, still bodies and swiveling heads. Lee shook his head. "One of the many reasons SWAT hates him."

"Oh?"

"Coles's private protective detail always changes on the fly— going places that haven't been advanced. Extra people in the car, heading into the crowd to shake hands. Shit like that. Guy's got a hard-on for screwing with the CPD."

"But if he has a private detail—"

"CPD's at the bottom of the food chain. SWAT recommends four snipers, Coles agrees to one. Then they hamstring him by demanding he follow Coles's team lead's directives. Asshole egomaniac won't even wear a vest."

"You sure?" I said. Coles seemed a bit meatier than normal. "Looks like he has one on today."

"I'm guessing new team lead or viable death threat."

I turned up the volume on the socialist pap Sean Hannity would be shredding in the following minutes. Coles stood at the podium, heiress wife, Zara, slightly behind his right side in a blush-colored Alexander McQueen pantsuit. The mayor raised his right fist, thumb tip up, gesturing for emphasis. "While my administration, in conjunction with the CPD, has made significant inroads into the criminal activity—"

Sure, you have.

"Golly," I said, "you don't think underreporting the number of homicides by incorrectly classifying sixteen percent as 'death investigations' had anything to do with it, do you?"

Lee opened another beer and handed it over. "Hard to build up momentum for a presidential run when you're the mayor of Murder Capital, USA."

Coles leaned over the podium in a sorrowful pose. "This weekend we witnessed yet another tragedy on our streets. The separate shooting deaths of not one, but two innocent teenagers and the wounding of a five-year-old boy in West Englewood. Our citizens deserve to live happy, healthy lives of opportunity. We must stop the lawless use of firearms!"

Blergehdy blerg blerg. I took a swig of beer.

"I've just signed a budget addendum," the mayor said, "adding fifty badly needed patrol officers to impact zones on the South and West Side."

The camera cut to a wide-angle crowd shot.

"But more than cops on the beat"—up came Coles's fist for emphasis—"we need community action and stronger gun laws to take back our city."

Yeah, because criminals really respond to stricter laws.

On-screen, a scrawny guy in a black polo shirt and khakis suddenly raised a fat black pistol. Coles stepped back from the podium, palms up.

Coles spun and dove on top of his wife, crashing them to the ground, covering her with his body a split second before the protective detail blanketed them.

The shooter landed two rounds into the podium as Poppa Dozen stepped behind the shooter, extended his arm, and blasted him in the back of the head with a shiny blue-black Taurus revolver.

The crowd erupted into an instant panic, scrambling and screaming.

Lee and I stared at each other. "Holy shit," he said.

"Yeah."

His phone was ringing and buzzing before the news crew synched up to replay the attempt.

"Lock it down," Lee said into the phone. "I'll be there in ten." He turned to me. "Gotta go, Bae."

Take me with you! "You do realize that *Bae* is Danish for 'poop.'"

Lee shrugged a wide shoulder. "None of the other girls seem to mind."

"Wow." I nodded. "Now, that's cute. Work pretty well for you?"

"It doesn't hurt. . . ." Lee bent over and kissed me on the cheek. "Bless your little Irish heart, and every other Irish part."

He chucked me under the chin and left.

Chapter 3

The assassination attempt was on every website and television and radio station throughout the country and the world. Slo-mo of Coles protecting his wife. Over and over and over.

Uuuuuugh.

Karma wasn't just lying down on the job; she was passed out on the floor letting Coles draw a permanent marker mustache on her face.

I couldn't bear it a second longer and switched to Apple TV and *Whitechapel* on Prime.

Around eight forty-five, half-rock star, half-super-nerd Dr. Williams came in and gave me the less-than-stellar news that he was releasing me late that afternoon. I'd been hoping for another day or two in my sterile prison of too much light and noise before my impending interrogation. The McGrane clan could break *Unbroken*'s Louis Zamperini in six weeks. Me? I'd shatter like cheap glass in sixty minutes or less.

I watched the clock, dreading each hop of the minute hand.

Nine twenty-five a.m.

The twins were the only ones who hadn't pulled guard duty. A safe bet they'd be here before noon, salvaging their rep with the family that yes, indeed, they had visited their poor baby sister.

Nine forty.

Any minute now.

A rap sounded on the door.

"Come in," I said.

The door swung open. An attractive, masculine-looking forty-something blonde in a violet bandage dress stepped into the room. Mob princess Violetta Veteratti.

Nostradamus, I'm not.

Consigliore Jimmy the Wolf was tight on her heels. The six-four, 280-pound enforcer bore an enormous fruit basket in his left hand. His right arm held a squat cardboard box tight to his chest, tied with string. The Wolf held out the basket for me to see before setting it on the bureau, mashing the vases of flowers together. "The Syndicate wishes you a full and speedy recovery." He gave me a surreptitious wink, skirted the bed, and still holding the box, pulled the armchair around for Vi.

She sat and crossed her long legs. "I appreciate you smoothin' things over with Renko for Eddie."

"Smoothing." I *guess that's one way to put it.* "Saving your brother's life" *would be another.*

Eddie Veteratti helped Coles hire a hitter to clip me. And while I'd held Stannis back from killing them both, it didn't mean I didn't hold a grudge.

I shrugged. "I'm sweet that way."

"You need anything, you come to me." She tapped her chest with a square-tipped nail. "Eddie's in Hazelden. Rehab. I'm running Chicago now."

"Bittersweet congratulations," I said, meaning it.

That stopped her. "Yeah, well, blood costs."

I nodded. "Sorry the heist didn't come off."

"Deals go bad and guys go down." She waved a hand. "It's business. So. You steppin' into Renko's shoes?"

Holy cat.

A free pass into the Syndicate. Talk about redemption.

"I'm not sure," I hedged. "I haven't talked to Stannis or seen the full extent of the CPD's damage to his infrastructure."

She glanced at Jimmy the Wolf, standing between her and the door, still holding the box. "How'd you skate? I figured to see you in bracelets with one at the door."

"I'm a freelance reporter for the *Chicago Sentinel.* Covers a great many sins."

"Oh yeah?" she asked. "Whaddya write?"

"Obituaries."

Vi gave a snort-laugh.

"My byline is 'Staff.'"

"Nice cover." The Wolf shook his head. "Friggin' Bannon's as sly as a spook."

"I'm starting to see why Hank's gone cock-eyed over you." Vi curled a finger and Jimmy the Wolf set the box on the wheeled table in front of me.

"Thank you?" I said.

"It's not from me." She stood and smoothed the violet fabric over her hips. "Lemme know if you and Renko wanna renew the Chicago deal."

"I need to see how things shake out."

"It's a limited time offer, kid."

"Six months?" I pressed.

"Three."

Jimmy the Wolf got the door and we both watched the new boss of Chicago walk out the door on the sharpest stilettos I'd ever seen.

I lifted the box. A solid ten pounds. I set it back down, carefully unknotted the string, and opened it.

A white envelope rested on the nest of excelsior. Inside was a vintage-orange Monopoly *Get Out of Jail Free* card.

I flipped it over and read:

Quit.

H

Hank. My alpha archangel.

A drop of water landed on the envelope.

I put a hand to my cheek. I hadn't realized I was crying. I slipped the card back into the envelope and set it aside. I scooped out the top layer of packing material and jerked my hand back when my fingers felt the familiar thick lead-glass and wooden lid.

Oh no. Please, no.
I lifted the lid, even though I already knew the contents.
Human finger bones.
More than two hundred ivory pieces filled the jar. Some taken in warning, others in retribution. Stannislav The Butcher's legacy. His everything.
My ticket in or out of Slajic's organization.
Because Hank always had my six.
I pinched the bridge of my nose and tried not to think. About anything.
Everything went back in the box, my fingers numb and clumsy as I knotted the string.
Jaysus Criminey.
By weight, those bones equaled a metric fuck-ton of evidence. Talbott Cottle Coles's finger aka traceable DNA was in there.
A rivulet of revulsion oozed down my spine.
Hank had trusted Violetta Veteratti to keep it safe.
Last time I checked, I lived in a house with four policemen and a former prosecutor.
Where the hell am I going to put it?

The twins—Declan, the devil, and Daicen, the saint—drew the short straw and came straight from court to pick me up at the hospital. Declan, perpetually in need of a haircut, maintained a style of mischievously rumpled. He snagged a Royal Verano pear from the fruit basket and left to hit on a pretty RN.
Where Declan was haphazard, Daicen was precise. Impeccably tailored, dark hair slicked back, shoes polished to a mirror shine. He pulled the cards from the flowers and noted what they were on the backs with his fountain pen so I could write thank-yous. Then he sent the posies via candy striper to the cancer ward before helping me pack.
"What's in the box?" Dacien asked.
A world of hurt.
"Candy jar. From work."

Daicen shook his head. "Not content to be bit once, stepping on the adder's tail surely will make it happen again."

What the hell kind of proverb is that?

My face scrunched as I deciphered the riddle. "Oh. Yeah. The *Sentinel*."

He laid a finger against his nose and winked. "I'll fetch the car." He picked up the fruit basket and gestured to the box. "Shall I?"

"Sure," I said, as casual as all get-out.

An orderly got me into a wheelchair and we waited.

Declan reappeared with the RN. She dismissed the orderly and dumped a plastic bag of my admittance belongings—clothes stiff with dried blood—and the folder of postop instructions into my lap, flirting as hard as she could with my brother.

Why yes, chopped liver IS my middle name.

The elevator ride was worse than an eHarmony commercial. Poor kid. She wouldn't rate more than two dates.

Daicen waited patiently next to his Audi in the circle.

He helped me out of the wheelchair and into the passenger's seat, closing the door behind me. Skirting the car, he took the suitcase from our brother's hand and put it in the trunk while the RN gave Declan her number.

Stannis's legacy sat on the floor next to Declan and the Chicago Syndicate's fruit basket.

Don't look. Don't look. Don't look.

"We've got you quite a present, Snap. Haven't we, Dai?"

Daicen's lips tightened.

"Oh?" I said.

"Christo Keck is our new client."

"Who?" *Jaysus Criminey. Can't a girl catch a break around here?*

Declan leaned forward and nuzzled his chin into my neck. "Tsk-tsk. Mustn't fib when we're going to take the heat off of you getting stabbed. Tell us about him."

Gee, let's see. Christo Keck ran Renko's prime chop shop. Oh yeah, and a couple of weeks ago, he helped me dispose of a body.

I swallowed hard. "He's guilty."

Declan laughed. "They always are."

"I can see why Mom has difficulty reconciling your aversion to law school." Daicen gave me a sideways look. "While collaborating with the same criminal element, we receive significantly higher compensation and suffer far fewer workplace injuries."

"Ha-ha."

"Point!" Declan ground his knuckles into my head. "You know we're here to take you *home* home, not Bannon's place, right?"

I nodded. Nicer to be coddled by the clan than hobbling around Hank's place, alone, fretting over him. "Uh . . . Hey guys? Do you think we could swing by Stannis's penthouse and pick up my car?" I let my voice go soft. "I'd rather not tempt Flynn and Rory with the chance to nose around."

"Certainly," Daicen said.

I opened the sealed plastic bag of the stuff I'd had on me at the time of the accident and rummaged around the blood-stained clothes and gear until I found the key fob to the Dodge Hellcat SRT. I handed it back to Declan.

"Whoa. It's true?" he breathed. "You let Bannon buy you a car?"

No, I hadn't, actually, but after the knife-in-the-leg incident, the chances of getting Hank to take it back were nonexistent.

"When's the wedding?"

"Funny how you guys are in such a rush to marry me off to a man none of you want me to date."

"Dai and I aren't on Team LEO, Snap. I, for one, welcome the opportunity to represent your future husband in any and all of his mercenary misadventures."

Cute.

I directed Daicen to Stannis's penthouse and told him the underground garage entry code.

Declan whistled as we pulled up next to the car. "Hell-o, Black Beauty."

"Easy, pally," I warned. "She's got a stonking V-8 Hemi and more guts than you."

He grinned and gave me a salute that ended in one finger. He got into the car and gunned the engine.

Daicen turned to me. "Would you rather I drive it home?"

I put my hand on his arm and squeezed. For Daicen to even offer was akin to loaning me a kidney. Declan drove like he dated: completely out of control. "Thanks, but one accident a week is about all I can handle."

"Are you all right, Maisie?" Daicen asked softly.

"Everything's aces."

He didn't believe me.

I didn't believe me, either.

It took me a solid six minutes to make it up the stairs to my bedroom. Thierry, our housekeeper/cook, offered to set up the guest room on the main floor, but I wanted to sleep in my own bed, and the more I walked, the faster I'd get back to one hundred percent formidable.

Yeah, baby.

Because what I was going to bring to Walt Sawyer was the brass fecking ring.

My room, pin-neat from my absence, was still wonderful; midcentury modern in rich taupes and grays with splashes of yellow. And I felt like a stranger in it.

I hobbled over to the bed and eased down. *Stupid ambulance driver.*

For the last month, I'd lived at Stannis's penthouse. Before that, Hank's. And now I was returning to the hotbed of Irish Catholic guilt and overprotective guard dogs. It was going to take some damn fancy footwork to keep my clan in the inky black bliss of unawareness.

Daicen, who kindly let me navigate the stairs solo, knocked on the door frame and came in with my suitcase and the box. He rolled the suitcase into the walk-in closet. "And this?"

The box.

"Nightstand?"

He tucked the box beneath the table farthest from the door

and took a seat in one of the mushroom-colored microfiber armchairs. He adjusted the crease in his suit pants and waited. I dry-swallowed an Oxy and closed my eyes. I wasn't sure for how long.

"One helluva car, Snap." Declan grinned from the doorway. "I wouldn't be giving it back, either."

Daicen glanced at his Rolex but said nothing.

"Funny thing . . ." Declan came in with a cardboard carton. "Aside from a pile of new clothes with the tags still on, I found this in your trunk." He dumped it out on the foot of my bed.

Time to lace up the ol' tap shoes.

As expected, I saw my Kimber-solo and Flashbang holster, ammo, and spare magazine, document scanner pen, signal detector watch, Swiss Army knife, and *Chicago Sentinel* credentials.

It was the pair of Belgian FN Herstal tactical Five-seveN MK2 handguns with additional mags and laser sights that popped my eyes saucer-wide. Well, that and the bank-wrapped stack of hundred-dollar bills.

Hank's Law Number Two: Respond to threats with complete confidence.

"I asked you to drive my car home. I don't recall giving you permission to toss it."

"Quid pro quo." Declan dropped his hands onto the bed and eyed me like an Eskimo over a baby seal. "You're an untapped resource of useful information about our new client and his relationship with your butcher boy toy."

Shite.

"I'm sensing a conflict of interest," Daicen said mildly.

"Huh?" Declan frowned at him.

"I have a fiduciary duty to protect my client's rights and interests." He turned to me. "I advise you not to answer any questions."

I smiled innocently at the older twin and shrugged.

"Like hell!" Declan's cheeks flushed. "This isn't over."

"Yes, it is. My duty to my client comes before your ambition.

If you'd like me to stay on as your partner, I advise you to let this lie."

Talk about a line in the sand.

Declan left, slamming the door behind him.

Daicen straightened his French cuff. "Would you like to talk?"

God, yes.

"No." I croaked.

With an inscrutable look, he nodded and stood. "Can I get you anything?"

"I'm fine, really," I said.

"Perhaps."

After he was gone, I riffled through the packet of hundreds. Ten thousand dollars. I was starting to appreciate Special Unit's "to the victor go the spoils" mentality. The Five-seveN pistols were bad boys, cocked and locked. I stashed everything in the nightstand drawer and pretended I didn't see the box.

If you can't be content with what you have received, be thankful for what you have escaped.

With a groan, I dragged the comforter over me. "Where are you, Hank?"

Chapter 4

My iPhone bleated a short alarm.

Sawyer. Beating me to the punch.

I grabbed it, checking the time before answering. Six-oh-two a.m. "Good morning, sir."

"There's been a development in the assassination attempt on Coles. A driver will pick you up in an hour. Wear your *Sentinel* credentials."

"Yessir."

He hung up.

I swung my legs over the side of the bed and cracked my neck.

Where the hell am I going to hide Stannis's legacy?

I stood up, gingerly, fetched the box, and limped into the bathroom. I set it on the counter and got in the shower. Normally hot water drumming on my head would have sent me into a Zen state of mental preparation for Sawyer. Today, my mind was running the infinity loop of where to hide the damn jar.

Ugh.

I couldn't make it into the attic, not like this. The garage was a no-go. So was Da's workshop. Hank's house was a fortress, but he'd chosen Vi to hold it. So that was out.

Into the closet, then. I stashed the bone jar inside a suitcase inside a suitcase inside a suitcase. The Russian doll horror-style of traveling.

Until I thought of something better.
Goddammit.

Going down stairs was far easier than going up. My pace had improved from radioactive beta decay to glacial.

Mom and Thierry were in the kitchen. Since the bastards at Amp energy drinks in their infinite wisdom had swapped out original sugar-free for the horrific blueberry-white-grape and equally awful watermelon flavors, I was a girl without a go-to breakfast.

Thierry slid a Go Girl energy drink across the counter.

"Thanks." As far as over-caffeinated drinks went, it was okay, but the name and hot pink can killed me.

Mom looked up from the stack of case files she was reading at the counter. She slid her reading glasses down her nose and gave me "the look."

"I have to check in at work," I said.

"In a Marc Jacobs original? A bit gauche for the communist collective, don't you think?"

"What can I say?" I popped the top of the energy drink. "I'm an ambassador of ever-expanding horizons."

She took a sip of green tea, eyes never leaving mine. "I seem to remember Dr. Williams mentioning something about light duty. . . ."

"I'm wearing flats."

"You're not driving."

"Already have a ride."

She pushed her glasses back up in resignation. "Thierry? Be a dear and bring Maisie her crutches."

For the love of—

Thierry came around the counter holding a pair of forearm crutches. And to my supreme irritation, fitted them to me.

"Gee, thanks, guys."

A horn sounded from the driveway. A driver stood waiting next to the passenger door of a black Chevy Impala. I shambled out of the house looking like the girl version of Jimmy from *South Park*.

Let's g-g-go g-g-get 'em, Tiger.

I crutched into the slogan-tee, skinny-jean, hipster hotbed of the *Chicago Sentinel,* lanyard ID around my neck. I waited my turn at reception and then again for Mr. Renick's assistant.

A dish of a girl in skinny black jeans, open-necked white blouse, cropped red blazer, and kitten heels came toward me. "Jenny Steager. Call me 'Juice.' You must be Maisie McGrane, the new Op Ed."

Op Ed? WTH? "Er . . . yes."

"Paul's reserved a conference room. Let's go." She led me to the elevator, swiped her pass, and pressed the Up button.

We got off on the thirty-second floor.

"Don't mind Lennon," she whisper-warned with a glance at the end of the elevator bank, where a guy so skinny you could grate cheese off his ribs leaned against the wall. "Dickheads make surprisingly good reporters."

Clad in a camel-colored V-neck sweater tucked into brown-belted, brown tapered trousers, he pushed off the wall as we approached.

"'Morning, Lennon," Juice said. "This is Maisie, the new Op Ed."

"Nice to meet you." I lifted a crutch in greeting.

He started at my feet and let his eyes calculate everything from my Stuart Weitzman flats, to the David Yurman earrings, lips crimping in a sneer at the total. "And what have you penned besides your signature on Daddy's checks?"

Other than parking tickets? Not much.

I gave him my best wide-eyed and innocent. "Is that Lenin with an 'i'?"

Hipster no likey.

"Friendly tip, *Miffy*"—he leaned in and I could smell the faint stink of chocolate vape from his e-cig—"stay out of the way of the real reporters,"

Juice gasped. "Geez, Lennon!"

"And the mayor's driver?" Nyx asked. "Chicago's hero?"

"We have Percival 'Poppa' Dozen in custody," Sawyer said. "A convicted felon, so not surprising that the Taurus 85 revolver he used to kill the shooter was unregistered."

Ditch Broady reached inside his pale gray suit coat and removed a tri-folded paper. He set it on the table and pushed it over to Walt. "Percival Dozen's full pardon."

"Apparently it takes more than an assassination attempt to slow Talbott Cottle Coles," Sawyer said wryly.

Nyx cleared his throat and said to me. "Water, please."

"Certainly." I got up and tried not to limp to the sideboard, which held a clear acrylic pail filled with sodas, water, and ice. I tipped the water bottle at Broady in question. He gave me a sympathetic half smile that said Nyx should have gotten his own water and shook his head.

I set the water in front of the Swede and sat down.

"The Justice Department has requested the DEA and ATF take over this investigation."

"Curious, how that came about, gentlemen . . ." Sawyer pressed the tips of his fingers together. "Seeing as the assassination attempt occurred in downtown Chicago."

"The Justice Department has zero tolerance for attempting to silence an American politician," Nyx said. "Especially one who's trying to clean up the nation's drug hub."

Riiight. Coles is so dirty he has to creep up on bathwater.

Nyx continued, "The shooter, Juan Echeverría, was known to the DEA as a *halcone* for the Grieco cartel."

"Echeverría was a U.S. citizen with no record." Sawyer looked skeptical. "But even if he was a *halcone,* or informant, I don't see him making the transition to hit man, or *sicario.*"

"Upward mobility. One can't climb the cartel ladder from *halcone* to lieutenant without a stint as a *sicario.*" Nyx smiled.

"A bit of a leap to a conspiracy involving the Grieco cartel, wouldn't you say?"

"Nope. Looky here." Broady tapped the safety on the pistol. "See the inset? A black diamond. That and the FN Five-seveN MK2s are the new status symbols of the Grieco *sicarios.*"

"The skill of Coles's would-be assassin hardly qualifies as elite," Sawyer said.

"Yes. Strange he was able to get past Chicago's finest, considering he had enough cocaine and heroin in his system to convulse a gorilla." Nyx paused, letting that sink in. He slid a length of blond hair behind his ear. "Grieco's got a stranglehold on the Tampico port. He's looking to ensure his place in the food chain, entrenching with his own private army."

"The DEA and the ATF are already partnering in joint special operation with the Federales to eliminate this threat," Broady said. "We heard your team has an 'in' with the Grieco cartel."

Sawyer raised a shoulder. "You were misinformed."

"We'll make that determination after we meet this field agent of yours," Nyx said. "Where is he?"

"She," Sawyer said. "And you're looking at her."

Holy cat. I wouldn't exactly call a couple of flirty conversations with El Cid an "in."

I raised my palm slightly above the table. "Hi."

"Nope." Broady pinched the bridge of his nose. "Ain't no way in hell."

Thanks for the resounding vote of confidence.

"Hold up," Nyx said.

Broady snorted. "Cartels are all balls, blood, and machismo. To them, women are whores, hostages, or breeders." He folded his arms across his chest and shook his head at Nyx. "No cartel is gonna deal weapons with her."

Aside from the fact that this assignment sounds less appealing by the second, Agent Broady, you seem pretty on board with the cartel mentality.

Broady started to get to his feet. "This meeting's a wash."

Nyx raised a hand to still him and said to Sawyer, "Explain the connection."

"Incidental. She successfully infiltrated the Srpska Mafija's Chicago operation," Sawyer said. "Which is the basis of her connection to Grieco's American-born lieutenant, AJ Rodriguez, aka El Cid."

"Last point of contact?" Broady asked.

Sawyer gave me a reluctant nod.

"El Cid sent me flowers last week." To the hospital. About the failed heist. With a card that read, *No hard feelings.* "A friendly gesture. Nothing more."

"Hmmm." Nyx leaned back in his chair and gave me an appraising once-over. "She has a certain naïve appeal." He shot a look at Broady. "She could solidify the relationship via drug buys, sleep her way into a position of trust."

WTF?

My cheeks flamed.

Think again, pal. Casual sex isn't in my job description or my repressed Catholic schoolgirl DNA.

Broady turned to Sawyer. "You send this cream puff in, you'll never see her again."

"Your chivalry is showing, Ditch," Nyx jibed.

"I'm afraid Agent Broady has the right of it." Sawyer made a clicking noise. "The Srpska Mafija connection won't hold."

"Why not?" Nyx asked.

I snatched up the lifeline Sawyer threw me. "The carjacking gig was a one-shot. My Serbian connection refuses to partner with anyone in the drug trade. El Cid knows this. He'd never take me with no backing."

"I guess that's it, then. Too bad." Nyx's smile turned sly. "Could have been a career maker."

As what, exactly?

Broady and Sawyer got up and walked to the door.

Nyx rose and held out his business card to me. "In case you hear from El Cid."

Sawyer returned to the table. He smiled mirthlessly. "A narrow escape, Maisie. If Nyx had wanted you, I'd have been hard-pressed not to send you in."

Jaysus Criminey.

He raked his fingers through his flaxen hair in a gesture totally unlike him. "Damn him."

"Sir?"

"Talbott Cottle Coles's connections at the DOJ run deep. Broady and Nyx are here to knock the Bureau of Organized Crime out of the loop and quite possibly Special Unit out of existence." He adjusted his tie. "On the plus side, your name won't leak back to Coles."

Special Unit's unique ability was to operate beneath the law enforcement radar. We sat in silence for several minutes.

"Violetta Veteratti came to see me in the hospital," I blurted.

"Oh?" Sawyer asked, his gaze slightly unfocused.

"She offered to work with me if I picked up the reins to Renko's organization."

He blinked the fog away, tawny eyes snapping to full alert. "Timeline?"

"I pushed her to three months."

"Right, then." He nodded. "Spend the next four weeks getting fit and solidifying your journalistic cover. I'll deal with Coles and the DOJ."

"Yessir."

He got up, retrieved my crutches, and set them next to me. "Thank your lucky stars Broady took a fancy to you and helped shut this down. He and Nyx don't play by the same rules we do."

Chapter 5

Juice returned a few moments after Sawyer left. "Paul's ready to see you now."

I crutched behind her wake into yet another conference room. This one, however, held a room full of people, including the ubiquitous Beatle wannabe.

Super.

"Welcome, welcome!" A jovial, portly man with a neatly trimmed black beard and frameless glasses stood at the head of the table. "Come in, we don't bite."

Lennon snapped his teeth together in my general direction, which sent the tubby woman next to him into a gale of giggles. A cross between Martha Stewart and *Grey Gardens,* she was wearing a hemp sweater that had gotten into a macramé fight and lost.

"I'm Paul, as you know." Renick waved sparkle fingers at the table. "Everyone, Maisie McGrane is our new Op-Ed. Maisie, this is everyone."

"Hi," I said.

A dozen people, each striving for individuality, dressed in various-colored stovepipe-legged pants and bagged-out V-neck sweaters, gave me the collective stink eye.

Nothing like being the new girl every other feckin' day.

"Aside from writing the Op-Ed, Maisie has another skill set she'll be sharing with the *Sentinel.*" Renick gave me a "take the floor" gesture and plopped down in his chair.

Neat-o. Newbie piñata at your service. Whack away!
I approached the table. "Any guesses?" I asked, hoping for a clue.

"Hmm. Op-Ed." Lennon stroked his chin, pretending to think. "What *does* the Republican minority do best?"

"Source the best consignment shops for Louis Vuitton?" snarked a diminutive Goth.

"Travel Section?" Grey Gardens batted her lashes over her Starbucks cup. "Where to go to avoid the common folk?"

Lennon raised an index finger, playing to the room. "Best ways to bribe your three-year-old's way into a preschool for gifted children."

Oh, my little Pravda pal, you have no idea where I cut my teeth.

"I'm the new small-arms specialist," I said. They stared at me, mouths open, even Renick.

"Why on earth would the *Sentinel* need that?" Lennon asked pleasantly.

The room waited on the edge of their seats, trembling like wet poodles for him to put the screws to me.

"To keep you from looking like the *HuffPo* reporter who mistook foam earplugs for rubber bullets. Or the *NY Times* staff writer unable to tell the difference between a Glock .40 and a Colt 1911. Or most newscasters, who think the *A* in an *AR* stands for *assault* or *automatic* when it's *ArmaLite*."

Lennon let loose his second shot. "Exactly what qualifies you as an expert, Ms. McGrane?"

I can shoot a Starbucks cup off your head at fifty paces. Wanna see?

"I've had my Firearm Owners ID since I was fourteen, concealed-carry permit since the day I turned twenty-one, and I can tell the difference between a Nerf gun and a double-action pistol."

Paul stood up. "All right, okay. Enough ribbing the newb. We're clear on the direction for the weekend magazine?"

The table agreed collectively.

"Let's get to work, everyone."

"If I may, Paul—I'd be happy to show Miss McGrane the ropes," Lennon volunteered. "I'll even edit her first piece."

Ick, no.

Luckily, Grey Gardens wasn't digging on that idea, either. "Really, Lennon, we're sharing a single office already. She'll have no place to sit, much less work."

"Exactly." Paul said. "That's why, starting next week, she's going to take the office next to Juice."

Which caught everyone by surprise.

"An office for an Op-Ed?" said the Goth under her breath as she kicked back her chair. She brushed past me, making sure to bump me with her shoulder. "Whose leg are you humping?"

Back at you, sweetheart.

Paul came over and rubbed his hands together. "Let's go get you set up, Maisie."

He led me through the corridors of the termite mound that was the *Sentinel*. "Want the nickel tour and travelogue?"

The crutches were killing my wrists. "Nah."

"Sawyer and I go way back. Now, I don't need much," Paul said. "But I do need you at the staff meeting every Monday whenever possible."

"Okay," I said, breathing heavily as I tried to keep up. For a tubby guy, he moved pretty fast.

"Nice work, by the way, with that small-arms comeback," Paul said. "How do you feel about illegal immigration?"

"As in?"

"Single-sentence, personal viewpoint."

"Um . . . Unfair to the people who are trying to emigrate the right way," I said, hating how my voice went up at the end like a question.

"Excellent. That'll give me a nice jump on next week."

"What?"

"If I'm writing opinion pieces under your name, I might as well take your actual positions on them." Paul clapped me on the back. We stopped in front of a tiny, windowless office. A battered Formica desk took up half the space. "This is you."

"Great. Thanks."

"You betcha." He high-stepped away, like a Santa leading a marching band.

* * *

There's something especially decadent about having a driver. Even more pleasant was the fact that he didn't utter a single word.

A block away from my house, I caught sight of a janky blue Ford pickup truck held together with rust, duct tape, and spit. *Oh no.*

"Stop." My voice came out in a whisper. "Please, stop."

The driver complied.

I got out in a rush. "Thanks for the ride."

I waited, knees shaking, until the Chevy Impala turned out of sight before crossing the street to the pickup. One of Hank's men, a six-foot-seven, long-haired, blond Viking got out of the truck and met me in the middle. "Hey, kid."

"Ragnar," I said, trying not to hyperventilate. "What's up?"

He snorted. "How long you gonna milk that goddamn paper cut?"

I looked down at the crutches. "Long enough."

"Hank figured you'd be back at his place by now."

He's okay.

I closed my eyes and let out a shaky breath. "Yeah? You talked to him?"

"Nah. He put a detail on you before he scrammed with that crazy bastard Renko."

I should have known.

"Detail's staying until he comes back. Easier for the boys when you're at his house. Fuck, every car in this neighborhood's a goddamn Porsche or Jag."

I guess covert rarely enters the equation when you're born the son of Odin.

"Gotta say, though, it's been boring as shit. Didn't fuckin' expect that from you." He jabbed a thick index finger into my chest.

"You're welcome." I smiled. "When's he due back?"

Ragnar slid a hand up under his hair and rubbed at the scar tissue that covered the left side of his neck and jaw. "He figured a month, maybe two of palling around with Renko."

Yeah. Just a couple of guys hanging out having fun, running guns for Goran Slajic.

"Relax, kid. He wants to leave Renko nice and easy. Make sure you're in the clear."

I cleared the lump in my throat. "I know."

"The company's monitoring his place. We're off the clock once you're there."

"Yeah."

Ragnar leaned down. "When?"

"End of next week?"

"That'll work. Text me, will ya, kid?" He started toward the truck.

"Sure thing." I rubbed my eyes with my fingers, pressing hard enough to swirl dark blues and purples beneath my lids.

Two months.

Hell, I can do that. In my sleep, right?

The pickup's engine rumbled to life.

I opened my eyes and sighed. The half block to the driveway spread before me like a country mile.

"Hey, kid!" Ragnar said from the window.

"What?"

"You gonna let me drive this piece of classic Americana up your fuckin' manor house drive, or do I gotta carry your god-damn candy-ass to the door?"

I crutched it up the sidewalk into the house, grateful for my aching forearms. I never would have made it without the damn sticks. Which is why everyone needs a mother, to tell you to put your jacket on when it gets chilly.

I eyed the stairs. Twenty steps and a long hallway to Oxy. Twelve into the great room.

No contest.

I hobbled into the kitchen, aiming for the wet bar.

"Maisie," Da said from the couch.

Aw hell.

"Hey, Da." The beer could wait. Best to keep a clear head. I balanced the crutches against the bar and limped into the room. I leaned against the back of the couch. Close enough to see Stannislav Renko's file on the coffee table.

No questions, huh?

"You look like shite," Da said.

Gee, thanks. "It didn't come easy."

He gave a bark of laughter. "Trouble always comes easy for you."

I nodded at the folder. "What's that?"

"Your penance that I'm serving." Da folded his arms across his barrel chest. "Sawyer made sure Homicide's following up on Renko's possible involvement in Coles's assassination attempt."

The orders came from the Grieco cartel in Tampico, Mexico.

I closed my eyes and blew out a slow sigh. "Don't waste your time."

"Eh?"

"If Stannis wanted him dead, he would be."

His face turned stony. "Nice class of people you're running with. Mercenaries and mobsters."

"So far none of them have cut my heart out and fed it to me, like you did."

"Keep telling yourself that, gel." Da picked up the file. "You're a feckin' babe in the woods."

That stung so bad I made it halfway up the stairs before my leg thought to fuss that it still had a helluva lot of stitches inside.

You didn't need Luminol to see the bad blood between us. Unable to bear the idea of something happening to his only daughter, Da had called in some heavy favors and had me expelled from the police academy on a technicality.

Sawyer stepping up and making me an undercover cop eased the hurt, but it sucked to have to lie to the clan. Even if I'd had permission to come clean, I wouldn't risk it. Da would do anything and everything to keep me off the force.

The front door swung open. "Hey, Snap!" Cash yelled. He was the hyper Labrador puppy the vet promises will settle down when it gets to be a year old, that pretty much runs and jumps its way into the grave thirteen high-energy years later. "Look who I brought home to cheer you up!"

Lee Sharpe stepped into the foyer.

Jaysus Criminey.

"How goes it, Lee?" I said.

He leaned his forearms against the banister. "Dark and dirty, baby."

No surprise there. He looked as handsome as ever in that harsh, über-fit way that was completely at odds with his happy-go-lucky attitude. A heady combination and he knew it.

He sent a soft wolf whistle my way. "Pretty sharp suit for a cub reporter." Giving me the tease because he could.

"I do all right."

My brother's phone chirped. "Yeah, yeah," Cash answered. "Lemme check." He trotted off down the hall.

"How's the leg?" Lee asked, coming up the stairs to meet me.

"Okay."

"Hmmm." He leaned in close, mouth in a flat line. "I'm not a doctor, but I'll take a peek."

The laugh that popped from my lips was embarrassingly high-pitched. Lee could serve up a line as neat as Louis C.K., but still . . .

I'm just a little over-done, that's all.

"When are you back at Special Unit?" he asked.

"Three weeks to solidify cover and get fit."

"Sawyer tell you what you're coming back to?"

"Not yet," I fibbed. "But I have a vague idea."

"Maybe I'll put in a request to partner up." He tucked a lock of hair behind my ear. "Raise a little hell together, yeah?"

No.

I was wrecked. I missed Hank.

I raised my chin. "Beat it, tough guy."

He left. Laughing.

Chapter 6

A week in Hank's place, and it still felt like an empty airplane hangar without him. And an eerie one, too. I knew Hank's company had, at the very least, the alarm system under surveillance, and probably the thermal cameras, but it was Hank's valet, Wilhelm, who made me edgy.

I'd never seen him.

Ever.

Hank had found him—a real English butler—chained up in the basement of a South American drug lord's mansion while on a deep clean mission. But after years of imprisonment, interacting with people was no longer Wilhelm's forte. The only person he could bear to be around was Hank. And so he'd given Wilhelm the run of his place.

I had no idea when Wilhelm came or where he went, but whenever I set a glass down and left the room, by the time I got back it was either in the dishwasher or there was a napkin under it. He was like a green lizard zipping across the floor in your beach cabana. You know it won't hurt you, but it still creeps you out.

Stannis's legacy kept niggling at me, too. Holding on to forensic trophy evidence didn't exactly give me that Xanax vibe.

Bell Jar? *Try the Bone Jar, Sylvia Plath. You ain't got nothing on me.*

I toyed with the idea of wrapping the whole mess up and asking Daicen to hold it for me, but making him an accessory was less than decent.

C'mon, Maisie, think.

Plain sight.

Twenty-four hours later, Amazon Prime delivered three pounds of salt-white aquarium sand to the house. I filled the jar, the bones disappeared, and Hank and I had a new coffee table decoration.

It made me miss him even more.

Hank's Law Number Thirteen: Anyone can endure expected pain.

For cripes' sake, it had only been three weeks.

Weirdly, I missed the hell out of Stannis, too.

Getting a lil' Stockholmey in here, kid. Best pour yourself a whiskey, sit in front of the fire, and read some Kipling.

Instead, I went down the hall into Hank's weight room and hit it as hard I could handle for the second time that day. Back to normal jogging, I was still sprint-shy.

And sure as hell looking forward to getting back to work. Even after a shower, blow-out, and fake tan, the clock had only crawled to 5:00 p.m.

What was I staying up for anyway?

I took one of the Ambien that Dr. Williams had sent me home with to combat the side effects of the painkillers I wasn't taking. Wearing one of Hank's shirts, I climbed in on his side of the bed, ready to sleep the sleep of a fingerless skeleton. And it would be lovely.

My iPhone buzzed and rattled on the nightstand. "Hello?" I fumbled with it, sitting up in the dark. "Hank?"

"Try again."

"Lee?"

"Who else cares enough to call at two a.m.?"

"Are you drunk?" I asked.

"No. Are you?"

Jaysus, is this some vintage comedy routine? "What do you want, Lee?"

"You. Naked. But I'd settle for a date."

How about a sock in the jaw?

"I can send a patrol car," he said, "but I'm betting a crack reporter like yourself won't want to miss us locking down the perimeter."

"Huh?"

"I'm inviting you to a SWAT bust, Bae. A three thirty-five a.m. no-knock entrance, followed by drinks at Hud's. On Cash."

Talk about a way to a girl's heart: flashbang grenades, take-downs, and beers on my brother.

"I'm in." I said.

I slid behind the wheel of the Hellcat.

Damn, it feels good to feel the blood pump.

Lee texted directions to a Marathon gas station in Little Village, the Mexican version of Englewood, where his man would be waiting.

Siri guided me through a mix of brick two- and three-flat buildings, cottages, and bungalows scattered among them. The closer I got to Lawndale and Ridgeway, the more bright colors and Santeria graffiti appeared. Santa Muerte statues—a bizarre hybrid of the Virgin Mary and the Grim Reaper—were in more windows than they weren't.

Even drug dealers need a patron saint.

I pulled into the Marathon gas station. A twentysomething guy in all black motioned for me to roll down the window. "Maisie?"

"Yes."

"Joe Hyne. Your ride." He directed me to park in front of the pumps closest to the station, and gave me a look over as I got into his unmarked Suburban. "So you're Sharpe's dove, eh?"

"Hardly. I'm a reporter," I said, trying out my new cover. "And a McGrane."

"No shit? You Cash's sister?"

"Yep. That's me."

"Damn." He shook his head. "Okay. Two gangs, the Caballeros and the Eight Six, pretty much run Little Village. We're heading into 'The Wasteland'—the zone they kill each other over every day—for a drug bust."

Lee's voice crackled over the radio. "Got the package?"

"En route," Joe said.

My phone rang. "Hello?"

"Hey, Lois Lane. Ready to see me in action?"

It's amazing what's funny at 3:00 a.m. "Cute. How long you been saving that one up?"

"Awww, Bae. Don't play that way," Lee said. "Joe's gonna put you with the ELSUR guys. Give you a bird's-eye view of the action."

"Okay."

"They got Cooky up there. Nervy little rat, but chatty. Give you a chance to practice your investigative journalist skills." Lee covered the mouthpiece of the phone, said something, and came back on. "Gotta go." He hung up.

Second thoughts squealed through my mind like microphone feedback. This felt more like some sort of test than a date.

Joe turned the Suburban down a dark alley along the back side of a squat three-story building, the ground-level windows boarded up with plywood, broken windows on the second and third. He killed the lights and stopped the SUV near the rear corner of the building. "This is it. Door's around back. Got a flashlight?"

"Yep." I reached into my messenger bag and dug out my Fenix PD35 Tactical flashlight.

"Sweet glowstick." Joe gave me a thumbs-up. "Head upstairs, use your light only in the stairwell. Three thirty-five they're gonna enter and it's gonna be loud."

"Can't wait." I got out and jogged around the corner of the building. A dented metal door, propped ajar with a rock, glinted in the bright harvest moonlight. The hinges squealed as I opened it far enough to slip inside. I turned the flashlight on low and kept the beam pointed at my feet as I searched for the stairwell.

It wasn't bad as far as abandoned slum buildings go. Mostly empty, the reek of urine and garbage dissipated the higher I went up the stairs. I hit the third floor, clicked off the flashlight, and stepped into the room. "Hello?" The space spanned the entire length of the building. A pair of men in T-shirts and jeans worked behind a camp table full of equipment, fronted by a black curtain hanging from the ceiling to prevent light from escaping. The electronic surveillance boys.

One pressed his headset. "I've tapped in to their camera feed. All quiet."

I approached the table. "Lee Sharpe sent me here."

"Maisie. The reporter, right?" Two said. He typed on the keyboard. "Wanna see what the good guys are up against?"

"Yes, please." I leaned forward to look at the video screens.

Two gestured toward the left monitor. "These are six of their camera feeds."

"Theirs?" I asked.

"The Eight-Six. They're running their own security. They got Wi-Fi cameras on the buildings, streetlights, you name it. Watching for the Cabeleros, riffraff, and of course, the police."

Whoa.

Sharp, unintelligible garble buzzed from their headsets.

Game time.

One leaned back in his chair and gave me the *sorry-but-you-need-to-get-out-of-the-way-now* smile.

I threw a thumb over my shoulder at the windows. "Over there?"

"Yeah," Two said. "Cooky'll fill you in."

I walked around the screen. A scrawny, long-haired Hispanic man stepped out from the shadows to meet me. "You Maisie?"

"Yeah."

He scratched his arm. "I'm Cooky."

"As in Chips Ahoy?" I whispered.

He giggled, a thin, shrill sound. "Thass a good one, *juera*. You funny." His arms were covered with scabs and puncture scars.

Someone's been riding the dragon a good long time.

Duh. *Cook*-y.

"You Lee's lady?" he said. "This make you all hot? Watching Captain SWAT busting ass?"

"Something like that." Grit crunched beneath my feet. Down below, dark figures moved in the shadows around the duplex next door. "What's the situation?"

"Stash house," Cooky volunteered. "Thass why I'm here, on account o' the Eight-Six. The friggin' *Nacos*." His nails scraped the underneath of his jaw. "Mexican Nationals. They ain't got no connect, they just fighting to get a piece, trickin' for their *paisa* cartels."

"*Paisa* cartels?"

"Lil' fish, like Soldados de Cristo and Grieco." He shook his head. "But the Eight-Six and the Cabeleros—they ain't gonna let no small-time junk dealers move into Lil' Village. No way."

"Keep a lock on the competition?"

Cooky let out another shrill giggle. "Shit, you funny." He tagged me on the shoulder. "The Cabeleros and the Eight Six, they in with El Eje. Deal smart. Keep Lil' Village clean, yo."

"Clean?" I said.

His fingers scrabbled like spiders across his chest. "You can't be smokin' crack or shooting H on the sidewalk 'round here. Gots to represent."

Riiight. I nodded. "An awful lot of people getting killed around here."

"Cuz it all gangbang. This ain't no drug hub, *juera*."

I moved closer to the window, bouncing on my toes. SWAT was moving into position, setting up a perimeter around the house. Five men at the rear, two in the alley on the side of the house.

My fingers tingled, the anticipation almost electric. I leaned back to get a view of the front of the house. Two unmarked Suburbans waited out of sight line of the duplex. The other SWAT squad I knew was there but couldn't see in position.

"*Psst!*" Cooky hissed, pointing. "Check it!"

The back porch light went on. A woman lugging a toddler stomped out, followed by a man tight on her heels, the Spanish zinging between them fast and loud.

Three thirty-two a.m. *Three minutes to go-time.*

"Sit-Rep," a voice demanded over the radio.

"Stand down," the guy with the headset answered. "We'll pick them up in the frozen zone."

The men at the rear of the duplex melted back into the night. The mission already in motion, the team couldn't risk alarming whoever was left inside.

The couple argued their way into a rusted Chevy Malibu and took off down the block.

The frozen zone—the outside ring perimeter—was manned by regular patrolmen. There'd be no chance for the couple in the Malibu to tip off the perps in the duplex.

"Stealth Two." I heard Lee's voice over the radio. Beneath us his SWAT squad lined up in snake formation on the back porch.

"Charge is hung," answered another man. "Standing by . . ."

"Move in," Lee said, his voice low.

The two SWAT on the side of the house raised the flashbang poles.

"Entry in five . . . four . . ."

The flashbang grenades went off like cherry bombs filled with lightning, blinding and disorienting.

The front and back doors blasted open simultaneously. SWAT entered the rear of the duplex like a black snake into a rabbit's warren. "Police officers in the door! Police officers in the door!"

Gunshots cracked. They were silenced by controlled bursts of SWAT's M-4s.

My ears rang. I strained to hear the radio.

"Get down! Get down! Get down!" Shouting blared from the receiver. "Safety clear!"

"Right side, clear."

The radio buzzed. "All clear, Squad Two."

"All clear, Squad One," Lee said.

And it was over. In less than one supercharged minute of peerless violence.

I shook out my arms and cracked my neck, trying to calm down.

"Shit," Cooky said. "They like the Black Ops version o' the Eight-Six."

Seriously? I tried not to laugh. *How high are you, anyway?*

The street was awash in the cruisers' red and blue flashers and spotlights. Outside the duplex, the uniforms took custody of SWAT's cable-cuffed perps.

The SWAT team moved off to the SUVs waiting at the mouth of the alley, the men shedding their heavy gear.

I recognized Lee's stocky frame. And my brother, rocking slowly back and forth on his heels, talking to a couple of the other team members. Everyone moving a little slow, hitting the wall.

Adrenal dump. When the forty-second super-juiced adrenaline burst abruptly ends.

I could relate.

The window glass was cool against my forehead. The evidence techs arrived and went to work. Within minutes, camera flashes glared against the broken windows of the duplex.

The ELSUR guys packed up behind me, while Cooky watched with me at the window, scratching.

"You cool to wait up here for Sharpe?" Two asked, laden with gear. He flicked a glance at Cooky.

I nodded. "You bet."

The guys nodded and left, lugging their gear.

Down below, Cash said something to Lee and started toward the back of the house. He slung his M-4 over his shoulder and unseeing, looked up at the building windows, threw me a salute, and walked down the alley.

I smiled. *The hummingbird with cement wings.*

The rear of the house remained dark, the evidence techs working front to back.

A section of lattice under the porch popped out onto the lawn. A man shimmied out from beneath it.

"Oooh, *Naco* better get his ass in gear!" Cooky giggled.

The man pulled a gun from his waistband.

Cash rounded the corner.

"Gun!" I banged my hands on the window. "Stop!"

The man raised the pistol and fired two shots.

"No!" I shouted.

Cash jerked spasmodically. He stood, weaving, dark head cocked to one side.

The man fired again.

Cash crumpled to his knees and fell facedown in the dirt.

Blood pulsed in my ears. *No!*

The man ran toward him, gun pointed low at Cash's head.

NoNoNo—

The man's hair flared up in a puff of red mist. A rifle shot echoed through the alleyway. He was dead before he hit the ground.

Rifle out, Lee ran to the body, kicked the handgun away, and went to Cash.

I turned and sprinted to the stairs. Cooky shouted at me.

I hit the stairwell blind, slipping and tripping on trash, somehow managing to keep on my feet. I slammed against the rear door and stumbled out into the alley, skidding around the corner at full speed.

"Cash!" I screamed. "Cash!"

Lee was on his knees beside him.

My brother wasn't moving.

I couldn't, either. Paralyzed with dread. *Cash . . .*

"Can you hear me?" Lee said.

Cash suddenly convulsed, coughing. His hands went to his stomach, and he curled onto his side. "Aww. Feck."

Lee's face was slack with relief. "He's all right."

I choked on a swallow of air, lungs already full of breath I'd been holding.

He's alive he's alive he's alive—

"Jaysus Criminey," Cash groaned. "What'd they hit me with?"

I glanced over at the guy who was missing a sizeable portion of his skull, the dark pool spreading beneath his head.

And then at the pistol Lee had kicked away from the dead man.

"A 5.7," I said, my head starting to spin.

An FN Five-seveN MK2, to be specific.

Sweet Jesus.

Chapter 7

"This feels strangely familiar." Lee winked at me and leaned back on the squad bench of the ambulance.

Always the joker.

"Yeah? How about you tell the driver to watch the road," I said, sharper than I meant to.

Cash, on the gurney, pale face turned toward us, spoke in between grunts. "Maisie? I won't tell . . . if you don't."

Seriously?

I ran a hand through my hair. "Do you actually think Da and the boys won't find out?"

"About you . . . on scene?" He made a growling sound. "Feck no."

Yeah. Because taking three in the chest is not nearly as troubling as me being here.

"You've got my word, Cash," Lee said.

"Ergh. Hurts like a sonuvabitch." He panted. "Don't call the clan."

"Mom'll kill me—"

Lee put his hand on my leg. "Cash is gonna be fine. Sometimes you take a hit to the vest and . . . nothing. Other times it feels like you got gored by a bull. Don't make it something it's not."

I glared at his hand on my thigh.

Don't you dare tell me it's part of the goddamn job.

He gave me a squeeze before letting go. "He's gonna be fine."

* * *

The smell was the same in every emergency room: disinfectant, blood, and the primal stink of fear.

Cash went to triage. Lee took me to the waiting room.

Cash's SWAT squad showed up, milling around, their voices loud and jocular.

"Give me your keys," Lee said. "Joe's gonna drive your car over."

I handed them to him. "Thanks."

He nudged me with his shoulder toward the waiting area. "You oughta sit down before you fall down."

I slumped down into one of the hard blue chairs. Lee walked over to the squad standing by the door. The high-pitched whine of *SpongeBob SquarePants* on the TV filled the waiting room for a solid sixty minutes. I was numb from fear. Numb from relief. My mind unable to track a children's cartoon.

A cheerful bear of a man in a white coat pushed through the ER doors and called, "Miss McGrane?"

"That's me." I walked over to meet the doctor, Lee on my heels.

The name on his gold badge read Dr. Greg Purchase. "Mr. McGrane has a bruised kidney, one large contusion, and some soft tissue damage. The vest saved his life, but he's got some BABT—behind-armor blunt trauma."

My mouth went dry. "What's that?"

"When the bullet strikes but doesn't perforate the vest, it can still penetrate soft tissue, pushing the bullet, vest, and clothing inward," Dr. Purchase said. "When the vest is removed, the vest material and bullet come back out, leaving a hole that looks remarkably like a bullet wound."

Lee squeezed my shoulder.

Dr. Purchase continued, "He'll have a tender couple of weeks and needs to take it easy. We're waiting on the results of another test, but he should be fine to go home within the hour."

Lee went over to tell the men.

I sat back down and started to shake. All over.

I couldn't stop.

Every time I closed my eyes, all I could see was Cash, his body jerking from the impact of the slugs, legs giving out beneath him as he fell flat on his face. The sickening certainty that he was dead.

He's okay, he's okay, he's okay.

I put my hands to my face. They were clammy and damp. Saliva ran down the back of my throat. My stomach heaved. I sprinted for the ladies' room.

And was sick. From both ends.

Spent and empty, I leaned against the sink, running cool water on my wrists.

At least I wasn't shaking anymore.

I rinsed my mouth out, washed my face, and stepped out.

Lee waited for me outside the door. He'd sent the rest of the team home. He walked me over to an empty bench and we sat down.

"You saved his life."

"No." Lee shook his head. "My fault. I let him go alone."

"What was he doing anyway?"

"He wanted to walk the length of the house. Said something in the interior felt off to him." Lee put his hand on mine. "Plenty of false walls and hidey-holes. Drug dealers are nothing if not ingenious."

We sat there another ten minutes, holding hands, not saying a word.

"Shouldn't be long now," he said.

I nodded, not trusting my voice.

He gave me a cockeyed smile. "Not much of a date."

"Jaysus, Lee. Give it a rest."

He put his arm around me and tugged me into his chest. I stiffened and tried to pull away, but he held my face to his chest, thumb stroking my cheek. The steady *thump* of his heart beat in my ear.

"He's all right," he said softly.

My mouth formed the words, "*I know,*" but all that came out was a sob.

Chapter 8

There was only one place to take Cash.

Hank's.

We'd keep the clan in the dark for as long as we were able.

Cash flipped through channels on DirecTV, halfway through the pint of Häagen-Dazs Swiss Almond in Hank's guest room. I handed him two OxyContins from Hank's medicine cabinet and a bottle of lemon-lime Gatorade.

"Thanks, Snap."

I sat next to him on the bed. "I'll pick up your prescriptions tomorrow morning. First thing." I couldn't stop smiling at him. I knew if I did, I'd start bawling.

"What do you wanna watch?"

I shrugged. "What's even on at ten thirty in the morning?"

He clicked the remote. Channels blurred in front of my eyes. "Sweet!" he said, stopping on Bill Murray carrying a pizza and dry cleaning. *Stripes*.

Carefully, I scooched up next to him. "Does it hurt?"

"Like a bitch." He gave a pained chuckle. "But it's the pissing a feckin' stream of gore that freaks me out the most."

Yeah, he was gonna be just fine.

I lay back on the pillow, watching the movie through half-closed eyes, and fell asleep.

Cold metal pressed against my cheek. My eyes snapped open.

"Tell me." Stannislav Renko loomed over me. "Tell me, *Vatra Andeo*."

Fire Angel.

I raised my chin slowly, the barrel of the gun sliding down along my jaw, knowing exactly what he wanted to hear.

"*Moj đavo,*" I rasped. *My devil.*

He grinned, crooked white teeth gleaming from his blue-black scruff. "For always." He straightened and put the gun to his temple.

An FN 5.7.

"No!" I jerked awake, panting. Stiff and cold and sweating. And furious.

Cash was passed out next to me, snoring softly. I slid my legs off the side of the bed and rubbed my eyes with the heels of my hands.

A little overdone, that's all. I'm just a little overdone.

Disoriented, I went into the kitchen, the midday sun jarring. I needed to pick up Cash's painkillers and antibiotics. I scribbled a Post-it Note for Wilhelm, who probably already knew Cash was here and why, then grabbed my keys and headed to the garage. Forcing myself to wait until I'd left the driveway before I made the call.

"Can't bear to be away from me for more than a couple hours, huh, Bae?" Lee answered.

"Yeah, that's it." I pinched the bridge of my nose. The street blurred in front of my eyes.

"Cash all right?"

"Yeah. Thanks for asking."

He let the silence stretch and warp before saying, "What's up?"

"Um . . ." The words seemed to wedge in my mouth. I cleared my throat. "I . . . uh . . . need a favor."

"Name it."

"Do you have the gun Cash was shot with?"

"Not on me," he said. "It's probably been logged in to evidence by now. Why?"

"I need a look at it."

"Hmm." Lee made a *clicking* sound with his mouth. "Any reason why you're not running this through Sawyer?"

"I need to know if I'm right first."

"As a McGrane, you're not exactly an unknown entity around here."

Duh. A little slow off the mark today.

"What are you looking for?" he asked casually.

"I'll know it when I see it."

He made the *clicking* sound again.

I winced. *What price this favor?*

"Okay," he said. "Lemme see what I can do."

He hung up.

"Huh." I clicked my phone off and pulled in to the Walgreens parking lot.

Go figure.

I drifted around the store, sipping a sugar-free Red Bull, wondering when the price of drugstore mascara made the leap to department store exorbitant and where they kept the Mini Chewy Sweetarts.

I scored the candy and a copy of *Car and Driver* and headed back to the pharmacy to wait for Cash's script.

I spent the next ten minutes next to an old guy who was more than happy to share his Nips Caramel for a debate on the merits of crossbow versus composite bow hunting.

My phone buzzed.

A text. From Lee.

Bae, I'll show you how heavy it was in person.

I laughed in spite of myself, and scrolled down. Attached were two pictures of the handgun and a single macro.

Lava filled my lungs.

Inset into the safety was a black diamond.

By the time I got in the car, I was in full alertness mode, breathing in through my nose and out my mouth. The shooter was one of Carlos Grieco's.

It was personal now.

I dug Special Agent Nyx's business card out of my wallet and dialed.

"Nyx."

"Er . . . This is Sawyer's field agent, sir." I said, carefully avoiding mentioning my name. "I met you at the *Sentinel*."

"Sure." I heard him lean back in his office chair. "Walt's pet."

Aww, you remember. "Sir, I'd like to be reconsidered for the assignment."

"Oh? You seemed reluctant at the meeting."

"I didn't feel comfortable talking about career advancement in another branch in front of my current boss."

"That was over two weeks ago."

"I wanted to be back to one hundred percent before calling, sir."

"I see."

Hank's Law Number Ten: Keep your mouth shut.

I waited.

C'mon, you sonuvagun.

"I appreciate ambition in my agents, but Sawyer's caution had merit," Nyx said. "Your only connection to the Grieco cartel was the Srpska Mafija. You have no legitimate backer. And I have neither the time nor the resources to establish that for an untested rookie."

Ouch.

"But, hey"—he gave a scoffing chuckle—"you find someone to vouch for you, and I'll set you up like a fatted calf at the county fair."

Aren't you just a lil' ray of sunshine? I bet all the girls are lining up to work for you.

Cash was lounging on the couch playing *Battlefield Hardline* on Xbox when I got home. Feet on the coffee table, an open Coors at his side, and a dead soldier on the floor.

Cripes.

I dropped my purse and the Walgreens bag next to him, then picked up the empty bottle and took it into the kitchen. "A little early in the day to be hitting it, don'tcha think, Captain Oxy?"

"Nah," he said, firing away. "Got anything to eat around here?"

The counter Post-it to Wilhelm was gone, as expected. I opened the fridge. Inside were two Saran-Wrapped plates of triangular-cut turkey club sandwiches complete with fringed toothpicks, dill pickles, and fruit salad.

"Wilhelm. You are a prince among men," I muttered. I took the plates out, snagged a bag of Tim's Jalapeño Chips and brought them over to the coffee table.

"That was fast," Cash said.

"Don't ask." I went back to the fridge for a couple more beers.

He set the remote down and pulled off the plastic. "I'm asking."

"Housekeeper."

Cash took a giant bite of sandwich before asking, "Is she hot?"

"He."

"Never mind."

I sat down carefully next to him. "You call Mom and Da yet?"

He shook his head.

"What was it like, besides horrific?"

"My last thought was *Aww, feck,* or more accurately, *Aww.*" His mouth curled wryly. He popped the top on the new beer and took a good long swallow before answering. "It felt like someone rigged my vest with M-80s." He shook his head. "Goddamn careless and stupid. FNG-type shit."

Fucking New Guy.

He opened the chips, took a handful, and propped the bag up against the bone jar. "That's the trouble with me and Koji being the two token non-former-military guys on SWAT. They already lived through all the dumb-ass mistakes we haven't made yet."

The gun that he'd been shot with was a military-grade weapon, the rounds illegal armor-piercing.

He'd been lucky. Damn lucky.

Without SWAT's ceramic-plated armored vests, the regular rank-and-file wouldn't be so fortunate. Men and women like my da and Flynn and Rory.

"You okay, Snap?" Cash popped me in the shoulder. "You don't look so good."

"Yeah. Switch it to multi-player." I picked up my purse and felt for my phone. "I need to send a text before I take you to school."

Cash hooted with laughter. "Bring it."

I pulled up Ragnar's number and typed.

I need you to set up a meet between me and Vi.

I hit Send and felt the fire in my chest fade ever so slightly.

Chapter 9

Ragnar insisted on driving. I insisted we take Hank's Mercedes G-Wagen.

He wasn't happy with me, but with Hank MIA, the Viking wasn't about to deny my request. "This is fucking ridiculous."

Gee, thanks for all the positivity.

I wore a vicious Parker black leather minidress, my hair in a sleek high pony. I armored up with Stannis's stainless Aquanaut Patek Philippe watch. It hung loose and chic at my wrist. Stannis, for all his violence, was a lean and lithe five-nine. Next came the Cartier engagement ring.

I flexed my fingers into a tight fist, crushing every second thought.

Ragnar pulled up hard to the curb and popped the G-Wagen into Park with a jerk, refusing to look at me, shaggy blond hair obscuring his face.

"It's all good," I said.

He grunted.

The valet opened the door. I got out feeling as badass as Bruce Lee and trotted up the stairs into The Storkling Club.

It defied belief that Eddie Veteratti, the uncouth cocaine cowboy, had re-created the original New York namesake with a better-than-perfect twist. Luxe, Old Hollywood style, complete with torch song singers, smoky back rooms, and champagne cocktails.

A beauty in a clingy sapphire blue dress met me when I

stepped inside. "Good evening, Ms. McGrane. So lovely to have you with us again. This way, please."

We walked down a long, dark hallway into the lounge. At 11:00 p.m., it was already a controlled crush. The lounge took reservations, but the club and dining room were members only.

She escorted me through a sea of gold velvet drapes into a world where the wealthy elite, celebrities, and sports stars rubbed elbows, free from reprisals. Jimmy the Wolf came at me, hand extended, smiling beneath his Satan goatee. His monstrous bulk was barely contained in his tuxedo jacket.

My hand disappeared in his. "Hello, Wolf."

"Vi's busy." He folded my hand over his arm and led me to a table at the edge of the dance floor. Siren Bobby Blaze warbled a sultry "Bye Bye Blackbird." "Drink?"

"No thanks." I took a seat.

"You sure?" The Wolf sat down too close. Crowding me. "Does Bannon know what you're getting into?"

"Yes."

He leaned in, his beard prickling my ear. "Because you sure as fuck don't know."

Lovely.

It wasn't enough to scare me. Nodding absently, I let my eyes drift across the room.

Fuuuuuuuugh.

The bad penny.

Talbott Cottle Coles.

Vengeance was not a feeling I was familiar with. Until now.

Hank's Law Number Three: Don't let your lizard brain go rogue.

"Wolf? About that drink . . ."

He raised a thick hand at a hovering, white-jacketed waiter. "Scotch."

"And for you, miss?"

"Rakija," I said, feeling mean enough to hunt a boar with a butter knife. "Bring the bottle."

Out of the corner of my eye, I took in the bastard who'd tried to have me killed.

Out of jealousy.

Coles was obsessed with Stannis. And while we'd tangled before, it wasn't until I became Stannis's beard that he wanted me dead. He couldn't stand the closeness between us. And so he'd used Vi Veteratti's coked-out brother, Eddie, to arrange a hit on me.

My skin rippled in revulsion.

At his arm was a delicately handsome Latino man wearing an Italian suit so snug, I was glad he was sitting down. Coles's fingers grazed the man's wrist.

Stannis might be gone, but Coles would never get over him.

The waiter returned and poured a shot tableside, set down the bottle of Žuta Osa, and left.

"You drink that Yellow Wasp shit?" Wolf asked.

"The bastard child of Manischewitz and Everclear? What's not to love?" I raised the glass, holding it delicately in my left hand, intact pinkie raised, Stannis's diamond engagement ring winking in the candlelight, and waited.

Wolf swung his heavy head to look over his shoulder.

Coles noticed me, then.

Message received.

His lip recoiled in a sneer, his overly white capped teeth gnashed the butt of his stout nub cigar.

I threw back the shot, not breaking eye contact. I held the glass out to him, turned it over, and planted it on the table.

Apparently I am petty enough to hold a grudge.

A dark chortle came from the Wolf. "I thought you Irish Catholic girls were all about forgiveness."

"Try eternal damnation."

He got up and pulled back my chair. He held out his arm, and we disappeared behind the velvet curtains. I could feel the slime and the fury of Coles's glare, felt it even when I knew he couldn't see me.

And I liked it.

Violetta Veteratti hadn't wasted any time transforming her twin's office from Italian cigar library to Palace of Caserta baroque. It leant a certain majesty to her hard, mannish face.

Jimmy the Wolf leaned against the wall, arms folded across his chest.

"So," the Mafia princess said from behind her desk. "You wanna head Renko's operation."

"Just until he gets back." *Tread gently.* This was the razor-fine edge between getting what I wanted and screwing things up for the Bureau of Organized Crime.

"Yeah?" she said. "When's that?"

"I'm not exactly sure." I tipped my head from side to side, ponytail swinging like some idiotic cheerleader. "He's, uh . . . gone to ground."

"What's the holdup?" Jimmy said.

I crossed my legs and adjusted my skirt. "Stannislav's best players are either in jail or under surveillance. I need time and—"

Vi smirked. "How much?"

"About that . . . I was wondering if I could call in my chit."

The favor. The one you promised me in return for not letting Stannis kill Eddie.

Her hatchet face turned keen. "How much you think my brother's worth?"

Not as much as mine.

"I want you to vouch for me with the Grieco cartel." The words came out as smooth as if I'd asked her to pick up my dry cleaning. A favor almost too small to be asked.

"Entering the narcotics market, are we?" Vi asked.

"Capital is necessary in every business."

"I can supply that," she offered silkily. "Lawyers on retainer, too."

I'm sure you can. With ankle shackles and iron chains. "Thing is, I'm one of those master-of-my-own-destiny kinda girls. I just need the nod."

She stared at me, evaluating. "Done."

"Thank you," I said.

Her pointed red tongue slid out and licked the center of her upper lip. "Bannon's gone to a helluva lotta trouble over you."

"Yes." I swallowed hard, aching for him like a whipped dog.

"But trouble doesn't put a ring on your finger."

She held out her hand and snapped her fingers. I extended my left hand. She moved it under the desk light. "Cartier?"

I nodded.

"Renko gives you the world, is that it?" She let go of my hand.

"Sure. And he sticks around to share it with me. That's the trick."

Vi nodded. "Ain't it, though."

"He'll be back. Sooner than later."

"Then we'll be seeing you around, Mrs. Renko."

Jimmy the Wolf pushed off the wall and opened the door.

I guess that's my cue.

We reentered the dining room, the Wolf with a firm grip on my elbow, reminding me that I was still an interloper.

He slowed as we neared the table we'd shared earlier. Everything remained as we'd left it, untouched. Coles and his date were nowhere to be seen.

"Another?" Wolf asked.

Practically giddy, I smiled up at him. "Why the hell not?"

Two shots and twenty minutes later, I remembered I'd left Ragnar out front. "I better scoot, Wolf."

His heavy brow creased and he started to get to his feet. I put my hand on his arm. "Stay. I know the way out."

I ambled through the dining room, recognizing a Bear, a Blackhawk, and an indicted city councilman drinking with a local newscaster.

I passed through the heavy drapes into the lounge.

A hand grabbed my ponytail and jerked me backward. Another jammed something against my throat and let go.

Fire.

I slapped my hand over my neck. Tripping over my own feet, I swung wildly through the gold fabric into the lounge. Blinded, I crashed into a bar table, sending glasses shattering on the floor.

I lay crumpled over the table, tears streaming down my face.

JaysusfeckingChrist, it hurts so goddamn bad!

I sucked in a deep breath. The stink of my own burning flesh filled my nose and mouth.

Oh god.

A cigar.

Coles, you sonuvabitch!

"Miss?" a waiter asked. "Are you okay?" His eyes widened as I pulled my hand away.

"Burn," I forced out through clenched teeth.

A heavy hand landed on my back. "Tell the kitchen," Jimmy the Wolf ordered and half-carried, half-walked me into the staff room.

A woman in a white sous chef uniform took one look at my neck and marched me into the staff room. "Put your head over the sink." She pulled out the sink hose and ran cool water over my throat. "You're in luck. Burns are my specialty."

The pain pulsed in constant, searing throbs. The agony so intense it was almost narcotic.

I stayed that way for five minutes, shaking. The Wolf watched, frowning.

"Sit." The sous chef opened a first-aid kit. She opened and put on disposable gloves, tore open an antiseptic packet. "Silver sulfadiazine." Ignoring my whimpers, she applied it with a swab before covering it with a 3M Tegaderm clear-gel dressing.

I felt light-headed. Equal parts shallow breathing and pain.

"You should see a plastic surgeon after it heals." She glanced at the Wolf. "I'll let the boss know."

He nodded and turned to me. "I'll drive you home."

"Actually," I said, "I have a ride."

The Wolf would have carried me out if I'd let him. Instead, I just trembled against his side.

"You are a guest of Violetta's. My responsibility," he said. "I'll make this right."

"No, you won't."

We walked to Hank's G-Wagen. He put his hand on the door, but didn't open it. "Who?"

For God's sake.

"Coles." I got into the car, trying not to look at Ragnar. "Let it go."

"No way," he said. "No how."

"Owe me, then."

The Wolf shut the door.

Ragnar pulled away from the club.

Hank's Law Number Thirteen: Anyone can endure expected pain.

I counted long, slow breaths. I got to one hundred sixty-seven.

He stayed quiet until we merged onto the freeway. "What happened to your neck?"

"Accident," I lied. Tears welled in my eyes.

"That's a burn dressing," he said in a voice so flat it might have been an airstrip.

"Yeah."

"I recognize the pong of sulfadiazine."

Of course he did. The whole left side of his neck and shoulder was covered in pink-puckered scar tissue.

Man up, Maisie. You don't know what pain is.

I cried all the way home.

Chapter 10

I spent from 5:00 a.m. to 8:00 a.m. resisting the siren song of Cash's OxyContin. I needed to stay sharp. Same side or not, Nyx was conger-eel slick and not a guy I wanted wrapping me up.

I swiped through my contacts and hit Call.

He answered on the third ring. "Gunther Nyx."

"Good morning, sir."

"And how is Sawyer's *liten Sötis?*" said the Swede.

Whatever the heck that is. "Very well, thank you. I have a backer."

"Really?" he said, stretching the word from surprised to skeptical. I heard him lean back in his chair. "Do tell."

"Violetta Veteratti."

There was a long silence. "How did you manage that?"

"She owed me a favor."

"I don't."

"No sir," I said. *Easy does it.* "Although you did say if I found a backer . . ."

"Yes." He went quiet.

And I went antsy. I covered my mouth with my hand.

C'mon, already.

Nyx hummed tunelessly for a moment. "Okay. Reach out to El Cid. Find out if he's amenable."

"Okay." I waited, pen in hand, for further instructions.

None came.

No pearls of wisdom. No rocks of crack. "I . . . er, need some kind of ballpark."

Nyx sighed. "Five kilos. Heroin. Push for purity and immediate delivery." He hung up.

The empty screen of my phone felt exactly like my insides. Blank with a hint of despair.

Coles, sandbagging me with the cigar. That's all it was.

Well, that and it's hard to feel like Mata Hari when you're hunger-striking like Mahatma Gandhi.

I went into the kitchen, got a Cherry Lime Xenergy drink out of the fridge, and popped a Quest brownie bar into the microwave for ten seconds. Cash was awake and on the couch, running and gunning on *Halo.* "You want anything?" I asked.

He glanced over at me. "Nah. Hank's invisible butler left me an awesome upgrade of an Egg McMuffin and corned beef hash."

I perched on the arm of the couch, eating my bar. "You're up early."

"Yeah. Shite's got me on the ropes."

"Second day's always the worst."

"Let's hope." He paused the game. "What happened to your neck?"

"Curling iron burn."

He tossed me his bottle of painkillers. "You look like you could use one." He tipped his head. "I'd advise you to either stay with bad hair or get a crew cut."

"Funny. You call Mom and Da?"

"Remember that favor you owed me? Well . . . we're good now."

I popped two tabs, washed them down with the energy drink, and waited.

It took almost three whole seconds before Cash started chirping. "Look. It was way easier to cover me being tagged with a little shrapnel by telling them Lee asked you along. On a date." He threw me a wide, closemouthed *I'm-not-sorry-at-all* smile.

"Nice try." I crumpled the paper towel and tossed it on the coffee table. "They couldn't possibly ignore the 'shrapnel.'"

"They didn't seem to remember that after I told 'em how confused you are, what with your mercenary MIA and your warm feelings for Lee." He fluttered his lashes at me. "And because I'm a prince of a guy, I offered to stay with you until you see the error of your ways."

"If Da didn't want me to end up with Hank, he shouldn't have gotten me kicked out of the police academy."

"Yeah, about that . . ." Cash rubbed his chin with the back of his hand. "Da sees those as two separate problems."

I sighed. "Of course he does."

"Hey, I like the guy, but what do you really know about him?"

"Everything I need to."

"Da, Flynn, and Rory see a decorated Ranger who did time at Leavenworth." Cash let his eyes drift around the room, dollar signs in his eyes. "No family. No known source of income. Working with the Veterattis. And he let you run with Renko."

They're compiling a jacket. The Quest brownie bar turned to granite in my stomach.

He shrugged. "There's badass and then there's just plain bad."

"Hank Bannon is the best man I've ever known," I said tightly. "Present company included."

Cash's mouth quirked in a condescending smile. "You may think you're Lara Croft, but you're Princess Peach, Maisie. Bannon's not even the same species."

A slow glaze of detachment filmed across my eyes. The Oxy kicking in. I picked up the other controller. "Let's see what you got."

Five miles on the treadmill listening to Craig Johnson's *The Dark Horse: A Longmire Mystery* and I was feeling Wyoming hard and cowboy strong.

Tough enough to change the dressing on my neck after a shower.

Or so I thought.

Hank's first-aid kit was better equipped than most third world hospitals. I peeled up the edge of the dressing.

Holy cat.

The burn was the size of a silver dollar. The outer rim a nasty bright pink going to a soft white fluid-filled center.

Well, that's a hell of a lot worse than I thought it was.

Smearing the silver sulfadiazine stung more than rubbing alcohol on a carpet burn. I eased on a new Tegaderm dressing.

Fecking Coles.

I went into the bedroom, flipped on TNT mute and closed-captioned, and curled up in the dark microfiber armchair. Time to see how lasting an impression I'd made with AJ "El Cid" Rodriguez, up-and-coming lieutenant of the Grieco cartel.

Thanks to Stannis, I'd met him twice. Although I'd talked to him less than a handful of times, we had a connection. Smart and funny, with a master's in business from UCLA, AJ had a thing for fast cars, faster women, and tough guy movies. I glanced at my watch. He ought to be up by now.

I texted him some *Tombstone.*

I'm your huckleberry.

And waited.

A half hour later my phone rang. "Hey, kid. It's AJ. How you feeling?"

His greeting told me two things: One, he was with a woman and two, he was stateside. "Hungry and broke."

"You sure ain't no daisy," he drawled and laughed. "Where are you?"

"Chicago. I need to see you."

"You're in luck. I'm in Vegas. At the Wynn. Flights run from Chi-town to LV every hour on the hour. How soon can I get you here?"

"Gee . . . nine? Maybe ten?"

"Perfect. We'll talk over dinner. Text me your reservation. I'll have someone pick you up."

That was fast. "Uh . . . sure thing." My voice must have been a little uncertain.

"Not going to stand me up now, are you?"

Oh, I'll be there, you sonuvagun. With bells on.

"Never."

* * *

The Wynn's SW Steakhouse was a candle-lit cloud of creams and whites. The waiter led me to El Cid's table. He rose to meet me, clad in an open-necked white Zegna dress shirt and black dress pants. A couple inches shy of six feet, Alphonso Raúl Rodriguez was lean-jawed with a shaved head, his aggressive, ambitious look tempered by velvet-brown eyes.

"Hello, gorgeous." He kissed my cheek. "I love a redhead in a red dress."

"You're looking all kinds of fine, El Cid."

A waiter pulled out my chair. "Thank you for the flowers," I said.

"*De nada.*" He reached across the table, lifted my left hand, and eyed the ring. "I take it you're not here for pleasure."

I dipped my head in acquiescence.

"I've already ordered," he warned.

All the easier to gauge my position. "It'll keep."

"Wine?" he asked.

"Martini?"

"Now you're talking."

We feasted on Japanese Ohmi Shiga Prefecture New York Strips, crisp potato rosti with sturgeon caviar, and black truffle creamed corn, each bite better than the last. Laughing like I hadn't in months, I let AJ steer the conversation to his favorite topic: movies.

I could feel myself getting full and loose. "You've gotta be kidding me. You've never seen *Slap Shot*? Duuuude."

AJ snorted a mouthful of martini. "*Madre de Cristo,* you called me 'dude.'"

"How's the Chevelle?"

He wiped his mouth on the linen napkin. "Goddamn thing of beauty. You oughta see her on the track."

"I'd like to," I said.

AJ let that linger. "How'd you slip the collar?"

"Stannis bought me cover at the *Sentinel* as a reporter. Wasn't even a hop-skip for my brother the lawyer to jump me."

He leaned his forearms on the table. "What do you want, Maisie?"

"Capital. Fast."

"Damn." He patted his chest. "I left my Wells Fargo name tag at home."

Here we go.

"Yeah. About that . . ." I bit my lip. "Let's just say I don't have the same sentiments as Stannis when it comes to dealing in powdered pleasures of a limited and sensory nature."

He shot me a look more skeptical than the Inquisition. "The cop's kid is gonna start running?"

I nodded.

"It's funny how many clichés are built on truth." AJ sipped his drink. "Such as, 'The apple doesn't fall far from the tree.'"

"True, but a man can pick it up and throw it a country mile."

He laughed.

"I have the seed money, AJ, but that's it. I'm in trouble." I smoothed the tablecloth in front of me. "Stannis is in Europe. Vi Veteratti's giving me a window to reboot the chop shops. I need to spring his crew or there'll be nothing for him to come back to."

With measured strokes, AJ cut into his New York Strip. "Renko's last deal didn't turn out so hot."

"Coles set him up."

"Man, I hate that prick." He bit the steak off his fork. "He's given us some headaches."

In all fairness, your uncle Grieco did just try to assassinate him.

"Yeah, well, driving my fiancé out of the country and destroying his livelihood is not something I'm prepared to live with."

"I like you, Maisie. I like you a lot. But I've had hotter tickets than you try to set me up."

"Baa-baa," I bleated. "I'm the original black sheep, baby."

AJ rolled his tongue in his cheek. Considering. "What do you want?"

"Heroin. Five kilos."

"Anything else?" He chuckled.

"Don't make me look like a chump, okay? Best purity. Best price."

He squinted. "And you have distribution for this?"

"I do." *Well, Gunther Nyx does.*

"Veteratti?"

I nodded.

Calculations flitted across AJ's face. "Okay. You bring me the money. I give you the product."

Easy as a blackbird whistling.

"Absolutely." I sat up a little straighter.

"Ah-ahh." He wagged a finger. "In Juárez."

Shite.

"And the product?" I asked.

"You'll pick up in Juárez." His smile gleamed in the candle-light. "Getting it stateside will be your responsibility."

Double shite.

"Cripes, AJ, I've never done this before. A little help, maybe?"

He tossed his napkin down on the table, stood up, and held out his hand to me. "Okay. A little."

Chapter 11

I spent the night playing party girl until AJ finally let me catch a midmorning flight. He sent me home first class, but hung over, and still wearing my red dress and heels, all I felt was used up and jaded.

The beauty of flying out of Midway was onsite parking. My feet were killing me. I flagged down a taxi cart. Fifteen bucks to my car was a bargain. I would have paid a hundred.

I started up the Hellcat, flattening my bare foot on the rubber-coated gas pedal, giving it a good rev, and headed for home.

"Call Cash," I ordered Siri.

"Yeah-'llo," he answered.

"I'm swinging by DMK Burger Bar. You want something, or has Wilhelm taken care of you?"

"Lemme check." I heard him groan as he pushed himself off the couch. "Third day's pretty fucky, too."

"Any time now," I said.

"He's got some kinda shrimp-penne casserole in the fridge. Huh. So yeah . . . Why don't you bring me a couple double cheeseburgers, fries, onion strings, and a chocolate shake."

"You trying for extended obesity leave?"

"Feck off." He laughed. "And make that two orders of fries."

I sped home, cranking The Killers and the air conditioner to stay alert, mouth watering from the smell of fried onions. I pulled into Hank's driveway and banged my head on the steering wheel.

No wonder Cash had ordered so much food.

A dirty Ford Mustang in Steve McQueen highland green was parked in front of the door.

Lee.

Ugh. I'm so not up for this.

I pulled into the garage and checked my reflection in the rearview—a tired, smeary version of sixteen hours ago. I dragged my index fingers under my eyes, wiping off mascara flakes, jammed my feet back in my heels, and went to face the music.

"Lunch delivery." I held up the paper sacks at Cash and Lee. "That'll be fifty-two, forty-two plus tip."

Ever grateful, Cash said, "About time."

Lee gave me a low whistle. "How long have they been serving cocktails in the drive-through?"

Not long enough.

"Good one." Cash tagged him in the shoulder.

I set their food on the coffee table, walked into the kitchen, and tossed my bag in the warming drawer. "I'm gonna take a shower."

"Thanks for sharing," Cash said around a mouthful of fries.

Lee opened his mouth with a smirk.

I jabbed an index finger at him. "Don't."

After a shower so long it turned my fingers pruny, I spent a shameless amount of time getting myself back into first gear. Hoping Lee would get his fill of my idiot brother and beat it.

Eventually, my stomach forced me out of my robe and into Lululemon yoga pants and a Chicago White Sox zip-up hoodie. I went into the kitchen.

"What the—?" My bare feet squeaked to a stop on the polished cement floor. "What the hell do you think you're doing?"

Cash was unabashedly pawing through my purse. He held up my boarding pass. "Vegas?"

Lee looked up from the armchair and asked in all nonchalance, "He there? Bannon?"

I smiled tightly. I wanted to say yes so bad it burned my

tongue. But as my mother was so fond of reminding us, a lie is a trap you set for yourself. "No."

"Who did you see?" Lee said.

"My bookie."

"Pfft." Cash crumpled the boarding pass and threw it at me. "Grab me another Coke, will you?"

"I'm gonna hit the road." Lee stood up. "How about you walk me to my car, Maisie?"

The way he said it wasn't negotiable.

"Yeah, sure." I fetched the soda pop for my brother.

"See you, Cash," Lee said.

His hand went to the small of my back as we walked out of the house and onto the driveway, stopping in front of the Mustang.

At five-foot-ten, Lee seemed taller than he was. Especially up close. He had the densely muscled frame that only a shorter guy could carry without drinking his weight in creatine and whey protein on a daily basis.

The cold driveway pavers felt like dry ice. I shivered and hugged myself. "So. What's up?"

"A little chilly for bare feet," he said, opening the passenger door. "Get in."

The car smelled of cedar, gun oil, and lime. The backseat was littered with gear and sports equipment. He got in on the driver's side, turned sideways in his seat, and rested his elbow on the steering wheel.

You wanna play ringleader? Go ahead and lead.

He gave me the stare-down. His eyes were the cool brown of creek mud, close set and long lashed. "Walt asked me to check up on you."

"Sawyer?" I gaped.

"Did you really think you're the only one working this jacket?"

Shite.

"No, but I'm pretty damn sure it wasn't assigned to you, either," I blurted like an idiot.

Hank's Law Number Eight: If they ask for the rope, give it to them.

And I'd just put the noose around my own neck. "I'm sorry, Lee. I'm beat."

"You asked me to get you a look at the gun that shot Cash. I did. The Bureau of Organized Crime runs the show when it comes to narcotics, gangs, and vice. No way in hell was Special Unit not going to hear about the shooting of a SWAT officer on a cleared stash-house scene."

I sighed. "Yeah. Okay."

"No, it's not," Lee said. "Who knows what kind of hellfire would be raining down on you if the old guy working Evidence hadn't tipped me off. 'Second Belgian-made tactical 5.7 in a month,' he said. But because I'm your own personal savior, I went to Walt with it. Directly."

Wow. Who needs brothers when I have you around?

Lee straightened his black nonreflective Luminox wristwatch. "Walt called up Ditch Broady from the ATF, who—although he didn't remember much about you except for your 'exceptional' ass—was able to shed considerable light on a shipment of stolen FN Five-seveNs with inset black diamonds and the Grieco cartel."

I banged my head gently against the headrest, waiting for it.

"So . . ." he said. "How long did it take for you to go running to the DEA and try to sign up?"

"I don't know what you're talking about," I stalled.

Walt was tighter with information than a Swiss bank. Unbelievable that he'd given up Broady's name, much less the rundown of the meeting to Lee.

"We're talking about your brother. McGranes take this kind of shit personally." His fingers circled my wrist. "You're already working undercover, Maisie. Not much of a leap for you to start thinking that maybe, just maybe, you could weasel your way into the Grieco cartel just far enough to make them pay."

I looked down at his fingers on my radial artery. "Monitoring my pulse, Mr. Human Lie Detector? What's next? Kiss me and measure my respiration rate?"

"You're gonna get yourself killed."

"Lee—"

His grip tightened. "Why'd you go to Vegas?"

I wasn't about to confirm or deny. "Bachelorette party."

"I knew it." He let go and threw himself against the back of the seat. "I told Sawyer the first thing you'd do was set up a drug buy."

DammitDammitDammit.

"Gee." I shrugged. "Hate to disappoint you, but what happens in Vegas . . ."

"You're not funny."

"Neither are you. How about the next time you feel the urge to rat me out to my boss, you give me a heads-up first?"

"*Our* boss."

Jaysus. Enough already. I rolled my eyes. "Okay, Mr. Part-time Muscle."

"Not for long."

"Lee . . ."

"Explosives expert with eight years' combat experience. Sawyer's definitely got a place for me on Special Unit."

Well, gee. You make months of fake-dating a Serbian mobster sound like a cakewalk.

"I'm five and a half years in on SWAT." His lips thinned. "Six is about the longest most of us last."

"Really? Why?"

"It's not just the three or four busts a night that get to you. It's the regular patrol work besides and lugging around and maintaining sixty pounds of gear. Always on call. Duty hours irrelevant." He shrugged. "Hard to keep a girlfriend, much less a wife with that kind of schedule."

Come to kettle, pot.

I laughed. "And you think going to work for Walt Sawyer would be different?"

"You tell me. I never had a partner I wanted to sleep with before."

Chapter 12

I texted Nyx the specifics I'd agreed to with AJ aka El Cid. He agreed to a 13:00 meet, which was a perfect way to end a morning that would rapidly disintegrate into chickenshit. First, the weekly check-in at the *Sentinel,* followed by the dreaded come-clean with Walt.

At best? Censured. At worst? Terminated.

Feck.

One thing that sucked about my new cover was the uniform. Dressing like the average *Sentinel* reporter was not my glass of whiskey. I'd be heading to Belmont Army, Futurgarb, and Hot Topic after my meet with Nyx.

If, of course, I wasn't filling out unemployment paperwork.

I went into the garage to retrieve my Caterpillar steel-toed work boots from the trunk. Somehow a bag of Stannislav's clothes had ended up in my car. Not surprisingly, Declan "missed" it when he'd dragged my belongings into the house a couple of weeks ago.

I rifled through it and scored a white dress shirt and black and red rep-striped tie. Back into the house, where I chose black leggings and a lace cami. A plaid micro-mini finished the look. Teasing my hair into a slapdash ponytail, I added a goth-level of eyeliner and so much mascara my lashes looked like furry caterpillars.

Bring it, angsty newsies. I'm ready to party.

I drove to the politburo aka the *Sentinel.*

The elevators and hallways were a thriving bustle of energy.

The bulk of the hustlers had opted for the Big Gulp–sized of overpriced Starbucks. I squeaked into the conference room just before Paul's assistant closed the doors and slid into the empty seat next to Juice. She gave my appearance the nod. "I like the tie," she said out of the side of her mouth. "Sexy prep-school. Hot."

The Santa-esque Paul Renick bounced about in the front of the room, praising the story ideas that appealed to him with the same boisterous enthusiasm as those he shot down.

The murderer suing the detective for ruining his reputation? *Sentinel gold.* Cat raising a litter of ducklings? *Bronze.* Green algae virus making people stupid? *Platinum.*

Grey Gardens and Lennon were the big story winners. The ad department put on a pointless five-minute PowerPoint dog-and-pony show, followed by the local happenings editor's recap.

"Let's move on to the *Talk Back* column." Paul pointed at me. "What's your take on the EPA? Go!"

"Aside from it being unconstitutional?" I asked. "It's a corrupt, useless agency that'll cost taxpayers eight billion dollars this year."

The table gave a collective gasp.

"Excellent angle, McGrane." Paul glanced around the table. "Who wants opposing?"

"I nominate Ava." Lennon put a skeletal arm around Grey Gardens. "I kicked McGrane's ass so bad on last week's op-ed, I'm surprised she has anything to sit on."

"Not quite certain about that," Paul said, stroking his beard.

Lennon, clueless his boss had actually penned my column, kept on digging. "Aside from the naïve ramblings of an inbred capitalist?" He shook his head in mock sorrow at me. "It's not the kind of thing we believe at the *Sentinel*. We bring news to the people. Not elitist propaganda."

I shrugged. *We were never gonna be pals, anyway.*

The door opened. "Ms. McGrane?" inquired an office assistant.

I raised a hand.

"Your ten o'clock is here."

Having an appointment announced didn't do me any favors with the hyenas. I collected my things and followed the assistant down the hall and across the lobby to the conference room where I'd met Nyx and Broady.

Inside, Sawyer stood at the picture window, dressed, as always, to the nines.

"Hello, sir." Ridiculous and underdressed was a hard combo for inner composure to beat. "How are you?"

"Very well, Maisie. I could ask you that same question, but I'm not sure you'd give the appropriate answer."

Sawyer had taken a chance on me when no one else would. And to repay him, I'd gone rogue. Time to man up. "I'm one hundred percent underwater. I'm sorry, sir."

"Shall we?" He gestured to the table and we sat down. "What happened to your neck?"

I got that sinking feeling. "Coles put his cigar out on me at The Storkling."

"Why?"

"He finds the sight of me provoking."

"Naturally. Will there be anyone pursuing recourse on your behalf?"

"No."

"Hmm." Sawyer leaned back in his chair and steepled his fingers. "The mayor's vendetta against you is disturbing and potentially problematic. How much so, remains to be seen." He dropped his hands abruptly. "Bring me up to speed on the past two weeks."

Floodgates open, I let the deluge pour out.

"Well done." A nostalgic sort of shadow passed across his thin face. "I, too, find that asking forgiveness has a significantly higher rate of return than permission."

It was hard not to sag in relief.

"The Bureau of Organized Crime's investigation into corruption within the mayor's office aside," Sawyer said, "I'm less than keen for you to become enmeshed with the joint task force."

"Oh?"

"The venality of these federal agencies is notorious. The influence of the Mexican drug cartels within them is as insidious as it is real." He gave a small sigh. "But what's done is done. Is Nyx aware of your transparency with me?"

"No sir. He thinks I'm making a run for a position with the DEA."

"Excellent. We'll keep this under wraps, then?"

"In the vault." I nodded, feeling the pressure ease in my chest. "Is there anything I should know about Nyx, sir?"

"Gunther's had a meteoric rise in the DEA. Too far, too fast, perhaps. He's become used to doing things his own way. A slippery slope in undercover work."

Yeah, well . . . Fair to say, I've experienced that firsthand.

I pinched the bridge of my nose. I still wasn't exactly over my last assignment.

"For a joint task force, Broady and Nyx are maintaining distinctly separate investigations," Sawyer said. "I sense a reluctance in Broady to involve his team too closely with Nyx. Watch yourself."

"Yessir." *Silly me. And to think I felt out of my depth before.*

"Is something troubling you?" he asked. "Aside from a federal turf war and becoming involved with the Grieco cartel?"

"I seem to end up actually liking my targets."

Sawyer grinned. "That's what makes you such an asset to Special Unit. Empathy, awareness, and compassion cannot be consistently faked." He made a minute adjustment to his cuff. "What else?"

"This assignment is larger in scope than I'm comfortable with." *Talk about the understatement of the year.* "I've never purchased illegal drugs before, much less smuggled them across the border. And I have to trust El Cid to get me stateside."

"He will." Sawyer nodded reassuringly. "The first time, everyone desires the deal to go smoothly. I find greed takes hold by the third." He raised a palm. "If the situation collapses, stay silent. Nyx has the resources to recover you."

"Got it."

"There's been another shooting. Two dead. Gun not recovered, but a 5.7x28 mm cartridge was. Special Unit will be liaising with Ditch Broady and the ATF regarding the original directive—recovering the FN Five-seveN MK2s. Any questions?"

Yeah. A big one. "Is Lee Sharpe transitioning to be a field agent for Special Unit?"

"Why?" Sawyer cocked his head. "Do you have a personal interest in Mr. Sharpe?"

"No sir." *But he's made no secret he has one in me.*

"Good. Have a care, Maisie. Intense bonds often form during stressful and perilous situations," he said carefully, not answering the question. "Speaking of attachments, there have been no known communications between Stannislav Renko and the Srpska Mafija, nor with any of his men in Chicago."

"He hasn't reached out to me." I bit back a smile at the confirmation that Stannis had gone to ground. Hank had the patience of a spider. It would be a good long while before he'd go near a phone and even longer before he'd let Stannis near one.

"Let me know when he does."

I parked in the ramp off of Clark Street and walked the two blocks to Giarrusso Dry Cleaners, where the sign said, *Drop your pants here and you'll receive prompt attention.*

A buzzer rang when I opened the door. A girl in full fifties pinup–style makeup took one look at me and called over her shoulder, "Wes!"

A podgy guy wearing a gray Men's Wearhouse suit came from the hallway behind the counter. "You Sawyer's?"

"Yes."

"I'm Wes Dorram. C'mon back." I followed him back through the hallway to a steel door. He knocked twice, then let us inside.

Nyx was on a cell phone, Ferragamos on the battered oak desk, working the long-limbed, long-haired Euro-look. "No, no, I haven't. Which doesn't mean I won't." He laughed.

I stood at attention, listening to Nyx talk, all flattery and platitudes.

Guess he saves the friendly patter for criminals.

Wes stood at the door, hands folded, placidly chewing the inside of his cheek.

Eventually, Nyx hung up. "Sawyer's *Liten Sötis.*" He came around to lean against the front of the desk. "Let's see what kind of middleman you are."

"Five kilos, sixty K," I said.

"Not too shabby," Wes muttered.

Nyx shot him a dirty look. "Product will be stepped to shit."

I gripped my wrist behind my back. "El Cid said it's the going rate for uncut in Juarez."

"Did he?"

Hank's Law Number Nine: Confidence is not competence.

Still, AJ wouldn't toy with me. I carried too much family baggage for sport. "Yes. It'd run seventy-five K stateside."

And now for the bad news. Because you made sharing the good news so very much fun already.

I squared my shoulders. "I . . . uh . . . have to deliver the money to Juarez. El Cid said he'd help me get the heroin across the border."

"Bargain shopping on behalf of the DEA?" He folded his arms across his chest. "How industrious."

"He didn't give me a choice, sir."

A Cheshire-cat smile wreathed Nyx's face. "You're in."

"A toehold," I cautioned.

"A test. And one you'll pass. I'll see to that." He sucked his lower lip. "Let's keep this out of Sawyer's field of vision. At least until the deal goes down. Or off. No point knocking over the hive if it's a washout."

"Yessir." The hubris of ego was a remarkable thing. He actually assumed I'd kept Sawyer in the dark. "Umm, Mr. Nyx? Don't you think you should know my name?"

He stepped into my space, leaned down, and whispered, "What makes you think I don't already know everything about you, Maisie?"

A tiny shiver skittered down my spine.

Nyx straightened and crossed the room. Wes opened the door for him.

"Put it in motion," Nyx said.

Wes nodded and closed the door behind him. He lumbered over and sat down heavily at a tiny table.

I took the chair opposite. "Hey—can I ask you something?"

"You betcha."

"What is *Liten Soot-ees?*"

"Little Sweetie."

"Really? Because the way Nyx says it, it sounds anything but."

Wes's lips twitched.

"I'm Maisie."

"Nice to know you. Alrighty then, you told Nyx that El Cid wants you to fly down on Thursday, right?"

I nodded. "One-way, first-class ticket."

"Which means you can't carry the cash. Too many variables with the airport. Sixty K isn't worth stressing our assets."

How much does it take to be cost-effective?

"The money will weigh around seven pounds." Wes chewed on a fingernail, thinking. "Where will you be staying?"

"Hotel Lucerna."

"No problem, then." He smiled. "I'll FedEx it to you."

Seriously? "Don't they have dogs trained to smell out currency ink?"

"Duh." Wes rolled his eyes. "That's why we coat the inside of the FedEx boxes with lynx urine."

"Ugh."

He gave a high-pitched but good-natured giggle. "The money will arrive scent-free, plastic-wrapped inside activated-charcoal deodorizer bags."

Sure thing. "And it'll just show up, unmolested at the hotel desk, no sweat?"

Wes looked at me like I'd lost my mind. "Of course. It'll arrive with the *Sentinel's* NAFTA certificate of origin and pro-forma invoice. Customs won't give it a second look."

"A Chicago newspaper has a duty-free custom's entrance number?"

"They will by this afternoon." He shook his head. "You are a green one, aren'tcha?"

That's me. The perpetual rookie.

"I'm betting he's planning to have you drive the product back. Weekends are the busiest border crossing times. The heavier the traffic flow, the less likely you are to get searched." Wes leaned forward and put a slightly sweaty hand on mine. "Don't think about what you're doing when you come back with the product. You're just returning a package to the DEA."

He gave my hand a damp squeeze.

I nodded, smiling, wanting to pull my hand away but standing firm. "Thanks for the advice."

He finally let go. "Anytime." He heaved himself to his feet and walked me out to the front of the store. "Have a good day, now."

Chapter 13

I gratefully took the scalp on the taxi limo to the Hotel Lucerna. Even with a spray tan, I stuck out more than a constitutionalist at a DNC rally. Ciudad Juárez had the highest murder rate in Mexico. But travel advisories don't mean jack to a Chi-town Irish gel working undercover.

Yeah, right.

The driver pulled up in front of the eight-story cream-colored resort hotel. I overtipped him and wheeled my black Victorinox Spectra hard-side into a lobby of marble-tiled arches and wrought-iron furniture with overstuffed cushions.

At 2:00 p.m., the place was empty except for a woman behind the front desk.

"Maisie McGrane. I have a reservation."

Her eyes were quick and nervous. "You spell please?"

I did. She typed it into the computer. "I'm sorry. There is nothing."

"Will you check again, please?"

She looked away.

"Señora Renko?" asked a man's voice from behind me.

Uh-oh.

The woman at the desk had moved farther down the counter, refusing to look at me.

I slipped my right hand into my jacket pocket and gripped the roll of quarters that served as traveling brass knuckles, before turning, blank-faced.

Three men in thick-rimmed spectacles stood behind me in jeans and plaid Western snap-shirts. The one in the center stepped forward. "You will come with us."

Not so fast, pal.

I eased my carry-on between us and widened my stance slightly. "Do I know you?"

"*Sí.*" He nodded. "I am Chac." He pointed at the other men. "Jefe and Esteban. We are the Hanseen brothers."

It took a minute to register. Han-*son* not Hanseen.

Feck me.

I grinned. *Slap Shot.* AJ had watched it. And sent his men with a coded message only I would understand.

"Yes," I said, realizing AJ had "married" me to Stannis for my own safety. "I am Mrs. Renko."

Jefe started for the door. Esteban took my suitcase and Chac moved toward me.

"Señora Renko—" The woman at the desk put two FedEx boxes on the counter and held out a clipboard. "Your packages."

Gee, thanks.

I signed.

Chac picked up my innocuous packages filled with sixty thousand dollars and we walked to out to the waiting black Acura MDX in the lobby turnout.

All three men replaced their fake, thick-rimmed glasses with sunglasses as soon as we were in the car. Jefe, the driver, and Chac sat in front. I was alone in the middle row with the FedEx boxes, while Esteban, his AK and my carry-on rode in the far back.

"Phone," Chac said. I leaned forward and handed him my iPhone, getting a nice look at his rifle, a Serbian Zastava M21. Jefe had one, too.

Chac popped the SIM card tray open with a paper clip and handed me the card back. "Music, *sí?*"

I nodded. Mexican rap filled the air.

Even with the heavily tinted windows, the bright desert sun

had me reaching for my Ray-Bans. I couldn't seem to get my fingers to work the zipper. I set the messenger bag to the side.

Hank's Law Number Five: Make it look easy.

I was freaked. And while they knew it, that didn't mean they got to see it.

We drove through the frenetic anthill of traffic and smog toward the northwest side of the city. The street sign—BOULEVARD MUNICIPIO LIBRE—reminded me that I hadn't been blindfolded.

Gonna take that the best way possible.

Which wasn't easy, especially as we passed a graveyard jampacked to overflowing that seemed to stretch for miles.

I settled back in the leather seat. Unlike me, Hank would have evaluated the strengths and weaknesses of the men in the car, memorized the terrain, running scenarios—hijacking, roadblocks, police, land mines, and planned contingencies.

Somehow awareness of my lack of situational awareness didn't make me feel real chipper, either.

"*Pila de la Chaveña.*" Chac pointed out the window at a large, dry fountain.

I nodded, absently sliding a thumbnail beneath the shipping label of one of the FedEx boxes. The edge raised. *Maybe I shouldn't leave this on there. . . .* I lifted the sticker carefully, a third of it raising neatly off the box.

"Not long." Chac frowned at me over his shoulder.

I pressed the sticker back down, resealing the adhesive.

The atmosphere in the car eased once we got past the center of the town. The men conversed but only briefly. They needn't have worried. With less than a semester of high school Spanish under my belt, I could barely order a burrito at Chipotle.

We left the city.

Barren mountains of scrub stretched out for miles. "Sierra de Juárez," Chac said. The MDX navigated a series of dirt roads until we arrived at a beat-up old cabin. Two men with identical Zastava M21s and glowering faces stared down at us from the wide wood porch.

AJ came out of the house looking tough as casing nails in mirrored sunglasses, black T-shirt, cargo shorts, and boots. He ran a hand over his shaved head, a good two-day beard covering the lower half of his face. "Maisie!"

I couldn't remember a time when I'd felt quite so happy to see someone. I mean, I had, but not recently.

AJ threw an arm over my shoulder and turned us toward the cabin. "How was your trip?" He raised his free hand and snapped his fingers at the Hanson brothers behind us.

"Easy." We took the six rickety steps up onto the high porch. "I like what you did with the guys. The glasses were a nice touch."

"Anything for you, baby."

The guards didn't look real friendly. There were a couple of chairs on either side of the door, a table on one end, a big blue Coleman cooler on the other.

AJ led me past them into the house. He gestured to an open bedroom on the right. "You want to rest? Take a shower?"

Gee. Let's see. I'm in a house with five men I don't know and one I kind of do. I think I'll pass.

"Nah. Let's get to it."

AJ laughed. "No hurry, Maisie. Your package won't be ready until tomorrow."

Esteban took my carry-on into the bedroom.

Yay, slumber party.

The living room opened onto a large kitchen. Chac followed with the FedEx boxes. "Those are for El Cid," I said.

He set them on the kitchen table. AJ pulled out a chair for me, as Chac, Jefe, and Esteban all tromped through the house and right out the back door. AJ sat down across from me. He slid his hands over the invoice sticker. "The *Sentinel* has a tariff number?"

"Of course they do," I said. "They publish *Sin Perjuicio.*"

"No shit?" He yanked the cardboard zip, pulled out one of the activated-charcoal black bags, and unwrapped it. The plastic-wrapped packets of cash slid out. He sliced one open and flipped through the bank-wrapped stacks of twenties. He smiled. "Nice and easy."

Together we sliced through all the plastic-wrapped packets and moved on to the second box. AJ scanned each one. I replaced them in the black bags.

"We're good." He called something at the front door. The two men from the porch came inside, M21s slung over their shoulders. Each man put the contents of a black bag into a backpack. A lot of Spanish crossed between them. The men took the backpacks and left. I was pretty sure they were done for the night.

The smell of burning charcoal wafted into the room. "C'mon," AJ said. "Let's go have a beer."

Or three. Or six.

We stepped out of the rear of the cabin into a flat yard, overlooking the arid scrub and mountains. The sun was just starting to set, the sky awash in vibrant orange and golden yellows.

Chac and Jefe were grilling beef on a makeshift open-mesh grill. Esteban disappeared into the kitchen.

"Beer or something stronger?" AJ asked.

"One of each." I took a seat at the picnic table.

"My kind of girl." He raised the lid on a sister ice chest to the one on the front porch and brought out a couple Negra Modelos.

AJ popped the caps off the edge of the table. Esteban came out with a bottle of Cava de Oro Extra Anejo and shot glasses, filling one for each of us.

AJ raised a glass. "*¡Salud, pestas y amor y tiempo para gozartos!*"

We drank. The tequila went straight to my shoulders, the easy, warm glow matching the sky. I sucked a lime and concentrated on the horizon. Getting tipsy with AJ was not the wisest course of action, but with no alternative, might as well enjoy the moment where the world was a laid-back and happy place.

Hank's Law Number Twenty-One: Never confuse politeness with civility.

Esteban went back into the kitchen and turned on some music. The tequila kept flowing. And with it, movie talk and the inevitable James Bond argument over our dinner of carne asada.

The Hansons were more disappointed than surprised when I sided with AJ that Sean Connery was and would be the only Bond, ever. Grumbling, they started clearing up.

"I was hoping we might talk about a couple other things tonight," I said as the Hansons milled around the table.

"Sure." AJ poured out two more shots of tequila.

No more, please. The tequila throat scorch isn't really my gig.

He reached into his pants pocket for his wallet, and took out a hundred-dollar bill. "Boys," he said. The Hermanos Hansons' heads swiveled toward him simultaneously like a pack of meerkats. "A hundred American for whoever kills the most scorpions in thirty minutes."

It was like he'd rung the school bell.

In seconds they were silhouettes in the twilight, their black-light penlights and blades glinting in the moonlight as they moved into the desert.

AJ shook his head. "I recruit the mutherfucking *Cinco-Sietes.* Some of the most badass killers in the world for my uncle Carlos. And what do I get? His half-retarded second cousins as my personal security force. *Madre de Christos.*" He gave a bark of laughter. "Okay, Maisie. Shoot."

"Funny you should say that, AJ. I'm actually in the market for some of those, as well."

"Some what?"

"Guns."

AJ rubbed his lower lip with his thumb. He got that really unpleasant fake-pleasant look that a smart guy gets when the wheels click and he knows he's being screwed with.

Only I couldn't figure out why he had that look.

"You got guts, Maisie. Ironclad, I'll give you that."

Uh-oh.

"That was sweet." His mouth split in a mean smile. "That little sob story about trying to save Renko. Coming here to deal with me all on your own?"

Shouting came from the desert. We turned. One of the Hermanos Hansons held up his knife. Something large on the tip. The other men yelled back.

"AJ—"

"That's El Cid to you, baby."

"El Cid, I don't know what you're talking about."

"You tell Renko, he wants to know if we're buying guns from someone other than the Slajic clan, then he best pick up the fucking phone and answer my goddamn calls."

"I don't know where he is." I put my hand on his. "Everything's in flux in Chicago. Eddie V's in rehab and Vi's cozying up to the Syndicate who's moving in on Renko's interests. The heroin was my idea." My voice splintered from the tequila-induced huskiness. "I'm just trying to keep it together."

He grabbed me by the back of my neck and brought my face in close, velvety eyes searching mine.

Oh Jaysus. "I'm not Fredo," I said. "I didn't break your heart."

"No." AJ grinned at the *Godfather* reference and slapped my cheek. "You're not." He put his index fingers in his mouth and gave a short whistle. "Time's up!"

The Hermanos Hansons jogged back to the table and presented their knives—Jefe with four, Esteban two, and Chac with a winning seven scorpions impaled on his blade. Some of the scorpions were still moving.

Eeew.

I excused myself, pushed open the cabin's screen door, and went into the tidy bathroom. I was half-cut, the kind where you grab the sink for a minute before you splash water on your face.

Steady on. Cartel killers aren't the type to hold your hair back when you're sick.

I checked myself in the mirror. My ponytail was tidy, mascara still fine after the face bath. But my pupils were dilated and my face wore a bad and reckless excitement.

"Settle down," I warned my reflection. "Just settle the feck down."

I stepped back into the kitchen and heard AJ's voice. "Get

the cooler off the front porch." He was talking to his men, but carrying a cooler might give me a little desperately needed centering.

"I got it!" I called from inside the kitchen, then spun toward the door and bumped my wrist hard on the back of a wooden chair. "Gah! Jaysus, Mary, and Joseph." I shook my hand out and walked out onto the front porch.

It was just as bewitchingly lonely in the front yard as the back. I could live in a place like this.

With Hank.

Moths flung themselves against the hot porch lights. Singeing their wings from their uncontrollable attraction. The air felt warm on my skin. Which meant, as a happy but chilly drunk, I was toasted. The big blue cooler was gone.

Huh. We must've cleaned that one out already, too.

Focus.

A battered red Playmate cooler sat at the top of the stairs. It didn't seem all that heavy.

Hermanos Hansons will be making a beer run if this is all we have left.

It was buzzing.

Like my head.

I carried it over to the wood table on the corner of the porch and set it down. The faint droning continued. I pressed in the white button of the cooler and pushed the lid up.

It stuck.

The stench was immediately recognizable. Through the three-inch strip of open cooler, a human head, corneas fogged to gray marbles, stared sightlessly outward. Flies buzzed at the nostrils and mouth.

Oh God.

I shoved the lid all the way back.

And heard an ominous, metallic *snick.*

Followed by a long hiss and a sharp *crack.*

The burning acrid reek of chemicals seared my nose and mouth. I turned to run and fell off the porch. Landing hard on my stomach, I rolled underneath, scrambling to tuck up tight against the house.

The explosion ripped above. The concussion jammed my eardrums into my head as it squashed the air out of my lungs.

Dust and splinters and shards of plastic and metal rained down on the porch above me. I felt it more than heard it.

I didn't realize I wasn't dead until seconds after.

Chapter 14

I fecking hate bombs.

I lay there. Not thinking, feeling more than hearing the ringing in my ears.

No flash, no fire, just a noxious chemical smell.

So that's what it feels like to be tackled by Reggie White's ghost.

I rolled onto my back and stared up through the porch slats. The lights had been shattered. My whole body smarted.

"Maisie!" AJ grabbed my leg.

"Is anyone hurt?"

He shook his head. "Are you?" It sounded like he was talking underwater.

"No." I crawled out from under the porch and dusted my hands off on my pants. My ears were ringing.

I surveyed the damage.

Chac and Jefe had flashlights out. Wood screws, hex nuts, nails, and pieces of the cooler were embedded in the siding of the house. Windows and porch lights were shattered.

Chac reached out to pull a wood screw buried head-in in the doorjamb.

"Don't!" AJ rubbed his forehead. "It's probably been soaked in rat poison. So even if the explosion didn't kill you, the shrapnel might."

Moonlight reflected off a small ivory piece on the porch. I looked closer.

Ugh. Mistake.

A human tooth.

"El Cid?" Esteban lifted half of the head with his knife. Jefe trained his flashlight beam on the sight. Viscous goop dripped from the head onto the steps.

"Oh Jesus." AJ put an arm around my shoulder, turning us away from the carnage. "We need to talk."

Yeah. We sure do.

We walked around to the back of the house. "Lucky Jefe parked the car back here," I said. The lights in the kitchen still worked.

"Always does," AJ said as we sat down. "What happened?"

I pointed at the second blue ice chest. "I heard you ask for the cooler from the front. I went to get it. A small red one was on the top step of the porch."

"Fucking assholes!" AJ spat. "They fucking droned us."

"You're serious? They dropped it off by remote control?"

"Yeah. We have eyes a mile away on either end of the dirt road. Assholes. These guys are all about the toys." He ran a hand over his shaved head. "Back to the cooler . . ."

"I saw the head inside before it blew. Hispanic male, he had little plus-sign tattoos on his cheekbones."

"Goddammit!" AJ braced his hands on his knees and dropped his head. He took several deep breaths. "Galo."

He dug his cell out of his pocket, dialed, and stood up. He turned away, talking triple-time into the phone.

I was glad I couldn't understand a word of it. My head was pounding and I was shivering. I grabbed the bottle of tequila. I had a hard enough time getting the cap off, so I skipped the glass and took a slug straight out of the bottle.

It tasted like chemicals.

AJ hung up. "I'm sorry this happened." He sat down next to me.

I slid the tequila in front of him. "Not your fault. I was lucky." *Damn lucky.* "No one got hurt."

"Except Galo." He took a swig. "Fucking El Eje."

"I'm not sure, but . . ." I cleared my throat. "I think his eyelids had been, er, removed."

AJ traced the wood grain of the table with his fingers for several seconds. "La Bestia Que Llora," he murmured. "Burn in hell."

La bestia que llora definitely sounded like something I needed to remember. I said it over and over and over in my head. He was rattled. *Who isn't?*

I pressed the advantage. "What's happening, AJ?"

"Colombia, Bolivia, Ecuador . . . They treated the Mexican cartels like shit, paying them nothing to get the drugs into the U.S. And so the cartels like El Eje and Grieco unified and waited. Waited until the South Americans became dependent upon their lines of distribution." AJ raised a shoulder. "Eventually, Mexicans said, '*No mas.* No more. You will pay us what we want or we will not distribute.' And it worked. For a time."

"But you think the drone was from El Eje."

"Oh, I know." He smacked his fist on the table. "Carlos and I believe a more civilized methodology works to the advantage of all. Tampico is safe, the people are happy. We take our cut but we're not greedy."

Stannis had a toast like that. *Be a bull or a bear but never the pig.*

"El Eje wants Tampico," AJ said. "They are as primitive and crude as an ISIS tribe. Which is who they're actually recruiting."

"How do you fight that?"

"Marketing. Every vicious South American mercenary I've ever met has watched Marvel, *The Matrix,* and all Tarantino's shit. The promise of technology and exclusivity is how I'm building Carlos's private army, Los Cinco-Sietes," AJ said. "The Five-seveNs."

"What's with the name?" I asked, even though I already knew.

"They're named after the guns. FN Five-seveNs. I wanted something specialized, sophisticated. Not the same old blinged-out shiny-shit Mexicali bang-bang. Slajic scored a shipment of The FN Five-seveNs M2Ks. Fucking beautiful guns, with thirty-round mags."

"That ammo's not easy to come by."

AJ nodded. "That turned out to be a benefit—moving us in a different direction."

Where, exactly?

"Which is why you're here. Isn't it?"

"I don't follow . . ."

"Fredo. Do you really think I don't know what you're doing here?"

The blood drained from my face.

Feck feck feck.

Hank's Law Number Ten: Keep your mouth shut.

I raised the tequila bottle to my lips.

AJ put his hand on my shoulder. "Stannislav Renko sent you here as a test." His mouth split in a mean, knowing smile. "And as your loyalty to him is absolute, so is my respect for him and the business interests we share. I did not send a Cinco-Siete to assassinate Coles."

Really? It wasn't me? That's the best you got? "I didn't say you did."

"The fact that you're here says that Renko does."

Sometimes having lawyers in the family was a win-win.

AJ opened up this avenue of inquiry, after all. I presented the facts. "The gun—Five-seveN with the Grieco custom black diamond on the safety—it's one of your Cinco-Siete's, yes?" I said. "The man who fired it, Grieco's."

"Juan Echeverría wasn't one of the Cinco-Sietes. Hell, he's not even a *sicario*," AJ protested. "Echeverría's aim was so bad, if he threw a rock at the ground he'd miss."

I nodded. Juan wouldn't have made my Top Ten list of potential assassins, either.

"If we wanted Coles dead, Maisie, he would be."

"You must see how this looks. Coles and Renko go way back."

"Echeverría's a fall guy. El Eje kidnapped his family, gave him the gun and orders to go after Coles." He sighed. "It's Diego Rivero Lavayén's gun."

"How do you know?"

"Because until last week, he's the only Cinco-Siete who'd gone missing. I recruited Lavayén from Bolivia. Disappeared about six weeks ago. We found his head in a cooler at the shipyard, naked body hanging from one of the Tamaulipas entry arches." He turned his head, throat working. "The torture Lavayén suffered . . . blessed by the damned." He closed his eyes. "*La bestia que llora.* Fucking bastards. They were careful to keep him alive. Made it last for days. . . ."

"Why would El Eje want Coles dead?"

"To put the heat on us. They want Tampico."

"C'mon, AJ. You're trying to tell me El Eje is trying to take over the Port of Tampico by assassinating an American politician? Really?"

"It's not about Coles." Color flared in his cheeks. "They're trying to discredit us with Renko and Slajic. If the Serbs blackball us, where the hell are we gonna get what we need?" He grabbed the tequila bottle and poured, swearing under his breath.

Jaysus Criminey. Now, that was an admission.

It didn't explain the Cinco-Sietes's gun that shot Cash. But one doesn't search for the squall behind a windfall.

I stood up and walked out from beneath the covered patio.

The *snap* of the glass in the cooler echoed in my head. I knew exactly how Cash felt coming around that corner.

I put my hands in my pockets, concentrating on looking nonchalant and not puking up tequila and Chac's carne asada. My fingers closed around a small plastic rectangle. "Hey, AJ." My right ear had a raspy, blown-speaker reverberation when I spoke. "Do you have a computer?"

"Yeah, but we're not on the grid, babe."

I pulled a thumb drive out of my jeans pocket. "Aww. That's too bad. I guess we won't be needing this."

"What's on it?"

"*Zero Effect, Time Bandits, The Unbelievable Truth,* and *Touch of Evil.*"

AJ grinned. "You're a pretty cool kitty."

We spent the night grim-faced and shoulder to shoulder on the sagging double bed watching movies.

AJ passed out at 4:27 a.m. I eased off the bed, picked up my travel vanity case, and snuck into the bathroom. After the bomb, they'd drawn straws and Chac ended up spending the night in the MDX. The other two sacked out on the couches in the front room.

I turned on my iPhone. Chac still had the SIM card, but the rest of it was still operational. I dug through my vanity case for an empty Ziploc bag and plastic gloves—equally useful for fake tanning or evidence gathering. Into the bag went cotton balls, Q-tips, Kleenex, and tweezers. I shook the three Oxys out of an RX bottle, rinsed, and dried it.

I slipped out the back door and crept around the empty side of the cabin. The sky was growing light, but the sun wasn't due up for a while. I flipped on the camera and snapped some orientation shots, then put the gloves on and went to work.

A chemical bomb.

Hank had given me a vague idea of how explosives worked, but it was a case of my da's that had me swiping down the door, table, and leftover base of the cooler for residue with every absorbent material on hand.

The Ziploc bag was filled in minutes.

A chemical bomb needed a detonator. The barest rays of sun were lightening the sky. I searched for a solid five minutes before finding the striker impaled in the porch post behind me. It took some convincing, but after shredding my gloves, I got it out and into the Rx bottle.

For good measure I threw in a couple of screws, hex nuts, and plastic shard of cooler.

And the tooth.

Chapter 15

After a somber brunch and good-byes with AJ, the Hermanos Hansons and I got into the MDX. Jefe, as before, behind the wheel. Esteban, riding shotgun this time, immediately turned on the music. Chac sat next to me. The M21s and AKs at their sides were just a fact of life, the atmosphere in the car as carefree as a sunny day.

In their minds, at least, I'd passed muster.

A position I wanted to stay in. "Did you see the movie El Cid named you after?"

"*Sí, yes,*" Chac said. "Is very funny. *Slap Shot!*"

"*Slap Shot!*" Jefe and Esteban echoed.

Chac said, "Mexico team is no good. They must see *Slap Shot.* They need Hermanos Hanseen."

Jefe and Esteban began shouting like the Hanson brothers—in the Spanish-dubbed version—which cracked us all up.

Guys. They're all the same.

"You are from Chicago, yes?" Chac nodded. "You have team?"

"Chicago Blackhawks." I gave a double bicep flex. "The best."

He smiled. "Would like to see game someday."

I didn't have the heart to tell him hockey had evolved since the 1970s. "You guys get to Chicago, I'll get you into a game."

Jefe said something. Chac and Esteban nodded in serious agreement.

"What?" I asked.

"He says Mr. Renko is lucky husband. But not"—he searched for the word—"careful with you." He shrugged. "This not a good business for a woman."

Tell me about it.

Chac, Jefe, and Esteban were, in fact, not brothers, but cousins. My Spanish was too weak to follow the lineage, but safe to say they knew a heckuva lot about Carlos Grieco and AJ Rodriguez.

"So El Cid is Carlos's son?"

"No. Nephew. Carlos's sister, his favorite, she marry the Spaniard. They live in New York City. El Cid is Americano. But his mother is killed on street like a dog. Very sad."

I knew the rest. AJ was sent to UCLA, where he graduated early and got his MBA in business.

We were back in Juarez before I was ready. Time flies when you're not sweating that you're about to be killed en route. And consciously avoiding any thoughts about smuggling eleven pounds of heroin across the border. And about whether Nyx actually had my back.

A fire extinguisher filled with Zantac couldn't put out the acid inferno in my chest.

"Chac?" I said in a voice too low for Jefe and Esteban to hear. "I've never done this before."

"What?"

"Taken drugs across the border."

"Have no worry, Señora Renko." He reached over and squeezed my hand. "El Cid make easy for you."

We pulled into a ranch. Or at least I assumed it was, from the horses and corral and trailers. Chac handed me my SIM card back. "Do not use until El Paso."

"Okay." I put it in the zippered pocket of my backpack. Chac and I got out and went to the house.

A man wearing a six-shooter on his hip, old-school John Wayne style, moved aside so we could knock on the battered screen door.

We entered a kitchen with peeling linoleum and cabinetry with so many layers of paint that the doors must've grown an inch in thickness over the years.

An old man as weathered and stringy as rawhide sat at a round kitchen table with an enameled blue tin coffee cup. There were no other chairs.

His rheumy brown eyes looked me over from head to toe.

I was wearing a Burberry Brit denim cropped jacket, white tee, and biscuit-colored jeans over my distressed calf-hair, square-toed Donald J Pliner boots.

He shook his head and called, "Consuela!"

A teenage girl in a shapeless print skirt and a Taylor Swift T-shirt came into the kitchen and went straight to his side. He said something. She straightened and waved a hand at me. "You come."

Consuela took me into a tiny bedroom. A single bed held a multicolored quilt with primitive appliqued pillows. A ratty teddy bear was the only decoration. There was no furniture except for a battered dresser. She opened the bottom drawer and took out a beaten pair of Wrangler jeans and an old, polyester-blend Western snap-shirt. "Put on."

I did. Snug, but not uncomfortable. The girl carefully folded up my old clothes while I put my boots on. I reached for my jean jacket. Consuela shook her head.

She gave a small sigh and pulled out a red canvas jacket from the top drawer. From the look on her face, it was a favorite. I slipped it on.

She held out my clothes to me.

I shook my head. "For you," I said without enthusiasm. I didn't want to trade my jacket, either.

She looked doubtfully at my clothes. "*Gracias.*"

When did this adventure become a D-level version of *Traffic*? I was still taking my suitcase home.

"Hang on." I dug my wallet out of my backpack. I had two thousand dollars in hundreds from Nyx for incidentals. I held up five hundred dollars and pointed at my clothes. "Can you get those in my suitcase?"

"*Sí!*" She took the money, went to the bed, and jammed it inside the moth-eaten teddy bear's leg. Still holding my clothes, she opened the window and put her leg over the sill. "You go back now."

Back in the kitchen, a pile of papers sat on the table.

The old man patted his hand on the stack, then removed a set of car keys from his shirt pocket. He tossed them on the table.

Chac picked up the papers and the keys. "*Gracias.*"

"*De nada.*"

We walked outside the small ranch house. I looked back over my shoulder to see Consuela climbing back into her bedroom window.

Chac and I passed several beat-up-looking junkers. "You drive *transmisión* manual, *sí?*"

"Sure thing."

He picked up the pace. We were almost trotting now, past the corral to a barn on the other side. "*Remolque, sí?*"

"I don't understand."

On the other side of the barn sat a faded tan Ford series pickup from the late eighties. Not quite old enough to be an antique. Attached to it was a five-foot-by-fourteen-foot rusted livestock trailer. Chac hit the trailer with his hand. "*Remolque.*"

Remolque me.

"Nope," I said. "I've never driven a trailer."

"Ah!" He waved a hand at me. "Is easy."

He handed me the keys and had me take it for a spin. I practiced backing it up to a sort of narrow pen, only messing up two out of three times, for cripe's sake, before Chac said, "Good. Stop now."

I got out of the truck, only mildly sweaty after my air-conditioning-free test run. "So, I'm good to go, yeah? Now what?"

Chac walked me around to the front of the truck. He handed me a hand-drawn map with no road names. He spread open a big paper map. "You keep in your head, *sí?*"

Random direction memorization. Gah!

Men's voices and metal *clanks* sounded in the background. I squinched my eyes shut, trying to focus. "No," I said. "No. I need to see."

He thought it over for a minute, then penciled in the names on the El Paso side. "You follow us to crossing at Juarez."

"Thank you."

A snorting bellow broke the air.

Then shouting. Lots of shouting.

I stepped to the side of the truck. To my abject horror, three men were prodding out one of the biggest, maddest animals I'd ever seen in my life. He'd turned broadside toward the chute and trailer, shaking his head from side to side, hair standing up on his back. He stopped, digging his horn into the dirt.

The men fell back.

"Is Miura fighting bull. Toro Bravo. The best," Chac said. "You drive careful, *sí?*"

Are you fecking kidding me?

A wave of heat splashed over me, like I was a lobster dropped in a pot.

This is a terrible idea.

Red heat shot up my neck and burst in my cheeks. I couldn't cool down. I moved away from Chac, fanning myself ineffectually with my hands.

"Chac, I don't think I—"

He raised a hand and dipped his head. "Is best way, Señora Renko." He tapped his nose. "The dogs they no smell the product."

I heard the metal *clinks* and *clangs,* then cheers.

Chac barked an order at a short, lard-tailed kid standing by the fence. He pointed at the steaming pile the bull had just dumped prior to trailer entry.

The kid waved, picked up a shovel, and jogged out to the pile. He scooped up a blade full of the manure, hay, and gravel. He squeezed through the open gate and the closed trailer, holding the full shovel high and close like it was going in a pizza oven. I watched as he walked straight up to me and tossed it on my shins and boots.

"*Gracias!*" Chac said to the lard-tailed kid.

"Wha!" I gaped, shaking my legs, trying to get the warm stink off me. "What the—"

Chac turned to me. "You are ready now."

In the cab of the truck was the map to my destination in El Paso, as well as the *veterinario* papers for El Toro Bravo. Who I was now calling Benicio, in the hopes that by sending him friendly karmic thoughts, he'd behave himself.

Benicio clattered from side to side in the trailer.

Should have named him Ferdinand.

I trailed the Hanson brothers back through Ciudad Juárez, damn glad I hadn't let Chac pawn me off with his not-to-scale scribble map. I wouldn't have made it ten blocks without getting lost.

As it was, I spent the half hour white-knuckling the wheel at the slightest sway of the trailer.

Up ahead, Chac rolled down the window and indicated that I should take the next right turn. With a honk and a wave they disappeared.

I turned and joined the massive traffic jam at the Paso del Norte Bridge.

I crawled past a dozen matte-black pickup trucks filled with soldiers in back, clad in full battle rattle and neoprene ski masks to hide their identity from drug traffickers.

Gee, that's . . . me.

I sat there, waiting my turn in the far lane, slow-baking in the cab like one of those asinine fake-news stories where they bake chocolate chip cookies on the dashboard. Hell, Benicio might be BBQ by the time we got to El Paso.

Hank's Law Number Four: Keep your head.

Surprisingly difficult to do when you had a couple of hours in line, watching Border Patrol search the vehicles ahead with mirrors on little rolley sticks and men with German shepherds.

Five kilos carry a minimum sentence of five to twenty-five years.

Feck off, clarity. No one asked for you.

I pulled forward another car length. And another.

Benicio gave a whopping triple kick into the side of the trailer. The *clangs* echoed through the holding lot.

A mustached border patrolman waved me forward. He approached my open window. "Good afternoon."

"Hi." I gave him a perky smile and handed over vet papers, truck and trailer permits, passport, and driver's license.

He took the stack back to his desk and did whatever it was that they do with them.

Benicio shuffled from side to side in the trailer. I could see it rocking in the rearview mirror.

Don't come a knockin' . . .

I gave a chuckle-gasp.

Panic giggles are frowned upon when working undercover.

Benicio bellowed and kicked some more. The two German shepherds whined and stutter-stepped.

Oh my God.

The bomb shrapnel in my backpack . . .

The guard looked up from my paperwork, disapproval creasing his face.

Panic giggles gone.

He went back to the papers.

On the plus side, I was already sweaty as hell with no AC. Minus side, the Border Patrol's two German shepherds were now going positively apeshit. Over which—the heroin or the bomb residue—I had no idea.

The border patrolman went to the side of the trailer, shaded his eyes, and peered in. Benicio's hoof kicked again. The patrolman came back to my window. "Señorita McGrane? Step out of the truck."

Here we go.

Hank's Law Number One: You are defined by your disasters.

I opened the door and hopped down from the seat, as chipper as all get-out. "Yes sir?"

"Come with me, please."

We walked around to the back of the trailer. He swung open the top panel of one of the doors. "Ma'am, this bull—he is sick, no?"

The bull chuffed and groaned. Benicio was in the head of the carrier, separated from the rear doors by a chest-high fence of open bars.

My eyes bulged.

Good Lord, what had they fed the poor beast? Sugar-free candy and Ex-Lax?

It looked as if an outhouse had exploded.

"Uh . . . Not sick-sick. Only carsick," I lied, hoping bulls could suffer from motion sickness. "Benicio doesn't like to ride."

"Benicio?"

I bit my lip and smiled. "Del Toro. Benicio del Toro . . ."

"Ha! I see," he said.

Benicio's tail raised, firing a spattering cannon. The guard raised his arm in front of me like a protective mother as we skittered backward.

He turned to me, eyes wide and mouth open. He began to chortle. "You should have named him *Rey de Mierda*."

One of the two dog handlers approached the rear of the trailer.

"No, no." My patrolman waved a hand in front of his face. "Egh. Carsick bull. Very angry."

The dog handler and his furry companion beat a hasty retreat.

The border patrolman walked me back to the cab of the truck, stopping at his station to retrieve my stack of paperwork. He opened the door for me. "You are a lovely *vaquera*, Señorita McGrane. We see you at the Paso del Norte Bridge again, *sí?*"

"*Sí.*"

I sure as hell hope not.

Chapter 16

The ranch was only a half hour outside of El Paso. I was getting the hang of the trailer now, and Benicio del Toro seemed to have calmed down some.

I pulled up to a scrub-looking ranch surrounded by splinter-wood fence posts and barbed wire. Everything about the desert was dry and mean, not a plant around without spikes or needles. The perfect home for 1,200 pounds of pissed-off beef.

I put the truck in Park, got out, and opened the gate. Ran back to the truck, pulled in, closed the gate, and then drove up to the house.

Nice of them to be waiting for me.

A seventy-something rancher with bowed toothpick legs and a potbelly came out of the clapboard farmhouse. He took off his hat and waved me off toward the barn, following behind.

I shut off the truck and rested my head on the steering wheel for a ten-count.

So far, so good.

I lifted the handle and climbed out of the truck.

"I see they don't teach you no manners in the city," the rancher barked at me. "You're supposed to honk a'fore you open the gate." The rancher peered in the back of the trailer. "Damn amateurs. Gave 'im too much mineral oil. I'll have to water an' salt him up plenty."

I could use a Gatorade myself, right about now. One half-filled with vodka.

The rancher glared at me. "He all choused up now. Turn on a dime and give me a nickel's worth." He shook his head. "Alrighty then. You go on and back into that corral over yonder. We let him get hisself out."

I looked at the tiny hole in the fence he wanted me to back the trailer through. "Uh, sir?" I held out the keys. "This is the first time I've ever driven a truck with a trailer."

He spat on the ground, inches from my foot. "Then you best pay attention to what yer doin'."

The rancher was far more intimidating than the Border Patrol. But after four false tries and a helluva lot of signals and swearing, I managed to back the trailer into the corral.

The rancher threw open the doors and hustled to the fence. Benicio stayed in the trailer.

"What now?" I said.

"I done tole you," he said, walking away to the house. "We let him get hisself out."

My gut gave the twinge that the rancher was jerking my chain. I followed him to the back porch. I didn't dare go up the steps with my filthy boots.

But it wasn't until he came out drinking a large, iced-up glass of lemonade that I knew for sure. He spent the next five minutes scolding me or telling me a story, I wasn't sure which. I just knew that I was about a half-a-hair from yanking that glass from his hand and guzzling it down.

"He's out now." The rancher set down his lemonade and we returned to the truck. He looked at the bull fondly. "Damn, if he ain't gonna cause a stir."

I nodded, figuring now was when he'd open the magic hideyhole in the truck, hand me the product, and give me a ride to El Paso.

"Go on, pull the truck up to barn."

I drove the truck and trailer to the side of the barn. He disappeared inside. I hopped out of the truck. "Um? Sir?"

He came out with a shovel. "You best call a cab." He threw the shovel at my feet. "And get yer shit outta my truck, you hear?"

Lovely.

I went into the trailer and almost passed out.

Poor Benicio.

I opted to start with the biggest pile. I slid the shovel up under the mound. It flipped over before I lifted it up.

The "shit" was actually *in* the shit.

"Thank you, baby Jesus." I bladed off as much manure as I could, then carried the package out of the truck to the water bib next to the barn. And no, I wasn't asking Rancher Crabbypants if I could borrow a little water.

I took a drink out of the tap. It was warm and tasted of iron, but I wasn't complaining. I rinsed off the top garbage bag. Getting braver, I tore it off. Beneath it was another thick black garbage bag. And who knew how many layers under that?

I didn't care. It was now fit to be stored in my black nylon LeSportsac backpack. I dried my hands on my jeans and called the taxi. I slipped the map from the truck cab into my pocket and spent the next ten minutes repacking my suitcase and backpack.

Wearing my backpack and hauling my carry-on, I hoofed my stinking, sweating self off the ranch and up to the main road.

I made the cabbie take me to the closest FedEx. Miracle of miracles, the FedEx guy had just arrived to pick up the six-thirty final drop-off.

"Please!" I begged. "Let me box it up, it'll only take a second."

"Ma'am, it's already ten after seven. I'm late."

I held up a fifty-dollar bill. "Please?"

"Okay," he said.

Thank God for private enterprise.

I took the smallest box they had back to the corner. I wrapped the evidence I'd taken from AJ's cabin in Consuela's jacket, shoved it in the carton, and sealed it up while the girl behind the counter typed in the address from Walt Sawyer's business card.

God knew I'd have liked nothing more than to send the heroin ahead, too, but there's luck and then there's my luck.

The cab dropped me at the DoubleTree Hilton in downtown

El Paso. Four stars. The best I could do. I checked in, went up, and called down to the concierge. I took my clothes off, threw them in a plastic laundry bag, and scribbled *TRASH* on it with a Sharpie marker. I put my boots in another one and wrote *SHOE REPAIR*—a girl can hope, can't she?—and set them outside.

Minibar, magical giver of alcohol, bestow your blessings upon me.

I gulped down enough Coke from the can for a mini-bottle of Bacardi to fit, took it in the shower, and stayed there for an hour. Afterward, I put on yoga pants and Hank's old army T-shirt, then ordered room service. With my third rum and Coke, I had to say, it wasn't bad as far as sixteen-dollar turkey sandwiches go.

I ached for Hank. Missed him so bad I could hardly see straight.

A mirror hung over the desk. My reflection was a stranger to me.

Would I be in El Paso if Hank were here?

The answer was unequivocally "no."

This misadventure was a knee-jerk reaction. To what had happened to Cash. To what had happened to me—joining Special Unit, choosing not to prosecute Coles after he tried to have me killed, getting stabbed by Hank.

I pointed at my reflection. "You, my friend, are a hot mess."

Not as hot as Benicio.

Holy cat.

I'd just smuggled eleven pounds of heroin over the Mexican border. Not bad for a graduate of St. Ignatius Catholic school. If Sister Mary Cecelia Clare could see me now . . .

Jaysus.

A giggle sprang from my lips. The thin, high-pitched, cuckoo-bananas kind.

Call him.

I dug my SIM card out of the zipper pocket in my backpack, completely ignoring the black garbage bag–wrapped brick. I inserted the SIM card, let my phone reload, then called Hank's office.

The sultry-voiced secretary answered the phone. "Good evening, Miss McGrane."

I hated her.

I'd never met her—hell, I didn't even know her name—but I hated her just the same. Hated her silky Southern drawl caressing the words my girly-voice ironed flat with my Chicago twang. But most of all, I hated that she knew more about Hank's past, present, and future than I did. And now I had to beg. "Can you please tell me the last time Mr. Bannon checked in?"

"His last message pickup was thirty-four days ago."

Over a month. I started to shake.

That's too long. Far too long.

"Ms. McGrane? Are you there?"

I pressed the phone tight to my ear. "Can you . . . please . . ." My voice splintered and I tried again. "Is there anything you can tell me? Anything at all?"

"The message Mr. Bannon last received was, 'M.M. stable. Full recovery expected.'"

"Who sent it?"

She hesitated before answering. "Randolph Acrey."

Ragnar.

"Thank you," I said and hung up.

Where are you, Hank?

My reflection had gone white-faced and glassy-eyed.

"Don't worry," I told it. "If something happened to him, you'd know."

I'd know.

Chapter 17

Twenty-one hours and fifty-three minutes.

My drive ahead from El Paso to Chicago.

Feck me.

It was hurting me not to rent the Daytona Sunrise Orange Corvette in the Hertz lot. "Do you have anything with a little more zip than a Ford Fusion?" I asked the clerk. "Anything?"

He typed away. "Well, there's an Infinity G37, but that's three times the rental fee."

"I'll take it."

"Ooh." He gave me the sad face that wasn't really. "I'm sorry. It's been returned but the interior hasn't been detailed yet."

I snapped my Visa on the counter. "I'll take it."

"But—"

"Write it up," I said. "Now."

A half hour later I was cruising through El Paso with *Eagles Live* playing from my iPhone. I was on my third extra-large, sugar-free Red Bull, hitting the full body rebellion where over-caffeinated allied with acid belly and demanded sleep. The plan for two twelve-hour driving days melting to ten and fourteen in front of my heavy eyes.

I crossed the border into Oklahoma, which had apparently changed its slogan to "The Road Construction State."

Oklahoma. You're killing me.

I was still driving around with eleven pounds of heroin in my car. Operating at full-crush depth of stress, I couldn't just pop the hatch and bleed out the pressure.

How did criminals do it? The rush of the moment, with so much to lose? It was like high stakes in Vegas, only since you were all in, the only thing you had to play with was your freedom.

I gave up and checked in to a Holiday Inn Express.

I took off my clothes and slid between the sheets. The iPhone played "Got to Give It Up."

Aww.

I grabbed my phone, which naturally was plugged in to the wall on a two-foot cable, and hung my head over the side of the bed. "Hi, Mom."

"Are you okay? Where are you and why haven't you called?"

Feck.

I sat up and slid off the bed onto the floor to keep the charge and fend off her voice-detection superpower.

Nothing like sitting on a hotel floor in your underpants.

"Mom. I'm great. I'm working."

"You're in Oklahoma?"

Stupid family locator.

"Yeah. I'm working on a . . . road construction-slash-public works scandal."

"Mmm-hmm," she said absently. "That's nice, honey."

Whew! This was not about me. *Little fishy off the hook.*

"Actually, I've been trying to get a hold of you to talk about Cash."

"Oh?" *Oh shite, more like.*

"About the shrapnel business. How bad was it?"

"Not that bad. Not that bad at all, really."

"Is that Mr. Sharpe's coaching I hear?"

July Pruitt-McGrane didn't miss a trick. I laughed. "No, Mom."

"Watch your step. Mr. Sharpe is not the kind of man to let something he wants go easily into that good night."

WTH, Mom? "The only reason he's interested is because I'm not. He's a player. That's why he and Cash are BFFs."

"Yes," she said, neatly coming around to where we left off. "About Cash. Why exactly is he hiding out at Hank's?"

"He's not. I need him." The lie came out so smoothly, I realized it was the truth. "I haven't heard from Hank since the—er—accident. Having Cash around makes it . . . less awful somehow."

"If something happened to Hank, baby, you'd know."

One of the million reasons why I loved my mother. As committed to logic and objective fact as she was, heart and instinct were all that mattered when it came down to brass tacks.

"Thanks, Mom."

"Try to get some rest. You sound exhausted."

My eyes snapped open at 2:30 a.m. If I was awake, I might as well be driving. I loaded my things in the car and headed for Chicago.

I braked at every speed limit sign. Like my brother Rory, I, too, was a serial speeder. I set the cruise control and flipped through my playlist to the ridiculously pleasing Spencer Day.

Somewhere in mid-Missouri I called Gunther Nyx. We agreed to meet the following day at the dry-cleaning drop.

I showed up at home sometime during the midnight hour.

Cash was a night owl. You had to be one if you worked SWAT. Most no-knock warrants were served between 2:00 and 5:00 a.m. I let myself in through the garage, backpack and carry-on in hand, and went directly into the bedroom. I slid the backpack under the bed.

Stannis's bone jar was in the great room. Nyx's heroin under the bed. And CPD SWAT was in the kitchen.

I'm a little out of my depth here, Hank.

Cash was living large, drinking my boyfriend's Highland Park single malt Scotch and eating a fist-sized chocolate molten-lava cake. From the debris, it appeared he'd gone through a jumbo shrimp cocktail, Caesar salad, French bread, and a New York strip with a baked potato.

"Hey, Snap!" he said. "Sit down—I'll have Wilhelm rustle something up for you."

"You've met Wilhelm?" I gathered up his dishes and carried them into the kitchen.

"Well, not exactly. I left him a note, so now we text so he can tell me when everything's ready and I can come back. I'm pretty sure it's one of those seen-not-heard British Empire kind of things."

"Oh yeah?" *Couldn't possibly be the "imprisoned in the basement of a Colombian cartel boss" thing.* "How'd you suss that out, Champ?"

"He made fries when I asked for chips."

"Wilhelm made fries. For you."

"Uh-huh." Cash tossed back a slug of Scotch. "They were great, but I really wanted Doritos."

Selfish dog. "Looks like you're feeling better."

"Yeah. Where were you, anyway?" He scraped the last bits of chocolate sauce off the dessert plate with his fork.

"Working."

"Hammering or sickling at the *Sentinel*?"

"Hammering." I gave him a saccharine smile before fibbing. "Didn't you read my Sunday op-ed?"

He sucked the chocolate off the fork and shrugged. "Lee wanted to know where you were."

"Seriously?" I snatched the empty lava-cake plate from his hand. "You're living Hank's life while you're hiding out from Mom and Da, and you don't feel even the slightest bit bad about trying to get me to date your SWAT squad leader? What the hell, Cash?"

He sank back against the leather couch. "I like 'em both." He let his dark head loll to the side and gave me an evil grin. "And so do you."

"Zip it."

Chapter 18

The heroin was in my backpack. I carried it in both arms from the parking lot, not daring to risk slinging it over one shoulder. The door of Giarrusso Cleaners buzzed as I entered. The fifties pin-up girl sat behind the register reading a *Star* magazine. She didn't bother looking up.

Wes clomped partway out of the hallway and waved me back to the open office door. "Hey there, Maisie. Good to see ya."

"Thanks."

The office was empty. "Where's Nyx?"

"He's a busy guy." Wes took a seat at the tiny table. "Okay, now. Let's start the debrief."

"Sure thing." I couldn't have cared less whether Gunther Nyx was there or not. I wanted to cut this iron anchor free from my neck.

I sat down, opened my backpack, and set the black-wrapped slab of heroin on the table.

Wes jumped up and away, his chair tipped over, and he almost tripped over it. He pointed at the parcel. "Wha-what the hell is that?"

What do you think it is, genius?

"What I purchased with the DEA's sixty grand. Pure-grade heroin, from El Cid."

"Oh no. Oh no, no, no." Wes picked up the chair. "You need to distribute this."

"What?"

He ran a finger inside his shirt collar. "You made the buy, see? So now the stuff has to hit the street. If it doesn't, the Grieco cartel will know it was a plant."

"So call Nyx. I don't have those kind of connections. You guys do. You're the DEA, for cripes' sake." I scoffed. "Call him."

Wes's cheeks flushed a painful pink. "I can't."

"Then I will."

"He's out of the country."

"So?"

The chunky guy plopped back down on the chair and heaved a sigh thick with chagrin. "I'm less an agent than a glorified secretary, Maisie. Gunther Nyx doesn't let anyone too far in the loop for security purposes. I know more than most, but unfortunately, that's not saying much."

Super-duper.

"Let's start the debrief. The sooner you're out of here, the better." He removed a small notebook and a pen from his suit coat and set them down, careful to avoid contact with the package on the table. "How did you possibly know it was safe to leave the hotel with those men?"

"AJ Rodriguez—El Cid—sent a message."

"What message?" he asked, pen poised to start scribbling.

"They identified themselves as Chac, Jefe, and Esteban Hanson, the trio of misfit brothers from the movie—"

"*Slap Shot!*" Wes said. "No way. Now, that is fucking funny." The cuss word seemed to change our entire dynamic.

"You've seen it?"

"Is there a hockey player alive who hasn't?"

I grinned. "Fake glasses and all."

"No shit?" Wes laughed. "I'd give anything to be in the field."

I raised a shoulder. "It's not all it's cracked up to be."

The look on his shovel-wide face said, *Sure, it is. But I get that you're trying to be nice.*

I told him about the money and transporting the bull from Mexico into El Paso. He was laughing so hard he had tears at the corner of his eyes. "And you're telling me that's not awesome?"

"It's slightly more fun on the retelling."

He laid his pen down on the notebook. "What haven't you told me?"

"El Cid's actively building Carlos Grieco's private army. They're known as Los Cinco-Sietes. The Five-seveNs. They're recruiting the most violent soldiers they can find from South and Central America. El Eje is trying to take over Tampico."

"We're aware of the current political situation."

"Thing is, the Five-seveNs are badass Black-Ops kind of guys. El Cid admitted their man tried to kill Coles, but claims Juan Echeverría hadn't earned the Five-seveN MK2 pistol, much less the black diamond in the safety. He says they were set up by El Eje to fracture their relationship with the Srpska Mafija."

"And you believe him?"

"I'm not sure. It's so outlandish I almost do."

"Huh." Wes's brows knit together and he scribbled a note. "Anything else?"

"El Cid believes the gun was stolen from Bolivian national Diego Rivero Lavayén. They found his head in a cooler at the shipyard, naked body hanging from one of the Tamaulipas entry arches. The torture Lavayén suffered was . . . extensive. Lasted for several days."

"Barbarians at the gate, McGrane."

"El Cid said he had been damned by the blessing of *la Bestia que Llora.*"

Wes stilled. "What does that mean?"

I thought you spoke Spanish. "According to Google Translate, 'The Weeping Beast.'"

"That's . . . a weird kind of colloquialism." He started writing again, not meeting my eyes. "Are you . . . ah . . . are you sure you heard him correctly?"

"Probably not." I shrugged.

Sweet. Wes is lying to me.

And Nyx left me holding the proverbial bag.

So, how much time do I have before they hang me out to dry?

"Okay . . ." I tapped the heroin. "What normally happens in this situation?"

Wes closed his notebook and slipped it in his inside breast pocket. "The mule hands off the drugs to the dealer, who will cut or 'step on it' with anything from powdered milk to Benadryl to inositol to dilute the product and make it go further. Next, the cut product is measured out and packaged in tiny waxed paper envelopes with a 'brand' name and design stamped on it, hence the term *stamp bag*." Wes raised a palm. "Then it's out to the street for distribution."

"What's the timeline?" I asked. "How fast does this happen?"

"You have seventy-two to ninety-six hours max before the new stamps should be ready for sale."

Lovely.

My jaw slid out in full pissed-off mode as I returned the plastic-wrapped slab to where it didn't belong—my backpack.

Goddammit!

"I'm sorry," Wes said. "I really am."

The tips of my fingers shot to my forehead. I snapped him a stiff salute.

Aren't we all?

I got back into the rental car, which now I couldn't return, because with the way my luck was running, I couldn't risk a cab *not* getting into an accident.

I pulled out of the parking garage, thinking hard. Where in the Sam Hill did one find a drug dealer who'd be willing to buy five kilos from a cop's kid? And not rip off or try to kill me?

The only person I knew with the organization and ability was Violetta Veteratti. And she was out. As far out of bounds as I could possibly imagine.

Going to Veteratti would jeopardize Special Unit's organized crime directive, not to mention the very real and horrific possibility that it could force me into becoming a drug nag for Nyx. I glanced at the backpack on the passenger seat, stomach churning.

I am now actively helping to destroy people's lives.

Malignant guilt gnawed at me from the inside out.

I drummed my hands on the steering wheel. *Fecking Nyx.*

After he cut me off at the knees, there was only one person in the world I'd like to work for less than him.

A limo pulled out in front of me at the stoplight.

Bingo.

Wearing a smart and sexy For Love & Lemons lace-embroidered black mesh cocktail dress, I pulled into the drive of the University Club of Chicago. I gave the valet the keys to the Hellcat and asked for a cab.

"Snap Gala, Ms. McGrane?" he asked and motioned for the cab to pull up.

"Yes." I climbed in the taxi.

"Chicago Art Institute," the valet told the driver and closed the door behind me. I probably could have walked the block and a half up Michigan Avenue, but I needed to be able to make a fast getaway.

Tonight was the Photography Department's Annual Snap Gala. My mother and the twins were hosting two $7,500 tables of their six top clients. The evening consisted of an overexposed whirlwind of who's who in fanciful "get snapped" moments that flashed across every social media platform within seconds of being taken. The place was an absolute crush.

Fine by me. I have no ticket and no intention of going inside.

"Pull up behind the limos, please." I held up a fifty. "I need to talk to someone, and I'm not sure for how long."

"You got it."

I got out of the taxi and walked down the line of limousines. There, leaning against a mini-stretch Escalade, smoking a Camel, was Percival "Poppa" Dozen. Talbott Cottle Coles's offensive lineman–size chauffeur. He looked equal parts ridiculous and intimidating in jodhpurs, jacket, high boots, and cap.

I raised my hands up. "Look who's comin' to Poppa."

"Damn, McGrane!" Poppa Dozen gave a low whistle. "You a dime piece."

"Got a minute?"

He took a final drag, considering. "A'ight." He flicked the cigarette onto the sidewalk.

I reached for the passenger side door. He caught my wrist. Shaking his head, he opened the door for me, closing it after I got in. He loped around the nose of the limo.

My stomach clenched.

Gee, I hope this isn't as bad of an idea as it feels right now.

Dozen slid behind the wheel. "Thass one serious-ass look on your face, girl."

I nodded. "I have five kilos of premium uncut Mexican heroin. I need to move it, fast."

"So you come lookin' for me. Cuz all black people sell drugs, right?" He poked me in the chest with a thick finger. "And I'm the only black mutherfucker you know."

"No," I said. "But you are the only *criminal* I know well enough who won't merk me over it."

Dozen threw back his head and laughed, streetlights reflecting off his gold crowns. "I'm just fuckin' with you, sweetness. I got it gully. A'course I can move that shit." He looked down his nose at me. "Question is, do I want to?"

"I want $115K for it. I'll pay you ten percent off the top. You able to move it for more, the gravy's all yours."

"A hunnert fifteen? Better be some beasty shit. Whose is it?"

"Er . . ." I squinted at him. "Mine?"

"Damn, McGrane." He shook his head, chuckling. "What's the stamp?"

"Doesn't have one."

"They all have a stamp." Dozen fingered his soul patch and said very slowly, "Who's sourcing it? Where'd it originate?"

"Grieco cartel."

Which was apparently the right and wrong answer simultaneously.

Dozen adjusted the brim of his driving cap, then the sleeve of his coat. Getting fidgety. "They the ones running Tampico."

"That's right," I said.

"Grieco's causin' a shitload of troubles in Señorita Land. You heard about that bloodbath? Goddamn. Grieco's death squad piled up twenty-two El Eje soldiers outside of La Burra. That ain't no small-time shit."

No, it certainly isn't. "How do you know that?"

"Girl, I drive this limo 'round all day and night. You think my ears is busted?"

"That's why this is a one-shot. An in-and-out."

"And if I wanted an introduction?"

Jaysus. I folded my arms across my chest. "I can try and arrange a meet, but no guarantees."

"How's a lil' piece of Wonder Bread like you get hooked up in the first place?"

"You sure you want me to say it?" I asked, not waiting for an answer. "Renko."

Dozen traced his fingers over the glossy Cadillac emblem inset in the steering wheel. "Goddamn, I was glad to see the back of that lil' badass mutherfucker."

"About that . . ." I sucked in my bottom lip. "I'm hoping to step in for Stannis, keep things copacetic until he comes back."

"Ahh. So that's why you needin' the lettuce." His fingers returned to the soul patch, plucking at the hairs on his chin. "No stamp means Grieco don't want it on the street you is working together, neither."

Hank's Law Number Ten: Keep your mouth shut.

He thought for a while, nodding slowly, grooving to an invisible rhythm in his head. "A'ight. You got a sample on you?"

"Yeah." I handed him an envelope.

He opened it and removed a Ziploc bag that held about a teaspoon of the white powder. "Fuck. This like, four grams, girl. Way too much for a sample. And you gotta wrap that shit in waxed paper, not fling it around in a sammich bag."

Well, you know what they say—once you stop learning, you start dying.

He took out his phone. "Gimme your digits." We exchanged numbers. "All we got left to do is come up with one kickass fuckin' name."

"Uh . . ."

"For the stamp bag. Sumpin' hot like, Criminal Damage, Pac Man, Raw Dope."

I tucked my hair behind my ears. "How about Sugar Skull?"

"Yeah! Sweet and deadly. That'll move like a mofo." His smile froze on his face. He pointed at me, eyes narrowed. "What happened to your neck?"

"Coles needed a place to stub out his cigar."

"Thass some faulty-ass shit, right there."

You got that right. "We good?"

"I'll call you," he said.

I opened the car door and got out. He whistled after me. "You got cake, McGrane. Yes, you do."

I spun around and leaned back in the limo. I jabbed a finger at him. "Watch it, pal!" I said in my best cop voice.

Poppa Dozen hooted with laughter. "You think you know what you're doing?"

I rolled my eyes skyward. "Not sure yet." I dragged a hand though my hair. "I know a lot about a little and a little about a lot."

"That may be," he said, "but you better recognize. You don't know shit about shit."

Chapter 19

My phone *pinged* from the nightstand. I grabbed it and squinted, the screen too bright in the darkened bedroom.

Lee Sharpe.

Range and shine, Bae!

Got 2 FN5.7 M2Ks locked & loaded

Pick you up at 0600

I flopped back onto the pillow. God, he was exhausting. I took a couple of breaths with my eyes closed, then sat up and looked at the clock.

Five fifteen a.m.

I rolled off the bed and hit the shower. The Hot Topic–style outfit I'd picked out to wear to the *Sentinel* was sitting on the chair. I put it on. It was always good to practice in real-life situations.

Lee arrived with two cups of coffee.

"Thanks, but I don't drink coffee."

"Really?"

"I hate the taste." I shuddered.

He leaned in across the armrest, slow and close. "Better kiss me now, then."

I raised my can of Mango-Guava Xenergy in between us and popped the top.

He let his eyes drift slowly down, over my old Chris Cornell concert tee, short red plaid skirt, and leggings tucked into Caterpillar steel-toe work boots. "Nice shirt." He sat back, clicked his phone, and said, "Play 'Nearly Forgot My Broken Heart.'" He grinned and pulled out of the driveway.

We hit the freeway as Cornell's whiskey yowl throbbed against the acoustic guitar.

Lee pulled into the lot of The Second Amendment. He grabbed the gear and we walked into the range. The delicate brunette behind the counter in an I HEART MARK LEVIN sweatshirt, was falling all over herself for Lee. "I saved the two end lanes for you, Mr. Sharpe."

I'm sure that's not all she's saved.

"Thanks," Lee said. "You're a sweetheart. Miss Coonan."

"Mary Beth," she corrected.

Ughhh. Bat those baby blues at him on your own time, sister.

We made our way back to the lanes, Lee discussing the upcoming drills as he unpacked the Herstal FNs and an excessively delicious number of loaded magazines.

"How'd you get a hold of these?" I asked.

"Let's just say, if you were my girlfriend, I wouldn't mind pimping you out to Ditch Broady every now and again."

"I'd rethink ticking off a girl with a loaded gun, Champ."

"Aww, Bae," he said. "I'd never sell you out."

I rolled my eyes and put in my earplugs, muffs on top.

"Ladies first," Lee said.

I moved up to the counter. Da's voice in my head from the very first time he took me to the range. *"You're not shooting at the target; you're shooting into it."* I took an isosceles stance, feet square, face flat to the target. Concentrating on keeping every action consistent and tight.

We started with a timed reload drill. Three shots, reload, three shots, reload, three shots.

Next up, the malfunction drill to clear a jammed weapon while shooting. We moved onto Delta and Chaos drills. Pouring through the ammo like water through a sieve.

When time gets small and stress goes up, you have to work as smart as you can.

We ended the drills with Mozambique—two shots to the chest, one to the head. Close-in shooting, using both hands as much as possible.

"Pretty sweet, aren't they?" Lee said.

"Pure sugar."

I cleaned up brass while he packed up the gear.

"Strong groupings, tight times." He gave a low whistle. "Not bad for a girl."

"Gee, thanks. You're not so sucky yourself." I felt that satisfyingly good kind of tired, looser and happier than I'd felt in months.

It must have showed in my face.

He laughed and held up his hands. "Glad I called?"

"Yeah. Thank you." I caught sight of the clock over his shoulder. *Holy cat. We've been here almost three hours.* "Uh, Lee? Any way you could drop me at the *Sentinel*?"

"Sure thing, Smiles."

Lee drove with a lead foot. I walked into the *Sentinel* a half hour before my sit-down with Walt. Which worked out perfectly, because I needed information. And fast.

I found Jennifer Steager working at a wall of file cabinets. "Juice?"

She turned. "Good morning, Maisie. How are you?"

"Living the dream."

"Aren't we all?" she said wryly.

"Hey, I was wondering if you could point me in the direction of an experienced researcher."

"Sure. What kind?"

"Mexico. Cartels. Specific. In-depth about a person."

Juice's nose crinkled, agate-brown eyes narrowing. "We have an expert on staff."

"Who?"

Juice tucked her chin and her shoulders hit her ears. "Lennon."

Totes awesome.

"He speaks fluent Spanish and he has a ton of connections."

"Lost cause?"

"Don't be silly." She waved me off. "It takes Lennon a long time to warm up to someone. You can't take it personally."

"Any ideas how to get him to help me?"

"Money."

Now that, I can do. "Lead the way."

I followed her trim figure down the hall to his office. She knocked on the open door. "Hi, Lennon. Do you have a few minutes?"

"For you? Sure."

"How about me?" I asked.

I saw Juice's reflection in the window, as she mouthed, "*Be nice*" and then left.

Lennon, gaunt enough to hang glide off a Dorito, turned back to his computer. "What do you want?"

"Research. I'll pay you fifty dollars an hour. Cash. Twenty hours, tops."

Just think, you could buy yourself a sandwich.

His side of the office was a pit. Portishead and The xx stickers, indie band fliers, and take-out menus were tacked up all over his wall. Every surface was covered in empty coffee cups, papers, and Post-its. The whole place reeked of vape and Febreze.

Grey Gardens's side, however, was spotless. The only ornamentation was a framed photo of her and Lennon.

He clicked his mouse, uninterested. "What kind?"

"Four Mexican drug cartel *sicarios*. Enforcers. Torture killers."

He turned his chair around. "What? Why?"

"I'd rather not say."

He thought that over for a long while. A petty smile creased his face. "Sixty an hour. Take it or leave it."

I pretended as though I was actually giving it a second thought. I rubbed my forehead. "Okay. Deal."

He grabbed a Post-it Note and a pen. "Any specifics?"

"Chilo, The Weeping Beast, Kah, and Águila. I want everything you can get on them. Neighbors, social workers, teachers. Real background from the day they were born until today."

"What are you going to do with the info?"

I'd been waiting for this. "I don't think I'm a good fit at the *Sentinel*. I'd like to move out to LA, but a handful of op-eds doesn't open doors."

He nodded happily. "Glad to help."

"Great. Thanks, Lennon." I left his office and went to see Walt, feeling a little weird to be so openly disliked.

My phone buzzed. I dug it out of my messenger bag. "Hello?"

"Snap!" Declan's voice, "Whatcha doin'?"

"Working."

"Maisie?" Daicen said. "We have you on speaker."

I figured as much. "Go ahead."

"We'd like to have a meet regarding a mutual acquaintance."

"Huh?" I glanced at my watch. Four minutes. I stopped in the hallway.

"Our client. Keck. Christo Keck," Declan interrupted. "Your pal Stannislav Renko is one helluva a heavy hitter—"

"Maisie," Daicen cut him off. "You are my uppermost priority. As this case has progressed, unsavory connections and events have come to light. Both Declan and I are deeply concerned for your safety."

"You're in the shite, Snap. Big-time."

"Guys, I've got a meeting. Can we talk about this later?"

"Sure," Declan said. "But don't wait too fecking long."

I disconnected and trotted down the hall into the conference room.

Nattily attired in a slim-fitting Armani windowpane gray wool suit and chestnut John Lobb shoes, Sawyer waited for me at the window. "None the worse for wear after an encounter with a binary chemical bomb, I see, Agent McGrane."

"Yes, I'm fine, sir. Thank you." We sat down.

"How is your assignment for Gunther Nyx proceeding?"

"Almost finished, sir." I traced the wood grain of the table with my finger, opting not to flesh out the undistributed-as-of-yet heroin angle. "Um, sir? I'm not sure that the Grieco cartel was involved with the assassination attempt on Coles."

"How's that?"

"They're aware that one of their soldiers' guns was used. And El Cid assumed Renko sent me to see if they were really responsible. He swears they aren't."

"That's . . . unexpected," Sawyer said. "What else?"

As I filled him in, his eyes focused on a far-off place over my shoulder, processing and evaluating the information.

"El Cid's men were armed with Serbian assault rifles," I said. "I'm not so sure that—"

A quick *rap* sounded, and the door opened. "Hello, Walt. Am I late?" Lee stepped inside and closed the door.

That sonuvagun played me like a chump all morning.

He'd changed from his jeans and tee from the range into navy suit pants and an open-necked blue dress shirt that had to have been custom-made. No off-the-rack shirt would fit that large a chest and shoulders and taper so closely to his waist.

"Not at all." Sawyer gestured toward the table. "Take a seat."

Lee took the chair next to mine and scooted too close.

"What are you doing here?" I asked, more abruptly than I meant to.

"Lee Sharpe's agreed to be your new partner."

You've gotta be kidding me.

I propped my elbow on the table just in time to catch my chin so I didn't pound the brains out of my head on the table.

Lee riding around in my back pocket was the very last thing I needed.

"Let's get you up to speed, Lee," Sawyer said. "Maisie has made significant progress fostering a relationship with AJ 'El Cid' Rodriguez, the Grieco cartel's number-one lieutenant. With the recent spate of diamond-chipped Five-seveNs recovered, we are critically concerned about the potential influx of the black-tip SS190 steel-core, armor-piercing rounds similar to those discovered at the attempted assassination site, as well as the SWAT bust in Little Village."

Lee's face hit high alert. He took Cash's shooting personally, too. "What's Maisie's involvement with El Cid?"

"At this point it is difficult to predict El Cid's intent with

Maisie. He believes her romantic connection to Stannislav Renko is still intact. As does Violetta Veteratti."

Lee's chiseled features turned stony. He knew who the mob princess was, too.

"Special Unit's preference is for Maisie's relationship with him to continue, but remain limited to an auxiliary partnership," Sawyer continued. "Which brings us to Special Unit's and your primary directive. Operation Summit. The Bureau of Organized Crime has decided to take on the single bastion left to the traditional Mafia. Their trade in drugs, human trafficking, and stolen goods wanes in comparison to the influence they wield over politicians and governmental services."

Lee and I exchanged glances.

"Over the course of the next several months, Maisie will operate as Renko's de facto proxy. During this time, she will establish you as her lieutenant," Sawyer said. "The two of you will move forward rebuilding Renko's chop trade with Violetta Vetteratti and further cementing connections with the NY Syndicate."

"Sir," I said, "I was wondering if you've had time to read my report?"

"In regard to Christo Keck?"

I nodded.

"Who's that?" Lee said.

"Stannislav's business manager," Sawyer answered. "Currently represented by Declan and Daicen McGrane against pending indictments."

Lee scoffed. "Christ, I knew you were a close family, but this is ridiculous."

I ignored him. "Keck's a critical player. I'll need him."

"That will be the trick, won't it?" Sawyer glanced at his watch. "Rest assured Special Unit is prepared to leverage the necessary assets." He looked from Lee to me. "I fully expect this assignment to last several months."

Lee held out his hand, with a smile that was more scowl. "Looking forward to working with you, *partner*."

We exchanged a short businesslike shake. "Me, too."

Not.

"That's all for now, Maisie," Sawyer said. "Thank you."

I guess that's my cue.

I left Walt and Lee—the sandbagging bastard—and walked back to my office.

Cash ought to be able to play taxi driver and give me a ride home. Since I was here, appropriately dressed, I might as well serve my time.

As I cruised past the aisles of cubicles and Formica desks, Juice, on the phone, spied me and raised a finger. I nodded and stopped. She wedged the phone between her ear and shoulder, and scribbled furiously on a yellow legal pad. After a minute, she glanced up at me. I gave her the "*I'll wait*" palm.

I shook out my arms, flexing my fingers, trying to figure out exactly why I was so angry with Lee. Special Unit was a dream come true for an adrenaline junkie. And what was SWAT but for that?

Juice hung up and came over. Her neoprene sheath clung to her like exactly what it was: a wet suit. The knee-high boots kept it civil. "Hi, Maisie. Let's go pick up your mail."

"Oh? I thought it was delivered."

"Regular mail is. Uh . . . fan mail isn't."

"I don't follow."

"The *Sentinel* mail room opens everything. When they find . . . um . . . aggressively interested mail, they scan and copy it. You need to sign off and file it."

"Are you saying I have *hate* mail? Me?"

Her mouth moved as she looked for a delicate way to say it. Finding none, she nodded.

How can that possibly be? I don't do anything here. . . .

Oh geez. The op-ed pieces Paul is writing under my name.

Juice led me down the hall. We got into an elevator. As the doors closed, the six-foot-one, 220-pound bulk of Ditch Broady passed by.

What the heck is he doing here?
And why aren't I included?

Juice and I got off two floors down and stopped in front of a large counter. "We're here for Maisie McGrane's fan mail."

The squat bottle blonde behind the counter rolled her eyes and waddled behind the counter. Juice schooled me during the insanely long wait.

"You need to do this a couple times a month. Most of the columnists prefer to do it weekly. That way you feel less . . ."

"Reviled?"

Juice smiled. "Exactly!"

The stack of letters the blonde slammed on the counter was quite a bit larger than I'd expected.

There were colored paper slips in between. Reds mostly, with some pink, orange, and a couple of blue. I thanked her and scooped it up.

We walked down the hall. "So what's with the colored paper?"

"Sliding hostility scale. Red hostile, blue friendly."

"Jaysus Criminey," I said, flipping through the folder as Juice pushed the elevator button. A lot of red.

"It's really not that bad. Our insurance company demands we print out all the e-mail responses, too, after we had that one reporter get stab—er . . . never mind."

Neato.

I kept flipping.

Juice's perky pace slowed to a slither. "Oh my God. Look at him."

Lee Sharpe, my own personal bad penny, leaned against the doorjamb of my office, grinning. In rolled-up shirtsleeves, hair slightly mussed, he looked positively rakish. "Waited for you downstairs. Thought you might need a ride home, Bae."

Oh, for God's sake. "No thanks. I'm good."

"You don't mind if I hang around, just to make sure."

"Lee?" I grabbed Juice by the arm. "This is my pal, Jenny Steager."

"Uh . . . Hi!" she said. "Everyone calls me Juice."

Lee took her hand in both of his and stared in her eyes. "Nice to meet you, *Juice.*"

For a second I thought she might swoon. "Easy, Captain Charming." I ducked past him, tossed the thick file in my in-box, and started searching through the drawers for a pen.

Lee followed me right in and made himself at home, taking the visitor's chair and rummaging through my in-box.

Juice stood in the doorway. "Later, Maisie." She pointed at Lee, fanned herself with a file folder, mouthed, "*Wow!*"

I threw her a small salute and she closed the door to my tiny office.

"I'm gonna kill you, you fucking corporate shill." Lee's forehead creased in a deep frown. "You can get down on all fours and suck my . . . er . . . whoa, you got some haters, kid."

"Admirers come in every stripe." Four colors of Post-its, seventeen mini-boxes of paper clips, manila folders, Scotch tape, and scissors. Not a pen to be found in the place.

He shook his head. "What is this shit?"

"Fan mail. From my op-ed pieces."

"Why isn't it on a police desk?"

"It's waiting for me to initial, and—if I decide not to notify the police—file. The red cover slip indicates high hostility. Blues are friendly." I gave up looking for a ballpoint and dug a couple of Ultra Fine Sharpies out of my messenger bag.

"I don't think this is as harmless as you make it out to be." Lee mashed through the stack of papers. "Christ. They're all red."

"Lee. I've got bigger fish to fry than a militant greenie living over his parents' garage who disagrees with the guy who's writing my column's stance on the EPA."

Although it might be prudent to ask Paul to tamp it down a bit.

He read through another one; this time the helpful fellow had glue-sticked the column to his angry letter. "I see this brave social justice warrior forgot to write his return address." The set of Lee's jaw was only slightly disturbing. "Might be fun to track Junior down, pay him a visit."

"Logic and facts have a tendency to anger and confuse those

who pass feeling-based judgments." I handed him a blue-tagged letter before he started getting any ideas.

He scanned it and laughed. "Which one of your brothers wrote this?"

"Cute. You're assuming they can spell."

Lee drummed his palms on my desk. "So. Can I give you a lift home, partner?"

"Sure." I threw him a pen. "Start initialing."

Chapter 20

"That was smooth. Real smooth, by the way," I said as Lee slid behind the wheel.

"Yeah? Which part?"

All of it. "Signing on to work for Sawyer as my secretary."

"Partner," he corrected. "But if makes you feel better, go right ahead and dictate something."

My iPhone pinged. Poppa Dozen.

Sweetness

CU 2nte @ 11

Dawes Park, S. Hoyne

Dawes Park was on South Damen Avenue. A mere five blocks away from West Englewood.

Because today just can't get any better.

Lee leaned in for a look. "Who's that?"

I clicked my phone off. "None of your business."

"Try again." He changed his grip on the steering wheel. "Tell me about the bomb."

"I don't see how that's relevant to your angle on this case."

"You're my partner. Everything pertaining to your mental state is pertinent to me."

Okay, tough guy. "Honestly? It was pretty scary. I was buzzed and not thinking clearly when I opened the cooler. And yeah, I'm pretty much lucky to be alive. So let's just get on with things. Okay?"

"It catches up with you." His brown eyes darkened. "When you least expect it."

Gee, thanks.

"We'll see." I wanted to get out of the car right then and there. "I got some pretty sick avoidance moves left in the ol' skull. . . ."

He shook his head slowly. "This isn't a fucking joke, Maisie."

"No. It isn't." I turned away to the window.

Lee took the hint and flipped on the stereo. Sublime played a little too loud all the way to Hank's. My breath came out in a shaky sigh as he put the car in Park.

Smarten up. He's messing with your head. Don't let him get to you.

I popped the button on the seat belt and moved to open the door. He reached across, lightning fast, boxing me in. "You're not cut out for this, Maisie."

"But you are?" The retort snapped from my mouth before I could stop it. I glanced down at Lee's ripped arm. Each muscle clearly defined, bicep, tricep, flexors, extensors.

He wasn't a little man.

"Thing is, kid, there's more than one type of lethal. The silent, detached kind. And then there's me. Happy-go-lucky, I'll crush your throat while you're laughing."

The insides of my cheeks trembled. "I already have a boyfriend and a job. When I need a life coach, Lee, I'll let you know. Thanks for the lift." I got out and went in the house. He sat in the driveway for several minutes before pulling out.

To heck with this garp. Hello, avoidance nap.

The alarm sounded at 9:30 p.m. I put on makeup and flat-ironed my hair. I had to leave it down, as the Tegaderm burn dressing made me look like a tween trying to hide a hickey left over from a basement vampire party.

Rat bastard Coles.

I popped a couple of Hank's modafinals to keep my edge and went into the closet to choose an outfit.

Hmm. What do I own that screams self-assured drug dealer, don't merk me?

Levi's, IDF tee, black TacShell jacket, steel-toed work boots, and the Kimber Ultra RCP II LG .45 ACP that Hank bought me, just because. A honey of a gun with a three-inch barrel and a matte-black finish. It was an "extreme melt" concealed-carry pistol. Everything on it snag-free and rounded. I checked the magazine and tucked it into the Galco holster at the small of my back.

I could hear the tease of Hank's deep voice in my ear, the feel of his chest and stomach tight against my back, his large hands over mine on the Kimber.

> *"One to make ready*
> *And two to prepare.*
> *Cocked, locked, and loaded,*
> *Let's go meet the bear."*

I grabbed the heroin out from under the bed.

God, Hank. Come home.

AC/DC's "Back in Black" blasted through the Hellcat's stereo. Heater cranked, windows down, I hit the freeway, crushing the speed limit exactly like a girl with three brothers and a father in the CPD would.

Arriving at Dawes Park with ten minutes to spare, I circled the grounds before turning into the South Hoyne Avenue dead end. I parked nose out, opened the door, and stepped into the crisp, clear October air. Eyes closed, I leaned against the car, feeling the modafinil, listening to the autumn leaves rustle and fall.

The lights from Poppa Dozen's headlights turned the insides of my eyelids orange. He put the car in Park. The electronic *hum* of the window rolled down. "Them some fucking manly rims for a sugar baby."

"Hey, Dozen." I fired him a salute. He sat behind the wheel of a shiny ruby-red Navigator. "You ain't doing so bad yourself."

"Get in."

I grabbed the backpack out of my car and got in his. He was wearing a suit, open-necked shirt, and a thick gold necklace. I got into the Lincoln. It reeked of cigarettes and Creed cologne. Music I didn't recognize reverberated in my chest.

Dozen ran a thick tongue over his lower lip. "Yo. Seat belt."

"Yeah, sorry."

"Gotta swing by the bando. Get Dafinest's locale from the baby gangstas."

He pulled up in front of a two-story, crumbling brick building. The ground level windows boarded shut with grafittied plywood.

Duh. Bando short for abandoned building.

I reached for the handle. Dozen thumped me in the chest. "Stay in the mutherfuckin' car, McGrane."

Ow. Don't have to tell me twice.

A hoard of walking dead addicts mobbed the door. One look at Dozen and they faded into the sides of the entrance, paying respect to his suit and size.

He approached the chipped cement entrance. A pair of men, twenties, in flashy athletic apparel, stepped out. The trio exchanged words and Dozen returned.

"We're goin' to Dafinest's G-Momma's." He started the SUV. *Okay?*

"Is that his name? Dafinest?" I asked carefully.

"Dafinest Johnson. But girl, he's Mr. Peanut to you." He sucked his teeth. "The kid's a mutherfuckin' genius. And ruthless. He's doin' this on the down low. On account of I helped his sister once. He ain't no child. And this better never come back on him. Unnerstand what I'm sayin'?"

Yeah, anyone who can buy twelve pounds of heroin and distribute it on the fly is more than a little connected.

I nodded. "Mr. Peanut. Got it."

He took Damsen to Eighty-seventh. "You still wearing Renko's ring."

"Yeah. Keeps the hounds at bay."

"Cuz 'The Bull' ain't fond of dogs, is he?"

I can play tough, too, Poppa. "Stannis hasn't been called 'The Bull' for years. But Coles preferred it to what they call him now."

"And wha's that?"

"'The Butcher.'"

"Shit, Sweetness. You don't gotta try an' scare me. I know crazy when I see it." He knocked on the ceiling as we turned onto South Greenwood and traversed into one of the upper circles of hell—Burnside.

We stopped in front of a small tan bungalow. Ordinary, if you didn't count the game cameras affixed to the corners of the roof, the blackened razor wire atop the wrought-iron fence, bars on the windows, dogs barking in the back, or the locked gate across the driveway to the left of the house.

Cripes.

Dozen honked twice, waited a five count, and honked twice again.

A midfifties woman in glasses and curlers and a pink housecoat stepped out onto the porch.

Dozen turned to me. "Out of the car, McGrane."

We approached the fence. He held up a hand. "Hey, G-Momma."

"Percy Dozen?" the woman asked. "Who that white girl with you?"

I held up the backpack. "UPS."

The woman came to the fence, a ring of keys in her hand. "You carrying?" she asked me.

Dozen rolled his eyes.

Then coughed in surprise when I unzipped my jacket and pulled the Kimber Ultra. "Yes, ma'am," I said.

She held out her hand.

I released the slide, removed the magazine, and handed it to her. I secured the gun back in the holster.

She didn't like it, but she unlocked the gate, securing it behind us before leading us up the sidewalk into the little house.

The inside was cleaner than most hotels and smelled of furniture polish and starch. Overstuffed, spindly-legged furniture was dwarfed by an enormous curved screen Samsung television in the center of the room. "Dafinest?" she called. "Your appointment is here."

"Thanks, G-Momma." A diminutive, freckle-faced, light-skinned teen came into the room. The resemblance to Mr. Peanut was evident, with a left eye noticeably smaller than his right. He was sixteen, tops, wearing low-slung jeans, high-tops, and a Bears jersey. He gave me a careful going-over, then nodded at Dozen. "C'mon."

We followed him down a hallway to a basement stairway that opened up into a laundry room and his grandma's pantry. He went to one of the built-in shelving units and pulled. The wall of cans opened onto a locked door, behind which was a twenty-foot-by-twenty-foot mini-laboratory and two clean-room attired workers.

We walked up to the counter. I opened my backpack and handed the heroin to Mr. Peanut. He set it on a butcher's scale. Eleven-point-oh-five kilos.

He motioned to the workers, who each came over with a milligram scale, sealed ampoule, packet of solution, and a skinny package. One unrolled a sheet of butcher paper. The other moved the heroin onto the paper and sliced open the package with a scalpel.

Both of the workers opened their ampoules, poured in the buffer solution, and unwrapped tiny spatulas. Precisely measuring out 20 milligrams of heroin into the weighing boat on their respective scales, they transferred the contents into the ampoules and snapped on the lid.

Each ampoule got a single shake.

The liquid inside instantly turned a dark orangey-brown.

"Ninety percent at least." Mr. Peanut nodded at the workers. "Cut it to seventy with mannitol." He sent a text, then turned to Dozen and me. "So we gonna start moving this quantity regular like, Meter Maid?"

Really? I shot Dozen a dirty look. *That's the drug dealer name I get? The worst fecking job I've ever had?*

Dozen grinned.

"Um, I'm not sure, Mr. Peanut. My Mexican connection is a little . . . er . . . unstable as of late."

"I hear you," he said. "Them *loco tacos* all up in our areous shooting up Humboldt Park. Doin' it with some hot four-poundas."

Actually, I think you mean five-poundas. Those are 5.7s not .45s.

"Wouldn't happen to got a line on some o' them, would you, Meter Maid?"

"Guns?" I asked.

"Yeah. Them flashy ones with the black diamond. Thass some class there, amiright, Doz?"

Dozen grunted.

"I'm sorry, Mr. Peanut. I don't."

"Okay. And now you know I got interest." Dafinest adjusted his jeans. "Lemme make somethin' clear. While this been a profitable exchange for both of us, I'm still doing you a solid 'cuz of Dozen, payin' you market value. So dontcha go bustin' my nut, a'ight? You get another quality load you come to me. And me alone."

"Agreed," I said and held out my hand.

"You wanna shake hands, bitch?" He laughed at me without a hint of malice. "Nah." He slapped my palm with the back of his hand and the back of my hand with his palm. "Hey, Dozen—let's take her up, have her do this lil' trained monkey shit in front of G-Momma."

Dozen pressed his fingertips to his forehead, the message *"you're embarrassing the hell out of me in front of Mr. Peanut"* unmistakable.

We followed the teenager out of the room and up the stairs.

G-Momma was at the kitchen table. Stacks of twenties, fifties, and hundreds were rubber-banded into two separate piles. 100K and 17K.

"Check it, Meter Maid." Mr. Peanut handed Dozen a plastic Nike bag, for the seventeen grand.

"Thanks, man," Dozen said.

I started flipping through the stacks. As soon as I finished a stack, G-Momma put it into a Macy's shopping bag. It wasn't like I was actually counting it, but I knew that me taking it as is would have been frowned upon.

Heavily.

I riffled the last stack of hundreds and tried not to breathe a sigh of relief as the cash went into the bag. My hands were filthy and my face itched. G-Momma laid a dishcloth over the top of the money, put the Kimber Ultra's magazine on top, and handed me the bag.

Mr. Peanut walked us out onto the front porch and whistled. Two black men carrying AR-15 pistols stepped out of the shadows.

Our escort to the car, not a hit squad, please, God.

"It was nice meeting you, Mr. Peanut," I said.

"Yeah. Dozen said you was a'ight and he was correct. I had G-Momma throw a lil' snowcap in. Celebrate our first deal."

Weed sprinkled with coke.

Aww, gee. How sweet.

"Thanks," I said. "Appreciate it."

Chapter 21

I reloaded the Kimber Ultra and wedged the shopping bag into my backpack as Dozen drove us to Dawes Park. "Meter Maid?" I asked. "That was the best you could come up with?"

"It was either that or Snow Bunny." He laughed. "When do I meet your Mexi-boys?" Dozen turned onto South Hoyne.

"Hey, I never prom—"

"What da hell?" He stomped on the brakes. The Navigator squealed to a hard stop.

At the dead end, under the streetlight, was a highland-green Mustang parked next to my black Hellcat. Lee leaned against the back bumper. Arms folded across his chest, looking pissed off as all get-out.

Great. Just great.

"He's my new bodyguard," I said trying to play it off. "What do you think?"

"Thas a mutherfuckin' cop."

"Marine," I said. "He's just a Marine. Everything's cool."

"Bullshit." Dozen shook his head. "Get out."

I reached for the handle. Dozen popped the locks. "Be seein' you, Meter Maid."

I hopped out of the SUV with the backpack. Dozen hit Reverse as I shut the door, and squealed off into the night.

Coward.

I loped to the cars, not in the mood to mix it up. "Hey, Lee. Funny seeing you here."

"We're partners." His voice was low and angry.

Better get used to it, baby. I'm not the kind that rolls over.
"That's sweet and all, but this?" I held up the backpack before
dropping it next to the door. "This isn't our particular gig."

"Burnside?"

"Whoa." He'd gone from tracking my car to tracking me.
"What?"

"You go into Burnside. With no backup except a known killer?"

Easy, Mr. Clean. "You're pretty much a known killer yourself, pal."

He squared his shoulders. "And you want your slice of the action, is that it?"

"Back off, Lee. I already live with the ultimate hard case."

"Do you? Seems like you moved in and he took off."

That stung. I gave him my sweetest come-hither smile and
looked up through my lashes. "I guess it takes a tough guy to
know a tough guy."

"Yeah? Well, maybe we're both as alpha as fuck, but the sim-
ilarity ends there."

"Does it?" Heat flushed my cheeks. "Because I can't wait to
hear how different you are from the man I'm in love with."

His lips thinned and his eyes turned cold. "I'll tell you one
thing, sweetheart." He grabbed the front of my jacket in his
fists. "There's no way in hell I'd ever let you do this shit alone."

I braced myself, waiting for him to knock me up against the
car to try to rattle some sense into me.

By the time I realized he was kissing me, I was kissing him
back.

I knew ten different ways to break the hold he had on me,
but I only shoved at his chest. He pressed against me. I turned
my head but his mouth followed mine.

His tongue slicked inside the roof of my mouth. Hot and
easy, it felt like a dance we'd danced a thousand times, just not
together.

Air sirens went off in my head.

I knocked him in the shin with my boot, not hard, but not
real sweet, either.

He took a step back, hands up. "If you wanted me to stop, all you had to do was quit kissing me back."

My hand sliced across his cheek. The slap so hard and fast my fingers went numb.

He didn't flinch, not a tic.

I'd never hit a guy. Not over something like that.

Not ever.

I stood there. Wanting to apologize and biting my lip not to.

His mouth twisted into a wry smirk. "What's in the backpack, Maisie?"

I swallowed. "A hundred thousand dollars, pot laced with cocaine, and a dish towel."

He picked up the backpack. "You're going to get in your car and follow me to Hud's. We'll have a couple drinks and square some things." He cocked his head, eyes searching mine in the streetlight. "Do you have your car keys and ID on you?"

"Yeah."

"Then let's go."

"No." I reached for the backpack.

He didn't move. "Who's going to have an easier time slipping the noose if they get stopped with this shit in their car?"

Goddammit.

"Maisie, you're going to have a hard enough time explaining that gun at the small of your back without blowing your cover. Get in your car."

I did.

He got into the Mustang and turned around. I followed him all the way to Hud's, my mind running all over hell's half acre. My hand still stung. Futility churned in my gut. And I could smell his cologne on my shirt.

Lee and I sat knee to knee at a booth in the back of the bar. A pitcher of beer on the table between us, the backpack with 100K beneath our feet. "You all right?" he asked.

I nodded. "Are you?"

"Butterfly kiss." He grinned and I took it like a knife in the lung.

He put his hand on mine. I gave it a beat, then started to slide away. Lee's fingers circled my wrist. "Hold up," he said, leaning forward. "Since we're going to be working together, it might not be a bad idea for us to be seen as a couple."

I ducked my head. Across the bar, a couple of detectives from Flynn and Rory's squad pretended not to notice us.

Even money they'd already texted my brothers.

Lovely.

I raised my left hand from beneath his and propped my chin on it. I tapped the Cartier wedding ring. "What do you propose I do about this?"

Lee shrugged. "Take it off."

"It's not that easy, Tiger. El Cid and Dozen think I'm carrying a torch for Renko." I sat back and tossed out a massive fib. "So does Vi Veteratti."

"Spoiled rich girls always sleep with their good-looking bodyguards."

"You wish."

"Yeah." He gave me the look. And it was a good one. "I do."

"I . . . I'm sorry I slapped you. I wasn't angry with you. I mean, I was . . . I am. But not like that. Not over that. I was mad at myself. Mad at Ha—"

"Shh." Lee pressed his beer glass to my mouth. "Be quiet."

I took the sip he offered and the out.

"Turn it up!" demanded a deep and intoxicated beat cop from across the bar. "Lemme hear how that sumbitch mayor's gonna fuck us up the ass again."

The bartender hit the volume on the main set.

Talbott Cottle Coles, wearing a terse and mannerly expression on multiple local news stations, now occupied more than half of the TV screens at Hud's. Wife on his right and on his left, the Latino guy he'd been with at The Storkling.

"Hello, Chicago!" He basked in the glow of public adoration for several seconds before raising his hands for quiet. "Recently I haven't been as accessible as I would have wished to both the American public as well as the news media. It would be a mistake for my critics to assume my absence was the result of the Grieco cartel's crude attempt to silence me and my war on drugs."

Let the spinning begin!

"As I covered the body of my wife, praying the mother of my children would live to see another day, I vowed that if I should live, I would not let my relationship with the Mexican people be tainted."

Two of the four local stations—obviously pre-pimped with his speech—preempted the live video, running a slow-motion reel of the assassination attempt over his voice.

"Our fair city is home to more than one-point-five million residents of Mexican descent," Coles said. "It is with pride I govern the city with the second largest Mexican population in the United States. The time for us to unleash the enormous potential for both of our fair nations is now. By expanding trade and tourism, and facilitating foreign direct investment, we will build a bigger, better Chicago."

Puke-alicious.

He put his arm around the shoulders of the fine-boned man. "This is Cesar Garza. The bright young son of—"

"That asshole," Lee said. "That fucking asshole!" He popped me in the shoulder. "You know who that is, right? That's Cesar Garza. The son of Álvaro Garza."

"Who?" I said blankly.

"Álvaro Garza runs El Eje," he said. "Christ, Maisie. You run a mission for the DEA and you don't know this? No debrief? No independent research? Are you kidding me?"

That got my back up. I gritted my teeth.

"Where the hell is your head?" he said, unable to let up. "Does Walt know how unprepared you were? Are?"

"It's not like that."

He smacked his palm against the table. "It's fucking *exactly* like that."

My cheeks burned like they were coated in Sterno and Lee had flicked a lit match at them. A humiliation bubble grew in my throat.

Rip me all you like, sport. It won't win you any tears.

I smoothed my hair back and refocused on the nearest flat screen.

"Questions?" Coles pointed at a particularly awestruck blond reporter.

"Mayor Coles," she asked, "how can you possibly ignore the fact that you are now on the hit list of a cartel?"

"Again, I must reiterate, the attempt on my life was not the fault of the Mexican people. I will not stand for the status quo or reliance on prejudicial racial profiling. Instead, I have seized this opportunity to develop a joint ATF and DEA task force to assist the Mexican government in ridding their nation of the scourge of these cartels."

Holy cat.

Maybe AJ wasn't so far off.

Another reporter stepped up. "How do you plan to stop any backlash against the Hispanic community?"

Coles's serious countenance couldn't disguise the spark of delight in his eyes. "At home, I will continue to press for police reforms, including deescalation training and mandatory body cameras. The true American tragedy is when we cannot trust our own, who have sworn to protect and serve."

I should have let Renko cut off his hand.

The mood within the bar had turned sick with disgust. Several cops closed out their tabs and split.

Coles finished up, demurely deflecting suggestions he run for higher office, but not closing the door, either.

Jerk.

My fingers strayed to the cigar burn. It was healing okay. Plastic surgery for the scar was going to cost me at least a wrist and a shin. Double when I'd have to explain it to my parents.

Lee pulled my hand away from my throat. Mouth tightening, he gave the dressing a once-over, his expression as forgiving as cured cement.

Super-duper.

Walt told him what happened.

I finished my beer, not meeting his eyes, hoping he'd take the hint.

"Tonight is going to end in one of two ways," Lee said. "Me at your place or you coming to mine. Either way, we deliver the money to Nyx tomorrow. Together."

From the set of his jaw, arguing was pointless. And I didn't feel right about having him stay overnight at Hank's.

I threw in the towel.

Lee lived in a neat little bungalow near a hip part of town. He pulled into the driveway and stopped, opting not to park in the detached garage. We walked up the sidewalk to the front door.

"I . . . uh, wasn't really counting on company," he said.

"Yeah?" I teased. "I thought Marines were always locked and loaded, forward-focused."

He unlocked the door. "Some habits die hard. Others need to be resuscitated on a daily basis."

He flipped on the living room light. It wasn't as bad as Cash's room, but it was close. I pointed at the couch serving double duty as a laundry room and newspaper recycling center. "Is that for me?"

"No." He shot me a dirty look. "Christ, Maisie. I have a guest bedroom."

"Oh, well . . . I wasn't sure if you were a scrapbooker or a quilter."

He slung an arm around my shoulders and mussed my hair. "God, you're just begging for it."

I clapped a hand over my mouth as my smart retort came out as a giant yawn. His easy smile and demeanor vanished. "Gimme a minute, okay?"

"Sure," I said and yawned again. He disappeared down a hallway.

I heard him rummaging around, and if the rest of his place was anything like this, he was going to be more than a few minutes unnecessarily picking up on my behalf.

A laundry basket by the couch held a hockey helmet and shoulder pads. A single glove lay by the stairs to the basement.

Down the hall, a hockey bag and sticks propped open a closet door. I put the gear in his bag, shoved the bag all the way into the closet so it cleared the jamb, and closed the door. The laundry from the couch and chair went into the basket, and a paper grocery bag from under the TV cabinet took care of the newspapers, junk mail, and old magazines.

I shivered, unable to stop yawning. I took off my jacket, pulled a red flannel shirt out of the laundry basket, and put it on. It carried the faint scent of Tide and cedar. I lay down on the couch, and using my jacket for a blanket, went to sleep.

"No. No!" I woke up, freaked and flailing, as Lee carried me down the hall.

"Easy," he said.

"Put me down."

He stopped and set me on my feet. "Sure."

"Sorry." Chagrined, I tried to quit shaking. "Thanks."

He pushed open a door on a spotless bedroom. A lamp on a nightstand illuminated a cream-colored room with dark wood wainscoting, a double bed with the sheet turned down, and a folded SWAT T-shirt and sweatpants on the end.

He pointed at the room down the hall. "That's me." Knocked his knuckles on the door ajar behind him. "Bathroom."

"Got it." I nodded. "Thanks."

I'm just a little shaken up, that's all. Sleeping too hard. That's all.

I moved toward the bedroom. He stepped in front of me and put his arms around me. His voice was low in my ear. "A lot has happened to you in a short amount of time. You want to sleep next to me now or later, that's okay. Hands off." He gave me a squeeze, then went down the hall to his room

I watched him go. Wanting to follow. Aching for "safe."

Knowing it wouldn't be right.

Chapter 22

I woke up without my phone. No clock on the bedside table and blackout curtains. I swung my legs over the side of the bed and pushed my hair off my face, feeling as groggy and disoriented as a moth in a mitten.

Jaysus. What time is it?

I got up and went into the bathroom. A new Colgate toothbrush and travel-size tube of toothpaste waited on the edge of the sink. My reflection had the healthy glow of a typhoid patient.

I crept on cat's feet into the sun-bright living room to find my backpack on the couch. Mr. Peanut's 100K and the snowcap were gone. As was my phone.

Apparently Bloodhound Jones was taking a shine to new partner duty, nosing around and marking his territory.

Too tired to give a good golly, I gathered up my remaining possessions and returned to the bathroom. Teeth brushed, hair and makeup salvaged, I put on my clothes from last night—including Lee's flannel shirt—and wandered into the kitchen.

"Yeah. She sweat it plenty, but stayed smooth from start to finish from what I could see," Lee said into his phone. "Figured she earned a decent kip." He paused, listening, and laughed. "Uh-huh, Roger that." He clicked off the phone and stood up.

"Hi," I said.

"Good morning." His grin was 1,000-watt bright, brown

eyes so lively I froze like a punch-drunk porcupine in the head-lights. "Sleep all right?"

I nodded, waiting for him to volunteer whom he'd been talking to.

He didn't. Without a smidge of guilt he went to the fridge. "So, Ms. No Coffee . . . What'll it be?" Lee swung open the door. "Juice, Coke, milk, or tea?"

"Coke."

He popped the top and handed me a can.

"Thanks. Haven't happened to see my phone?"

He pulled it from his shirt pocket and gave it to me. "Brunch or lunch? It's eleven forty. We debrief with Nyx at nineteen hundred."

What the what?

"Since when are you coming with me to see Nyx?" I said.

"Aside from serving as your personal secretary, *partner*"—he moved in close and gripped my waist, thumbs pressing my hip bones, face inches from mine—"my talents include armed currency transport, negotiation, and personal protection."

Talk about being screwed six ways to Sunday.

"I'm guessing that's not all they include," I said.

Lee's mouth hovered above mine. "Yeah?"

"Lunch. Definitely."

His eyes narrowed, hands fell away. "Let's go."

We went for hamburgers and Horse's Necks at the charmingly moody Au Cheval. The 100K, transferred into a well-used Chicago White Sox duffel bag, always infant-safe between us. After lunch we hit Weegee's Lounge, where hours passed like minutes playing table shuffleboard and trading smart-aleck remarks.

With the patience of an ice-angler, I resisted checking my incoming call log until Lee finally took a call in the car while we were en route to Giarrusso Cleaners.

I swiped through the screens. Wes had called and talked to Lee at 9:03 a.m. for four minutes. After which, Lee had called Cash for an eleven-minute chat, and—*sweet Jiminey Christmas*—

fielded a call from my mother that lasted more than twenty minutes.

God only knew what that had been about. And I wasn't about to ask.

Still talking, Lee parked in the handicapped space. He hung up and tossed a placard on the dash.

"You do realize those are for physically not mentally handicapped drivers?"

"Admit it, Meter Maid. You just want to show me your ticket book."

"You're adorable," I said flatly and got out of the car.

He grabbed the duffel and followed me into the dry cleaner's.

Pin-up girl glanced up from an *OK!* magazine, and started to yell, "Weh—!" but then laid eyes on Lee and changed her tune. "—ell, hell-o." She put down the tabloid and fluttered her eyelashes. "How can I help you?"

"Wes Dorram," I said. "Please."

Pin-up sashayed out from behind the counter, gave Lee a lascivious ogle, and disappeared down the hall, tight red skirt straining at the seams.

"You take me to all the best places," Lee murmured in my ear.

Pin-up returned. Wes lumbered behind, like a bear at a bank meeting. "Who's this?"

"My deliveryman," I said. "Let's go."

Wes didn't like it. But he could see Lee had him beat.

Lee and I followed him to the back office.

Gunther Nyx lounged behind the desk. The tiny table and chairs were full of boxes, invoices, and envelopes. It wasn't going to be a chatty meeting.

"Maisie." Nyx's smile went horizon flat when Lee stepped into the room behind me. "And Lee Sharpe."

"Gunther." Lee scanned the cramped, dingy office. "Looks like business-as-usual."

Nyx popped his chin up at the hit. "While your taste in women has improved, I see your career choices have not. How is SWAT?"

"Suits me just fine. I never had your taste for an altered mental state." Lee's eyes sparked. "I'm man enough to live with my sins."

"Is a life half-lived even a life at all?" Nyx's thin lips parted. His instantaneous resemblance to an albino python was remarkable. "But it is difficult for a soldier boy to resist the toys, eh?"

"Not at all," Lee tossed the duffel bag onto the desk.

Nyx was as interested in the bag as if it was full of dirty laundry. "Just as expected, *Liten Sötis*." His eyes drifted down my body, slowly, insolently, wanting to see how far Lee would let it go.

Lee's hands hung loose at his sides, but his weight shifted to the balls of his feet.

"Kennel your guard dog, Maisie."

No one moved.

Lee reached over and gripped my butt. I jerked upright, stung. "I'll wait for you out front, Bae," he said.

Lee sailed out of the office as carefree as a sunny day. Wes closed the door behind him, then walked over to the desk and removed the duffel bag.

Nyx's pale brows tipped down at the corners. "Anything you'd care to share, Maisie? Say . . . Sharpe joining Sawyer's team?"

"How should I know? You kinda left me high and dry, *sir*. Selling five kilos of heroin without a distribution line? Not to mention, 100K is an awful lot of cash for a girl to carry around on the mean streets of Chi-town. I had to use what resources I had to hand."

"Is Sharpe working with the Special Unit?"

I lifted an uncaring shoulder. "He hasn't mentioned it."

"You sure about that, ma'am?" Wes said. "The two of you seem awfully close."

Look who's not so sweet now. Throwing shade over my shoulder, I rolled my eyes at the beefy agent. "Nah. I just use him for sex."

Wes gave a strangled cough.

"Will you be able to operate independently from your . . . partner?" Nyx asked.

"Of course."

Hank's Law Number Twenty-Two: When among wolves, act the wolf.

Itching to leave, "I'm afraid I haven't had time to write up a report yet on the contacts or who I sold the heroin to," I said demurely.

Gunther Nyx adjusted the line of his trousers. "Wes will see to that."

Sawyer wasn't kidding about him playing fast and loose.

"It'll be my pleasure," Wes said. "You're too valuable to waste on paperwork. Especially since SWAT and the CPD have recently cleared three more stash houses. The composition and packaging of the heroin traces directly to the Grieco cartel."

And now, apparently, from me, as well.

"Also found at the stash houses were black-tipped, armor-piercing solid core 28mm rounds. Always pleasant to have a field confirmation." Nyx spun slightly in his chair. "An excellent report on El Cid, Maisie." He propped his feet up on the desk. "I think it's time we file a temporary personnel reassignment request for Miss McGrane with Special Unit, Wes."

"Yessir," the agent said.

What?

"If the DEA is going to continue to use you, it's only sporting we foot the bill," Nyx said. "See if El Cid is amenable to another deal. Four times the product."

My spine went ramrod-rigid—which had nothing on my heart, which had quit beating.

Oh, feck me.

"It sounds as though you already have the evidence you need, sir." I shook my head. "I think Ditch Broady of the ATF had the right of it. I can't see how this effort will be of any real use."

"Building an international case is a tenuous process, Maisie. One never knows exactly which weights and balances will prove useful."

Wes gave a small cough. "Unless you're not up for the task."

You want to see sparks, pal? Go put a fork in an electrical socket.

"Making a deal with El Cid won't be a problem, sir." I folded my arms across my chest. "Stateside distribution, however . . ."

"I'm sorry you were inconvenienced, Maisie," Nyx said silkily. "You have my word that will not happen again."

We swung by Hud's to pick up my car. "I need a drink," Lee said. "You in?"

Hell, yes. "Sure thing."

We took over the same booth as the night before. Only, instead of sitting across from me, this time Lee slid in next to me. We spent forty minutes studiously not rehashing the meeting or talking about Nyx, Sawyer, the DEA, or the BOC.

Lee took two showers a day, had three Marine Corps tattoos, preferred winter to summer, sci-fi, Italian food, and his favorite color was, unsurprisingly, navy blue.

"You gonna call him or what?" he said.

Who? "Er . . . Cash?"

"El Cid, dopey-face. Nyx wants another buy, doesn't he?"

My mouth opened, closed, and opened again. "How did you—"

"Call him."

Derp. Two Bud Lights and I'm out of sync faster than a dubbed Chinese action flick. "Here? Now? In a cop bar?"

"Yeah," Lee said. "I like the irony."

I don't.

"What's the matter?" Lee knocked his knee against mine. "You scared?"

A hundred smart-ass remarks bubbled up to the surface. Instead I said, "Yes."

He hadn't expected that.

Neither had I.

Awesome. Way to admit to your hotshot partner you can't hack it.

I grabbed the phone from my pocket, tapped AJ's contact icon, and dialed. He answered on the first ring. "El Cid."

"Hi," I said. "You busy?"

"Nah. Just crushing my enemies, seeing them driven before me, and listening to the lamentations of their women."

"Nice, Conan." As in the Barbarian.

How close is that to reality?

"You get me, Valeria. You really get me." AJ chuckled. "What's up?"

"You know the vacation I took to see you? The five days?"

"How could I forget?"

"Maybe it's time for a longer return visit." The words were stilted and off, sticking in my mouth. It was impossible to flirt under Lee's intent stare.

"Miss me?" AJ said, genteelly filling the conversational void.

"Desperately." I made a face at Lee.

"How long can you hang with me?"

"Two and a half weeks."

"Now, that's something I can get behind." AJ paused. "When?"

"Well, that's up to you, isn't it? I mean, if I'm coming all that way, I'd like for us to spend some quality time together."

"You should know by now, you never have to ask, Maisie." He let that settle. "You come back, I'll make it extra-special."

Lee's jaw slid to one side.

"You're a king among men, baby," I said as throatily as I could.

"Later, princess."

I swiped the phone off and took a sip of beer to keep the smirk off my face.

"You talk a good game. But that's all it is. Talk." Lee leaned back. His arm still rode across the back of the bench behind my head, but he was as far from me as possible. "Shouldn't play like that."

I felt a perverse rush. "Oh? Why's that?"

"Doesn't work out so well when you need to put up or shut up."

Hank's Law Number Nine: Confidence is not competence.

"Brass tacks or brass knuckles, Lee. I can hold my own."

"I know you think you can."

Maybe he had a point. "Gee, is this the pep-talk part of our partnership?" I laughed but it was high-pitched and nervy.

"You're not built for this."

"Thanks," I said. "But I'll take my chances."

"Not if I can help it."

He was angry with me, with the situation.

But there was more to it than that. Lee carried around a molten red core of fury inside. About what, who knew? But it'd take a more than a little "opening up" from me to make that happen. The quid pro quo would be exorbitant.

My beer had gone flat.

Propping my elbows on the table, I dropped my head in my hands and rubbed my eyes with the heels of my hands.

Hank.

Lee's warm hand slid up the nape of my neck, stopping where my neck and skull connected, and started kneading.

Pressure hissed out of me like the release valve on an engine. His thumb and middle finger rotated in small, firm circles.

My lower lip trembled.

I jumped up with a jerk, knocking into the table, tipping over my half-empty beer bottle.

Lee caught it before it hit the table. "Easy now."

But there was nothing easy about any of this.

"Hang on." He dug a twenty out of his pocket and tossed it on the table. "I'll walk you out."

"Please," I said hoarsely. "I'd rather you didn't."

Chapter 23

"Snap!" Cash said, shaking my leg. "Wake up!"

I rolled over and covered my head with a pillow. "What do you want?"

"Declan's on the phone."

"Unnnngh. So, talk to him."

"He's been calling you all morning. Your phone's off."

"Tell him I'm busy." Cash's grip on my calf turned into a claw.

"Aiiiiigh!" My foot kicked involuntarily. "Let go. Let go! Alright. Geez."

I sat up and he slapped his iPhone into my palm. "Hello?"

"What're you doing, Snap?"

"Sleeping."

"Get up. I need you to fill in for Mom at the club. We're in a mixed-doubles tournament."

Are you fecking kidding me? "Declan, you do remember I'm recovering from a stab wound to the leg?"

"Cash told me you're right as rain, running on the tread."

Goddammit.

"I haven't held a racquet in six months. And all my tennis gear's at home."

"Jaysus, can you fuss any louder?" Declan said. "Our opponents had the option to reschedule and wait for Mom or accept you, an erratic 3.6. They chose you."

Naturally. Mom was a strong 5.0.

"I'll be there in thirty. Mom packed your tennis bag." He hung up before I had the chance to say no.

Eighty-two minutes later, Declan picked me up in his black F-Type S Jag, which meant I got to change into my tennis whites in the front seat of his convertible. We sped to the Midtown Athletic Club, Declan spoon-feeding me strategy the entire way. "Okay, Snap. Here's the thing, these guys work for Hobbs, Aspen, and Mooney. Good guys, but crappy tennis players. Bad enough to where they can throw your game by their sheer ineptitude to get a ball back over the net." He smirked at me. "Which is great, because you'll be playing at about the same level."

I batted my lashes at him. "Gee, you're swell."

Declan popped me in the arm. "Thing is, Mom and I are gunning for the finals. No one has the balls to take on Avirett and Beaumont from the state attorney's office. We're gonna crush those asshats. They're trying to rape us on your pal Keck's case. Mom's seeing red, sweating that it might blow back on you. Ha." He shook his head. "Like we'd let that happen."

The gears in my head shifted into overdrive. Special Unit was going to need Christo Keck out and about and daisy-fresh if Lee and I were going to infiltrate the Veterattis. "What are you talking about?"

Declan turned on the stereo and shuffled to Mom's Mix. Prince's "Kiss" pulsated through the car. "Gotta have Mom here, in spirit, as God knows your game will need a little divine intervention." He grooved behind the wheel. "Fecking ASA Avirett is giving Daicen the shivering fits."

Typical. Christo Keck was more his client than Daicen's. Which was truly the "devil's gift." When Declan let someone else shoulder the responsibility, he let go and never looked back.

"How?" I said.

"Aside from the fact that he's a goddamn vindictive bastard? He's trying to swaddle us up in a piss and puke blanket."

"A natural-born poet, Declan." I toyed with the strings on my racquet. "Richard Avirett's gunning for you, huh? Who'd you sleep with? His wife, mother, or sister?"

He shot me a sideways glance. "Mistress."

Cripes. "Does Daicen know?"

"He should've figured it out by now." Declan shrugged. "First Avirett dismisses, then refiles and re-arrests, forcing Keck to make a new bond. Only now, in addition to the increased bail, Avirett's demanding a surety package. So Keck's back in lockup, needing proof his source for bail is legitimate."

I chewed a knuckle, thinking. Declan's philandering aside, Coles's mark on Keck's case was as puerile and obvious as red PETA paint on a fur coat. If Coles couldn't have Stannis, he'd do everything in his power to watch him burn.

Can't anything be easy? Ever?

We pulled into the parking lot of Midtown Athletic Club with its eighteen indoor tennis courts.

I was pretty edgy, actually. Not about the match as much as my leg. I stopped in front of the pro shop. "Hey, Dec? I'm gonna grab a pair of compression shorts before we start."

"Hustle up," he said. "You're making us late." I held out my bag. "Jaysus." He rolled his eyes and grabbed the duffel.

Vintage Declan. Pick me up an hour late and it's my fault.

"Court eight," he called at my back.

I billed the compression shorts to his account, and put them on in the pro shop dressing room. I yanked up my Bolle under-shorts and finally my Fila tennis skirt, and trotted down to the courts, telling myself that tennis was going to be great for my recovery.

Declan was on the court warming up, his serves smooth, fast, and perfectly placed. Across the net were two men. Also warm-ing up. I jogged onto the court. "What the hell, Deck? Those are guys."

"Oh?" He tossed me a ball. Then another.

"You said mixed doubles."

"Did I?" He tugged my ponytail. "Well, I didn't wanna hurt your feelings. . . . Last man off the line and all that."

"Wow." I served the ball. Then another. At least they made it over the net. "Aren't you sweet as an Easter Peep."

"Six months since you held a racquet? Are you sure it wasn't six years?" Declan threw me another tennis ball, this one slightly out of reach. I lunged and caught it, sucking in my breath at the sharp pain that zinged through my thigh.

"Get it together, crybaby," he said.

All I ever wanted was a sister. Just one.

But no. I got five brothers. Five.

And they all suck.

I smacked the racquet against my palm. "Come a little closer and say that."

He grinned and tossed his dark hair out of his eyes. "Poach like an East-Ender at a highbrow pheasant shoot, and I'll put 'em away."

The duo from Hobbs, Aspen, and Mooney weren't a tennis powerhouse by any stretch of the imagination. We were up four games to zip within thirty minutes, and things picked up from there. I cozied up tight to the net and let Declan do all the leg-work.

Serves him right.

Literally.

My leg was throbbing. I needed a stiff drink and an Oxy. Declan nudged me with his elbow over the armrest. "Nice work, Snap. Mom would have had my head if we'd lost."

"Now you tell me."

"After watching you warm up, I wasn't sure you could take the additional pressure."

"Ha-ha."

He turned the wrong way at the stoplight.

"Where are you taking me?"

"Well, you're gonna take a victory lap with me and Dai, yeah?"

"Of course," I said, basking in the warm glow of brotherly love. All I had to look forward to at Hank's was watching Cash eat and squabbling with him over the TV remote.

Declan parked the Jaguar in the underground parking garage. We took the elevator up to the tenth-floor apartment he shared with Daicen. Declan fished out his keys as we walked down the hall. "That was fun today," he said. "We haven't done that in a donkey's age."

"Yeah." I nodded, finishing the pun. "Long years."

He fit the key in the lock and swung open the door. Music and voices washed out of the foyer into the hallway.

"A victory party?" I said.

"I can't help it if I live at Delta House. After you."

I limped into the apartment. Flynn, Rory, Cash, Mom, and Daicen were chasing Jameson Caskmates Stout with Stella Artois. Or at least that's what the near-empty whiskey bottle on the counter suggested.

"Maisie!" they chorused.

Daicen popped the cap off with a bottle opener and slid a Stella across the counter.

"Thanks," I said.

"Well?" Mom demanded. "Did we win?"

Declan clasped his hands, held them up, and shook them first on one side then the other, like a 1930s prizefighter. "Was there ever any doubt?"

"Thanks for filling in for me, baby," Mom said to me. "How's the leg?"

"Stiff, but I'll live."

She patted the armchair next to the sectional she was on. "Come sit down."

Beer in hand, I did as requested and put my foot up on the coffee table. Flynn stood up and turned the stereo down. The rest of the guys swarmed into the great room.

It took a few seconds for it to sink in.

"Jaysus, Mary, and Joseph." I slouched down in the chair. "It's an Irish intervention."

"Very perceptive, darling," Mom said.

I waved my beer at them. "Go ahead. Have at me."

"That's not funny," Mom said. "My connection to Walt Sawyer is the only reason you're not in jail."

I slid my thumbnail under the paper Stella label, quashing the litany of responses building inside my chest. It wasn't the actual undercover work that ate away at me as much as the constant lying.

"It's like you're out, tin cup in hand, begging for trouble, Snap." Cash moved in and perched on the edge of the coffee table.

"Don't call her Snap," Mom said automatically.

Cash put his hand on my leg. "Lee told me about the truckload of hate mail you're receiving over your op-eds."

Gee, Cash. I'm not sure whose knife is sunk deeper in my back—yours or Lee's.

Mom took over. "You promised to be home when Hank wasn't around. You've gone back on your word."

"Yeah, well, after Da betrayed me, I guess words aren't worth the breath they're given anymore. I know at least a couple of you knew he was behind my expulsion from the police academy. And not one of you did a damn thing about it."

"I suspected." Flynn ran a hand over his face. "And I owe you an apology for that." He locked his dark eyes with mine. "I'm sorry."

"I'm not," Rory said bluntly. "Da's had the right of it all along."

No one saw that bare-assed admission coming. Least of all me.

"Just look at the feckin' mess you've made of your life last year. You fecked up as a meter maid, pissed off the mayor, and played kissing cousins with a goddamn Serbian enforcer called 'The Butcher.' And now? Stabbed in the leg in the middle of a Class X felony while playin' gel reporter at that commie shite news rag."

Gee, when you put it like that . . .

Cash gave the wide-eyed look-away that said he thought Rory was off his rocker.

Everyone else seemed to think he had a point.

Lovely.

"Real sweet of you to fill in for Da, Rory," I said flatly. "Seeing as he's not here."

"This ain't about Da, though, is it?" The corner of his mouth curled in a snarl. "Last time I checked it weren't Da that let a Leavenworth mercenary buy you a car and keep you as a mistress in his house."

He looked at each of my brothers in turn. "Did I miss anything?"

Not much. Only that Hank was everything to me.

My lungs collapsed, shrink-wrapping my heart into a tight, smothering knot of anger "Would it make any difference if I told you Hank asked me to marry him?"

Mom caught that one before it hit the floor. "And your answer?"

"Contrary to the McGrane Clan Bylaws, getting engaged isn't a family decision." I raised the beer to my mouth and took a swallow.

Six pairs of dark eyes lasered in on the Cartier band on my ring finger. They looked at me like I'd smothered a puppy.

Ughhhhh.

Stannis's ring. I forgot I'd had it on.

"Looks like the decision's already been made," Flynn said.

Except it wasn't. "It's not like that."

Cash patted my leg. "A test run. Right, Snap?"

"No. The ring was a gift, not an engagement."

Because when you're staked out on an anthill, you might as well have extra honey.

Daicen cleared his throat. "This discussion has devolved to unhelpful. The tennis play has taken a visible toll on Maisie." He rose to his feet and exchanged a long look with Mom. "I'll return her to Bannon's." Daicen faced the rest of our brothers. "Our youngest sibling is a gainfully employed adult who is considering becoming engaged to a financially stable independent contractor. Tempest in a teapot comes to mind."

He held out his hand. "Shall we?"

"Thanks, Daicen." I fastened my seat belt in his Audi.

"Yes," he said as he latched his buckle, "well, I am the nice one."

It was hard to breathe.

He pulled a roll of Wint O Green Life Savers from the center console and handed it over. "Are you engaged?"

I slid the foil from the candy. "No."

"The ring?"

"A gift. From Stannis." I handed the candy back.

He separated one with his thumbnail and flipped it into his mouth. "But Hank did ask you to marry him."

"Mmm-hmm."

Daicen didn't turn his head to look at me. Didn't say a word. So I did.

"It didn't happen how I thought it . . . I didn't expect . . . I mean, I didn't think it would be so—"

My brother focused on the road ahead, saying nothing.

"Hank asked me if a license and a ring would help." The confession poured out of me like new ketchup—halting and slow at first, then rushing out in a gloppy mess. "He asked me to quit. Everything. To just be with him. And when he asked me like that, I knew if I said 'yes' he'd have gone ahead and married me any which way I wanted it. But I wanted him to *want* to marry me."

"Yes," Daicen said quietly.

Unshed tears crept up my throat. "By the time I realized Hank loved me all the way enough to do that—for me—because to him nothing mattered except us . . . It was too late. And he had to go."

My brother remained impassive.

"I can hear how so completely stupid I sound." My fingers plucked at the pleats of my tennis skirt. "It's just . . . Things don't matter the same way to Hank as they do to our clan."

"No. They don't." He put his hand over mine. "You don't always have to play it so tough, Maisie." The heat from his hand was overwhelming, his words lighting my hair on fire.

I flexed my fingers and he returned his hand to the steering wheel.

"Thanks," I said. "Declan told me you want to meet about Keck's case."

"Not tonight. You've had enough."

We drove the rest of the way to Hank's in silence. He pulled up close to the sidewalk. I opened the car door.

"Maisie?" he said. "Cry about it tonight. Fix it tomorrow."

"I just might."

He waited until I was in the house before driving away. I pressed my forehead against the transom window, watching his taillights disappear into the night.

Crying was for babies.

I opted for Vanilla Swiss Almond Häagen-Dazs, Oxy, and *Gunga Din* with Douglas Fairbanks Jr.

Definitely.

Chapter 24

A yellow Post-it waited on my desk chair at the *Sentinel*:

Pay up.

Sweet. Lennon had finished my research.

Twenty hours—because no way was Lennon the kind of guy who was going to finish early—at $60 an hour. I counted twelve hundreds from my wallet and put them in an envelope. Time to go see what he'd found out about the scourge of the Grieco cartel, The Weeping Beast. I was banking it'd be a good deal more than Nyx's puppet, Wes.

I stowed my messenger bag in the file drawer, jammed the envelope in the back pocket of my jeans, and went to meet the human rake.

Lennon rocked behind his desk on a bright red yoga ball chair, typing. His shoulder blades poked painfully from his thin wool sweater. So scrawny, he could use ChapStick for deodorant.

I rapped on the open office door. "Got your note."

Lennon jerked his head toward his old desk chair in the corner and kept typing.

Thanks, but I can do without my clothes reeking of vape.

I walked over to the small window. "Hi," I said to Grey Gardens, who was wearing a mustard- and mud-colored tie-dyed outfit that a roadie for Phish would have rejected.

Grey Gardens wrinkled her nose as if I smelled far worse

than the trash can filled to overflowing with fast food wrappers.

"I'll get us a Starbucks, ya?"

"Tall Caffè Misto with soy milk," Lennon said still typing.

"Geez, I know, I know," she fawned. "You have the same thing every day!"

If there was anything sadder than a chubby, middle-aged woman crushing on a snobbish hipster, I couldn't think of it.

Grey Gardens wafted out on a cloud of Febreze, housecat, and White Diamonds perfume.

Lennon took his time before spinning around on the clown nose yoga chair. He held a manila folder tight to his thin chest and thrust out his palm. "Cash?"

Taking a Saf-T-Pop from a toddler would have been more challenging. I sucked in my lips, stifling a mouthful of snark, and handed him the envelope.

Awkwardly, he opened it with one hand and riffled the bills with his thumb. Satisfied, he wedged the envelope beneath his keyboard. "Now," he said, "we're going to get something straight."

"Ooo-kay."

"What are you planning to do with this research?"

"Not really your concern, is it?"

A shrewd, unpleasant look settled over his face. "What story exactly?"

"I don't feel comfortable sharing that with you."

"This report contains information you would never have been able to find, much less access and—"

Jaysus, let's get this show on the road.

"Yes, thank you. Which is why"—I pointed at the keyboard—"payment for services rendered."

His ears lit up like traffic flares. "I'm clarifying, for the record, that we had an agreement for research, not content. Background for a story? You use one sentence in its entirety, and I want co-writing credit."

Seriously? "A little cart before the horse, don't you think? You're assuming what you've done is useful to me." I held out my hand for the folder.

"It will be." His concave chest puffed out almost all the way to normal human. "Pro tip: Plagiarism is a journalistic career-ender."

Ignoring my hand, he tossed the folder onto his desk return, bounced back on his ball to the keyboard, and started typing. "Thanks. I'll take that under advisement."

I forced myself to wait until I was back in my office with the door closed before opening the file. I paged quickly through the atrocities of the three other hitters, Chilo, Kah, and Águila, before getting to The Weeping Beast.

Naturally, it was the shortest report.

Aside from a two-page collage of gruesome victim photos, there was only a single picture of "The Beast." A grainy, pixelated three-inch-by-two-inch square. The bridge of the man's nose was warped and flattened. A strange sort of round scar the size of a dime sat at the corner of his left eye, while a finger-width weal descended from the scar past the corner of his mouth, off his chin.

Lennon had roughly translated scans of an ER and police report:

> Iago García Falto aka The Weeping Beast (La Bestia Que Llora) was approximately fourteen years old when he was presented at ER by police with his nose crushed by length of pipe. Blow apparently administered by father.
>
> Due to prior damage, perforated nasal septum due to daily cocaine use, this injury resulted in permanent blockage of his nasolacrimal (tear) ducts. While these would ordinarily drain through the nose, he now has only his left eye as a point of discharge. Hence the nickname The Weeping Beast.

"Ergh." I turned the page.

The police report was worse.

Iago apparently returned to the apartment to dis-
cover his infant sister unconscious and mother
beaten to death by his father. Iago attacked his father, knocking him unconscious with a chair, and
for unknown reasons tried to resuscitate his battered sister, María Fernanda, in the bath.

At some point, his father regained consciousness,
and hit Iago repeatedly with a lead pipe. Iago re-
taliated, stabbing his father multiple times with a
kitchen knife, killing him, but not before his father crushed his nose with the lead pipe.

Neighbors found Iago barely alive, the rest of the
family dead, María Fernanda having drowned in
the bath.

After his release from the hospital, Iago García
Falto began working for El Eje as a low-level gang
enforcer, followed by what can only be termed as a
meteoric rise as a contract torturer for hire.

A horrible and par-for-the-course sadist's history.

Easy pickings for the El Eje cartel.

The rest of the report focused on Iago's favored techniques.
Of moderate intelligence, he had an unusually high aptitude
for keeping his victims alive. His modus operandi was to make
them suffer for days, sometimes even weeks, before death.

Nauseated, I shut the file and stowed it in my bag. Lennon's
information was stronger than I'd hoped. I owed Juice dinner
for middle-manning. Somewhere great.

Heck, maybe I'll give her a thrill and ask Lee to come along.

Reaching for the *Sentinel*'s directory, my phone went off.
"Tank!" by the band Seatbelts.

Walt Saywer.

"Good afternoon, sir," I answered.

"I received your message and I've a short break in my schedule. Where are you, Maisie?"

"The *Sentinel*."

"Excellent. Meet me outside in twenty minutes." He hung up.

A young man in a suit waved at me as I stepped out of the *Sentinel*. He stood in front of a sleek, short BMW 550i 30 limousine and opened the door as I approached.

The black leather interior and ultra-dark windows gave it the sophisticated chic of a vampire lair. I slid into the seat, waited for the door to close, and brought Sawyer up to speed.

He listened intently to the news about Christo Keck and Declan and Daicen's representational woes from ASA Avirett. "An unpleasant development, yes," Sawyer said, nodding, "But not unexpected. Coles's temper is nothing if not unforgiving."

"Keck is a critical player to Stannis's chop-shop operation. Without him overseeing the garages, I'm not sure how to proceed. I'm not even certain he'll go into business with me without direct contact with Renko."

"Leave the ASA and Keck to me," Sawyer said. "And you'll be the first to know when Renko makes contact with his men or the Srpska Mafija."

My iPhone buzzed. Inside the vacuum-sealed BMW it sounded like a hive of hornets.

Idiot.

I'd turned it to vibrate, not all the way off. "I apologize, sir." I dug my phone out of my messenger bag.

AJ Rodriguez.

"It's El Cid, sir."

"Take it." Sawyer removed a report from his briefcase and started reading. I hit Speaker.

"Hey, girl," AJ said, his voice honey-sweet.

"Hello, handsome," I said. "What's up?"

"Do you really want me to answer that?" He chuckled. "Listen, Carlos is throwing a party next weekend. It'd be a really good idea if you were there. Not to mention, looks like a cold front is moving into the Windy City. A little sun might set you right up."

"I'll be there."

Sawyer took a pen from inside his breast pocket, twisted it open, scribbled on the back of a report page, and held it up:

$$+1$$

"AJ, I'm afraid I'll be a plus-one. Will that be a problem?"

"Did you go all Beverly Hills and get a fucking Chihuahua? Or are you bringing down your twin sister? 'Cause I know you're smart enough not to mess around on Renko."

"Aww, aren't you sweet to worry," I teased. "Let's just say that while the dark angel was pleased as punch at the effort I went to for his operation, in his infinite wisdom, he now believes a minder would be . . . prudent."

"And our latest business arrangement?"

"Under wraps."

"Easier to bend the iron will once he sees what a lucrative partner I can be, is that it?"

I let my voice go husky. "Let's just say that asking for forgiveness falls within my skill set."

"I'll bet it does." AJ paused. "Carlos wants to meet you."

Sawyer's head snapped up.

"I beg your pardon?" I said.

"You saved my life, Maisie. Technically, at least. Who's to say I wouldn't have opened the cooler? Carlos is going all out. Limo, jet, the works. What's your address?"

Uh-oh.

Sawyer wrote beneath the number *1*:

Renko's Apt.

I gave AJ the address.

"I'll text you with the deets."

"I'll be waiting. With bells on." I switched the phone off.

"Well done, Maisie," Sawyer said. "Well done, indeed."

My cheeks got warm. "Thank you, sir."

"An excellent head start toward cementing a cohesive back-story for Veteratti and the NY Syndicate. People will get used to seeing Sharpe as not only your shadow but as your subordinate." He cocked his head. "Obviously, Renko's apartment is the most natural place of residence during Operation Summit. It bolsters your legitimate claim to Renko's holdings, as well."

Oh God.

Other than using acid for eye drops, I couldn't think of anything I'd rather do than explain to the clan how I was moving out of Hank's and into Renko's extravagant penthouse apartment.

Which I couldn't possibly afford on my fictitious *Sentinel* pay. Not without dipping into my trust fund.

Feck.

At least Hank would understand. *Sort of.*

"Yessir."

"Well then." He pressed a button on the armrest. "It appears as though you and Mr. Sharpe have some packing to do."

Before I could close my gaping mouth, the driver opened my door.

Chapter 25

Coin toss of awesomeness.

What to do first? Kick Cash out or tell Lee we were moving in together?

Whee.

I stepped into the foyer. "Goddammit! What the feck?" Cash shouted.

I came around the corner into the great room. *H1Z1* was on the TV screen.

"Seriously, man. What the feck?" He tossed the controller onto the coffee table. "Yeah? Well, take your head outta your ass next time, Koji. I'm out." Cash jerked the wireless headset off and dropped it on the couch.

"Cash?" I said.

He rolled his eyes at me. "Jaysus, everybody knows you can't friggin' multi-play with a girl sitting on your lap. I mean, what the hell is he thinking?"

Maybe you should rewind the last five seconds and figure it out yourself.

I went to the fridge and got out a Coke. "We've gotta talk."

"Sure. What's up?"

"That ol' highway's a callin'. You need to move home."

"Did I piss you off or something?" His face crinkled in confusion. "This is, like, the most fun we've had in a long time."

"Yeah, it's been great and all, but . . ." I hedged.

"Is Hank coming home?"

"No." I walked over, sat on the couch, and opened the box of Maisie-brand Whoppers. "Lee asked me to go away for a couple of days with him."

Cash's eyes went the size of silver dollars. "What did you say?"

"Yeah."

"Shit," he breathed. "I can't believe he didn't ask me first."

"Ask you to go?"

He snorted. "For permission."

Response to this level of self-aggrandizement is impossible.

My brother got up and strode over to the wet bar. Without another word, he took out a bottle of Bud, twisted off the cap, and drank a third of it in one go. He came back to the couch and flopped down next to me. "What's Wilhelm gonna do without me?"

"Seriously?"

"It's just that he makes my meals, runs my errands . . . You know, any ones that don't require direct contact. I mean, he's gotten pretty attached to me."

Really? You can't understand your best friend choosing a live girlfriend over a video game and you, a guy he spends twelve hours a day with every day, but yet you're completely in psychological sync with Hank's reclusive valet.

"I'm sure he has," I said. "But even you, Captain Sensitive, has to see that you staying at Hank's while I take a trip with Lee is nowhere near close to appropriate."

Cash scratched behind his ear. "How is this even happening?"

"You threw him at me over and over again. What did you think would happen?"

"Maisie . . ." He shook his head.

"Lee invited me as a friend."

"Like hell." He rubbed his hands on his thighs. "I'm supposed to go back to work on Thursday. Would it bum you out if I left tonight?"

Yeah, as much as a free phone to a welfare mother.

"I think I can handle it."

Cash grabbed me around the neck and ground his knuckles into my head. "We'll see, Snap."

Roughhousing aside, I was feeling more *Why me?* than *Try me* to man up and call Lee.

After all, Cash needed help hauling his gear to the car. He'd accumulated a surprisingly large amount, considering his only activity here had consisted of being waited on hand and foot.

Sawyer beat me to the punch.

Lee Sharpe flashed on my phone screen as Cash drove away. "Hello?"

"One night with me," Lee teased, "and you're pulling out all the stops to get me under the same roof."

"A live-in secretary is essential for a girl in my position. I never know when I might feel the need to give dictation."

His chuckle was warm and intimate. "All you have to do is whistle."

I'll keep that in mind.

"So," Lee said. "How do you wanna play this?"

"Smart. I'll finish up here, swing by, and help you pack."

"Uhhh . . . You wanna roll my socks, Bae?" he kidded, uncertain.

Nice to have him on the defensive for once.

"You're employed by Mr. Renko now. And Mr. Renko likes things just so."

Lee swung open the door. He was wearing jeans, a black tee, and square-toed Harley-Davidson boots. He gave me a slow wolf whistle.

"Gee, thanks," I said and stepped inside and around the three duffel bags of gear. "How long until you're ready to go?"

"Now."

"Not like that, you're not." His couch had returned to "handy storage" mode. I tossed a sweatshirt to one side and moved enough newspapers to sit down.

"Since when does moving in require a jacket?"

"See this?" I smoothed the hip of my ancient red Misook

sheath. "This is my moving outfit. We're not leaving until you change."

"Quit jerking my chain."

"Mr. Renko requires every member of his team properly attired at all times."

Lee looked mulish.

I folded my arms and crossed my legs. "Go put on a suit."

"Are you fucking kidding me?"

I tapped Stannis's Philippe Patek. "Ticktock, darling."

For five minutes I fought the urge to tidy up Lee's living room. Normally I would've, because we're partners and I'm helpful like that. But he was going to be my bodyguard, and he was going to have to start treating me like an employer, whether he wanted to or not.

Lee returned to the living room in a navy Brooks Brothers suit with enough room in front to hide a pregnant panda. "You work that hard to have a flat belly and you actually wear that?"

"Easy to hide the piece." He flashed his palms at me. "Christ, it was for a wedding. I never wear a suit. Ever. I have two dress uniforms."

"Open the jacket."

Inside, he was wearing a shoulder holster and another custom-made dress shirt.

"How in God's name does one purchase custom-made dress shirts and then cover them up with an off-the-rack suit made for a man who weighs at least a hundred pounds more than you?"

Lee rolled his tongue inside his cheek. "I didn't. My ex-girlfriend, who studied fashion design at the School of the Art Institute of Chicago, did."

"Why'd she leave you? The suit?"

"C'mere and ask me that."

I don't know how he did it, the way he turned a silly remark into something hypercharged and sexual. "Thanks, but I don't wanna risk suffocation in all the extra fabric."

"Good enough?" he demanded.

"For now." I balled my hands into fists and walked past his gear at the door, feeling like a bitch, but explaining to him that this was how it was going to be from here on in would be worse.

I waited until Lee was following behind in his Mustang before asking Siri to call Daicen for the number of his contact at Nicholas Joseph Custom Tailors. I booked an appointment for Lee at 7 a.m. the following morning. Although it would be egregiously expensive, he would look like one of Stannis's regulars by Friday.

Stannislav Renko's penthouse apartment was in a midrise rehabbed industrial building in the trendy West Loop. I circled around the building to give Lee an idea of where we were. I pulled up to the underground parking, and swiped my key card in front of the electric eye. The steel garage doors opened, and Lee and I descended into the dimly lit depths. I pulled into Stannis's spot, one of five where a yellow *PH* had been stenciled onto the cement wall.

Lee parked alongside, popped the trunk, and got out. He walked to the rear of the Mustang to get his gear.

I waited patiently behind the wheel.

Lee set two his bags on the ground, reached for the third as the light clicked. He marched over and opened my door. I swung my legs out, stood up, and pressed the car keys into his hand. "Thank you. There should be a bellhop cart nearby."

His eyes narrowed. I opened the rear door and lifted the box I'd wrapped up the night before. Stannis's legacy, now with added sand.

Back home where it belonged.

Sort of.

"Walk with me to the elevator, please, Lee. I'd rather not wait for you to get the bags."

"Oh?"

My God, it was fun to mess with him.

"I'll admit it's a bit of a hassle," I said. "But Mr. Renko insists on top-notch security." I glanced up at one of the many golf ball–sized video cameras.

Lee's mouth twisted in understanding. "Yes, Miss Mc—"

"Mrs. Renko," I corrected. I swiped the key card, pressed PH, and handed him the card as the elevator doors closed.

I hugged the box to my chest, crumpling the cardboard at the familiarity of it all.

I stepped into the black granite foyer of Stannis's penthouse. It felt oddly, distressingly empty with no bodyguards. Each reverberating *click* of my heels spookily foreboding.

Getting nervy.

Hank's Law Number Four: Keep your head.

The living room was just as it had been, spartan. Ebony hardwood floors, stone-gray walls, and everything else, from countertops to furniture, a pristine and brilliant white.

Sawyer said Special Unit personnel had removed every trace of my presence, but not Stannis's.

Passing through the great room I swiped a finger over the bar. Spotless. Apparently the cleaners were still being paid. I stopped in the kitchen, set down the box, and opened the Sub-Zero refrigerator. Half a dozen bottles of Bollinger champagne, three vacuum-sealed jars of beluga caviar, Voss bottled water and *sweet Jiminey Christmas,* the vegetable crisper was full of Original Sugar Free Amps.

"God, I miss you, Stannis." And I did. Especially when I ignored that splinter in time when Hank stopped him from shooting me in the head.

Vodka, rakija, and a box of caramelized pineapple Freezer Monkeys frozen dessert bars made up the contents of the freezer.

I picked up the box, walked past Stannis's room, where I'd be bunking, and started down the separate hallway to his office. The hardwood turned to quicksand beneath my feet as I approached the white enameled French doors with his legacy.

Apparently cowardice is filling in for discretion as the better part of valor today.

I hustled back to Stannis's room and wedged the box under the bed.

I'd be sleeping with the bone jar.

Again.

I trotted down the main hallway and down to the other en suite and gave it a quick once-over. No trace of my presence remained in the pale gray and silver guest bedroom.

The faint *ding* of the elevator chimed.

I went out to meet Lee. He'd found the bellhop cart.

"Where would you like them, Mrs. Renko?"

You wanna role-play, baby? "This way."

The text ring on my iPhone played the whistle from *The Good, The Bad and The Ugly*. AJ had sent our travel plans.

I handed my phone to Lee.

Here we go.

Chapter 26

We sat at the smooth white quartz table drinking Peroni and eating Coalfire pepperoni pizza straight from the box like a couple of heathens. I'd changed into Lululemon sweats and Gold-Toe athletic socks. "Thanks for getting this," I said around a hot mouthful of extra tomato-saucy heaven.

"Thanks for allowing me to dine at the table, princess." Lee's arms bulged from the short-sleeved heather-gray T-shirt with UMD Hockey emblazoned across it and a pair of jeans faded to butter soft. He shook some more red pepper flakes onto his slice, eyes surveying the room. "I can see why you dragged this assignment out."

"Gee, you're a sweetheart."

His jaw slid sideways. "You wanna see how sweet I can be?"

Funny, I don't remember poking the bear.

I got up from the table and went into the kitchen, rummaged around, and returned with two cut-crystal lowball glasses, ice, and the bottle of Tovaritch! vodka from the freezer.

Lee kept eating while I poured out two healthy slugs.

I slid a glass in front of him and raised my own, Stannis's words rolling smoothly off my tongue, "Because one must burn a candle for the devil now and again."

Lee threw his pizza crust in the box. He picked up his vodka with a scoff and drained it.

Ooookay.

I poured him another. And another.

He still drank like a Marine. Steadily and with purpose.

Lee held out his glass.

I slid the bottle out of reach. "What gives?"

"Did you fuck him?"

Hank's Law Number Eight: If they ask for the rope, give it to them.

"No," I said, patiently. "Stannis is gay."

"So?" He set down his glass, eyes scanning the room. "I wasn't asking about him. Yet."

"What?"

"Did. You. Fuck. Sawyer?"

My mouth dropped open in a perfect O. "Walt? *Walt Sawyer?*"

He stared at me, alert and watchful, looking for any hint, any give. There weren't any.

Jerk. "I never figured you for the kind of guy who liked to be slapped around."

"How'd you hook Renko?"

I didn't exactly feel like sharing. "I reminded him of his sister."

"Sure you did."

"See this?" I wound a strand of copper-colored hair around my finger. "She was a redhead."

"You fall for The Butcher? Is that why you claimed the blame for Coles's finger? Or was it just to get ahead in Special Unit?"

"Screw you, Sharpe."

His brown eyes went flinty. "You offering?"

"Get up." I walked past him and turned down the hall to Stannis's study. Anger churned in my gut. I grabbed the levers and threw back the doors, Lee tight on my heels.

I flipped on the dim recessed lights. The office was huge, and matched the house in masculine sophistication: Wood walls were stained a misty pewter; a thick charcoal rug anchored black leather seating in front of a sleek fireplace. One end of the room remained in shadows. I pointed to the far end of the room, at the raw steel desk in front of the wall of sleek cabinetry.

"Stannis use to have this big glass jar"—I patted the desk—"right here. He called it 'his legacy.'"

Lee went behind the desk, sat down, and put his feet up. "What'd he have in it?"

"Torture trophies. Bones of the fingers he'd taken."

"Nice."

"Which way do you want it, Lee? That I cut Coles's finger off? Or that I'm too sweet to have done it?"

"The truth."

I tipped my head at the chair. "Coles was restrained there. Cable-tied."

Lee ran his hands along the sides of the leather arm pads of the chair, feeling for ridges left from the cable ties, frowning when he felt them. "So?"

The room narrowed, dimming at the edges. The malodorous stink of Coles's fear clogged my nose as my mind crashed through the chasm in time.

Stannis had gone still, but energy hummed off him like a leaking nuclear reactor. "I am *Mesar*. The Butcher. You have choice to make, Talbott," he had said flatly. "Maisie will take finger or I will take your hand."

The mayor sagged forward, his voice more a moan than a mumble. "Giveherit."

"What?" Stannis asked politely.

"Give her the goddamn knife!" Coles's face went a dark mottled red. He put his left pinkie on the chopping block.

Stannis's bright blues filled with emotion as he turned to me. "Claim your place, *Vatra Andeo*."

I walked to the edge of the desk, as stiff and jerky as a bird. "I don't think I can do this."

Stannis placed the battered handle of the hoary iron cleaver in my hand. It was heavy and vicious, with a strange two-sided blade.

I squeezed my eyes shut.

"Open your goddamn eyes!" Coles snapped.

I raised the cleaver up past my chin. Stannis reached out,

lowered my wrists down to slightly beneath my shoulders, and nodded.

Oh God. I took a deep breath. *One . . .*

Feck it.

I swung the blade down as hard as I could.

It felt like chopping a piece of ballistics gel with a piece of glass in the middle.

Coles screamed and jerked up his arm, spittle and blood spraying as he cursed. Stannis grabbed his forearm and wrapped his hand in a white cotton towel.

Stannis grinned at me, the enormous, closemouthed smile of a proud parent. He nodded and reached out his hand to my face. "*Vatra Andeo.*" He wiped his thumb across my cheek, then held his hand away to show me the blood he'd rubbed off.

My vision dimmed at the edges. I knew what he wanted me to say. So I did. "*Moj đavo.*"

And all the while, Coles kept swearing, the pristine white towel on his hand soaking bright red with blood.

"Hey! Hello?" Lee rapped on the desktop. "Maisie?"

I blinked and shook my head. "Sorry."

Maybe it was Lee, or the time that had passed, or that after stubbing his cigar out on my neck Coles deserved any and everything he got, but somehow the intensity of the recollection felt . . . less. Smaller and more faded than it had since it happened.

I cleared my throat. "Coles put out a hit on me. Stannis took it personally. He told Coles I would take his finger or he'd take his hand."

Lee gave that chin-lifting *I'm not buying, but go ahead with your pitch* nod. "Coles, I'm assuming, opted for the loss of a digit?"

I nodded.

"Where is it? The finger?"

"Gone."

He nodded. "Convenient."

"Last time I saw it, it was over here." I strode to the darkened end of the room, to the granite plinth that the clear glass cube rested on. Lee followed tight behind. I felt along the side for the light switch and turned it on. The large glass aquarium atop the column lit up.

The floor of the cage was covered in cedar shavings and dead black beetles.

He knocked his knuckle against the glass. "What are those?"

"*Staphylinidae.* Corpse beetles." I slid open the top of the cage and pointed at the right rear corner. "I put Coles's finger there. It was . . . still warm."

Lee's brows knit together, mouth sinking at the corners. He believed me and he didn't like it.

I don't much care for it, either, sport.

"And the jar?" he asked.

"Maybe someday, sometime, if you're real nice, I'll show it to you."

I was up long before my four-thirty alarm. I took the elevator down and knocked out a four-mile run on the treadmill in the empty gym. Showered and snappy in a DVF navy V-neck dress and Pliner heels.

I waited until six fifteen to wake him.

Door open, I peeked my head inside.

Lee slept on his side, head buried in the crook of his arm, breathing heavily. Shirtless, he was an impressive sight. A Marine Corps tattoo on his left shoulder blade, and high on his left bicep another ink of a senior explosive ordnance disposal badge. The duvet was a crumpled pile at the foot of the bed, the top sheet a twisted mass that barely covered his butt and wound around the calves of a man who obviously never skipped leg days at the gym.

He slept as he lived. Messily.

"Rise and shine, Captain Sunshine." I shook his ankle and turned away, not taking the odds that he had anything on beneath the sheet. "We leave for an appointment in twenty minutes."

He groaned.

Enough for me, I spun on my heel and walked to the door. "Gah!" A pillow hit me in the back of the head. For a split second I thought about turning around and giving him what for.

His voice dropped into a deep, sexy lilt. "C'mon back, Bae."

"You got nineteen. And bring your shoulder and back holsters," I said without turning around, and closed the door behind me.

Twenty-two minutes later, Lee was behind the wheel of his Mustang wearing his awful suit and bitching about the subpar breakfast of a Quest bar and water, as I had no intention of sharing my newfound stash of sugar-free Amps.

"How in the hell can there not be any coffee in those digs?"

"I'm sure they'll give you some when we get there."

"Where are we going, anyway?"

"Nicholas Joseph's."

"Who's that?"

"Turn onto West Grand," I said, "and park."

He saw the navy blue awning with the white lettering. "Christ, Maisie. I got up for this?" We got out of the car and went to the door. "They don't even open until ten."

At that moment, the door swung open. "Maisie McGrane? Steven Schoeneck," said a young guy in a perfectly tailored suit. He ushered us into the store and nodded at Lee. "And you must be Mr. Sharpe. Can I get either of you anything to drink?"

"Coffee'd be great," he said and cracked a couple of knuckles.

"Tea would be lovely, Steven," I said, "please."

The clerk disappeared, and Lee scanned the showroom, rocking back and forth on the balls of his feet. Oriental rugs dotted the hardwood floors. Suited mannequins and elegant display cases of fabric swatches and ties rounded out the showroom.

Lee cracked a couple more fingers. "What is this place, anyway?"

"The best custom tailor in Chicago."

"Uh . . . yeah." He moved his hand in a circle. "This is a lot."

"Don't worry, Daicen said Steven's the best and I know exactly how you need to look."

"I meant expensive."

"Oh! No worries there. Special Unit's picking up the tab."

The look on Lee's face was priceless. Half-relief, half-skeptical. "What?"

"The wardrobe isn't just for Grieco's benefit." *Although maybe Sawyer can get Nyx to foot part of the bill.* "You have to walk the walk of Renko's men for Operation Summit."

He nodded.

Steven came back, with coffee and an abbreviated tea service on a tray. "Has anything leapt out and grabbed you yet?"

Lee grunted.

Which Steven and I both took to mean "no."

The clerk gestured toward a room in the back. "Mr. Sharpe, why don't we step into the changing room, and begin taking your measurements?"

With an apprehensive glower, Lee disappeared.

Steven popped his head out of the door within seconds. "Miss McGrane, perhaps you wouldn't mind joining us?"

Covering a giggle with a cough, I went into the dressing room.

The changing room was more like a study from *Masterpiece Theatre.* A desk and two chairs at one end. An English tufted sofa, three-way mirror at the other.

Lee stood on an elevated three-foot-by-three-foot box, an uncomfortable and impressive sight in boxer briefs and a wife-beater. A small notebook at his feet, Steven held the pencil in his mouth and wound the tape measure around Lee's bicep.

"Mr. Sharpe, do you prefer French cuffs to standard?"

Lee glowered at me. "I don't know. Do I?"

"French cuffs on the tuxedo only," I said.

"Are you quite certain?" Steven asked. "We could do an eight and four split of the dozen."

"Dozen what?" Lee asked.

"Shirts, of course," I said. "No. Standard cuffs."

And it went on from there.

Measured within an inch of his patience, Lee promptly abandoned ship when Steven went to fetch the fabric swatches. "You choose." He yanked on his shirt and pants.

"Lee?"

"I gotta get some breakfast." He jammed his feet in his shoes, grabbed his suit coat, and left. His tie remained behind, forgotten on the chair.

Steven and I spent a delightful hour paging through swatches, discussing fashion trends.

Four suits with extra pants, a dozen dress shirts and ties, sports coat, trousers, topcoat, and a complete tuxedo later, I left the shop eight grand lighter and with Steven's solemn promise that one of the suits and two shirts would be done possibly by Wednesday night, Thursday afternoon at the latest.

I went outside.

Sitting behind the wheel of the Mustang, Lee was reading *The Hockey News*.

I opened the door. A plastic Subway bag of crumpled wrappers was on my seat. I tossed the bag onto the backseat and got in.

"Where to?" He closed the magazine.

"Walt wants us at the *Sentinel*."

Chapter 27

Lee and I took our places at the conference room table. We'd walked in on something and it wasn't pretty. Walt Sawyer looked carved from stone, Ditch Broady from fire, and Gunther Nyx from ice.

Sawyer said, "Agent McGrane has been working in conjunction with the DEA. The strides she's made in such a short time have been considerable, notably the invitation El Cid has extended to her to attend Carlos Grieco's birthday celebration. While the Special Unit is amenable to her pursuing leads on the 5.7s and steel-core rounds, her work for the DEA will cease upon commission of this latest drug purchase."

Nyx didn't like it but he wasn't much bothered, either. I had the distinct feeling that after I returned from Tampico, I'd have a lucrative offer from the DEA waiting. "What's Sharpe doing here?" he asked.

"Sharpe's transferring from SWAT to Special Unit. He will be accompanying Agent McGrane as her bodyguard."

"Excellent," Broady said.

Nyx huffed a breath from his nose and raked a hand through his hair. "Are you kidding me? He's as subtle as a cement truck."

I chirped up. "El Cid is expecting him."

Nyx spoke as if Lee and I weren't there. "Sharpe's a mistake, Walt. And you know it."

Sawyer shook his head. "He's in."

SHOOT 'EM UP   195

"Heavy is the head . . ." Nyx stood. He dropped a hand on my shoulder. "Connect with Wes. I'll approve the funds."

He left.

Ditch Broady tipped back in his chair. "You dug yourself in, missy, like a fat tick on a blue hound. I'll give you that."

My, aren't you sweet?

"Why don't we discuss the ATF's objectives?" Sawyer smiled thinly.

Ditch nodded. "We've got satellite and drone observations. We want confirmation, numbers, weapons, and intention. You may be in the belly of the beast, ma'am, but we don't want you danglin' ass-out from a tree, you understand?"

Not really, no.

Lee said, "Getting the drugs stateside to build a case against the Grieco cartel and Chicago distribution lines is more important than putting yourself and the ATF's objectives at risk by overreaching surveillance objectives."

Broady rapped his knuckles on the table. "Ain't that what I just said?"

"Agent McGrane," Sawyer said. "As an established field agent, we're confident you understand what's required of you. However, this is Agent Sharpe's first assignment, so if you wouldn't mind giving us a few minutes?"

The snark-polite smile split my lips before I could stop it.

I get us in, so now it's a man's job, is that it? "Certainly, sir."

Except for the very real part of me that was damn happy to get up and walk out and let Lee carry the cross for a bit.

I closed the door behind me and leaned my forehead against it. My hands were shaking.

Back in my office I chugged a couple cans of Coke and calmed the feck down. And turned my attention toward finding a solution to my most looming problem.

What exactly does one give the head of a Mexican drug cartel for a birthday gift?

I cycled through Neiman Marcus and Sharper Image and Cabela's.

Zip. Zero. Nada.

As someone who defended big-time baddies, Mom, naturally, would have the perfect gift idea, except that she was the very last person I needed asking me about my weekend plans. Now that conversation would be supes terrif.

Hey, Mom. Nothing, just chillin' with the head of the Grieco cartel, running a little rekkie for the DEA and ATF. No biggie.

I started cycling through eBay, randomly searching for crazy, blinged-out shite, refusing to let my brain start running on the rusty hamster wheel of worry over Hank and Stannis. Sawyer and the BOC would alert me to the moment that they made contact with the Srpska Mafija.

Hank had the patience of a sniper.

I wish I did.

After taking the full score with Sawyer and Nyx, Lee drove us home from the *Sentinel* and thankfully put a leash on the flirting.

We spent the next eight days working out, drying out, and de-carbing like prize fighters trying to make weight.

And we spent hours at the range.

Every day.

"You don't suck, Maisie." Lee pulled off his ear covers after I finally outshot him by a hair after a mind-numbing set of combat reaction drills. *Speed reload from holster. 2 in weapon; 9 in pouch. Fill mag with 7. Analyze and repair.* Over and over and over. "You ever compete?"

"Sure. But I never did as well against another kid as I did going up against my brothers. Taunting and pressure gives me focus." I knocked him with my shoulder. "Thanks for the assist."

He winked. "How about a little Five-seveN action?"

We finished with them every day.

It helped and he knew it. Even more when he changed the load to steel-core armor-piercing rounds. Like the kind that hit Cash.

I may not bring you down, Grieco, but I'm sure as hell gonna do my part.

After the range, Lee and I swung by Mon Ami Gabi for a superlative meal that neither of us could taste. Tomorrow's mission an ever-expanding wall between us, we ate in quiet and drove home in silence.

A man leaned against the wall of the entrance to the underground parking garage, smoking a cigarette. I almost didn't recognize Stannislav's right-hand man, Christo Keck.

Uh-oh.

Lee drove us inside without a second look. He parked and started unloading the guns and equipment from the trunk.

I dug the mail key from my satchel and stepped out of the Mustang. "Hey, Lee? I think I'll go check the mail, unless you need a hand."

"Nah, I'm good." He slung a duffel bag over his shoulder.

Careful to keep it nonchalant, I hustled to the elevator, and jabbed the button for the lobby.

Hank's Law Number Four: Keep your head.

Keck was the asset the Bureau of Organized Crime couldn't get along without. He needed to believe I was all in or the Syndicate sting would never get off the ground.

The doors opened. I stepped out with a wave at the security guard behind the desk and opened the front door. Christo Keck stepped in before I could step out. "We need to talk," he said in a low voice.

I took him across the lobby and down the hall to the workout room. I swiped my card and took a quick peek inside the empty space, before pushing the door wide for him to enter.

Keck had shaved his beard, gotten a haircut, and looked about twenty years younger. The cool fifteen pounds the stress of a trial knocked off his five-foot-eight frame off hadn't hurt much, either. I might have thought he was his own kid brother, except for the cunning in those close-set, slanted hazel eyes.

"You are well, Maisie?" He walked slowly around the pristine mirrored and matted private gym.

"Yes." *Time to go fishing.* "And pleased Stannis had you hire my brothers to represent you."

"No," Keck said. "I have not heard from Renko since the job went bad. I had men watching the hospital. Following what the police did with you. From this, I chose your brothers to represent me."

Yikes. "I'm glad you did. Saved me the trouble of doing it for you."

His eyes narrowed. "Oh?"

"I want Stannis to have something to come home to. I'm in negotiations with Vi Veratti and the Grieco cartel." I raised my palms to him. "I'm getting the band back together, baby. Whaddya say?"

"What about your brothers?"

"Declan and Daicen are defending you, aren't they?" I said.

The corner of his mouth raised in a smirk. "The other brothers. The cops."

"Never bothered Stannis."

He mulled that over. "Who's the new driver?"

"My bodyguard. Lee Sharpe."

"Renko's?"

"No. Mine."

Keck paced in front of a rack of free weights, gripping his wrist behind his back. He stopped and faced me. "My case is not going well. The ASA is Coles's personal attack dog."

Sawyer would get Keck out of hot water. And pay the twins' fees. And I was sure as hell going to use that to my advantage. I smiled. "Leave it to me."

He nodded in relief, eyes lingering on the engagement ring on my finger. "Better for the men if you are already Stannislav's wife."

I shrugged. "If you say so, Christo."

"I do, Mrs. Renko."

Chapter 28

I rode the elevator up to the penthouse, breathing easy. I shot Sawyer a text about my unexpected run-in with Keck and the state of his case.

Lee lounged on the couch watching a Blackhawks game. "Mail traveling by Pony Express nowadays?"

"Cute." I fanned myself with the stack of junk mail I'd retrieved. "I ran into the quicksand neighbor. The more I struggled to get away, the deeper I sank into conversation."

He smiled thinly. "In less than fourteen hours, we'll be on our way to Tampico. We gonna watch a movie, or what?"

"Yeah. Gimme five minutes to change, okay?"

We spent the night like we had every night for the past week: watching movies from opposite ends of Stannis's dove-white sectional. Tonight was Lee's choice. *Predator.* Which was terrific because, well . . . *Predator.*

Stannis was a glorious and platonic cuddler. The reality that I missed him chilled me from the inside out.

Getting a lil' nervy. That's all.

With a bellyful of bees on bath salts, I got up and opened the cabinet beneath the wall-mounted television. Inside was a mink throw so soft it made water feel rough.

Back on the couch, I snuggled into it, the silk satin lining rubbing against my cheek.

Lee glowered at me.

"What's wrong?" I said.

"You were lucky to have survived Renko, you know."

More than you could possibly imagine. I tipped my head in a half-nod, half-shake. "Maybe so, maybe no."

"This is reckless and stupid, Maisie."

A little pre-mission aggression, Lee? "Let a girl put her seat belt on first, sport."

Lee left his end of the couch for the coffee table in front of me. Up close and personal. Hands on his knees, the expression on his face wasn't real sweet. "These cartel guys aren't like regular criminals."

"Oh yeah? How do you know?"

"Because I've killed my share of goddamn Hajji sand-crawlers. They torture for sport, rape and murder women and children. Who the fuck do you think the cartels are importing for their private armies?"

Errh . . . No real response to that.

"So." Lee bared his teeth. "What are you gonna do when one of them wants to fuck you?"

"They won't." I crossed my fingers behind my back.

I hope.

He snorted. "Wake up."

"I'll hop that puddle when I come to it."

"Yeah? How's Bannon going to feel about that?"

"Gee, you're awfully worried about my love life," I said and lied, "He'd understand."

"Then he's a bigger man than me."

"Yeah, he is. You through?"

Lee's jaw slid forward. He folded his arms across his chest. "Sure, Bae."

I went to my room. A sick, twisty knot tightened in my belly. Did I think Hank would cheat on me? Maybe. If he needed to preserve his cover.

But not like this.

Not that it mattered. Good little Catholic girls—even lapsed ones—aren't built that way. Skipping confession is a helluva lot different from skipping off to bed with someone else, just because you're lonesome.

Shake it off, kid. You got work to do.
The suitcase taunted me from the bed.

Packing sucks. And there's nothing worse than the conundrum of outfit selection when you have no idea of the situation or duration. According to *Vogue*'s "Pack Like a Parisienne on Holiday" article, I was right on target.

Fingers crossed.

Last into the suitcase went the spy-tech kit we'd been sent from Special Unit, which included bugs, locator disks, spare SIM cards, camera pens, and hi-tech watches that did more than I could remember, as well as my decidedly non-tech, point-and-shoot Kimber Ultra and extra mags. Lee would be gunned up to the teeth.

Beneath the liner of my small clutch, I packed the volcanic glass knife that Hank had given me. I stowed the clutch in my carry-on satchel and, yawning, gave up.

It'll be what it'll be.

The digital clock read 12:07 a.m.

I oughta ask Lee about bringing another gun.

The hardwood floors were silk smooth beneath my feet. I raised my hand to knock on his door and stopped. He might be sleeping. I put my ear to the door.

Lee was moving around inside, talking in that easy, sexy, teasing voice. He was talking to a woman. He laughed that deep, warm chuckle.

Which inexplicably seemed to chip away at my flinty heart. Why was he always pressing me when he already had someone else?

Hound or sonuvabitch. I was opting for the latter.

I snuck back down the hall to Stannis's room and got into bed. Forty minutes of staring at the ceiling didn't seem to help.

Goddamn mission nerves.

The soft *ding* of the elevator pealed from the foyer.

I'd set the security system. The elevator couldn't come up without someone entering the code. But it could go down.

Lee. Leaving.

I kicked off the covers, went out, and turned off the system so Lee could get back into the penthouse.

Hound.

Shaking my head, I padded into the bathroom and raided Stannis's medicine cabinet. "Geez, guy," I muttered, pushing around bottles that were the hot ticket in Serbia but banned or phased out in the States. I landed on Halcion.

I shook one out, snapped it in half, and dry-swallowed it.

Five minutes later I was encased in the sweet glow of utter relaxation, realizing just as I dropped off to sleep, why "the halcyon days" were something to be revered.

Chapter 29

Lee took our bags down to the lobby. With only seven luxury apartments in the building, the front desk was unmanned before eight. I heard the elevator *ding* when he came back up. "Car's here, Maisie! Are we leaving or what?"

I walked out of Stannis's bedroom, fastening my diamond drop earrings, heels echoing when they hit the black granite tile of the foyer. Lee held the elevator door open, and then we descended to the lobby.

He looked fantastic in his new black Nicholas Joseph suit, egg-white shirt, and a black- and amber-striped tie. "Feels strange." He rolled his shoulders. "Tight, but not exactly. Snug."

"Makes my heart go pitter-pat," I teased.

"Of course it does." He grinned, back to his jocular, teasing self.

Ah, the power of the booty call.

It irked me, like a rock stuck in the tread of my running shoe.

"But you, Bae . . . You look too buttoned-up to pet a puppy, much less swing a drug deal."

"Oooh! Thanks for the confidence booster, partner." I knew I looked great. For luck, I'd chosen my black St. John dress and jacket that Stanislav bought me for our first meeting with El Cid.

Lee played bodyguard perfectly, stepping in front of the driver to check the limo, before letting me in. He sat down beside me. "Is this all right, ma'am? Or would you prefer I rode up front?"

"Assssssss," I hissed.

He turned his face to the window, but not before we traded smiles. The ride to the airfield was silent, each of us trying to hit that level of calm for the upcoming assignment.

There is nothing quite as wonderful as flying via private jet. No lines, no security, just a drive right up to the tarmac and a drop-off at the plane. A hot little number in a short navy-blue suit waited for us. She introduced herself as our flight attendant before walking us to the tail of the plane to introduce us to our pilot. "This is Captain Hester."

A dark-haired, rangy, five-foot-eleven man shook hands with us. "Please, call me Walker." Flyboy charm hung from his shoulders like an overcoat. "That'll be all for now, Mia."

Mia climbed the steps into the plane.

"Mrs. Renko?" Walker asked, "El Cid mentioned you're bringing a special birthday gift for Mr. Grieco. One that weighs around ten pounds and might best be transported in the . . . ah . . . special storage compartment."

"And where might that be?" Lee said.

The pilot frowned, but answered, "Wing compartment. Grieco's own design."

Lee handed him the duffel bag of 250K.

"Thanks." Walker eyed him. "What branch?"

"Marine Corps," Lee said. "You?"

"Navy. A-4 Skyhawks."

Lee escorted me up the stairs of the aircraft, while Walker disappeared around the other side of the plane.

Grieco's Lear 60XR had a cavernous stand-up cabin, ebony wood veneers, supple ivory leather seats, Wi-Fi, and every electronic convenience.

Lee gave a low whistle. "It's good to be king."

"You think?"

We stowed our carry-ons and took our seats, facing each

other across a small table. In less than ten minutes we were in the air. Destination: Tampico.

The flight attendant sauntered down the aisle. "Would either of you like to see the cockpit?"

"Very much." Lee stood. I gave a slight shake of my head.

After depositing Lee in the cockpit, she stopped to ask me, "Can I get you anything?"

"Vodka on the rocks, please." I peered around her at the cockpit. The door was open. Lee and Captain Hester were animatedly talking.

Apparently my bodyguard was going to remain with our dashing pilot for the whole flight.

Fine by me.

I stretched and opened my carry-on. *Let the McGrane flight ritual begin.*

Package of chalky King mints. *Check.* Set of urBeats into iPhone, playlist: Schubert. *Check.* Kindle Paperwhite, opened to chapter 10 of Kipling's *Kim,* Hank's favorite. *Check.*

The flight attendant returned with my drink and a fruit and cheese plate.

Sipping the icy vodka, I settled in to the story with a happy sigh.

Too soon, Lee came back and flopped down across the table from me. Amped, he drummed his hands bongo-style on the table. "What's Tampico? A six-hour flight?"

I nodded and he proceeded to devour the fruit and cheese plate.

Captain Hester came on overhead. "We will be landing in San Luis Potosiat at the Ponciano Arriaga International Airport in approximately two and a half hours."

"That doesn't sound like we're going to Tampico." Lee frowned.

"You're in the cockpit for the better part of the trip and you didn't talk about the flight plan?"

Lee reached across the table for my drink, took a swallow, and coughed. "Vodka?"

"I prefer to call it 'heavy water.'"

"Christ, Maisie," he hissed. "We're on mission."

"Exactly."

"You're cool with this?"

I took pity on him. "Ponciano is the closest airport to Autódromo Potosino."

"What's that?"

"A NASCAR track that Carlos Grieco doesn't own, but is a major holder in the consortium that does." I leaned in. "Grieco is an old-school muscle car freak. His life is all about racing and restoring seventies-style racers. We're talking badass legends like Pearson, Petty, Yarborough, Earnhardt Sr. Not a big surprise that we're stopping there. Either to watch Grieco race or to pick him or El Cid up on the way back to Tampico."

We landed and taxied to a separate hangar, bypassing the main terminal.

I packed my gear into my satchel, after loading my Christian Louboutin clutch with my phone, passport, and wallet.

Lee stopped to glad-hand with Captain Hester. "Thanks for the ride, squid."

"Keep an eye on him, Mrs. Renko," Walker said as I moved to the exit. "You know Marines are sailors who can't read."

"Oh, I'm well aware." I stepped out onto the stairs.

On the ground, in front of the MDX, stood the Hanson brothers. Serbian Zastava M21s slung over their shoulders, they wore plaid Western shirts tucked into jeans over exaggerated pointy-toed cowboy boots. And, just for me, they were all wearing oversized eyeglasses. "Hey, Chicago!" they shouted.

Lee growled behind me, "Who the fuck are these clowns?"

"Easy, guy. They're the Hermanos Hanson. El Cid's crew, and from the looks of it, our transportation."

I introduced Lee to Chac, Jefe, and Esteban. We piled into the SUV, Esteban behind the wheel, Chac riding shotgun, while Jefe sat in the far back row behind us. "We go to Villa Zara Zaragoza," Chac said over his shoulder, "to the Autódromo."

The sun was bright and merciless. Esteban turned onto Route

70. Thorn scrub and desert stretched for miles on either side of the highway. Thirty minutes later, the circuit appeared on our right-hand side.

"So, Grieco's a NASCAR superfan?" Lee said, as Esteban turned into the Autódromo.

"No." I shook my head to the side. "More accurately, an old-school American muscle car freak."

"What's the difference?"

"Muscle cars are dangerous."

"And old," Chac piped up. "Full of temper."

"Cars built in the sixties and seventies?" Lee gave Chac a doubtful smile. "How dangerous can they be?"

Chac waved a finger at him. "Too much power for the body."

"You're talking cast-iron V8, big-engine beasts," I said. "The steering's either nonexistent or overboosted. The name 'muscle' came from the engine and from the pipes you get changing gears—no hydraulic assist for the clutch. And brakes?" I laughed. "Hey, Chac—what are those things used for again?"

"I do not know. What is brakes?" Chac winked at me. "All I know is crack-up."

"Reckless power, Lee. You'll love it," I said. "And Grieco races these bad boys on a short half-mile oval track."

Esteban stopped the SUV. Lee hopped out and took my elbow as I stepped down onto the asphalt. Out of the side of his mouth, he said, "You're pretty cute when you think you know what you're talking about."

I pretended to stumble and dug my elbow into his side. "Gee, thanks."

Autódromo Potosino was a short seven-tenths of a mile long, low-speed course, the entire circuit visible to the stands. Chac escorted us down close to the track. A small grouping of people was in the metal bleachers with umbrellas, balloons, and signs that said *Feliz Cumpleaños, Carlos!*

A private birthday race; six cars were on the track, but only two were contending. A metallic-orange Chevelle, I recognized instantly as the one Special Unit and I had acquired for AJ, and a glorious yellow Plymouth Superbird I was pretty certain Carlos was driving.

Lee stood at the edge of the bleachers, head on a swivel, eyes continually scanning for threat, while Chac and I took a front-row seat.

I'd forgotten how much fun watching a race was. It was exactly the same as when Da had taken us as kids. Thunder pulsing up from the ground as the cars flew past, the tang of melting rubber and brake dust. Flashes of brilliant colors and the whine and *whump* of the engines.

Five laps to go, hitting speeds around 110 mph, AJ's Chevelle dropped low on the track riding the apron, as Carlos and the Superbird took the high line and ultimately the checkered flag. Everyone cheered as he took a victory lap, including me.

Chac gestured for me to walk with him toward the track. "Come, we see El Cid."

I glanced back at Lee, who gave me the nod. We crossed the track to the pits. AJ, leaning against the Chevelle in his black Nomex Crow racing suit, pushed off and came toward us stripping off his gloves, then he kissed me on both cheeks. "Gimme some sugar, baby."

Army of Darkness. "Hail to the king, baby." I grinned and kissed him back.

"Damn, you're good." AJ threw a salute over my shoulder. "Here he is, the man of the hour."

Carlos Grieco left his adoring throng and was coming our way. His NASCAR-style jumpsuit was bright yellow. Unzipped to the waist, a tight Under Armour T-shirt stretched across his barrel chest. He'd pulled his arms out of the sleeves, letting them swing.

At five-foot-seven, he was my height, but with a good seventy pounds on me, easy. The jewelry added another two. From the look of his arms, he was heavily muscled beneath his layer of indulgence. He stank of sweat, gasoline, and a heavy, flowery cologne.

AJ's hand went to the small of my back. "*Tío,* this is Maisie Renko."

"Yes, I see." Carlos nodded at his nephew. "Go tell Miguel to check the secondary air valve tension."

"You got it." AJ jogged off down the track.

"Mr. Grieco," I said. "It is a pleasure, indeed, to meet you."

He gave me a once-over that was less than pleasant, smoothed his sweaty mustache, then extended his hand.

Ick.

I put my fingers in his.

"I extend my hospitality to you, for the inconvenience you suffered in Juárez," he said.

Oh, so the bomb in the cooler was an "inconvenience." Got it.

"Thank you."

He clenched my hand, letting me feel the threat. "Women should not be involved in this type of enterprise, Señora Renko."

"I agree."

"I accept your influence over your husband." Grieco's mustache flared up at the corner, exposing smoke-stained teeth, and he jabbed me in the chest with a thick middle finger. "But not my nephew, yes?"

I looked down at his finger resting just above the V of the neckline of my dress. "We're business associates first. Friends second."

"El Cid has *fiebre del Ártico.*"

Talk about lost in translation. "Oh?"

"Arctic fever." He slid his finger far down between my breasts, rough knuckle grating against my skin. "He likes only the whitest women."

My pasted-on smile dried up and crumbled off.

We all may have sprung from apes, but you didn't spring far enough.

At least he was out of Lee's line of sight. I didn't flinch, just stared back with a blasé look on my face and said blandly, "Then we'll have to find him one, won't we?"

Grieco removed his finger. "You leave that to me."

AJ trotted back. Grieco threw a playful arm around his neck. "I thought for sure you had me. Then you turn chicken."

AJ grinned, teeth flashing against his dirty, swarthy face. "Thank your lucky stars, old man. You woulda been eating the wall except"—he glanced over his shoulder at the Chevelle—"I love my baby too much."

Grieco slapped his cheek. "Women and cars. Things you must learn to keep in perspective."

Somehow I knew at that moment, Lee was smiling.

Chapter 30

The Lear made the hop from Ponciano to Tampico at full capacity. The rear of the plane held Grieco's protection squad wearing ballistic vests, FN Five-seveN MK2 handguns, Ingram MAC 11 spray-and-pray submachine guns at their sides.

Lee and I rode facing backward, while Grieco and AJ sat across the table from us. The music pulsing, booze flowing as Grieco lit a celebratory cigar.

"You." He pointed his glass at Lee. "You are not Eastern bloc. Who are you to Renko?"

Lee jerked his chin in my direction. "I'm the containment squad."

Grieco thought that was hilarious. "You were soldier, yes?"

"Yes sir. I've served."

"That is why Americans go to war. To learn geography." Grieco paused for our obligatory chuckle and snatched up my hand. "This ring. It is too small for a brave woman."

Lee's warning flashed in my mind.

Awesome. Time for the charm.

Lee didn't move a muscle, but he didn't like Grieco touching me. I didn't much care for it, either.

"And you are very brave," Grieco said. "Here? Alone? Dealing with El Cid, when Renko made it clear that he would not soil his hands with narcotics."

AJ took a sip of his drink before steering the conversation back to the ring. "It's the European aesthetic, *Tío*."

"So? She's a fucking American." Grieco turned my hand in his. "I send the boy to school, and now he takes me for some blinged-out *paisa*. What do you think, Maisie?"

I refused to let my gaze drop to his stubby, ridiculous, ring-encrusted fingers, holding mine. Instead, I glanced around the Lear and his men. "How could anyone possibly find a man with this level of sophistication and the control of the most important Mexican port city primitive?"

"Yes. Yes," he said, finally letting go of my hand. "How do you come to deal with El Cid?"

I smiled demurely. "Stannis is a man who allows himself the occasional uncomfortable luxury of changing his mind."

As soon as the words left my mouth, I knew I'd made a mistake.

Grieco's face darkened.

"Ahhh! You see? You see, *Tío?* Renko, too." AJ laughed, smoothly transitioning my comment from incendiary to harmless. "I'm not the only one with *fiebre del Ártico*. Although, to be fair, Renko's a polar bear himself."

Grieco laughed, raised his arm, and snapped his fingers.

Moments later, our flight attendant returned with a tray of six fat lines of cocaine and three short black straws.

Feck.

The birthday boy snorted the first two, then gestured for me to take a turn.

I'd never done it. Never even been curious. And I really didn't want to give it a go right now.

"Mr. Renko prefers she doesn't," Lee said.

Grieco ignored him and handed me a straw. "I prefer you do."

Nice and easy does it.

I didn't dare glance at Lee.

Mimicking our host, I sucked a single line up into my nose. It burned like I'd snorted champagne up my nose, only my nose went numb before I felt the burn hit the back of my throat and slide down.

"Thank you." I set the straw down and muffled the desperate hawking throat-clear with a cough. "I think one's enough for now."

AJ swooped down for the other two. The remaining line went back to Grieco.

What I really wanted was water, but as I'd already wussed out, I raised my drink. "*Salut.*" I took a swig of vodka. I couldn't feel myself swallow.

Why would anyone ever do this shite?

The rush hit.

Wow. I get it.

Who would have thought increasing the neural activity in the nucleus accumbens in the mid-brain could be this mind-blowingly awesome?

From the looks of it, Grieco and AJ. I was smart and witty and the world was fantastic and Carlos was actually pretty decent. And funny.

I grinned at Lee, who pinned me with a fierce glare, then ran his thumb slowly over his mouth.

Zip it the hell up, Maisie.

Roger that.

I spent the rest of the trip chewing the insides of my cheeks to keep from talking.

We landed on Carlos's private airstrip just outside of Tampico.

"I will see you at the party tomorrow, Maisie." Carlos raised a hand and the three men in the back of the plane followed him out.

AJ raised his hand to the flight attendant signaling for another round. "Let's give him time to get gone."

Out the window a crew of four heavily armed men waited at two black Lincoln Navigators at the edge of the hangar. Standard Grieco cartel projection—power and muscle. Identically equipped to the men who rode in the back of the plane.

Carlos said something and laughed as he and his men packed into the SUVs and drove off.

After our drinks, we left the aircraft. One of the Five-sevenS waited for us with a silver Navigator. Odds Carlos's fleet was stolen from the U.S.? Dead even.

AJ and I got in the backseat while Lee and the man stowed our luggage. The driver was up front, Lee riding shotgun.

"So, how long to Carlos's house?" I asked.

"We're on my uncle's property right now," AJ said. "He owns everything within a ten-mile radius."

We were coastal now, right off the Gulf. Tropical savannah, the AC protecting us from the 90-degree heat. The land was sandy one side, sodden with small lagoons on the other. The fortification was impressive. Barbed wire, game cameras, watch towers. I recognized one of the outlying buildings. Lee scanned the landscape, eyes calculating distance, noting everything as we drove leisurely through the compound.

"Is that a horse barn?" I asked, pointing at the smaller of two large buildings. Several cars were parked outside. Some spectacular, others barely hanging together.

"Yes. But neither building is used for livestock any longer. The horses prefer to hear the sea, from their air-conditioned and heated paddocks. Those are used for car maintenance, servant parking, etcetera."

The rooftop of the mansion came into view. "Take us to the laguna first," AJ said. The driver slowed and turned down a gravel road. He stopped the Navigator at a sort of beach house at the edge of a mangrove swamp.

AJ hopped out. "C'mon, I want to introduce you to my baby."

Lee was out, opening my door before I even reached for the handle.

"C-Rey! Where are you?" AJ opened the small bar fridge built into the outside of the patio kitchen. He took out a cleaned chicken carcass and walked down to the water.

A grayish brown crocodile with yellowish bands and dark spots on its body heaved itself slowly up onto the edge of the inlet.

AJ waved me over. "It's cool, Maisie. Pacific crocs aren't aggressive."

I left my heels on the grass and trotted barefoot to his side at the freshwater lagoon.

"He's a Morelet's. Bigger than most, at ten feet, three inches long, aren't you, C-Rey?" AJ offered me the raw chicken. "Wanna feed him?"

No. Not even a little bit.

I pointed at a red fleshy circle the size of a nickel on the croc's stubby arm. "What happened to his elbow? Was he in a fight?"

Shadows crossed AJ's soft brown eyes. "Go back to the car, please."

I did as AJ lured C-Rey up onto the grass. The croc had two more wounds—one on his side, another on his tail. Tossing the giant reptile the chicken, AJ squatted and took a closer look at the injuries. He straightened, threw back his shoulders, and washed his hands at the outdoor sink.

"Let's go." AJ climbed into the Navigator. Deep grooves now bracketed his mouth.

We drove past heavy cement statues and through iron gates up to the mansion. Decorative protection against everything from suicide bombers to murder squads.

"Wow," I said. "Gorgeous."

"The estate is typical of the French and Spanish 'grandiose style,'" AJ said mechanically. "Tampico and its architecture were heavily influenced by New Orleans oil barons."

"The east wing is original," he continued on autopilot. "It was built during the oil boom in the early nineteen hundreds. And it will boom again. Tampico is rich with shale oil deposits. Buried gold in the backyard."

Uniformed servants were waiting in the drive. We got out of the car, AJ rattling off a list of directions in Spanish to a woman in a long black skirt and white shirt.

"Dinner is at seven, Maisie," AJ said, swiping through his smartphone. "Anyone in uniform will get you whatever you need. Please feel free to explore the house until then." He put the phone to his ear, his voice low and harsh as he walked away.

The woman walked Lee and myself through the main floor before taking us up a sweeping staircase to our rooms. Two bedrooms, each with their own bath, a connecting balcony and door between them. The furniture was hand-wrought iron and wood, the linens Egyptian. Our luggage was already there.

I opened my suitcase and started unpacking, counting down in my head. *Five . . . four . . . three . . .*

Without knocking, Lee stepped into my room and closed the connecting door behind him. He hit his watch, checking for bugs, Wi-Fi signal tracking, and found none. "Why don't you tell me what the hell you think you were doing on that plane?"

The fleeting euphoria I'd experienced from the coke was long gone, leaving a comet's tail trail of a headache. "If it makes you feel any better, I feel quite horrible now."

"It doesn't." He rubbed his eyes with his hand. "You are spectacularly unmatched for undercover operations. Did you even see what those guys are carrying? On his own fucking property? Christ, Maisie. And where is the 250K?"

I shrugged. "I'm sure one of Carlos's men retrieved it from the plane."

"When will we see the heroin?" He folded his arms across his chest, tapping his foot.

"I'm sure Captain Hester will sock it away in the plane wing on our return flight."

"You're not checking purity or quantity?"

"Oh my God," I groaned, letting my head roll back. "Look. I'm not gonna act like an ass and freak out about the drugs, because if AJ and Carlos are cool to screw with Renko and the Srpska Mafija, well then, Nyx can consider this ransom money, and Broady some expensive recon."

"Are you fucking kidding me, you can't just—"

"Lee. It's been a long, dehydrating day. I've had several drinks and my first line of coke. I have a headache, my throat is killing me, and I really, really, really wanna lie down. So, how 'bout you go in your room, unpack, and go do whatcha gotta do?" I pulled the suitcase off the bed with a *thump* and flopped down on top of the quilt.

"Smarten up. We have a goddamn assignment," Lee growled. Stiff-legged, he left the room, only to return five minutes later, wearing black cargo pants, T-shirt, and Bates boots. "Where's your gun?"

I didn't open my eyes. "In my satchel."

He rummaged through it, came back, jammed the Kimber under the pillow, and dropped my phone by my head. "Have you taken any aspirin? Drunk any water?"

No, Da, I haven't.

I rolled over onto my stomach. "I'm getting up in a minute."

He snorted and left.

Thank God.

Chapter 31

Lee knocked on my door.

"Come in." I swiped on the last of the war paint in the bathroom. "How was dinner?"

"Not bad for a staff mess, other than it was too early. I got some up-close-and-personal shots of personnel. At my count Grieco's carrying twenty minimum to a shift. Pros, not the kind that get squirrely. If your pal El Cid's recruiting, he's doing a damn fine job."

I dabbed Must de Cartier on my pulse points.

"You've got just under five," Lee said.

Not everyone runs on military time.

"Thanks." I turned off the bathroom lights and walked into the bedroom. Because Stannis preferred me to look as feminine as possible, I'd chosen a navy, sleeveless BCBG stretch-jersey cowl-neck dress with back-baring cutouts. I gave a quick spin. "Wish me luck."

"You don't need it. You look beautiful." His mouth quirked up at the corner. "And that's the least interesting thing about you."

Gee.

Cocaine had nothing on the rush that shot all the way up from my toes to my cheeks. "Thanks."

He opened the door for me. "I'll be close."

* * *

AJ, in taupe linen pants and a cream shirt, was waiting for me in the foyer. He turned on the Euro-charm with a kiss on each cheek, before walking me outside, far past the hotel-size flagstone veranda with requisite swimming pool, spa, and water features. We kept going, over the koi pond bridge and up two sets of stairs to a private, open-air cabana overlooking the ocean. A formal table was set for two.

As soon as we were seated, a waiter brought out champagne, champagne bucket, and a stand. AJ nodded for him to open and pour.

"How is C-Rey?"

"A specialist from Lake Carpintero Sanctuary will see him in the morning."

"He was shot, wasn't he?"

"Yeah." AJ's jaw turned to granite. "And I'll have physical proof of that fucktard by the end of dinner." He said something in Spanish to the waiter, who left immediately. AJ raised his glass. "You do the honors, kid."

"For some crimes, there is only blood reckoning."

AJ grinned. "Hell, yeah."

"Stannis. He has the best toasts of all time."

We talked movies over butter lettuce salads and stuffed crab. Halfway through the sea bass, he circled back around to C-Rey.

"I've told Carlos over and over that goddamned Raúl can't be trusted," AJ said. "I mean, who the fuck shoots someone's pet?"

"Not to put too fine a point on it, but C-Rey's not exactly a fast-moving target. Not much sport in that."

He slid his chair forward. "Do you hunt, Maisie?"

"Only rich and powerful men."

AJ laughed.

"The closest I've been to hunting is skeet. Although I know my way around rifles, pistols, and the occasional AK."

"Part of your charm," AJ said. "I ran a credit check on you, Maisie. You have plenty of resources at your disposal. You didn't need sixty thousand dollars' worth of heroin from me."

"You know my family. Four cops and three lawyers. Do you honestly think I can tap in to my trust fund without them finding out? I'm having a hard enough time just being engaged to Renko," I fibbed. "My clan hates him."

He took a bite of sea bass, then said with a passable Italian accent, "Don't ever take sides with anyone against the family."

"It'd be funny if it wasn't so true." I smoothed the section of tablecloth in front of my plate. "What are you doing here, AJ?"

"I ask myself that more often than you can imagine." He heaved a mighty sigh. "Family. When I first came here, it was all adrenaline and machismo—cars and women and drugs and money and shooting guns. But now?" He shook his head. "It's about saving Tampico. Mexico is fucking insane."

Gee, you think? Cartels, private armies, corrupt police, jungle death squads, and jihadi foot soldiers . . .

"You have no idea, kid. It's like a fucking B-movie version of the Holocaust. El Eje moves in and massacres a town—an entire fucking town—of some three hundred people, then loots, bulldozes, and leaves not a goddamn trace. You think anybody'd ever come to *Me-hi-co* if they had the slightest fucking clue?"

"Yeah, no," I said, "but—"

"No, nothing. Look, I'm not saying we haven't done some bad shit. Horrible shit. But fuck, we are not murdering grandmas and raping babies and running some fucked-up ISIL pogrom purge. The Five-sevenS captured one of their *sicarios*." His velvet brown eyes went flat. "I went down with Carlos to find out what happened. They imprisoned them in the church, he says, and then they killed them. The entire village. Three hundred thirty-six people."

He smiled horribly. "Then he told us how they disposed of them. Loading the bodies into fifty-five-gallon drums. Burning the corpses with diesel fuel and pieces of old tires until they were nothing but ash." He rubbed his chin. "He was our guest for several weeks. The guy wouldn't eat anything except vegetables. Said the smell of burning bodies was too much like chicken."

"Jaysus Criminey," I breathed.

"El Eje wants Tampico. But we're not some *paisan* unprotected desert village, and the last thing they want to do is kill the golden goose and destroy the port, pissing off the very people they want to do business with."

"So, how did I end up here, AJ?"

"We need our supply lines flowing in Chicago. And we'd like to deal weapons and men with the Srpska Mafija."

Lovely.

The next morning, Lee and I were up and at 'em at 0500, dressed for a run. While we agreed it would have been better to split up, neither one of us was comfortable with the idea of me running alone. We planned for six miles—three out and three back.

Before we headed out, Lee and I sat on the end of my bed, eating the Quest brownie bars from my suitcase while he outlined our route.

Only the servants were up before the sun, already starting to decorate for Carlos's birthday party. The color of the day? Yellow.

Lee jogged us out the way we'd come in, toward the airstrip. As we ran, I told him about C-Rey and El Eje.

Lee said, "How does it feel to be playing around in the middle of a drug war?"

"Not real great," I said. "Drug mule is my least favorite assignment so far."

He made a face. "What was your worst job prior?"

"Meter maid. Still, I pretty much have the career trajectory of a downhill Slip 'N Slide."

"I'm not exactly riding high myself. Trophy wife's boy toy."

"You wish!" I laughed.

"That's right." Lee sprinted ahead. "Keep your eye on the prize, Bae," he said, looking back over his shoulder. "Me."

The first fingers of sunshine splayed across the horizon as we jogged into the gravel parking lot between the two renovated barns. Carlos's two black Navigators were parked there along with a few others.

"I want a closer look." Lee steered us to the rear of the barn near a rusting red aboveground diesel fuel tank. "Keep an eye out."

"Say cheese." I raised my arms above my head and walked in a couple of lazy circles, spotting a couple security cameras. "Big Brother has three of them as far as I can see."

Lee stretched his Achilles, getting a glance inside the barn, before walking back over. He came in real close and put his mouth against my ear. "I want a closer look." His fingers hooked inside the elastic of my shorts. "Let's give them something to see." He pulled the elastic and let it snap.

"Jerk!" I said, chasing after him.

He bobbed and wove, and we reconnoitered the barn and the stable, playing tag, flirting around.

Lee stopped me at the window of the stable.

"What do you see?"

"Nothing. They're black. Trip alarms. I'm guessing garage where they fix the cars."

"Then we should move this to the back of the barn." I ducked beneath his arm and took off.

He caught me before I hit the corner, and edged me over to the windows. He raised my arms over my head and held me by the wrists. "What do you see?"

"Hand presses." He started kissing my neck. "Mmm. Pallets of gunpowder."

Nothing for me to see except the rusted diesel tank supplying the generator and the security camera on the edge of the barn.

Lee's mouth on my neck was . . . *oh, so damn good.*

My lips parted in a breathy sigh and his mouth was on mine, kissing me. Playful and trusting and somewhere the playful heat turned scorching. I didn't remember him letting go of my wrists, or wrapping my arms around his neck.

But the alarm bells went off when his fingers edged beneath my sports bra, up inside my shirt. "Stop. I can't do this."

"Sure thing, boss lady," he said in a voice that was anything but sweet.

It stung, more than it should have.

Muddled and confused, it took a good mile on the way back to the main house before I felt like talking to him. "How do Nyx and Broady plan to use this information anyway?"

"What does it matter? Whatever they do, it won't be good."

Chapter 32

Carlos's party started in the afternoon. On the front golf course of a lawn, was a luxe carnival with rides, bounce houses, food carts, and animal rides. This was for his children and guests not important enough to attend his wife's sophisticated starting event on the back veranda—tea and canapés.

AJ told me that while his aunt Grieco's occasional afternoon teas were infamously tedious, Carlos appreciated the additional intimidation and respect that upper-class manners demanded.

A white-gloved and jacketed staff worked silently and tirelessly beneath white tents. It was a surprisingly intimate party for the eighty or so adults, two-thirds of them men.

Lee, while technically not a guest, got the nod from AJ and floated in between Grieco's bodyguards and the Five-seveNs on the fringe of the property.

Red-gowned and raven-haired, Grieco's wife took Carlos's arm and swept him over to a raised dais where a pair of gilt chairs waited. Trays of French champagne were distributed, and we toasted his health and benevolence.

The string quartet played *"Feliz Cumpleaños."* The guests all sang and cheered.

And then came the gifts.

Trays of tiny cakes and champagne were passed around, yet no one dared speak. In front of his captive audience, Carlos opened each and every present like a child.

I started to get that sinking feeling.

He opened bottles of alcohol in every shape and variety, boxes of cigars, cuff links, and leather goods. The highlight was the matte-black Colt 1911 from AJ with black mother-of-pearl grips.

AJ drifted over to me and whispered in my ear, "Bored yet?"

Hardly. I could feel Lee glowering at me through his sunglasses from the edge of the pool.

"This is the smallest birthday party Carlos has had since he took over Tampico." AJ lowered his sunglasses. "Family only."

El Eje.

Carlos got to my gift, in the subdued matte silver paper and gray satin bow. He pointed at me before looking at the gift tag. "From you, yes?"

"Yes." I ducked my head, my smile as tight as a compression sock on a fat woman's ankle.

Why hadn't I gone with something more . . . conventional? That's the trouble with thinking you're clever. Not everyone else does.

Carlos shredded the paper. Inside was a silky cherrywood box. "Humidor." He nodded and made to hand it to the servant, then changed his mind and looked inside.

Dammit.

He frowned and jabbed a finger at me. "You chose this for me?"

I nodded.

He whooped with delight, then turned it around to show it to everyone. Inside were, according to eBay and DiecastMan, "a Rare Set of 1:24 Dale Earnhardt Sr & Jr 24-karat gold-plated 1998 Elite die-cast cars," both numbered one hundred of one hundred, complete with certificates of authenticity and commemorative coins.

It set Nyx and the DEA back a cool $4K on eBay, plus shipping.

Señora Grieco gave me a showy clap of hands. The glass of champagne I'd ignored had gone utterly flat. But it became nectar of the gods when mixed with the fizz of giving the perfect gift.

"Goddammit!" AJ seethed, jostling my arm and spilling champagne down the front of my little black dress. "Who the fuck does Raúl think he is coming here?"

The man who'd used C-Rey for target practice was young and wiry with a long, narrow head. His small-irised brown eyes were an unhealthy mix of eagerness and arrogance, the whites as yellow as tea-stained teeth.

He sauntered up to the dais, followed by two men, and gave a showy bow, then reached back to one of his men, who handed him a box, which Raúl opened and presented to Carlos.

AJ jammed his hands in his pockets, teeth gritted together. Waiting.

Carlos held up a pair of pointy-toed cowboy boots.

Crocodile.

I thought AJ's head would explode. I put my hand on his forearm. He jerked it away and strode over to his cousin.

"You think this is funny, *Pelotuvo?*" he demanded.

"I would have put your name on the card, too, cousin." A smug smile lit on Raúl's piranha mouth. "But C-Rey's belly was too yellow. So I had to choose another. I can't have *Tío* Carlos walking around in yellow boots."

"How is C-Rey?" Carlos asked AJ.

"The vet thinks he'll recover."

Carlos tipped his head. "Raúl will pay for the vet."

"And a new enclosure," AJ said.

Raúl spat. "*Deje de ser tan pendejo.*"

"We settle it at the Autódromo," AJ said. "Tomorrow."

"*Tío* Carlos." Raúl tossed his palms in appeal. "El Cid is a track rat." He moued. "I need time to find a driver. It will not be easy to find one with your skills, *Tío* Carlos. And as you know, the next two weeks will be busy for me and my men."

The drug lord thought that over. "Shooting contest. Three rounds. Best score of two," Carlos said, enjoying playing King Solomon more than any gift he received. "The winner determines C-Rey's fate. Wallet and belts for Raúl and his men, or a crocodile casita for El Cid."

Well, that's about as fair as a three-sided square.

"Choose your champion, Raúl," Carlos said.

Raúl raised his hands high in the air. "My best man is me."

AJ's lips flattened. It didn't matter who won the shooting contest. He'd been outplayed. So he did what any of my brothers would have done: He diminished the victory by flipping the situation to be the most insulting thing he could think of.

"Me? Shoot?" He grabbed one of the many gift bottles off the gift table. "When there's so much tequila to be drunk?" With a nonchalant spin, he viewed the crowd, then pointed the bottle in my general direction. "I choose her. She will be my champion."

"Me?" I squeaked.

Everyone laughed. Raúl went scarlet with fury.

Gee, thanks, AJ.

Nothing like being the star of the show when you're undercover.

AJ came back. "You're gonna do it, right?"

"Of course."

"You're one cool kitty," he said. "And Raúl's the son of a motherless dog."

"Easy, *El Guapo*. Let's not get carried away here."

His chuckle didn't touch the sadness in his eyes. "No worries, Maisie. This isn't on you."

"How good is he?"

AJ put his hands on my shoulders. "If it is C-Rey's time to die, so be it. Raúl has already lost face."

"Okay," I said. "What are we shooting at?"

"Plate racks. With the Five-sevenS all ex-military and cops, shooting contests are a weekly event."

"Where do we go?"

"Nowhere." AJ jerked his thumb toward Carlos's favorite bodyguard, firing orders into a walkie-talkie. "We'll be set up in less than twenty minutes."

The servants began immediately clearing the far end of the veranda. Lee came up behind me. "The rules?"

"Nothing to it. Just hit down your plates first," AJ said. Carlos called out to him and held up a tequila bottle. With a wince he went off to get a drink.

Around the corner a man drove a glossy yellow Can-Am 6x6 ATV onto the veranda. He pulled a small trailer with two deluxe plate racks in it. The frames, about five feet high, looked exactly like empty swing sets at a playground. Only instead of swings hanging from the crossbar, each rack had six five-inch round white steel plates sitting on top, like birds on a telephone wire.

Two of Carlos's guests helped the man set up the targets, while another handed out packages of disposable foam 3M earplugs to the crowd.

At Carlos's top man's directions, the servants set up two small tables about twenty-five yards back with earmuffs, earplugs, and safety glasses. This apparently was where we'd be shooting from.

Except I had no gun.

Raúl approached the table and removed a Colt .38 Super Automatic from his shoulder holster. His gun was pimped-out to the extreme. Gold- and silver-plated, engraved within an inch of its useful life.

Utterly ridiculous and tragically cliché.

I rapped on the underside of the table. "Hear that?" I murmured to Lee. "Liberace's ghost wants his gun back."

Lee glared at me. "Forward-focused. Don't fuck around with these people."

"Easy, guy. I'm trying to stay loose here."

Lee reached into his jacket for his Colt 1911. I gave him the barest hint of a shake and he stopped.

"Um . . . El Cid?" I called. "I don't have a gun?" I pointed at Raúl's pig-mess of a Colt and asked innocently, "Is there another one as pretty as yours?"

At least a dozen of Carlos's male party guests pulled their pieces and held them out.

The magnanimous King Carlos waved a hand across all his guests. "Choose any gun you wish, Señora Renko."

I pointed at the small sentry in full gear at the far edge of the veranda. One of Carlos's Five-seveNs. "I want his."

That shut everyone up.

Carlos, eyes twinkling, called the man over. In Spanish he asked for the gun and extra magazines. The man complied without the slightest twitch. Carlos weighed the pistol in his hand before handing it over. "Why this one?"

"Because," I let my voice go husky, "if I can't have the prettiest gun, I want the scariest-looking one."

Carlos ate that up with a spoon. His attention to me further rattled Raúl, who realized that not only did he have to beat me, he needed to mop the floor with me to salvage what was left of his machismo.

I thanked Carlos and the Five-seveN and walked over to the table I was shooting from. Lee was already there.

The soldier's FN 5.7 MK2 felt like exactly like the one I'd practiced with at home. As I'd suspected, the man had chosen the smallest back strap—a slim nylon piece used to customize the grip—to fit his hand better. I handed the gun and magazines to Lee. "Any tips?"

"Exactly like we practiced last week," he said softly, checking the gun. "Shoot, move on, come back if necessary. Eyes first, then sights to target. Take your time, make clean shots. Worry about speed in the next round." He ran his thumb over the chamber indicator, and handed it to me, cocked and chambered, ready to fire.

Covertly, I eased the black diamond-chipped safety to On. "May I have a practice shot?"

Raúl leered. "Of course."

I didn't bother with the earplugs, just the muffs and glasses. I raised the gun, pointed at the target, and pulled the trigger. Which didn't budge. I tried it again and again.

"It's not working," I complained to Lee.

Raúl covered his eyes with his hand, shoulders shaking. His men laughed aloud. AJ blanched.

"A little heavy-handed, don't you think?" Lee said under his breath. He reached over and turned the safety Off, and said loud enough for Carlos to hear, "Try again."

I aimed a good three feet above the target, fired, and missed. The man they'd chosen to referee explained the rules to the crowd in both Spanish and English. The horn would sound and we'd shoot; the horn would sound again when someone won.

No sweat.

I stepped out of my sky-high Jimmy Choos, feeling the sandy grit on the flagstone tiles beneath my bare feet. No sense risking the contest on a pair of sandals, no matter how cute.

I took off the muffs and rolled the earplugs between my fingers. "You work for Carlos?" I said, trying for a little innocent conversation to distract him further.

"Yes." Raúl sneered. "And you? What is it a woman like you . . . *does?*"

Ahh. The language of the smack. My favorite part of any contest.

"Aside from crossword puzzles in ink and sweating glitter?" I asked full of chirp and sunshine. "I watch a lot of cowboy movies."

Raúl looked at me like I was insane.

He might have a point.

We plugged and muffed up. The referee stepped between us. "Shooters make ready. Stand by." He blew the air horn.

I squeezed the trigger. *Clang.* Target down.

Clang. Clang.

Da's voice sounded in my head, "Aim small, hit small."

Clonk.

The fourth one stayed up. I took down the fifth, sixth, and went back to clean up number four.

Clang.

The air horn blew.

Raúl had a target up. And now, his dander.

The only thing that kept me from doing a winner dance was that Lee would have kicked me in the shins.

Raúl didn't like to lose. He especially didn't like being sandbagged by a honey. And he hated the flurry of activity between the men behind us making bets. "*¡No me jodas! Puta!*"

I glanced up at Lee, impassively surveying the crowd. "Any advice?"

"Let him win this round."

Agreed. Every time Raúl looked at me, my dress felt as though it was made of ants.

Sorry, C-Rey.

The ref blew the air horn. I knocked down the first three in a row and committed the cardinal sin of a glance to see how he was doing.

Even.

I hit number four, missed five and six on purpose, and hit five just as the horn sounded.

Raúl won round two. Chest puffed and haughty, he nodded at the crowd. "*¡Me cago en todo lo que se menea!*"

I didn't know what that meant, but the venom was . . . disturbing. He kept spewing, like a PMS-ing progressive.

I visualized a big fat strip of silver duct tape across his mouth.

AJ, sitting next to his uncle, raised a glass to me with an *it's-okay-to-lose* chaser face.

"What are you gonna do?" Lee asked quietly, loading the 5.7.

"Save C-Rey."

"Okay." Underneath the table, Lee locked his pinkie with mine and squeezed twice. "Bang bang."

I squared up to the table, cracked my neck, and put on the glasses and muffs. I exhaled in a slow hiss, the pounding in my chest matching my pulse, vision narrowing into tunnel-focus.

"Shooters make ready," the referee called, "Stand by."

The horn sounded and I took those targets down like all my brothers were watching.

The referee blasted the horn as I dropped the last one.

I looked over. Raúl nailed number five. But he was too late. I'd won.

There were cheers and jeers, but they were between the gamblers in the crowd. Two men stepped forward, calling for the referee to set up the plates and let them have a go.

AJ walked to me, arms extended. "*Madre de Cristo,* Maisie!" He picked me up and spun me around with a laugh. "If you shot them any faster, it would have sounded like an alarm clock!"

Raúl walked over and offered his hand. "Where did Señora Renko learn to shoot, El Cid?"

I genteelly put my fingers in his and lied. "My husband, Stannislav."

"I must commend him on his excellent instruction."

Yeah, never mind my mad skillz, bro.

He raised my hand to his mouth.

Now I know what bait feels like.

"Carlos is waiting," AJ said. Raúl let go and together they walked over to Carlos, still on the dais.

I gave a little shudder and stepped back into my shoes while Lee returned the gun to the Five-seveN.

AJ and Raúl made peace in front of Carlos, laughing and smiling. Although if anyone thought that made any difference, they were as wet behind the ears as a newborn calf.

Chapter 33

After the competition, Lee and I headed back up to our rooms for a siesta, as did all of the guests who were staying over. The house was packed.

The children had gone home and a small army of servants dissembled the carnival in the front yard. The real birthday party started at 8:00 p.m. and was scheduled to go all night.

Lee held out his hand. In it was one of the Five-seveN's rounds. He held up his smartphone. "Wanna read the ballistics report? I'm guessing it'll have markers similar to the ones that Cash took."

I really don't want to think about that at all.

At least he was on the ball.

"Nice work." I sat down on the bed and pulled off my shoes. "My case-building skills went out the window at the first sight of piranha-mouthed Raúl."

"A real nasty piece of work."

"AJ and I won't be anywhere near him."

"Raúl's going to be waiting for his chance to slip the blade in," Lee said.

Gee, you think?

I grabbed the throw on the end of the bed and lay down. "That's why AJ and I are going to be joined at the hip. And you?"

"Me? I'm on duty." His face hardened. "Watching you walk neck-deep into shit and wondering how far you plan on going."

"We're at Carlos Grieco's Tampico estate. Surrounded by his

elite Five-seveN army. My plan is to take it easy tonight, maybe get a little sun tomorrow, and jet back to Chicago on Monday. So, honestly, Lee? How 'bout you have a couple of drinks and chill out?"

He leaned in the doorway, forearm on the jamb, considering. I closed my eyes.

"Yeah," he said after a long pause, his voice sounding like it came from a far-off place, "Maybe I'll do just that."

After he left, I heard him turn on the shower in his bathroom.

The man was born in a barn—the door connecting our rooms was still open. But getting off the bed to close it seemed like an overwhelmingly onerous chore. Until I caught a glimpse of him—unaware or uncaring—padding naked into his bathroom.

Then I was sorry I hadn't.

Carlos turning fifty-three was like Bud Light Party Town meets *Scarface* only without the giant snow pile of coke. Instead tidy trays of lines and pills were served by women in itty-bitty nurse costumes.

Acrobats and a band in the front, a light show and a band in the back, and a full casino in the main house. Ice sculptures, martini towers, the most ostentatious food stations imaginable, and half-naked women everywhere you looked.

AJ was higher than high after besting Raúl. A speedball of coke didn't hurt, either.

Everywhere we went, people thumped me on the back and congratulated El Cid for his clever way of saving C-Rey. After more small talk than at a nervous insurance salesmen's support group, AJ led me onto the black-and-white dance floor set up on the back veranda. The sparkles on my Sue Wong cocktail dress flared and fluttered as he gave me a whirl. "Did I mention I'm in love with you?"

My eyes bulged like a soft thing being held in *The Grapes of Wrath.*

"For saving C-Rey." He laughed. "I may have *fiebre del Ártico,* but it'd take more than your sweet face to make me cross swords with Stannislav Renko."

"The fake-out with the safety . . ." He shook his head, still chuckling. "I thought Raúl was gonna blow a gasket. Goddamn pissant motherfucker. You're like that fucking kid from *Paper Moon*."

"I want my two hunnert dollars!"

He laughed and pulled me in. "Damn, Maisie," he murmured. "What are you doing marrying Renko?"

Raúl approached us, a stunning young woman on his arm. Eighteen, nineteen tops. They stopped inches from us. The blonde let go, prowled over to AJ, and slid her hands up his chest. "Happy birthday."

AJ caught her wrists and held them away from him. "It's not my birthday."

Eyes flashing, the teenager jerked away and returned to Raúl's side. Hate radiated off her.

Which was weird, because AJ was a good-looking guy and he hadn't been impolite.

"A mistake anyone could make, right, cousin?" Raúl's nostrils flattened in smug repose, making him look more than ever like a piranha. "Tell Carlos I'm waiting with his other birthday present in the wine cellar."

"Yes." AJ's hands curled into fists at his sides.

Raúl and the girl sauntered into the kitchen.

"Why did you do that?" I asked. "Agree to tell Carlos?"

"Easy. If I don't tell Carlos, Raúl tells him I'm making decisions for Carlos's life. How soon until I'm making decisions he doesn't know about the business?"

"I see your point."

"Either way, my dear, our night is at an end."

"Why?"

"I have to tell Carlos about the gift. After which, one of two things will happen." He counted off on his fingers. "One, Carlos wants the girl. I spend the night entertaining my delightful *Tía* Grieco." He snapped out his second finger. "Two, Carlos wants the girl gone. Which means I must extricate her from here as quietly and pleasantly as possible. Raúl, naturally, would prefer she make a scene."

I nodded. "Got it."

"Where's Sharpe?"

"Why?" I asked. "Do you need some help?"

AJ shook his head. "But you do."

"I don't get—"

"You don't actually think Raúl is going to let that contest lie." AJ grasped my upper arms and put his nose inches from mine. "You can't be alone tonight."

I winced. "I kind of gave Sharpe the night off."

"Okay." He saw a Five-seveN at the edge of the pool and waved him over. "Señora Renko is in your charge. Do not leave her side. No matter what Raúl says." The soldier nodded. AJ rattled off another series of orders, this time in Spanish, then kissed my cheek. "I have a very special day planned for the two of us tomorrow."

"Can't wait," I said.

The Five-seveN watched him leave. His focus switched to me.

"I think it's time for a drink," I said, moving toward one of the bars. I actually had two Cuba libres, and picked up some interesting background on my step-in bodyguard's South American childhood of murder and mayhem. Around 2:00 a.m., I started yawning and couldn't stop.

The Five-seveN escorted me to my room.

Lee wasn't in his room. He wasn't answering his phone, either.

"Will you help me find him?"

The Five-seveN nodded vigorously. "*Sí*."

After fighting our way back through the casino crush on the main floor, we slid out a side door and I walked the perimeter of the backyard, looking for Lee.

He was nowhere to be found.

We crossed the pool area and walked down to the beach. I kicked off my shoes and walked down along the sand, the Five-seveN keeping a moderate distance from me. The sand was smooth, but after the day I'd had, too much work. I moved down to the water's edge, the beach easier to navigate. Cool, salty water splashed up against my ankles. I shivered.

This wasn't like Lee. I tried to feel annoyed, but rising unease was the only sensation I could generate.

Where the hell is he?

Five jaunty beachfront cabanas were just up ahead. Over my shoulder the Five-seveN was getting nervy as I strayed farther than his comfort zone.

Yawning, I turned back at the last one.

Against the whisper *shush* of the surf came Lee's laugh. Half-chuckle, half-purr. A panty-melter. Followed by a high-pitched titter.

Okay, then.

"Señora Renko," the Five-seveN shouted.

Shite.

I backed away from the tent to the water. The flapping of canvas was unmistakable. Lee stumbled out, shirt completely unbuttoned, shoulder holster, gun, and jacket still on, feet bare. "Maisie?"

Go back. Go back to the tent.

"Maisie?" He caught up to me and snagged my arm. "You okay?"

AJ's guard came at us. I waved him back. "Sure."

He stood, weaving slightly. "Isths—it's not what you thi—"

"Wanted to let you know I'm turning in."

Lee put a heavy hand on my shoulder. "Lessgo."

"Don't you want to say good night?" I pointed at the tent.

"Nah." He reeked of tequila. Like he'd taken a shower in it. "Lessgo."

"Shoes might not be a bad idea."

"Shit." He gave that traitorous laugh. "Hang on."

I didn't wait, but I didn't exactly run, either. He caught up, stumbling, grabbing my arm and knocking us both down into the sand.

The Five-seveN was at my side, helping me to my feet before I'd even pushed myself up.

"Aww, fuck." Lee got to his feet, leaning slightly. "I'm sorry."

I swiped the sand off my dress. "No worries, Lee."

I bent to pick up his shoes—his combat boots actually, more comfortable to be sure, although not exactly apropos—but he beat me to it. "Lead on." A goofy smile split his mouth, his teeth gleaming in the moonlight.

It took several minutes to make it back to the main house. The Five-seveN torn between trying to help Lee and trying to protect me. Inside, the gambling and partying were as wild and loud as when it started. The three of us garnered not even the slightest glance as we made it to the central staircase.

"Thanks, but I got it from here," I told the Five-seveN.

He followed us at a short distance.

Lee and I started up the stairs. Getting him upstairs was hard work, and he had no problem letting me do the bulk of it. "Geez, you're so sweaty. What have you been doing?" I said, instantly regretting the words once they left my mouth.

"Uh . . ." He knocked into the railing.

God only knew what happened to his key, so we stumbled to my room and then into his through the open en suite door.

"You're pretty."

"Come on." I walked him backward to the bed. His legs bumped up against it. I slid off his jacket, helped him out of his holster, and set them both on the nightstand.

"I mean it." His hand slid to my butt. "I reallyreallylikeyou."

"Lee, seriously. Knock it off." I caught his wrist and tried to force his hand down. "Your whole mad-crush-credibility rolled back to zero after you ran out for your last-minute booty call."

"Booty call?" The haze left his eyes for a moment. "I just wanted to crash for a minute," he said. "How was I supposed to know there was a girl in the tent?"

"That's not what I'm talking about. . . ." There's no reasoning with a drunk. "Oh, never mind!"

"I do. Mind." He dropped backward onto the bed, pulling me down on top of him, hand still on my butt, the other around my waist, his mouth warm and tasting faintly of tequila and lime. "I mind a lot."

I tried to push myself off of him. His hand left my waist and slid up the nape of my neck, my hair, pinning me to his chest. I wasn't going anywhere.

"C'mon, Maisie. Tell me what you're talking about."

I had no right to press it. But he was trashed. And I wasn't above taking advantage.

Just ask Raúl.

"The night before we left Chicago," I said. "At the apartment. I wanted to ask you something and you were on the phone, laughing that laugh of yours, and . . . And then you left."

"Admit it. You like me," he teased. "You think I'm hot."

"Jaysus, Lee. You're drunk."

"Jaysus, Maisie. You're jealous." He laughed, deep and warm, and it popped something inside me. His fingers traced around my ear, down my jawline to catch my chin. "I was talking to my sister."

Sure, you were.

"Easy, Cowboy. There's a fine line between cuddling and holding someone down so they can't get away."

"Yeah," he said. "I made that mistake at the barn." He shook his head. "Cuddle, no. Hold down, yes."

"Where did you go that night, Lee?"

He craned his neck and buried his face in the deep V of my dress. "To . . . er . . . uh . . . pick up a prescription."

Liar.

"Okay, darlin'," I said, swinging into the McGrane boys' patented "*let 'em down easy*" Western drawl. "Time to turn in."

I rolled off of him and he let me. With a groan.

His jacket was on the nightstand. I hung it up. By the time I crossed the room to my own, he was out.

I closed the door.

For as much as I hated his lie, a part of me liked that he didn't want to hurt my feelings, even when he was drunk.

Heady stuff, being pursued like that. Risky and reckless in that overly open sort of way. No girl's above that kind of compliment.

And for that, he didn't deserve to suffer too terribly.

I snuck out into the hall, found a member of the staff, and requested four bottles of Gatorade, a roast beef sandwich, chips, and some birthday cake if there was any left.

By the time I was ready for bed, there was a scratching at my door. The server brought the domed tray into my room and put it on the bed. I gave him a twenty. I didn't know if American dollars were okay or even if I should tip, but he seemed okay with it.

I added one of my mini travel bottles of Excedrin, a couple of B-12 tabs, and a note.

Rest and recover, Champ.

Up early, I went down to the pool.

A maid caught sight of me and said in pigeon English, "El Cid is out-of-doors."

I found him on his phone. AJ disconnected, looked at me, and grinned. "Have you had breakfast yet?"

"Nope."

"C'mon." He took my arm and walked me back into the house. "Then we'll go see C-Rey and the vet. You can feed him the chicken this time."

"Great." I hoped my frozen smile didn't fall off and shatter. It was one thing saving C-Rey in the metaphorical sense, but something different altogether to be that close to him.

AJ's crocodile seemed in as good spirits as any other prehistoric reptile. I tossed C-Rey the raw chicken, then retreated up the bank while AJ and the vet lingered at the lagoon's edge.

One day, someday, I'll tell this story to my brothers and they'll believe it.

We were back at the house a little after nine, with plans to go out to lunch, shopping, and to the special place AJ had promised to take me.

The only buzzkill was that if we went somewhere along the coast, the humidity would make my hair insane. I scraped my hair into a tight ponytail and changed into my jeans, black knee-high boots, and black Mack Truck T-shirt.

Forgoing a wallet, I slipped a couple hundred bucks, Swiss Army knife, and iPhone into my lightweight cargo-pocketed jacket and locator disc into the coin pocket of my jeans. I crossed the room and carefully pushed open the door to Lee's room.

A shaft of light landed on his shins. The lid from the tray upside down on the foot of the bed. Gatorade bottles and empty dishes on the floor and nightstand.

Lee lay on his back. Chest rising and falling in deep and even breaths.

I shut the door, catching it just before it hit the jamb, and released the lever with nary a sound.

Freedom.

I practically skipped down the drive.

AJ was waiting with the Hanson brothers in front of a black MDX. "I slipped the leash, baby! Let's roll!"

Chapter 34

Tampico is a seafood paradise. AJ took us all to the unpretentious El Porvenir for an obscenely leisurely lunch. Like Poseidon's children, we dined on spicy ceviche, oysters, shrimp, and the spectacular rich *Jaibas ala Frank*—crab wrapped up in paper-thin slices of cheese—and icy cane sugar Coca-Cola.

We talked movies, laughing and swearing, Chac and AJ translating every few minutes for Esteban and Jefe.

"I'm so getting you guys into a Blackhawks game," I promised. "You get them to Chicago, El Cid, and I'll babysit."

Babysit, which after AJ translated, sent them into gales of boyish giggles.

Chac pointed at me. "We are Hansons, and you are Coach . . . you are Reggie!"

Esteban and Jefe pounded the table. "Reg-gie! Reg-gie!"

"Change your mind yet, Maisie?" AJ waved his fork at the lot of them. "Remember, they haven't even had a beer yet."

After lunch, AJ and I walked in the park, two brothers on the street behind us, while Jefe waited for us behind the wheel.

"Now I'm going to take you somewhere special," AJ said.

"It'll be tough to beat El Porvenir," I said.

"It's a bit of a drive, so if you want to call your bodyguard, you need to do it right now. Reception's pretty spotty."

"Nah. I'll text him, though." I got out my phone. "How far away is this special destination?"

"Two hours. Inland."

The faint alarm "*Lee is going to kill me*" pinged in the back of my head. We wouldn't even arrive wherever it was until after four o'clock. But from AJ's face, I could tell it was something special. "We'll be back in time for dinner," he said, raising two fingers. "Scout's honor."

"Sure." No Eagle Scout myself, I chickened out and texted Lee. *Hope you're feeling A-1. Out with AJ. Inland. Back by 8pm. Don't be mad.*

I reread the text before sending it and deleted the last line. I needed to keep Hangover Bear as poke-free as I could manage.

Jefe drove us out of Tampico, keeping the SUV cruising at a steady eighty-five mph. Esteban rode shotgun, with AJ and me in the middle and Chac in the far back.

The air was salty and dry, the terrain a bizarre mixture of scrubby desert plants and lush palms, as surreal as a David Lynch movie. After an hour and a quarter, we turned onto a dirt road and the remaining drive time stretched out like purgatory.

"C'mon, give me a hint, AJ."

"Have you ever heard of Spanish Reales?"

"As in pirate pieces of eight?"

"Exactly. The coins were considered the world's money standard from the time that the Mexico mint began striking coins in the late 1530s until the 1850s."

I waited for the punch line. "Okay."

"As the Port of Tampico has expanded, we've undertaken massive underwater construction, and recovered more of these coins than anyone ever thought existed. The person we're going to see is a silversmith."

"Oh?"

"C-Rey wants you to have a necklace made from them," AJ said. "I want you to choose the pieces."

"That's . . . Wow." I shook my head. "Thank you. You really don't have to do this—I was glad to help C-Rey." *And stick it to that slime ball Raúl.*

"You have no idea." AJ paused and wove his fingers together. "We're friends, right?" he said.

"Absolutely."

"So, if I was to give you some advice, you'd take it in the spirit it was intended, right?"

"Sure." I nodded, waiting for the slow, overarching tail of his preamble flare to explode and wreck my life. "Fire away."

"Your bodyguard. Sharpe."

"Yes?"

AJ sucked his upper lip. "The footage of the two of you . . . at the barn . . . was brought to my attention."

Feck me. "Oh?"

"Whether Renko is out of town or not, you've gotta be more careful."

What?

"I get you haven't seen him for a long time, and dealing with people like Carlos isn't easy. And under pressure . . ." He blew out a breath. "Look, banging your bodyguard is a recipe for disaster."

"You're right." The implication worked its way through my brain. On the plus side, our rekkie had gone unnoticed. Minus side, Carlos now thought he had leverage. "Who else knows?"

"My guard. The footage is gone. I purged the week's worth before the party."

"Thanks, AJ."

"I got your—"

"Seat belts!" shouted Esteban.

"*Estar atento!*" Chac yelled from the back.

I pitched forward hard against my seat belt, knocking my forehead against the back of the driver's seat.

Jefe hit the gas.

Through the rear window, a big blue Silverado was coming up fast. Esteban shouted at Jefe. The truck hit us again. Harder this time.

"Get off the road!" AJ pointed out the windshield. Oversized jacks littered the dirt road ahead. "*Salir de la carretera!*"

Jefe hit the brakes. Too late.

The SUV heaved and bucked, tires shredding, tread slapping against the wheel wells, jerking and grating as it ran down to the rims.

And stopped.

Behind us, the Silverado skidded to a tee across the road, halting before the spikes.

Two black Chevy Tahoes sped toward us from the front.

Ambushed.

"Jammed." AJ threw his satellite phone down on the seat. "Fuck."

My iPhone showed no bars.

Hank's Law Number Two: Respond to threats with complete confidence.

I had Lee's emergency signal. I edged the dime-sized locator out of the tiny coin pocket in my jeans, snapped it, and tucked it into the side of my underpants.

AJ put a hand on my arm. "You okay?"

I nodded. "You guys all right?"

Jefe and Esteban popped their seat belts.

"Everybody stay put," AJ ordered.

The cousins looked at each other and jumped out of the car, firing their AKs as they walked out to meet the Tahoes.

Outmanned and outgunned.

AJ smacked his fist against the window. "Goddammit!"

Chac moved behind us, reseating the magazine in his weapon.

"You're gonna stay in the fucking car, Chac." AJ dragged a hand over his face and gave me a tight smile.

He put his hand on my neck and pushed me down in the seat well, then crouched down across from me. "Put your head down and cover your ears. Jefe and Esteban are going to die."

The sharp bursts of their AKs rang out.

They were echoed by more, many more.

I burrowed into the rubber floor mat, flinching as bullets sprayed and thudded against the MDX.

Grim-faced, AJ and I held eye contact. Sweat broke out across his forehead. He started Zen breathing: quick, measured inhales through his nose; long, slow exhales from his mouth.

Chac prayed aloud, "*Dios te salve, María, plena eres de gracia . . .*"

The shooting continued. Then came the slaps of bullets hitting flesh.

I jammed my fingers in my ears, but I could still hear the bullets, the shouts, Chac's Hail Marys and AJ's Zen breathing.

A single cartel news story was enough for the average American to know these men were as violent and barbaric as the average ISIS tribe.

What was coming up was going to be worse.

I pressed my side where the locator disc ought to be wailing to the skies by now.

C'mon, Lee.

It's going from brawn to bone here.

The guns stopped firing. A moaning wail came from Jefe or Esteban. It wasn't the sound of someone who was going to recover.

My legs started to shake, cramping from hunkering down behind the seat. A bead of sweat trickled down AJ's temple. Grim and furious, I couldn't tell if he was angrier at the indignity of being ambushed, Jefe and Esteban's not following orders, or their subsequent deaths.

The moaning outside grew keener, more desperate.

Chac kept praying.

I heard the metal-on-metal of a car door closing. The muffled sounds of boots crunching sand and grit.

The single finality of a shot.

Hank's Law Number Three: Don't let your lizard brain go rogue.

The boots came for us next. Only this time, several pairs. Fists drummed on the window. A man shouted for us to get out. AJ raised his hands above his head, showing empty palms.

The man at the window pointed at the door lock.

Slowly, AJ reached one hand down and popped the locks.

The car doors flew open, back hatch, too.

More shouting. I started to uncoil. Someone grabbed the back of my jacket and dragged me out of the car and onto my butt in the dirt. I kept my head down.

Two men had Chac at the tail of the MDX. Knocking him around, yelling.

Under the car, I could see the boots of three more men and AJ's feet. He stood motionless, silent, waiting for it to unfold.

Sitting in the dirt, I weighed my chances. Scrub savannah with green spiky succulents. No real cover for miles. Or a four-foot dive beneath the car, where I could scramble underneath from side to side. Not good.

"Señorita?"

I looked up over my shoulder into a smiling harvest moon of a face. A precise trowel-shaped beard only emphasized the full-ness of his sallow cheeks. His eyes were a contradiction of sad and merry, as though he regretted our plight, but there was still adventure to be had. He held out his hand and pulled me to my feet.

Without preamble, Moon-Face shove-walked me around the tail of the MDX. Dozens of tire spikes pronged out of what was left of the SUV's tires.

AJ and Chac were surrounded by a pack of armed men.

A rail-thin scarecrow of a man wearing a black straw cowboy hat and reflective sunglasses nodded at Moon-Face, then raised his hand.

A nine- or ten-year-old boy scrambled out of the Silverado that had forced us into the tire spikes. He wore an empty canvas bags across his chest like bandoliers. He jogged past us to Jefe and Esteban, collected their guns, and started going through their pockets.

I turned away. The boy returned, dropped a filled canvas bag in front of Scarecrow, then climbed into the MDX to scavenge.

Scarecrow pointed at Chac. "Not him."

A man with the rifle stepped from the crew with a nonchalant nod. "¡Ándale!" He pointed his weapon at Chac and gestured for him to walk into the savannah.

Oh God.

The rifleman had marched Chac a good hundred and fifty yards into the enemy landscape. Scarecrow whistled and they stopped.

Rifleman must have given a command, because Chac awkwardly hopped on one foot, pulling off one cowboy boot then the other. The man said something and Chac dropped to his knees, facing the lonely, endless vista, and clasped his hands behind his head.

Even though I couldn't see him, I knew Chac's lips were moving, hailing help from Saint Mary.

I waited for the shot.

None came.

The man with the gun picked up Chac's boots in one hand and walked back toward the SUVs.

Cicadas buzzed in my ears. The burst of adrenaline disappeared, replaced with sickening exhaustion and mind-numbing fear.

The kid got out of the MDX, duffel bulging at the seams with Chac and AJ's guns, extra magazines, cell phones, and whatever else he could find. He locked the car and came back to the Scarecrow.

The Scarecrow jerked his head at the Silverado. The boy grabbed the bags and jogged back to the truck.

"Let's go," Moon-Face said.

The pack of armed men spread out. Some drifted slowly back toward the Silverado. The others took a wide berth ahead of us toward the two Tahoes.

Scarecrow pulled a Glock and pointed it at AJ. *"Vamos, cabrone."*

AJ glanced at me and walked. Scarecrow followed close, smart enough to stay out of AJ's circle of influence.

Seasoned.

Moon-Face gripped my bicep, and we fell in behind AJ and Scarecrow.

They walked us past Esteban and Jefe nice and slow, making sure we got a good, close look on the way to the Tahoes.

Esteban had been the one to take the bullet to the head. Jefe lay facedown, a dull skin forming on the blood puddle beneath his shoulders.

Two men already waited inside the Tahoe. The driver and another teenager in the far back.

Scarecrow held AJ off to the side, while Moon-Face patted me down and with the clinical disinterest of a doctor. He ran his hands over and underneath my jacket, taking the money, knife, and iPhone. He felt down my arms, and around my breasts, checking the underwire of my bra. Hips, legs, and even the shafts of my boots were checked before banishing me to the far back of the Tahoe with the teen who reeked of cologne and body odor.

Moon-Face slid into the front passenger seat, while Scarecrow, after completing AJ's pat-down, pushed the two of them into the middle seats of the SUV.

From his tight T-shirt and jeans, I could tell the teen wasn't carrying. His tennis shoes with low athletic socks further diminished the chance he had a blade.

I turned in my seat and he flinched.

Aww. Did I scare you, sport?

Out the rear window, the Silverado circled around and drove off in the direction from which it had come. The Tahoes U-turned to their original routes, too. I watched from the rearview as we left Chac on his knees in the scrub, with no shoes, no water, and the merciless afternoon sun overhead.

Chapter 35

Moon-Face handed back black bandannas. "Put on."

AJ and I tied our own blindfolds.

The driver drove in fits, starting and stopping for random amounts of time. We turned often. Three hundred sixty degrees at least twice counterclockwise, and as many as five times clockwise, before I lost count.

Hank's Law Number Ten: Keep your mouth shut.

The pointless urge to kick and scream strained at the seams. I focused on how desperately thirsty I was. My mouth was so dry, I would have done just about anything for a drink of water: lapped it up out of a sandy puddle, licked it off of a cactus.

The men were civil, pleasant almost. Chatting with AJ about Federación Mexicana de Fútbol Asociación and their favorite telenovelas.

It gave our abduction an ethereal feel—that for these men, it was just a job. We were a package to be picked up and taken somewhere else, and they would go home and not give us another thought.

After an hour of boredom on a bed of pins and needles, I succumbed to the luxury of a little rationalization.

AJ was important. Carlos Grieco's nephew was worth a lot. They knew I was American. They could ransom me. Especially when they found out how much I was worth.

Moon-Face said something to either the man sitting next to AJ or the teen.

Ears straining, I heard the sound of plastic on plastic, and felt the man in the middle's arm as he handed something back to the teen.

I heard the instantly recognizable snap of a plastic lid cracking open from its seal.

The teen touched my arm and I jerked. He put a cold plastic bottle in my hand, slick with condensation. "*Agua.*"

As badly as I wanted it, I hesitated. *What if it's drugged?*

Feck it.

I hope it is.

The water was so cold and so good, tears pricked my eyes. I could feel the icy wave all the way down the back of my throat.

Hank's chiseled face swam in front of mine. "People that make it, believe it." I could feel his hands on my shoulders, cement-gray eyes boring into mine. "Stay positive, proactive, and know you are going to make it."

Moon-Face asked if we were okay with him turning on the radio. AJ said yes. We'd been in the car for an hour and a half at the bare minimum.

I shivered in the air-conditioned car.

Hank's Law Number Six: Do not fear fear.

I gripped the water bottle tighter, forcing myself not to double-check the locator badge at my hip.

Fear makes you nervous, and nervous people make mistakes.

Moon-Face said something. AJ translated. "You can take the blindfold off, Maisie."

The dark was replaced by sky deepened to a twilight purple. I saw AJ's face and almost wished I hadn't removed the blindfold. He looked worse than sick.

He looked defeated.

We drove on, night falling with an inky blackness as mariachi music played at a comfortable volume.

"Do you come from a large family, Señorita?" asked Moon-Face.

"Yes," I said, chest going tight.

Nice try, Moon-Pie, you're not gonna take me there.

I cleared my throat. "Five older brothers."

Hank's Law Number Nineteen: Show no mercy. Ask for none.

"No wonder you are . . . *tranquilo*," he said. "You understand the tears of women are worth less than sweat."

Gee, thanks, Attila the philosopher.

"She's my wife," AJ said.

Moon-Face chuckled. "This is not so."

"Same difference." AJ shook his head. "She's going to be."

"No," the man said. "She wears the ring of Stannislav Renko. You think we do not know this, El Cid?"

AJ turned his face away and stared out into the night.

Feck times a million.

"Are we close?" AJ asked.

Moon-Face turned in his seat. "Why do you ask this?"

"I know where you're taking us," AJ said calmly.

"This is not my choice for you, you understand," he said.

AJ nodded. "You will allow me the respect of a stop before we arrive?"

"Yes, El Cid." Moon-Face nodded. "That, I can do." We drove on another mile or so before he told the driver to pull over.

We all got out.

Moon-Face and Thug each held a gun. The driver and the teen walked off a short distance, stretching.

"Maisie," AJ said. "Take a piss."

"What?"

"Trust me. This will be your last chance for a while."

"El Cid," Moon-Face warned.

AJ walked a short distance into the scrub. "Stop."

I could hear AJ unzip his jeans and the flat sound of him peeing into the dirt. He finished, zipped up, and came back. "Go."

"I can't," I said.

"She doesn't understand," AJ said.

Moon-Face waved his gun at me. "Go to the back of the car. Do not run. If you make us run, you will be sorry."

His voice was so matter-of-fact, I almost had to go. I went to the back of the Tahoe.

There's a reason I hate camping. This pretty much sums it up.

"*¡Deprisa!*" Moon-Face said.

Fingers numb, I fumbled with the button on my jeans and yanked my pants down. The locater disc flipped out of my underpants and into the desert night.

Dammit dammit dammit.

I felt around with my fingers in the dirt. Nothing.

"Hurry," Moon-Face said.

"I'm trying." I squatted.

Just relax.

I went a horrifyingly large amount. Followed by the ignominy of the drip.

Oh god, I hope I didn't just short out the locater.

I pulled my jeans up and got back into the Tahoe, telling myself that if we were close enough to pee, Lee'd find us, no sweat.

In less than a quarter mile, the faint lights of a squat building appeared on the horizon.

We pulled up next to the other Tahoe in front of the squat stucco building. Two other cars were parked up close to the entry.

A group of men leaned against the Tahoe, passing a bottle around. It was apparent they'd been waiting for a goodly amount of time.

Moon-Face pivoted in his seat. "There is a chance she will not be on the list," he said to AJ.

"She'll be on it," AJ said bleakly.

"This you do not know, El Cid. I give you my word I will return her to the city if she is not."

"*Gracias.*" AJ forced the word out.

I knew from both of their faces the whole exchange was a charade, for my benefit.

What was coming was going to be unpleasant.

Scarecrow drew his gun. Together, he and Moon-Face escorted AJ and me into the building.

We entered a nasty little reception area, with two splintery wooden chairs, a desk, and a foul smell. A portable transistor radio, the kind my grandpa kept in the garage as a joke, hung from a nail in the corner, blaring at an ear-shattering volume. It wasn't quite tuned correctly. Another pulsing set of voices was audible in the undercurrent.

AJ gave an imperceptible shake of his head and muttered, "Fucking *conjunto norteño*. Typical."

Moon-Face crossed the room to a solid metal door and beat his fist on it.

I considered trying to get the jump on him. Scarecrow caught my eye and shook his head.

It's never a good feeling, going up against someone who knows their shit.

A man with the slick sheen of a fatted leopard seal and wide mustache edged from behind the steel door into the room and locked it behind him. He wore a khaki uniform without any identification tags.

"El Cid Rodriguez," Scarecrow shouted over the music.

Fatted Seal opened the desk drawer and removed a makeshift clipboard made from a piece of particleboard and a clothespin securing a handwritten list on cheap notebook paper. He cycled through the pages, found AJ's name on the last one, and drew a line through it. He swung the clipboard, and all the pages fell back into place.

"Maisie Renko," Moon-Face yelled.

Fatted Seal went through the notebook sheets again slowly, this time glancing at me and licking his finger each time, leaving a dirty smear on the bottom of each page.

There, on the last page, was my name. Beneath AJ's.

He drew a line through it, then waddled to the steel door and hit it with his fist four times.

Fatted Seal went back to the desk and swapped out the clipboard for an ancient receipt book. He wrote *El Cid Rodriguez* on one and *Maisie Renko* on another, then spun the pad around on the desk for Scarecrow and Moon-Face to initial.

Two metallic *clangs* sounded on the metal door. Then two more.

Fatted Seal lumbered over and unlocked the door, letting two guards with nightsticks in khaki uniforms into the room before locking it again.

Fatted Seal reached into the desk drawer and brought out two pairs of steel, police-issue handcuffs. He threw one to each guard.

They came for AJ and me. Cuffed us, hands behind our backs.

Once AJ and I were cuffed, Fatted Seal tore off the top copies and handed them to our kidnappers, who left us without a backward glance.

My guard stepped up with the keys secured to his belt.

And opened the door to hell.

They shoved us forward into the dank stench of death and blood and raw sewage and fear. The noise was horrific—wailing and shouting. We were in an old jail. Three cells were jammed full of people.

There must have been twelve to a cell, built to hold one, maybe two people. Some stood, pressed up against the bars, while others sat with their knees drawn up, arms over their heads, crying, rocking back and forth.

The floor in front of us was slick with urine, the condemned prisoners choosing to piss outside of their cells.

The guards marched us through to where a fourth cell had obviously been, but it no longer had any bars. A thick support post rose out of the floor into the ceiling.

My guard took me in first. He pointed at the ground and the post until I understood I was to sit up against it. My hands cuffed behind my back allowed me the slight dignity of having my back to the prisoners. Ahead of me was another heavy iron door, this one barricaded from the cell side with a heavy wood beam across it.

I didn't want to know what was behind it.

AJ sat on the opposite side of the post, facing the cells and the door we'd come in, his hands cuffed above mine.

"Maisie? Everything's gonna be okay," AJ said, as much to himself as to me. "This is SOP for Mexico. Shit like this happens all the time. Carlos will pay a fat ransom, and then they'll let us go."

"Yeah," I said, trying to put a positive spin on it. "I mean, we're Americans, for chrissakes."

"Exactly."

Except I'm pretty sure they don't hold you hostage in a kill house.

Chapter 36

AJ said something in Spanish to the prisoners. Several voices answered at once. He asked another question.

The prisoner rattled on, "*La bestia que llora . . .*"

"Oh my God." My lungs collapsed. Unable to suck any air in or out, I wheezed, "The Weeping Beast? We're in a goddamn kill house with The Weeping Beast?"

"I'm sorry, Maisie. I'm so fucking sorry."

"It's not your fault," I whispered. "But why didn't we try to make a run for it?"

"We didn't have a chance. They were courteous as long as we remained compliant. I didn't feel like being rifle-raped before getting dumped here," he said glumly.

Awfully chivalrous of you to put it that way, champ.

"They wouldn't have used a rifle on me, would they?" I asked.

He ignored the question. "You did good. Keeping your mouth shut kept you safe."

"What about Chac?" I said, unwilling to share my rapidly dwindling hope that Lee would track us down. "Is there any way he can get help?"

"Nah. He's useless." AJ gave a bitter laugh. "One of the reasons why I never made him a Five-seveN."

Against my back, AJ's hands had turned to ice. "At first I thought . . . I thought it was a kidnap," he said softly.

I leaned forward, twisting my neck to try to get a look at him.

People in the next cell mashed their sweat-stained, tear-streaked, grimy faces against the bars to get a look at us. They were filthy, and smelled of fear and defeat.

I'm sure we looked no better.

Hank's Law Number Fourteen: A good plan violently executed immediately is better than a perfect plan executed later.

Start from the beginning. What had Lennon's report said?

I'd skimmed it. The brutality had been too stomach-turning to memorize. Except I had.

Slow, mentally damaged, cocaine addict, Santeria follower. The magic rabbit would appear when I needed it.

Hank's Law Number Thirteen: Anyone can endure expected pain.

I wasn't sure exactly how that applied to being tortured to death, one thing that definitely wasn't on my bucket list.

AJ's wrists had gone slack; the full weight of his arms rested on mine.

He was giving up.

Like hell.

Not on my watch, sweet pea.

"AJ." I grabbed the tail of his shirt and tugged. "Can you get the barrette out of my hair?"

"What?"

"There's a clip, a barrette underneath my ponytail. Can you reach it?"

He leaned forward, grunting, his shackled wrists sliding up the post. Chilly fingers fumbled against my bra strap before sliding up between my shoulder blades.

I scooched my butt forward and thrust my hip to the side. My ponytail landed neatly in his hands.

"It's a snap clip," I said. "Press it in the middle and it'll snap open."

His fingers found the barrette and tugged it free, strands of my hair coming with it. "Now what?"

"Get it into my hands."

He managed to get on his knees and move until we were

shoulder to shoulder. He pressed his mouth to my forehead and murmured, "We have an audience that will sell our souls for the momentary dream of freedom."

"Surely, Carlos Grieco will come for us," I said loudly. His hands covered mine and he dropped the clip into my palm.

"Yes." He moved back to where he had started, hiding my hands from view.

I craned my neck to look back over my shoulder at our audience. Whether it was the mention of Carlos or my naïveté that we would be rescued, the other prisoners had lost interest.

You don't grow up in a cop family with five older brothers and not experience the joy of hazing. I'd been handcuffed, cable-tied, and duct-taped so often that Da had finally taken pity on me, and taught me several rudimentary escape moves.

And I'd used every one. Multiple times.

I worked the teardrop-shaped snap clip between my fingers, bending it back and forth until the bottom broke off, leaving me with the two thin metal pieces joined at the hinge. I slipped the bottom into AJ's back pocket, then felt the broken ends. There's always one smoother than the other. "I got this, AJ. Start thinking about what we're going to need to do to get outta here."

"On it."

Hank's Law Number Twelve: Improvise, adapt, and overcome.

The wailing from the cells was painful to listen to. Throbbing and pulsing behind my eyes.

Can't you people just shut the feck up so I can think?

A metallic sound rang out.

AJ tipped his head back against mine. "Guard's coming."

I palmed the piece of the clip and glanced over my shoulder.

Both guards were coming, actually. Banging their nightsticks against the rails. Laughing, jabbing them through the bars, the prisoners ducking and shirking but taking hits with no room to evade.

"Mighty El Cid, ha!" The first guard kicked AJ's feet. "You won't last the night."

The second guard put his knee on my back, forcing my head

down, then bent and unlocked AJ's right cuff. AJ swung his arms around and threw himself at the first guard, catching him around the legs, knocking him to the floor.

The second guard got off of me and landed two shots with the nightstick.

"No!" shouted the guard on the ground. "*La bestia* likes them unhurt."

Everyone stopped then. Even the prisoners went momentarily silent.

The two guards raised AJ to his feet and hauled him past me. The first guard jerked AJ's cuffs high up his back, while the second, grunting, lifted off the wood barricade, setting it to one side, before he opened the door.

AJ looked back at me over his shoulder, his velvet brown eyes sick and empty as they both shoved him through the opening. The door swung slowly shut, and the prisoners started shouting again.

I got the piece of clip between my fingers and went to work.

Handcuffs work on a ratchet-and-pawl mechanism. A spring engages the teeth of the hinged arm. I wedged my flat little piece of barrette into the space between the arm and the mouth of the cuff, squeezed the cuff one notch tighter, engaging the shim and *voilà*.

The cuff sprung open. I felt the metallic *click* more than heard it as the yowling continued.

I puffed my cheeks out in relief and went to work on the second cuff.

Within twenty seconds my other hand was free.

I jumped to my feet, grabbed the heavy wooden beam, and re-barricaded the door, trapping the two guards, AJ, The Weeping Beast, and God knew what else back there.

The prisoners went apeshit.

I got that fuzzy, light-headed feeling. The one that makes it impossible to think of a decent plan.

Stay focused.

Fatted Seal had the keys. Even if he fell for my *two-knock pause two-knock* kicks, he wouldn't open the door wide enough for me to give him the bum's rush.

He needed to come into the cells.

But how?

For the love of Mike! It sounded like a herd of feral cats trapped in a Dumpster.

What was it Mom said? *I never minded you guys screaming and yelling—it was when you were quiet, I knew there was trouble.*

I walked between the cells, finger to my lips, shushing the prisoners. Their hands grabbed at me through the bars, panicked and disoriented and still fecking yelling.

Shit.

I went and sat back down at the post, facing them this time.

They screamed at me to get up.

Fine. We'll just wait for Fatted Seal to notice the missing guards and come after them. Except what if there is another door?

The Weeping Beast preferred to keep his victims alive for a long time, and with AJ being Carlos Grieco's nephew, it was a given his would be a slow and grueling journey toward the light.

Savage beast, more like.

That's it.

"Okay, guys, time to step it up if you wanna get out of here," I said loudly and clapped my hands. "Catholic? Santeria? I know you know this." I started singing, "Jesus loves me, this I know. For the Bible tells me so . . ."

A woman in the cell facing me picked it up and continued in Spanish. Pretty soon all the prisoners in the cells were either quiet or singing.

The guards banged on the barricaded door.

The prisoners sang louder, covering the racket.

"C'mon, Fatted Seal," I said, staring at the front cell door, clenching and unclenching my fists behind my back, running through Hank's training. *Throat, groin, knee . . .* "Come on, you sonuvabitch."

The door opened.

Fatted Seal peeped around the edge before pulling it wide, slapping the nightstick against his hand. "*Silencio!*"

He hit his nightstick against the bars. The prisoners kept singing. I kept singing.

Smiling, he switched the stick to his left hand and waved it as though he were a conductor. "*Silencio!*" He pulled a pistol from his belt and indiscriminately fired two shots into the first two cells.

The singing stopped.

I kept going. Knowing he would come for me.

Hank's Law Number Fourteen: A good plan violently executed immediately is better than a perfect plan executed later.

I sang, "They are weak, but he is strong."

Fatted Seal kicked my feet apart. Bent over, huffing slightly, he put the revolver under my chin. "*Silencio.*"

I stilled.

He laughed and straightened, still pointing the revolver at my head. He rubbed his crotch with his left hand. "*Jesús esta.*"

I wet my upper lip with the tip of my tongue.

He leered.

"Fuck you, *el gordito.*"

The prisoners howled with laughter.

Close enough.

Fatted Seal's eyes widened in rage. "I fuck *you,* bitch!" He grabbed me by the front of my shirt and pulled me upright.

I hit him in the throat with the best punch I've ever thrown. He dropped the gun, frozen from the shock of it. He keeled over. He made a rasping gasp, and I kneed him in the face, feeling his nose shatter.

Eyes bulging, face bright red, he fell back against the bars, bucking and gasping.

The prisoners grabbed him, holding him tight against the bars. One man got his arm around the Fatted Seal's throat. Finishing the job.

I picked up his revolver, jammed it in my jeans, and went back, avoiding his kicking legs for the nightstick and the fat ring of keys snapped to his waist.

He was dead before I unhooked the keys.

The guards on the other side banged on the door.

"Oh yeah." I winced. "You guys."

I checked the gun. One bullet.

"What the feck?"

Who keeps a revolver with only one bullet in it?

I hadn't quite got that far with the plan. I needed a little muscle. I glanced back at the cells behind me, the panicked faces pleading and yelling.

This wasn't *Ben Hur*. We weren't pals.

I ran for the door, unlocked it, and went into the lobby. I rifled through the desk. Nothing. No bullets. No phone.

I ripped the blaring transistor radio off the nail and clicked it off, feeling the seconds fly by.

"C'mon, Lee. Where the hell are you?"

Here goes nothing.

Grabbing a chair, I tipped it on its side, propping open the door to the cells, telling myself not to expect a miracle—great favors earn ingratitude.

At the first cell, I started cycling through the keys. People grabbed at me through the bars, chattering, crying. "Hey!" I tore myself from their grasp and held the keys up and away. "No!"

The prisoners in the first cell fell back.

You can just chill the heck out.

I went to the cell across and opened it. The prisoners ran out in a herd, slipping on the piss-covered floor, knocking into each other as they scrambled to get the hell out.

I turned back to the first cell.

They let me open the door, choruses of "*Gracias, gracias*" and other things I couldn't understand. A man and a woman jerked at my shirt, pulling at me, trying to get me to go, to leave the last cell. I shrugged them off and pointed at the door.

The third cell waited for me to open the door. The man who'd killed Fatted Seal held them at bay. The prisoners filed out quickly, quietly thanking me and hustling out the door.

The man, short and barrel-chested, was last to leave the cell.

He stopped at the chair serving as a doorstop and smashed his foot down on the leg. It splintered off.

He picked up the leg and pointed at the door.

A friend.

I nodded. He crossed the room and looked back at me. I drew the revolver. He shoved the barricade off with a *thud* and stepped back next to me.

The guards burst in, relief on their pale and sweating faces fading as they realized they weren't nearly out of it.

Barrel Chest took their nightsticks and patted them down. With the revolver, I motioned them into the third cell and locked the door.

I put the revolver in my left hand and threw a salute at Barrel Chest.

He returned it and headed for the door out.

I'm coming for you, AJ.

Chapter 37

Hank's Law Number Twenty: The most dangerous enemy is the one with nothing left to lose.

If that wasn't AJ and me, I don't know what was. I took a couple breaths and stepped inside.

And gagged.

Oh God. And I thought the cells smelled bad.

The hallway was dark with black shadows, and it stank of fear and offal, curdled and greasy.

Holding the revolver down at my side, I stayed tight to the wall. At the corner, I edged out and took a peek.

AJ's wrists and ankles were strapped to the arms of a wooden chair that looked like it had been stolen from a medieval mental institution. The Weeping Beast pulled a plastic bag off of AJ's face and slapped him with a meaty paw.

AJ was unresponsive.

C'mon, guy. Don't give up.

The Beast was a giant, with thick, trunk-like legs and a lumpy torso made of scrap cement. He crossed the room to a large metal vat and dipped in a plastic pail, filling it, and trudged back to throw it on AJ.

Nothing.

With a grunt, he slapped the unconscious man hard enough to split his lip. The Weeping Beast picked up a thick black cord. Jumper cables. Connected at the opposite end to a Sears Die-Hard battery charger. He touched the ends to AJ's chest.

The horrible *spark-zap* and the stink of burning flesh.

Oh Jesus.

AJ's head bobbed, body jerked, then went still. He groaned.

Thank God.

Water dripped from AJ's torn and bloodied shirt onto the floor. His head lolled in my direction. His left eye was swollen shut, and the lobes of each of his ears hung loose, bleeding.

One bullet. It would have to be a kill shot.

Back pressed tight to the wall, my breath came hard and fast. "Hank?" His name spilled from my mouth in a silent prayer.

"Put him down, Peaches," Hank said in my head. *"You'll only feel one thing. Recoil."*

The Weeping Beast folded his massive arms over his chest and frowned at AJ, shaking his head. He wiped his cheek and mouth off on the back of his arm and went to rummage through a rusted toolbox. The mucus on his forearm glistened in the bare bulb light. He raised a pair of pliers and clicked them together, absently, thinking.

AJ didn't move.

The Beast put them down and picked up a scalpel.

"Iago," I said softly. "Iago."

He spun toward AJ.

I stepped into his private chamber of horror, revolver pointed at his chest. "Iago García Falto."

He turned slowly and peered at me like I was some sort of alien. *"Quién?"*

I motioned him away from the tools, to the near corner. He moved obediently, a surprised, openmouthed smile on his mouth, lower lip tucked to avoid the drip.

I backed slowly across the room to AJ, and without taking my eyes off him, went to work on AJ's wrist cuff. "AJ," I said. "AJ. Wake up."

Nothing.

I moved to the other wrist cuff. Fumbling, taking forever be-cause I couldn't take my eye off the Beast. I knocked AJ's hand in his lap. "AJ."

The Weeping Beast cocked his head, closed his good eye, and opened his dripping eye wide with his thumb and index finger. "*Quién?*"

I dropped to a squat and started on the ankle cuff. Sweat ran down my back. The revolver was getting heavy. My hand shook. "AJ."

AJ coughed, and his head sagged forward. "Okay," he whispered.

I moved to the last cuff.

The Beast frowned and demanded, "*Quién eres?*"

I rolled the dice, banking on Lennon's report. My Spanish stilted and slow as I tried to say I was his dead sister's guardian angel. "*Un amigo ángel de María.*" I hoisted AJ to his feet, ducking under his arm.

The Beast's face crumpled in concentration. He wiped the drip off his chin. "*Que María?*"

"*Tu hermana.*" I edged AJ and me toward the door. "María Fernanda Falto."

He began to laugh. A harsh, snuffling sound of the sort a wild boar made, bumping and rubbing its snout into the earth.

Oh God. The report got it wrong.

"I kill her. For the crying." He came slowly toward us. "All the time, the crying."

"No closer." We were almost to the door.

"Then I must kill them all, *sí?*"

I let go of AJ to grip the revolver, wrapping my thumbs over and pulling tight as I'd been taught. "Stop!"

The Beast didn't stop.

I aimed directly at his head. AJ stumbled, knocking into me as I pulled the trigger.

The bullet grazed the side of The Beast's skull.

I kept pulling the trigger.

Click.

Knowing there were no bullets left in the gun.

Click. Click. Click.

The Beast yanked the gun from my hand and threw it across the floor. Grinning, a gelatinous bubble of teary mucus dribbled down his cheek, and hung off his upper lip before dripping onto his shirt.

"Run, AJ!" I shoved him toward the hall.

The Beast grabbed me around the waist. He picked me up and threw me over the side of the vat as effortlessly as though I was a child.

Headfirst, dunking me into the filthy water. Eyes stinging, I inhaled a mouthful of water, choking beneath the surface.

He hauled me up by my hair.

I broke the surface, gasping and spluttering to his sick, grunting snuffles.

He held me over the tank, letting me getting my breath back. Knowing he was going to put me under again.

"María Fernanda . . . María Fernanda . . . María Fernanda." He sang the name, the syllables singsong guttural, the rage beneath them building. "María Fernanda . . . MaríaMaríaMaría . . ."

He jammed my head underwater.

My feet scrabbled uselessly against the sides of the vat. His weight pinned my waist over the rim. I arched backward, arms reaching over my head, clawing feebly at The Beast.

Eighty-seven seconds to break point. The moment when you're on the verge of losing consciousness and you inhale water.

Lights sparked behind my eyes. I thrust my arms inside the tank, feeling for anything to either pull myself in or to push myself out.

The sparks faded to a pinprick.

Arms grabbed me around the waist, forcing dirty water up and out of my lungs. Heaving and spasming, I heard Lee's voice in my ear. "I got you, you're okay."

Took you long enough, cavalry.

When my paroxysm of coughing had eddied down to tremors, Lee turned me into his chest. I sucked in giant lungfuls of him. Sweat and gun grease and the tang of diesel fuel never smelled so good.

The Weeping Beast groaned, semiconscious on the ground. Three Five-seveNs had their rifles trained on him, another two had AJ up and walking.

Lee let go.

"You all right?" I asked AJ.

His velvet eyes had turned to stone. "I owe you, kid."

"Time to go," I said. "Please."

"Not yet." AJ gestured with a hand to the Five-seveNs and cracked his knuckles. "Get him up." He turned to Lee. "Get her out of here."

"AJ—" I began.

"Beat it." He picked up the pliers and smiled. It was one of the most awful things I'd ever seen. "Zed's dead, baby."

Lee and I left the kill house in one of the Grieco cartel's armored Humvees. I sat in the middle of the rear seat bench, in between Lee and one of the Five-seveNs.

"Is good, what you did, Señora Renko." The Five-seveN nodded at me. "You save many people. *La bestia que llora* will die as he lived."

Violently.

Lee stared out the window. The frown on his face cut so harsh he looked like a fury.

I wanted to say something. Anything.

But what was there to say, really?

I felt exhausted and ancient. Beyond the years of a human being.

My body didn't seem to get the message. I couldn't stop my knees from bouncing, hands robotically clenching and unclenching the hem of my jacket.

The Five-seveN put his hand on my knee to still it. "You are okay now." He smiled at me. "Okay."

"Take your goddamn hand off her," Lee's voice sliced through the air. He threw a rough arm around my shoulders. I scooted up close to him. His hard, muscled body felt as unforgiving as his face looked.

It's a helluva lot nicer cozying up to an angry statue than being tortured in a kill house.

I sighed.

It came out a shudder.

Lee growled, "You stink of death."

The tears came then, silently sliding down my cheeks, dripping onto my chest. I didn't have the strength to move out from under his heavy arm, much less raise a hand to wipe them away.

Chapter 38

Carlos and his men were on the driveway when we pulled up. Floodlights and panic and the acrid smell of chemicals wafted gently through the air.

He met us at the Humvee, eyes shiny with unshed tears, took me by the shoulders, and kissed me on each cheek. "The angel who saved El Cid. We talk tomorrow, yes?"

I nodded.

Lee frog-marched me up the stairs to our rooms, gripping my elbow hard enough to leave a mark. Didn't bother me a bit.

He checked the bedroom, bathroom, and made sure the balcony and bedroom doors were locked. "Good night." He disappeared through the en suite door between our rooms, closing it firmly behind him.

Without a second thought, I stripped down and got in the shower and stayed until my fingers and toes pruned. Feeling remarkably peppy, I put on a tank top and underpants and blow-dried my hair. Amped, I glossed and flat-ironed it to a silk curtain before going back to the bedroom.

The lamp on the nightstand would barely qualify as a kid's nightlight. I clicked on all the lights. It still felt dark.

TV on.

Univision was rebroadcasting a soccer match.

I'm so not tired.

I splayed my fingers. Not a tremor.

The world's a happy place. Mani-pedi's chipped, though.

Back to the bathroom for fire-engine red nail polish. Waiting for the polish to cure, I turned on my phone and followed along with a YouTube contouring makeup tutorial.

Huh. That really worked.

I cracked my neck.

Time for a little yoga, maybe.

Univision had switched over to a telenovela. I turned it up, dropped onto the floor, and raised my legs into Boat pose.

Lee flung open the door between our rooms. "What the *hell* is going on in here?"

"Nothing." I wiggled my toes.

The red looks fantastic.

"Maisie!" His short brown hair was sticking up in the back. Indian feathers.

"Geez. I'm sorry . . . I didn't mean to wake you."

"You did." He stomped over to the bathroom.

I guess when you have a body like that, you've pretty much earned the right to walk around in boxer briefs whenever you want.

"Do you have any idea what time it is?" He turned off the light and shut the door. "You have every fucking light on. Every goddamn cabinet open. What the hell are you doing?"

He turned everything off, came closer, and squinted at me. "Are you wearing makeup at three forty a.m.?"

"Yes?"

"Why?"

"Uh . . . I'm a little off the rails, maybe?" I guessed.

"Yeah." He picked up the remote and turned off the television. "You are." He loomed over me. "Get up."

I stood.

He marched over to the bed and whipped back the covers. "Get in."

I obeyed and slid under the sheets.

Like an angry parent, he pulled the covers up under my chin, brisk and firm, before switching off the light. I watched his silhouette push the door between our rooms all the way open to the wall and disappear into his room.

I stared at the ceiling, humming. Legs restless beneath the sheets.

"Maisie?" Lee called.

"Yes?"

"Be quiet and go the fuck to sleep."

Lee leaned against the doorway a scant five hours later, waking me from a light and fitful sleep. "Grieco wants to see you."

"Okay. What about?"

Lee shrugged and went back into his room, closing the door behind him.

I got up, brushed my teeth, and took stock.

Bing, bing! Two steps ahead. Hair and makeup still passed muster.

I put on a Halston Heritage asymmetrical pencil skirt in a soft lead gray, matching Pliner wedge booties, and pale blue work shirt knotted at the waist.

Casual chic.

I grabbed my Louboutin clutch and knocked on the adjoining door, pushing it open at his grunt.

Lee, fully suited up, was in 100 percent bodyguard mode. "You packed?"

"Not at all."

He closed his eyes in that long-suffering way he wasn't close to owning. "Okay. Let's go."

A maid waited for us in the foyer. "Señora Renko, please come this way."

We followed her out to the front drive, where an empty dark-green two-seater LandMaster Utility Vehicle waited.

"Mr. Grieco is at old barn," the maid said. "You know the way, *sí?*"

"*Sí.*" I climbed in. Two unopened water bottles waited in the cup holders.

Lee got behind the wheel, and we zipped off down the drive. It was sunny. Searingly so, even at nine. I opened my clutch, dug out my sunglasses, and took stock. Travel bottle of Excedrin, camera/scanner pen, package of Dentyne Fire, two lip glosses, and a travel mascara. Add to that Hank's volcanic glass knife beneath the liner, and we were talking save-the-world travel kit.

I opened the Excedrin, peeled off the foil, pulled out the never-ending wad of cotton bigger than the bottle itself, and shook out two tablets. "Want some?"

Lee held out his hand. I shook out two more.

He dry-swallowed while I opted for the Evian.

"It's pretty creepy when you think about it," I said. "Obviously the whole idea of a kill house, of course, but the fact that we were like, what, less than an hour and change away? That's pretty damn close to the estate. I mean—"

"Grieco is going to ask you about the locator tag," Lee interrupted. "I told him Renko insisted you carry one at all times."

My knee started bouncing. "Okay."

"You should have never fucking left."

Great. A parental lecture from a non-parent. Whee!

"Yeah," I said, "but—"

"Zip it," he barked.

My mouth disconnected from my brain and I blurted, "I can't help wondering if Raúl had anything to do with this."

Lee jammed on the brakes and stopped the UTV short. He glared at me. "You need to lock it down, sweetheart. Right fucking now."

Congratulations! You're a shoo-in when it comes to the pissed-off partner taking on the father figure role.

He wasn't done. Not nearly. "No chirping off like little robin redbreast when you meet with Grieco. Do you follow?"

I nodded.

"No helpful comments. No friendly suggestions. We clear?" He jabbed a finger at me. "Grieco is a fucking drug kingpin, and the shit that went down in that kill house—well, guess what? He and your buddy El Cid have done that same shit to other people. For real. Do you get that?"

I tried to take a sip of water, but it wouldn't go down, so I sat there with it in my mouth as Lee drove us to the barn.

We came around the bend and I gasped, swallowing the water

into my lungs, choking and coughing. The barn was a charred skeleton, one where a death-eating monster had taken a jagged bite out of the center.

Lee steered the UTV through the sodden sandy soil up to the repurposed stable. The coastal breeze coating us in the stink of charred wood, burnt rubber, and plastic.

"There was a fire last night?" The lights and men all over the estate last night fell into place. It hadn't been only about AJ.

"Looks like it," Lee said.

The Five-seveN who'd sat by me in the Humvee on the drive back to the estate, approached. "Señora Renko? You come with me, yes?"

Clutch in hand, I stepped out.

He said to Lee, "I will see to her, personally."

Lee started up the UTV and took off.

The Five-seveN walked me to the near edge of the barn. "You wait here, *sí?*"

"*Sí.*" I surveyed the yard. The stucco on the stable was scorched, surrounding trees blackened on the side closest the barn. There had been a fire all right, a big one.

And an explosion.

The rusty diesel fuel tank was a distant memory. Shiny bits of debris were scattered as far as four hundred yards away.

The closest of the two Lincoln Navigators appeared to have taken the brunt of the explosion's blow back. The SUV was peppered with shrapnel and spall, and sticking out like a knife in the armor plate, was the three-inch butt of a metal striker.

Scarily similar to the one that I'd dug out of the porch in Juárez.

His back to me, the Five-seveN waited patiently at the edge of the barn to notify Grieco of my arrival.

When gifted with a NY minute, you sure as hell had better take it, because there isn't a return policy.

Nearing the SUV, I dug out the camera-pen I'd made fun of and started clicking away. Finishing with a couple tight shots of the striker, I slipped the pen behind my ear.

I grabbed the wad of cotton from the Excedrin bottle and tried unsuccessfully to pull the striker from the door. It needed pliers and some serious muscle.

Maybe the cotton collected a little residue.

I shook out the rest of the aspirin and jammed the swiped cotton back into the bottle, keeping an eye on my Five-seveN, who still hadn't moved. The ground was littered with pieces of wood, bits of plastic, tiny shards of broken glass, and brass casings everywhere.

Five-point-seven casings to be exact. I grinned.

Looks like my work here is done. Obligatory hat tip to Raúl and/or El Eje.

I pocketed some of the 5.7 casings. A ribbon of aluminum lay inches from my foot. At the bottom, a black letter *W* sat on a "warning" yellow background.

"Señora Renko?" The Five-seveN waved at me.

I waved back and dropped the piece of metal into the clutch, then gingerly picked my way around the edge of the barn. Black, wet dust drifted through the air, settling into my lungs.

Carlos stood in the middle of the barn talking to an old man as weathered and creased as an old tractor tire.

The old man examined a machine that resembled a drill press and shook his head. There were a half dozen other machines, including a grinder, all bent and warped and burnt.

Carlos gripped his temples, listening to the old man. He caught sight of me, gave the old man a clap on the shoulder, and strode over.

"Maisie Renko, I see how you bewitched Stannislav." He kissed me on both cheeks.

"Thank you, Carlos. What happened here?"

"*Un regalito.*" He spat. "A gift from El Eje." He took my elbow. "Come, let us go into the other building."

The Five-seveN followed behind at a respectful distance.

We entered the repurposed stable through an old wooden door. I followed Carlos through a short hallway to another set of glass doors, into his private showroom.

Six of the fiercest muscle cars ever were parked on a glossy terrazzo floor.

"Good Lord," I breathed as we passed a rally-red Corvette L88. "Is that a 1969 Chevrolet Camaro ZL-1?"

Carlos's chin lifted. "Yes. Only sixty-nine were made."

Stretching behind the cars, almost as an afterthought, was a six-foot-high, curvaceous S-shaped wave of polished steel. I was pretty sure it was a Richard Serra sculpture.

And from the vivid paintings of pills and capsules on the far gallery wall, it was safe to assume he was a Damien Hirst fan, as well.

A faint humming droned overhead.

Carlos pointed at the ceiling. "A computer-controlled HVAC system maintains twenty-one degrees Celcius and fifty percent humidity environmental conditions year-round. Special filters remove the sea salt from the air."

"Wow."

"Do you know they told me you cannot store muscle cars this close to the sea? They will rust out before your eyes." He gave a snorting chortle. "I told them science and money makes everything possible."

We walked to the archway at end of the showroom. It opened into the ultimate man cave. As if any man needed more than that showroom full of fury.

A sleek marble bar with a dozen stools, lounge area with big-screen TV, and a rectangular marble-topped conference table. Six of the Five-seveNs, all in black, stood waiting. Carlos led me to one end of the table. A Five-seveN pulled out the chair for me. After I was seated, the men followed suit, Carlos at the head.

AJ walked into the room, wearing tan pants and a loose raw-linen shirt, two more Five-sevenS at his heels.

I could see the square shape of bandages beneath his shirt as he moved. His face was a rainbow of bruises. Tiny strips of skin-colored stitch tape were above his eye, on his cheekbone and chin. His earlobes had been reattached.

But as rough as he looked, it was nothing compared to the dead in his eyes. He was El Cid. AJ was no more.

"Maisie Renko," El Cid said. "I am in your debt."

He reached into his pocket and stepped behind me.

I closed my eyes as a shard of pure irrational fear stabbed my lungs.

Something cold and heavy went around my neck, sliding down my décolletage.

I opened my eyes. Spanish Reals. Pieces of eight, each one wired in white gold, strung together in a thick and powerful web. "*Gracias,* El Cid."

Carlos set a heavy case onto the table. "I, too, am in your debt." He pushed the case a foot in front of him. The two FiveseveNs each laid their left hands on the case and crossed themselves. They pushed the case to the next men. It happened twice more before the case was in front of me.

El Cid put his hand on it and crossed himself, then popped the locks. "You are one of us now." He lifted the lid.

An FN Herstal 5.7 MK2 pistol.

Hank's Law Number Twenty-Four: Never, ever ignore your gut.

I stood up. "It is a great honor you bestow upon me." I put my fist over my heart and kept talking. "Retaliations must be made. This, I understand. But I urge you to move forward with caution and deliberate intent."

El Cid scowled. But Carlos's lips pursed. "Why do you say this?"

"I believe more than El Eje are involved." *Like your other nephew, Raúl.* "But I have no proof."

"Ahh, the evidence of a woman's intuition." El Cid chuffed.

Geez. Could you act a little more like a dink, AJ?

Carlos stroked his chin. "A *bendición* from *la Santa Muerte.*" He nodded. "This we will heed."

Chapter 39

Lee slid into the seat next to me in the Lincoln Navigator on the way to the hangar. A Five-seveN rode shotgun. After the kidnapping and the loss of the munitions factory, the Grieco estate was locked down, on high alert.

Lee gave my throat a slow going-over. "Nice necklace."

"Spanish Reales," I said. "Pirate treasure."

He scoffed. "Fitting."

The necklace was heavy, but I liked it that way. Armor.

Instead of the flight attendant, Grieco's dapper private pilot met us at the hangar entrance. "I'm sorry, Mrs. Renko, but I'm afraid our departure will be delayed."

"Oh?" Lee said.

Captain Hester nodded. "Seems we're missing a couple halon canisters. Which, if they were hoping for nitrous, are gonna make those poor bastards very unhappy."

"What's halon?" I asked.

"A liquefied, compressed gas that stops the spread of fire by chemically disrupting combustion. Aviation law—you can't fly without them. The Lear has three tanks. One in the nose for the electrical system, and the missing two, which were stolen from the storage hold."

"Oh?"

"Exactly. Stealing from Carlos Grieco on his estate?" Hester said. "Had to be drug addicts. No one else is that out of their mind."

Lee squinted into the horizon. "Any idea how long of a delay?"

"Shouldn't be more than an hour. Would you prefer to return to the house?"

Lee and I exchanged a glance.

Hell, no.

"I'm quite all right to wait here," I said and we boarded the jet.

Across the table, Lee watched me with a raised brow as I unpacked and set up my travel ritual. Something was niggling at me, and it wasn't the bits I'd recovered from the bombed barn. I was tired, that was all. It'd come to me if I let it alone.

"I called in your missing phone to Walt," he said.

"Thank you."

He offered me his phone. "Want to check your messages?"

"I can't think of anything I'd like to do less," I lied, aching to check on Hank, but unwilling to give Lee a traceable record.

Eventually the halon arrived and we took off. A new, equally attractive attendant came over for our drink order. "Stoli on ice, three olives."

"Ginger ale," Lee said.

I hit my head against the seat back in exasperation. "Oh, for God's sake, Lee. Have a drink."

"Ginger ale."

It took him a half can of ginger ale before he asked in a quiet voice, "What did Carlos say to you?"

"You know, the ol' 'You're awesome. Wanna take some drugs home for free?'"

He popped his cheek out with his tongue. "Very funny."

No harm in showing him. I wriggled the black molded-plastic case out of my satchel, popped the locks, and slid it across the table to him.

Lee raised the lid.

Inside was the 5.7 MK2 complete with a black diamond chip in the safety. Mine had also been modified to fully automatic, exactly like the one used in the assassination attempt on Coles. The case also held two standard-load twenty-round magazines, as well as a modified forty-round magazine, plus two hundred rounds of the Five-seveN's handmade steel-core black-tipped armor-piercing cartridges.

Lee's lips pursed in a low whistle.

"I'm an honorary Five-seveN. And get a load of this—" I reached over and showed him the detachable back straps. The smallest one, just my size, had been engraved with two microscopically delicate pictures. One face with the name Jesús Malverde. The other was a skull of *La Santa Muerte*. "The patron saint of drug dealers and the angel of death, blessed by the local priest. Pretty neat, huh?"

"Slick," he said, but he didn't sound like himself.

He didn't look like himself, either. The skin across his cheekbones seemed stretched too tight, and he'd missed a spot at the back of his jaw shaving. Bone weary.

It made my throat hurt. "You all right?"

"We won't be honeymooning here, if that what's you're asking."

"Yeah." I looked out the window.

I don't think I need to visit Mexico again. Ever.

We landed, went through Customs, where we got the salute-wave and rubber stamp while Grieco's jet with our guns and heroin was towed back to the hangar, unmolested.

AJ had a limo waiting. The driver loaded our luggage, then drove us over to the hangar, where Lee retrieved the contraband from the Lear and loaded it in the trunk.

The car returned us to Stannis's apartment.

"Stay in the car," Lee said. He came back with a bell cart, and he and the driver loaded it with our 250K worth of heroin, my new 5.7, and the rest of the luggage before opening my door.

I stepped out into the cold black Chicago night and shivered. Frigid wind whipping my cheeks never felt so good.

Lee and I rode up the elevator in silence. Stepping into the black granite foyer, I felt overwhelmingly sad. Lee rolled the cart in behind me and unloaded it.

"Are you in for the night?" I asked.

"What?" Lee squinted. "Of course."

"I'll set the alarm."

"Wait." He yawned. "Lemme run the cart down."

Rocking on my heels like an empty cradle, brain numb, my fingers and the tip of my nose turned to ice.

Lee came back up and picked up my things. He shot me a sideways look. "Get me a beer?"

I went into the kitchen. The only thing in the Sub-Zero was water, sugar-free Amp, and Bollinger.

If Miller High Life is the champagne of beers, does that make Bollinger the beer of champagne?

I giggled and got out two flutes, wincing as I knocked them together too hard. The miracle that they hadn't shattered made me giggle more. But the sound of me—so odd to my own ears— had me laughing for real then, while I peeled the foil and untwisted the wire cage over the cork.

Maybe it was because my hands were too cold, or I was laughing too hard, but the cork would not come out of the bottle. Holding the bottle between my knees, I pulled harder and felt the cork turn slightly.

Bang! It popped like a 5.7. The cork whizzed past my cheek, shattering the hanging task light over the counter.

Scaring the shit out of me, making me laugh even harder.

"Christ!" Lee's eyes were saucer-wide.

The champagne ran over my hands, pouring onto my shoes and the floor in a waterfall of foamy wine. "There wasn't any beer."

He dropped the duffel bag of heroin on the table. "I can honestly say I've never known a girl like you before." He came into the kitchen and yanked the bottle from my hands.

I took off the sodden suede wedge booties, my bare feet sticky on the smooth floor. "I think I'll change."

In my room, I went straight for my backup iPhone in the Ziploc bag under the top layer of sand in Stannis's bone jar.

I checked our electronic connection points. Nothing.

Screw it. With a shaky breath, I called Hank's office.

The sultry-voiced secretary wasn't her usual languorous self. "I'm sorry to inform you," she said stiffly, "Mr. Bannon has still not been in contact."

"Maybe you should rethink using the phrase, '*I'm sorry to inform you,*'" I snapped.

"I beg your pardon, Miss McGrane. I apologize. Is there anything else?"

"Yeah," I said. "You tell Ragnar—er—Randolph Acrey I want to see him. ASAP." I hung up.

I put the phone back and went into the bathroom. Washing my face, I leaned into the mirror for a closer look.

Funny.

Not a mark on me.

None that showed, anyway.

By the time I pulled myself together, Lee had cleaned up the kitchen havoc, showered, shaved, and changed into sweatpants and a T-shirt. He raised a champagne flute to me. "Sweet pants, Bae."

Holding the edges of the flannel *Halo*-patterned pajama pants, I did a slow pirouette. "A gaming incentive Christmas present. From Cash."

"Hungry?"

"Sure."

"Good." He nodded at the Bollinger in a champagne bucket. "We got less than twenty to drink this swill before dinner."

I sat down across from him. "What are we having?"

"Tacos."

I raised three fingers tight together. "Read between the lines."

Lee grinned.

Gee, he's a doll.

I took a swig of champagne. "Now what?"

"Debrief with Walt."

"It seems so . . . I don't know . . . anticlimactic." I sighed. "The futility of it. I went into this for Cash. To help the cops on the street. To make a difference, and it's over because El Eje stepped in and blew up Grieco's bullet factory? It's like it's all been for nothing. And I don't know how to take that."

"Hey." Lee put his hand on mine and squeezed. "You've scored direct evidence with the modified 5.7, the handmade steel-core rounds, and have definitive proof Grieco and El Cid are running drugs in Chicago. That's not nothing."

I took a sip of champagne and shook my head. "The munitions dump is gone, and you managed to survive." Lee cocked his head. "Nyx couldn't ask for more."

"That's just it. He can and he will ask for more. Sawyer, too." I spun my champagne glass slowly by the stem. "Can I tell you something?"

He nodded. "Yes."

I knew I shouldn't, but I couldn't hold the blackness in another second. "I feel . . . shredded." I gripped the back of my neck. "These assignments. They each demand their share of heart and blood. I like AJ. A lot. Hell, I even like Grieco. And Jimmy the Wolf and Vi Veteratti. And I really"—I swallowed hard—"really like Stannis."

His brown eyes squinted back into mine, mouth compressed into a hard line. "And Hank."

"What?"

"Aren't we listing all the criminals you care about?"

My mouth slid to one side, ready to fight, but not sure how.

The lobby buzzed.

"Food's here." Lee left to pick it up.

I pressed my eyes hard with the heels of my hands. *Where are you, Hank? Where are you?*

"Maisie?" Lee said softly, startling me. I hadn't heard him come back up. "You all right?"

"As rain." I looked up and laughed.

Idiot.

He really had ordered tacos.

Chapter 40

Monday morning, I cracked open one of the few precious sugar-free Amps left in existence from the vegetable crisper, forcing myself not to guzzle down the glorious goodness. "Mmm."

Lee came into the kitchen and jerked his chin at me. "Got another one of those?"

"Uh . . ." Aware that it was the height of churlishness to deny the guy who'd saved my life an energy drink, I said, "Why don't you try a sip first?"

He came around the counter and took the can from my hands. He raised the can to his mouth and took a swallow, eyes never leaving mine. "Wow. That's fantastic."

Dammit.

"Let me get you one." I got one out of the fridge and offered it to him.

Lee burst into laughter. "Your face!"

"What?" Heat flushed my cheeks. "You don't want it?"

"No, Bae." He chuckled. "It tastes like sour Mountain Dew." He glanced at his watch. "You ready? Maybe I can swing by Starbucks and get a coffee since you're not a sharer."

My mouth opened in mock indignation.

He tapped his cheek. "C'mon. Pay up."

I felt shy and silly and . . . light.

I leaned in and he turned his head, taking it on the mouth. He caught my face before I could pull away and he was kissing me so hard and it felt so good.

Stop. I need to stop. I need—

He edged me back against the counter, and yanked my shirt out of my pants. Knocking over the can. He swore against my mouth, trying to right it.

Energy drink flooded the counter and dripped down the back of my pants. "Gah!"

What the hell am I doing?

I ducked under his arm, grabbed my satchel and coat off the bar, and ran for the elevator.

"Maisie. Maisie, wait. Goddammit!"

I leaned against Lee's Steve-McQueen-Highland-Green Mustang. Before we'd left, I'd called down to the concierge, and without his knowledge or permission, had it washed, waxed, and detailed.

I'd meant to be sweet, but I could see how it could be taken as presumptuous. Especially after what had just happened.

Oh God.

Maybe he won't notice.

Nine minutes later, Lee came down, smart as hell in his new black Nicholas Joseph suit, white shirt, and charcoal tie. Duffel bag of heroin slung over his shoulder, black 5.7 gun case in one hand, sugar-free Amp in the other. He halted. "What happened to my car?"

Feck.

I stared at the ground. "I had it cleaned."

He popped the locks and the trunk. Inside were five card-board file boxes. Three filled with gear and clothes and the last two with the paper tiger he could never seem to tame: mail, work, and magazines.

God only knew how many bags of trash the car wash guys threw out.

Lee put the drugs and the gun in and closed the trunk. Without a word he came around and opened my door. I slid in and set my purse down.

"Ahem." He wagged the can in front of my face.

I took it and he closed the door on me before I could thank him.

I shook the can. Things were looking up. He'd managed to salvage more than half of the energy drink.

Lee started the car. We were halfway to the *Sentinel* for the debrief before I shook the blur from my brain. "We should have driven separately," I apologized. "My schedule's gonna hamstring you."

"I don't think you understand, ma'am. We're in full undercover mode. What part of Stannislav Renko would let you drive to work solo?"

He had me, and he knew it.

"Whatever," I muttered.

He dropped me off in the front of the paper. It was one thing for the hammer-and-sickle crew to think I had a love-sodden, muscle-head boy toy, something else entirely for them to think I had a bodyguard.

I rode the elevator up, checking my reflection in the silver doors.

In seconds I'd know whether my attempt to social justice warrior-ize Phillip Lim slim pants with a boxy cropped Tokyo sweater was successful. I figured the Soviet Bloc vintage wool gray military long coat prepaid the points my kitten heels would cost.

Because girls cannot live on Goth alone.

I couldn't bear the idea of a debrief with the suave Sawyer while wearing high-tops.

"You're in early," Jenny Steager said as I passed by her desk. "Didn't you get my e-mail that Renick bumped the weekly meeting to this afternoon?"

"Yes, thanks," I fibbed. "Lots of busywork to catch up on."

She nodded, glossy chestnut hair tumbling into her eyes. "Speaking of which, I brought up your . . . ah . . . fan mail. The response to your 'More Guns Mean Less Crime' op-ed was insan-o."

"Ughhhhh."

Goddammit, Renick.

Publicity was not the goal here. One more thing to talk to Sawyer about. "Thanks, Juice." I said. "Keep an eye out for my guy, Lee, will you? He oughta be coming up any minute, and I could use a few to get my gear together."

Her face lit up. "You bet."

I cut toward my office.

"Lurv the coat!" she called to my back.

I raised a hand and unlocked my door. As soon as this gig was over, I'd invite her and her pals over for the great Goth closet cleansing. I hung up my coat, took my satchel and the black case with the 5.7, and trotted to the conference room.

Sawyer was waiting at the conference table. "How are you, Maisie?"

He'd seen my report. And Lee's. And I hadn't.

"Not a mark on me, sir." I closed the door, set the case in front of him, and sat down.

He perused the 5.7, the modifications and extended magazine, while I explained about the engraved back straps, the handmade ammunition.

"I'll have ballistics standing by." He closed the case and slid it back to me. I put it at my feet and set out the evidence bags I'd pulled from the explosion. The Excedrin bottle, bullet casings, aluminum ribbon.

I handed Sawyer the camera/pen. "The bomb was set off with a similar striker to the one in the cooler. But it was embedded in the side of an armored Lincoln Navigator. There was no way it was coming out without a blowtorch and a pair of pliers. But I did get pictures."

"Of the scene." He pressed the tips of his fingers together.

"And the striker."

"Excellent." His cognac-colored eyes seemed to glow as he secreted the pen inside his breast pocket. He picked up the bag with the aluminum ribbon and tapped the pill bottle. "And this?"

"Whatever residue I could get off the striker. Unfortunately, there was aspirin dust in the cotton."

"Nicely done, Maisie." The two bags disappeared into the flap pockets of his suit coat.

"Thank you, sir."

"As for Operation Summit," Sawyer said. "Renko's ghosted. Goran Slajic and the Srpska Mafija don't seem concerned he's in the wind. Thoughts?"

"He's gone to ground with the Russians?" I guessed. *Or, more exactly, Hank and his two Russian mercenaries.*

"My thoughts exactly. Lucky for us, they're proving to be a cagey bunch and I plan on using every spare second to our advantage."

"Yessir," I said. Just hearing Sawyer agree that Stannis—*and Hank*—were dug in was a fifty-pound weight off my chest.

Sawyer checked his watch. "I'd prefer Sharpe takes the lead in the group debrief." His slim, foxy face gave nothing away. "We're going to play this close to the vest."

"Sir?"

The door swung open. I put the gun case at my feet. In strode Lee with ATF agent Ditch Broady and the DEA's Gunther Nyx, all sharp-suited and skinny-tied, Kray brothers style.

I was, yet again, underdressed.

Lee took the seat next to mine, then turned it on and turned it up. Way up. "The mission objectives were met."

"I hear you acquired a gun," Broady said. "Definitive proof of the Grieco cartel's involvement in Coles's assassination attempt."

"Maisie did." Lee put the case on the table and opened it. "This one's been modified to the same extent as the one used in the attempt on the mayor."

"Damn!" Broady held up one of the boxes of cartridges. "Golly-goddamned if you weren't right, Nyx. Y'all catch more flies with honey. Bears, too. Nice work." Excitement crossed Broady's face. "I think we have what we need to proceed."

"Yes," Lee said. "It was good working with you, Ditch."

"If either of y'all get a wild hair and want to work for the

ATF down Mexico way, you gimme a call, you hear?" Broady closed the case, flipped the locks, and stood up.

Sawyer put his hand on the case. "The handgun and its accoutrements will remain with the CPD, for the time being. Multiple open murder cases, as well as the attempted murder of a dedicated SWAT officer, using 5.7s and steel-core rounds, demand it."

"But—"

"Mayor Coles and the ATF know better than to disrupt open murder cases because someone wants a trophy."

Nyx shrugged. "The price of doing business, Ditch."

"I don't think y'all realize how important this evidence is to the ATF."

"Perhaps not," Walt said. "However, I personally guarantee the gun will be under guard at all times, not merely locked slapdash away in Evidence."

Ditch's smile turned to treacle. "Good. Warms my heart to hear you're on top of it. See you around." He left the office, closing the door a little too firmly behind him.

Gunther Nyx's straight blond hair fell forward. "There is the little matter of the heroin—250K dollars' worth. Where is it?"

I started to answer. Lee thumped his knee against mine.

"Special Unit has taken custody," Sawyer said smoothly. "The most advantageous route for Operation Summit would be to allow Agent McGrane and Agent Sharpe to further establish an obvious stream of income by continuing to move product within West Englewood and Burnside. The DEA can consider the distribution a consistent measureable control within those zones. Plus, it's a bit of a luxury to have an operation you can clamp down on when needed."

Nyx tossed his head. "The proceeds?"

"Well," Sawyer demurred. "Special Unit's agents are doing all the work."

"The collar?"

"All yours, Gunther," Sawyer said silkily. "Did you even have to ask?"

Nyx's smile turned snakelike. "I suggest the next transaction is reduced to half of McGrane's last sale. Essentially, that will secure at least eight fifty to sixty K deliverables." He squinted at Sawyer. "I look forward to a series of successful arrests."

"As do I," Sawyer said, shaking hands with Nyx. "As do I."

Lee, not saddled with a *Sentinel* weekend magazine meeting, took off and hit the gym. He returned wearing jeans, boots, white tee, and a SWAT nylon baseball jacket, which I assumed had been retrieved from one of the boxes in the trunk of his car.

He came around my desk and hiked a hip on the inside. "Just think, Russkie—we start going out and maybe I'll let you wear my jacket."

"Gee, I'm pretty sure I have a cuter one that says *Homicide* across the back." I slid through the final setup screen on my new BOC iPhone. "Finally."

It buzzed immediately with Mom's preset text ring, scaring me. I tapped on iChat. "Ughhhhhh."

"What?"

I flipped the phone to show him Mom's text:
Dinner. Tonight. Or else.

"I'm in." Lee threw his arm around my neck in a jocular hug and kissed the top of my head. "Thanks for the invite."

"That wasn't—"

"Of course it was."

We drove to my house. "Thanks for cleaning my car," he said, eyes focused straight ahead. "Sweet of you." He stopped at a red light and tapped his phone. Bobby Hebb's "Sunny" came on.

One of Mom's favorites. It always made me smile.

With no small amount of chagrin, I could admit I was rather pleased Lee had invited himself along. There would be far less of the clan giving me the what for with a fellow CPD member seated next to me.

The driveway of my parents' enormous house was filled with cars.

Hail, hail, the gang's all here.

Cash met us at the door. "Hey, man! Good to see you." He clapped Lee on the back, steering him toward the great room, and called over his shoulder, "Snap, heaven and hell are waiting for you in Da's study."

Yippee!

I dumped my coat in the hall closet and walked to the den. Daicen and Declan were kicked back on the couch, drinking and arguing.

"Hiya. What's up?"

"Our client," Declan said. "Pacing the floors."

"Oookay." I knew a sandbag when I walked into one. "So, what does that have to do with me?"

"Why don't you tell us?" Declan said.

"Tomorrow." Daicen stepped in. "At the office. There are a few discrepancies that you might be able to shed some light on. Say, a quarter to nine?"

About time to find out how Sawyer was progressing on Christo Keck's case.

"Certainly," I said. *Because really, why the hell not?*

Talk done, we joined the party.

"Okay," Flynn said. "We get the call last week. Sixty-eight-year-old guy killed as he's getting ready to go to work. His wife finds out he's been two-timing her, and is out in the driveway, trying to cut his brakes. Only the guy sneaks up on her, grabs her, and spins her around. She trips and falls, stabbing the bastard in the lower ventricle of the heart." He snapped his fingers. "Guy dies instantly."

"Accidental," Declan said. "She was only going to cut the brakes to scare him."

"Boo!" Cash zinged a beer cap at his head. "Premeditated."

Declan ducked, and it caromed off the lampshade.

Mom toyed with the loose cork on the bar. "Lee? I apologize in advance for the uncouth and savage behavior on display here."

"No worries, ma'am," Lee said.

Da winked at Mom. "Cash?"

He turned to look at Da and Mom hurled the cork, nailing Cash in the back of the head.

"Hey!" he said.

My phone buzzed with "If I Had a Heart" by Fever Ray.

Ragnar.

"Excuse me, I have to take this."

Lee started like he was going to follow me. Mom put her hand on his forearm. "If you thought Flynn's story was funny, you ain't heard nothing yet."

Saint July Pruitt McGrane aka Best Mom Ever.

I left the room, answering the phone, "Hang on." I took the stairs two at a time to my room. "Hello?"

"I'm on a job," Ragnar said. "What do you need?"

"I need to know where Hank is."

I could hear the muted sound of a helicopter in the background.

"Ragnar?"

He blew out a short breath. "So do I, kid."

"Now what?"

"I'll put some feelers out. Sit tight. He'll turn up when you need him most. Always does." He hung up.

I went downstairs. Everyone had moved into the dining room. I took the only open seat, next to Lee.

"Everything all right?" he asked.

"Same ol'. Just a pal with a problem."

"Sure."

Dinner was cedar-planked salmon and wild mushrooms with creamed kale and smashed goat-cheese potatoes paired with a supple and silky pinot noir.

When the plates had been cleared and the cognac came out, Lee said, "Thank you so much for having me, July and Conn. This has been fantastic."

"You're very welcome, Lee." Mom smiled demurely and gave me the look. The one that said, *Have you considered dating this man?*

The healthy slug of cognac I threw back did not go unnoticed by Da or Flynn.

"Do you want to tell them, darling? Or should I?" Lee said, with that smug smirk.

I wasn't sure what he was up to, but I knew I wasn't gonna like it. I forced my shoulders down from my ears, my smile razor-wire tight. "Oh, you go right ahead, sport."

"You're all aware that things with Bannon haven't been exactly"—he searched for the right word—"smooth sailing."

My family of trained seals all nodded their heads.

Cripes.

"Maisie and I've been spending a lot of time together, and well, frankly, after Cash left, neither one of us felt comfortable with her staying at Bannon's empty house." Lee put arm over the back of my chair.

Not all men are this annoying. Some are dead.

His hand dropped to my shoulder as he tipped his head to mine. "Maisie's helped me to realize I've had a damn good run with the Marines and SWAT. So when the Bureau of Organized Crime offered me a desk job, I took it."

All five pairs of my brothers' eyes flicked so quickly between me and Lee, we'd be having seizures for dessert.

"Congratulations, Lee," Mom said. "I'm so happy for you."

Da smiled a little too wide, his eyes a little too bright. "And what does that have to do with my daughter?"

"The last guy on the job had an ironclad lease on a three-bedroom apartment in the West Loop," Lee said. "Maisie's moving in with me."

"Platonically," I said, before they all collapsed in shock.

Ugh. Not how I'd have presented our new situation. At all.

Unable to free my shoulder from his hand, I discreetly elbowed him in the ribs. "Lee's such a kidder."

"Is he, now?" Da said.

I glanced around the table. From the looks of it, Team Lee had strong support. "It's a great place, Da. Cheap rent, and I was certain you'd approve of a Chicago police officer as my personal security guard."

He didn't.

But Cash stepped in and then the rest of them, teasing me to the nubs. Letting up to dish out the occasional heaping helping on Lee.

I laughed like I hadn't in months. We all did. It felt good to be home. And not at odds.

Well, not long ones, at least.

Chapter 41

Douglas, Corrigan, and Pruitt was an all-star law firm, the kind where the players have played for both sides successfully and now played for themselves. For the money as much as the sheer love of the win. Which was why I was in head-to-toe Prada with Mom's ridiculously heavy (and hence, cast-off) enormous Prada convertible tote.

The receptionist, whom I'd never met, came out from behind the desk and greeted me by name. "Miss McGrane, it is such a pleasure to meet you. May I get you a coffee, tea, or soft drink?"

She was so practiced, I almost felt bad saying, "No, thank you." I pointed down the hallway. "Are my brothers in?"

"Yes, miss." She crossed the lobby and led me to a posh conference room, knocking and waiting before opening the door.

I walked in.

Tie askew, Declan lounged haphazardly in a chair, one foot braced against the spit-polished cherrywood conference table.

Daicen sat at the opposite end, four neat stacks of files in front of him.

There was only one chair, waiting at the center of the table. Funny that. The table held eight comfortably.

"Hi, guys." I took the seat. "You wanted to see me?"

Declan rocked in his chair, moving the table ever so slightly with every push off.

Daicen ignored it. After a moment he looked up from his paperwork. "Yes."

Nothing else was forthcoming.

This was the game. Who would crack first. And as I didn't have much to say after my weekend with a Mexican drug lord, they were spit outta luck.

Declan cracked first. "What are you up to, Snap?"

"I'm afraid I don't know what you're referring to."

"Like hell, you don't." Declan dropped his foot and leaned his elbows on the table. "You wanna dance, that it?"

I puckered up my lips and gave him a showy air-kiss. "I love it when you try to play rough."

"Maisie," Daicen said softly. "We're in an untenable position."

"How so?"

"Ha," Declan said. "That sly feck ASA Avirette dropped the case against Keck."

"Oh?" I might not have cracked a smile, but it was written all over my face.

Daicen raised a piece of paper and read, "Pursuant to new evidence presented to The People and in the interest of Justice, The People no longer wish to pursue any further action against Christo Keck and respectfully request the charges and allegations be dismissed at this time."

"Congratulations," I said. "Always fun to defend an innocent man."

"No such thing, Snap, as well you know." Declan's chin popped up. "Keck's on his way in now to settle our exorbitant fee."

"Oooh." I moued. "That's why I'm here."

Daicen said quietly, "I beg your pardon?"

"To settle his account." I rubbed the bridge of my nose. "Christo Keck is my employee. I am in control of Stannislav Renko's holdings until he returns."

"Holy Christ, Maisie," Declan marveled. "How the hell do you go from wanting to be a cop to running an underworld chop shop?"

"Every Irish family needs a black sheep. And seeing as you guys are a bunch of straight-arrow choirboys, I had to man up and fill the gap."

Daicen surveyed me over steepled fingers. He knew there was more to this. Far more. His dark eyes flickered between our brother and me, and I knew he was deciding whether or not to keep Declan in the loop.

A soft rap on the door was followed by the receptionist showing Keck in. To Declan's consternation, he came straight up to me and took my hand in both of his. "It's good to see you."

"And you," I said as the receptionist rolled over a chair from the wall.

"Get us some glasses, please," I ordered the receptionist in a blasé tone that had my brothers looking like they'd traded in their eyes for silver dollar pancakes.

"Yes . . . certainly, Ms. McGrane."

"Mrs. Renko," Keck corrected. "She is Mrs. Renko now." The receptionist left.

Declan's head exploded. "Snap? Are you outta your goddamn mind?" He smacked his fist on the table. "You're fucking married? To Stannislav Renko?"

I lifted a stilling finger to my lips. "That's just between us, *boyos*."

Declan threw himself back against his chair, wanting to let me have it but heeding Daicen's still and silent lead.

The receptionist returned with four lowball glasses in chunky leaded crystal. I pulled a bottle of Žuta Osa, Serbian rakija, from the Prada tote, and cracked the label.

I poured four hefty glasses.

Keck and I toasted first. "To Stannis." We turned and toasted my brothers. "To a long and prosperous legal relationship."

Keck set his glass on the table and removed his wallet from his jacket pocket. "I will settle our account."

I put my hand on his checkbook. "What's the going rate, boys?"

"Twenty grand," Declan said, throwing down the gauntlet.

Keck choked.

I took two bank-wrapped stacks of hundred-dollar bills out of my bag and set them in the center of the table. "Services rendered."

I put down two more stacks of hundreds. "Our retainer."

They'd been ready for a lot of things, but cash on the barrel wasn't one of them.

"I'm sure you guys wouldn't mind giving Christo and me a few minutes?"

Declan swiped the money off the table. Daicen remained expressionless, but from the set of his shoulders as he exited the room, he would have preferred Declan left the money.

Keck put his hand on mine and squeezed. "Stannis chose his successor very well."

Time to roll the dice.

"Keeping you out of prison is one thing. Moving Stannislav's organization forward is something else entirely." I stared into his eyes and spoke very quietly. "You need to decide. Work for me as you would for him or walk away. No strings."

"I'm in, Mrs. Renko. One hundred percent." He gave me an appraising glance. "May I bring some of the men to meet you? To see you sitting behind Stannis's desk would be . . . beneficial."

"Yes, thanks. I'll expect you on Friday at seven o'clock."

Daicen waited for me in the lobby. "Maisie? My office, please."

"I'm kind of in a rush—"

Keck lingered at the door. I waved him off.

Daicen leaned in. "As your attorney, I highly advise against disregarding my advice."

Super-duper.

I followed him back to his office. He opted for the desk instead of the seating area. "That drink was atrocious." He pinched his temples.

"Yellow Wasp," I said helpfully. "It's been known to sting."

"Yes." He opened a folder and slid it across the desk. "Sign at the Post-it flags."

I signed the client retainer forms and handed them back. "Thank you."

"As your attorney, I may neither be compelled to nor voluntarily disclose matters conveyed in confidence." He checked the forms, closed the folder, and set his pen on top. "Prudent, to formalize the attorney-client privilege, but I did rather think our relationship transcended this sort of thing."

"It does. But I won't drag you down with me."

He weighed that over. "Thank you. Stannislav Renko?"

"My perversely close friend." I took a long breath. If anyone needed to know, it might as well be Daicen. "He gave me the ring. I was engaged—as his beard. Now, if Stannis's associates assumed we married before he left the country, who am I to correct them?"

"So you intend to take over his business interests, which consist primarily of criminal pursuits."

"Temporarily. I want him to have something to come home to."

"As a Serbian national, it is doubtful Mr. Renko's permanent home will ever be Chicago," Daicen said evenly. "Although, I see the penthouse apartment you listed as your home address belongs to him."

"Home is where your family is."

He flinched as if I'd struck him. "Fair enough. I assume Lee Sharpe is aware Renko owns the penthouse."

"Sort of." As badly as I wanted to confide in Daicen, it wasn't right to have him shoulder my load. "He's under the impression that Stannis rented the apartment under my name."

"And Mr. Bannon?"

I twisted Stannis's ring on my finger. My voice went husky. "I haven't heard from Hank."

"That is the nature of his business, is it not?" he asked gently.

I nodded. *I hope to God it is.*

"Sharpe presents as the type of man who will not be content to maintain a platonic relationship. Would you like me to draw up a sublease?"

A hiccup of a laugh popped from my mouth. "No, thank you."

"Would you care to discuss your relationship with Walt Sawyer or your employment at the *Sentinel*?"

Yikes. "Not right now. I'm still sorting things out."

His dark eyes clouded and morose, Daicen reached into his jacket pocket and removed a business card. He pushed it across the desk. It was blank except for a phone number.

"What's this?"

"The number of a therapist."

Whoa.

"The freedom of the confession without the judgment." My brother smiled wistfully. "You're carrying far more than your fair share, Maisie. I'm deeply concerned."

Chapter 42

Walt's text came in over my phone only moments after I'd returned to the apartment.

Sending material for your immediate perusal.

The concierge buzzed me from down below. I ran down and picked up the envelope addressed to Maisie Renko.

Perched on a bar stool, I pulled the zip tab and took out the contents. Several packets had been clipped together. The first was a detailed report and an eight-by-ten high-res picture of the blown munitions barn. Along with it were several pictures of the striker sticking out from the Navigator's armor plating. They'd been cropped in, microscope tight.

The other packet had a photo of the striker I'd recovered from the post of El Cid's Juárez stash house. As well as others, cropped in close.

I paged through memos and forensic reports until I hit the yellow-highlighted portions.

Identical chemical-residue markers. Strikers from the same lots.

"Whatcha looking at?" Lee loomed over my shoulder, scaring the tar out of me.

"I'm not quite sure. Walt sent this over." I shrugged as he scanned the report. "Confirmation, I guess, that El Eje was responsible for both bombs."

Lee's face went white. "That's not possible." He shouldered

me out of the way, flipping to the photos. "That goddamn motherfucking sonofa . . ." He walked away, raking his fingers through his hair, cursing low and fast under his breath.

"Lee?"

"It's not El Eje, Maisie," he said. "It's the fucking ATF."

"What?"

"The strikers. They're not easy to come by." He rubbed his forehead. "The numbers on the strikers are NSN numbers."

"What are those?"

"If the American government does one thing well, it's label the shit out of everything. Those are American tracking numbers on American strikers."

"So? Lee, you and I both know stuff like this gets stolen all the time. And nobody wants the gen pop to know it's missing."

His voice was low and bitter. "They weren't stolen."

"How can you possibly know that?"

He jabbed a finger at the second NSN striker number on the report. "Because I used that one when I blew the barn."

What? "How?" I stared at him like he was an alien. "Why?"

Lee slumped onto the stool next to mine. "Ditch Broady requested I partner with you. It was a natural fit, for a lot of reasons."

Including thinking I was too stupid to figure it out, which was apparently correct.

Hank's Law Number Ten: Keep your mouth shut.

I clamped my teeth down on the insides of my cheeks and waited.

Lee started, slowly at first. "The night before we left . . . The 'prescription' I picked up was two canisters of chemical explosives and the striker. I swapped out the halon in the storage hold on Grieco's jet."

I gaped at him. "You replaced fire extinguishers with chemical explosives?"

"Only the two tanks for the cabin. Without a detonator, it's not as risky as it sounds. I left the halon for the electronics alone."

Awesome. OSHA winner of the year.

"So . . . the night of the party?" I said, retracing his steps. "You weren't drunk, were you?"

"No. I retrieved the tanks." He gave a boyish smile. "I really didn't know there was a girl in the tent."

"Cute," I said, ignoring the sunny little butterfly in my chest. "And when I took off with El Cid—"

"I blew the barn at the night guard shift change."

Well, that explains the diesel smell. "You sonuvabitch. All that bullshit about 'being a partner' was just that. Bullshit."

He jabbed a finger at my face. "You never should have left the fucking estate."

"And you should've told me what the hell you were doing."

The cords stood out on his neck. "I didn't see you'd snapped the locator until I got back and saw my phone," he said, throat working. "Christ, Maisie. A minute later and you'd have been . . ."

The fury flaring inside me was snuffed as effectively as a canister of halon at the thought of The Weeping Beast.

"Okay. Okay." I sighed. "We both messed up. Now what?"

"Forward-focused. We're gonna lock this shit down." Lee got up and grabbed a couple bottles of water out of the fridge. On the way back, he picked up the television remote and turned it to the news.

"Mind if I check the weather, Bae?"

Even if I did, I wouldn't have said a thing.

He clicked the channel to the news and turned it up. "Christ, I hate that prick."

Talbott Cottle Coles and his weird, overly white, horse-sized caps leered at us from the screen.

How do these dinks continually get elected? They're not someone you'd want to eat lunch next to, much less trust with your lunch money.

Coles fairly pranced across the stage.

"Look at that asshole. Still not wearing a goddamn vest." Lee shook his head. "We're at square one. Broady's the lynchpin. What set all this in motion?"

"I got involved when Cash was shot. . . ." My voice trailed off as I stared at the TV. "No. That's not it. The assassination attempt on Coles. That's when Sawyer and I got called in to meet with Coles's ATF-DEA-BOC joint task force. Broady didn't want me."

"So, after Cash," Lee said, "you went to Nyx."

"It was a win-win for Sawyer and the BOC. Solidifies my cover for the upcoming Operation Summit, and puts the DEA in the owe column." I squinted at him. "But why the bomb at AJ's stash house?"

Lee frowned. "Trying to draw Carlos out? El Cid's his obvious favorite. Either that or the ATF was trying to force an El Eje link? It doesn't fit. Not yet."

"Next step?"

"We find out how, where, and why Ditch Broady got those strikers."

Lee and I started where the majority of crimes are solved: paperwork. Sawyer had secured the necessary warrants and systems log-ins.

"Ahh, the glamour of police work," Lee said. "Hardly need more than a credit check, tax return, and a couple of Visa statements nowadays. Two years ago, Broady was in the red. Bright red."

"Stoplight red," I said.

"Police-siren red." Lee gave my ponytail a playful tug. "And now he's black as pitch. He paid back slow, but not slow enough. There's no way he could have paid this off this fast."

Takeout of every ethnic variation covered the kitchen and bar counter. Empty beer bottles, energy drinks, coffee cups, and soda cans were overflowing from the garbage can. Stannis's kitchen was thoroughly trashed. We didn't look much better.

Lee hadn't shaved in two days.

And I was not one to talk. Unwashed hair tied up in a ponytail, and somehow my outfit had degenerated to cotton gym shorts, a green Jameson whiskey tee, Lee's dirty flannel shirt, and thick white socks crumpled at my ankles. Our two laptops and Stannis's laser printer were working triple-time.

"Here we go." Lee hit Print. "The strikers."

The ATF was actually the Bureau of Alcohol, Tobacco, Fire-arms, *and* Explosives. And as such, they have a normal, procedural need for detonators. While some old or unstable explosives like dynamite could be disposed of during slow burns, others had to be blown.

The printer beeped. Out of paper. I pushed my chair back.

"I got it." Lee got to his feet. "I know you don't like going in the study."

Pink exploded in my cheeks. "Don't be silly."

"Chill, Bae." He put his hand on the back of my neck. "You're still the most badass partner I've ever had."

The color didn't leave my cheeks, but the embarrassment morphed into happy-happy joy-joy.

Within minutes, the reloaded printer was spitting out government forms. I started highlighting. The two known detonators were from a lot of twelve, purchased from a government contractor.

The next pages that came out were the ATF records.

"We got him." Lee fanned himself with a printed, scanned-in form. "Broady's signature. He signed out the detonators."

My highlighter stopped mid–yellow streak. *Uh-oh.* "Lee? It says here, the entire lot of detonators were used. There are literally five separate signatures attesting to this, including a local fire chief and the—"

"What? Where?"

"Elmhurst, Illinois."

"Road trip," Lee said. "Race you."

Lee parked just north of the Union Pacific Railroad tracks in front of the Elmhurst PD. Clean, friendly, and well-run, it felt more like small-town store than a police station.

Lee flashed his badge, and within moments, an officer took us back to Police Chief Delbert Guptill's office. White-haired and smiling, he adjusted his tinted eyeglasses and waved us to the chairs in front of his desk. "Now, what can I do for a couple of the Bureau of Organized Crime's top cops?"

"Do you remember an ATF agent detonating a series of explosions?"

"You'll have to be a little more specific, son." Guptill hooted with laughter. "We got some o' them alphabet boys out here every other month, don'tcha know."

"Sir?" I said. "I don't follow."

"Elmhurst has a quarry pit. And our boys sure don't mind earning a little OT watching a fireworks show."

I handed across a copy of the form that Chief Guptill, two other officers, and two firemen had signed.

"Well, that's my signature, sure enough. If the ATF needs somethin' blown up, you know, they'd rather come here than take it over to the army range."

"Why?" Lee said.

"The paperwork alone, eh? You got OSHA and the EPA and God knows who has to sign off, chain of command and all that. And I imagine we're a fair bit cheaper."

I tucked my hair behind my ear. "So, they call you and say, 'Hey, I got some stuff to blow up?' A couple cops and firemen show up to watch the show, and . . . ?"

"They blow up their explosives, and we sign the paperwork and then go knock down a few pints at Manny's."

I'd seen the look on Lee's face before. On the National Geographic Channel. Right after the tiger brings the antelope down. "We got him," he said.

Once we were back in the car, Lee said, "Where's the best place to hide something?"

"Plain sight."

"And what's plainer than proof the strikers have been destroyed?"

On the way back to Chicago, he explained his theory of what Ditch Broady had done. "He files a phony report, tells them he found a bunch of stuff that needs to be disposed of. His boss signs off on the detonators. He reserves quarry time at Elmhurst. Then, sweet as pie, the Podunk police and firemen show up. Broady tells him it's pretty unstable and it'd be best if everyone kept their distance."

Lee's brown eyes sparked with the excitement of the chase. "He's an explosives expert, after all, so he makes some home-grown bomb, blows it to smithereens in front of the audience, who then sign off as witnesses." He slugged me gently in the shoulder. "No detonators, no accountability. Get it?"

"Tidy. Concise. Logical. You sure you don't want to be an attorney?"

"I'll give Walt the heads-up, check in on the ballistic report. Our next step: Find out who's bankrolling him. Yeah?" Lee flashed me a smile. "Whaddya think?"

A dirty ATF agent with God only knew who was pulling his strings?

I think I'm going to be sick.

Chapter 43

I jerked awake, panting and fumbling for my Kimber Ultra. I sat up and rested my elbows on my knees, gun dangling loosely in my hand.

I'm losing it.

Only the truly wicked or the truly good can sleep the sleep of the dead. Which is why I slept the hitching, twitching sleep of the neurotic.

The digital clock showed 6:21. Like some sort of challenge. I stared at my reflection in the mirror at the end of the bed.

Yikes.

Looks like hell wants its handbasket back.

I knew exactly how I was going to spend my day. I pulled on jeans and a tee, and in less then twenty minutes I was out the door en route to the salon.

It took Lee until 9:30 to wake up and call me.

Show-off.

"Hang on." I held up a palm to my nail tech, Luba. "You're going to love this." I hit Speaker on my iPhone and held it up so she could hear it.

The woman next to me and her tech leaned in.

"Where are you?" Lee demanded. "You just took off?"

"There's a note."

A bumping noise. "Nope." Lee paused, swallowing. "Nothing here."

"Are you drinking the milk straight from the carton?"

"Uh . . . no?"

Luba snorted and covered her mouth.

"Baby?" I said, laying it on thick for the girls. "Put the carton down. Turn it around until you see the note."

"Smart-ass."

"You're welcome." I moved to click off the speakerphone. The women waved at me not to.

"How long does a spa day last anyway?" Lee said. "And who are Sonia and Guma?"

"The cleaners. Their check is on the coffee table in the living room. Just get everything off the floor."

No response.

"Lee?"

"Yeah. I guess I'll see you when I see you."

" 'Bye-ee." I hung up.

"A deep voice," said the woman at the next station, eyeing me up and down. "How old is your son?"

"That's not my son." I started giggling.

Her nail tech opened a bottle of topcoat. "Husband?"

"Boyfriend," corrected Luba. "A husband would've called to ask *where* the milk is."

Sometimes a girl just needs a girl day. At the spa.

Hours later, I rode up the elevator, feeling better than brand new after a mani-pedi, massage, spray tan, and haircut. The outrageously charming navy Nanette Lepore jacket and power pencil skirt in a Saks shopping bag didn't hurt, either.

I went to my room and hung up my new outfit. There was something I was forgetting, but I couldn't put my finger on it. Stannis's watch read five thirty. An hour and a half until Christo Keck and company came over.

I lay down.

My eyes snapped open.

Stannis's legacy. The bone jar.

Dammit.

I made crying noises for about twenty seconds. It helped, surprisingly.

After lugging Stannis's legacy into the kitchen and setting it on the counter, I double-bagged a black trash bag and wedged a mesh strainer in the top.

I pried off the thick wooden lid.

Gently, I poured the white sand through the mesh, stopping to sift every so often. Eventually, the strainer was full of ivory pieces.

But the sand hadn't come off the bones as quickly or easily as I had hoped.

Dammit.

I Windex-ed the jar, desperately trying to think of an alternative solution, because wiping off all those human finger bones might actually make me vomit.

What would Martha Stewart do? Besides commit securities fraud?

Aha! Blow-dryer.

Set on cool, my Conair blasted clean Stannis's wind-blown sin.

Mine, too.

Coles's finger was in there, somewhere.

Cripes.

I returned the bones to the jar. The fine aquarium sand had settled into the deep grooves of the wood lid. I held it over the trash can and blew on it. The sand slid into a tiny rectangular outline. I pressed it with my fingertip.

It popped open. Inside was a minute black USB drive. Three-quarters of an inch wide by one and a half inches long.

Focus. Finish the jar.

I put the lid on and slipped the drive in my pocket. Stannis's legacy was impressively ghoulish. And the fact that it didn't weird me out that much, would hopefully instill confidence in their new leader.

The double doors were open.

An ESPN rerun of a classic football game droned on the TV over the fireplace. Lee was sound asleep on the couch. He loved Stannis's office. Partially because it made me uncomfortable, but mostly because it was sublime.

I crossed the room and returned Stannis's legacy to the desktop. Even money, it would escape Mr. *You-didn't-leave-a-note*'s notice.

I gazed down at his sharply planed cheekbones, the hard lines of his mouth. The corners tipped up naturally. Even sleeping, he was a good sport. I picked up a cashmere throw and covered him. He might as well get a solid half hour while I tried to find out what in the hell was on this drive.

The password code blinked at me. Unruffled, unbothered. The scurvy bastard.

I took a break to call The Storkling and make a request to see Violetta Veteratti personally that evening, as well as two bizarre reservations, one in the club for two or three and another in the bar for two or four or possibly six, and was assured complete satisfaction.

That's the lovely thing about power. Wielding it.

I looked at the notebook where I'd listed the passwords I'd already tried:

Mesar, Bik, Renko, Rakija, Maisie, Andeo, Vatra. Serbia, Goran, Slajic.

Nothing.

Safe to say I was more Hacky Sack than hacker.

Whatever.

The alarm on my MacBook went off. I shut down the laptop and put the drive away, loathe to disclose its existence to Lee or Sawyer until I knew what was on it.

Time to get ready.

"Lee?" I called, fastening Stannis's Patek Philippe on my wrist as I walked into the living room in my new Nanette Lepore. "Game time."

He was waiting for me in a charcoal suit and dark tie. "Wow. Setting the world on fire, are we?"

I gave a showy spin, so I could hide my ridiculous smile, then turned on the stereo and cycled through to Chopin.

At seven on the dot, Christo Keck called up from the lobby. I buzzed him and his men up.

Lee leaned against the wall. "You look good enough to eat."

"Easy, tiger. Ready to play muscle?"

"Yes, ma'am, Mrs. Renko."

"I'll be in the office."

Straight-backed, I perched on the edge of the desk chair. Not a big believer in the previous life thing, I wouldn't mind channeling Queen Elizabeth I or a lil' Margaret Thatcher.

Lee showed the men in. Christo Keck and three men, all in dark suits, entered the room. Two of the men looked to be brothers. Early thirties, six-four and six-two, hovering around 190 pounds with coal-black hair, long, pale faces, and identical aquiline noses. The third was five-ten, in his midtwenties, ropy and rugged, and somewhat adorable with deep dimples in his cheeks.

Stannis would never have let me stand or shake hands, so I didn't. "It is good to see you, Christo, out from under."

He bowed his head. "I thank you for all that you have done, Mrs. Renko."

My, so formal. "And who have we here?"

Christo introduced them from shortest to tallest. "Srecko, Miljan, and Vladimir."

"You are too young and beautiful to meet with men such as us." Srecko smiled, popping those dimples, dismissing me. "This business is for the strong."

"Awww." I propped my elbows on the desk, rested my chin on my hands, and smiled right back. "You are very sweet. But you forget your place, Srecko. Do not let it happen again."

The dimples disappeared. "*Šta?*"

I turned to Keck. "Would you be a darling and translate for Srecko?"

"I understand perfectly," Srecko said.

"Do you?" I looked up through my lashes. "Then pay me the respect due the wife of *Mesar* Renko."

"He is not here. Where is the proof that you are able to take the reins?"

I rested my fingertips on the edge of the jar. "In here is the mayor of Chicago's little finger. I took it. As I will take those of the people who disappoint me. As I was taught by my husband."

Uncertainty crossed Srecko's eyes.

"I know this to be true," Christo said.

Ignoring Srecko, I smiled at the two taller men. "Miljan, Vladimir. It is very nice to meet you."

"*Drago mi je da smo se upoznali,*" Miljan said.

I could feel Srecko's fuse burning. Lee's weight shifted to the balls of his feet. "I look forward to a strong and prosperous relationship."

Vladimir nodded. "*G-da Renko.*"

3 . . . 2 . . .

Srecko slammed his fist on the desk. "You know noth—"

Lee had a hand on the kid's belt and his Sig Sauer at the base of his skull. Eyes on Miljan and Vladimir.

Keck's face was shuttered.

"You are a killer, Srecko, of this I have no doubt. But beware the old man in a profession where most men die young." I opened the desk drawer and took out the kitchen cleaver I'd put there just in case. "I am young, too, Srecko. I do not want to make a mistake." I tapped the blade against my palm. "I do not wish to maim a young and talented man in my employ. But I will not have him mistake my wisdom for weakness."

"Take his finger," Keck said. "He's could use a reminder."

Not the answer I was hoping for, Mr. Keck, for feck's sake.

What would Stannis do?

I knew what he would do, goddammit. And it hurt me. And doing it in front of Lee was going to hurt even worse.

Hank's Law Number Thirteen: Anyone can endure expected pain.

"I have something else in mind. And this is far too clumsy." I dropped the cleaver into the desk drawer. "Does anyone have a knife?"

Miljan and Vladimir each held out a blade.

"No," Srecko said, eyes glowing with defiance. "You use mine."

Lee let go of the belt, reached around, pulled the blade from his pocket, and handed it to me.

I fecking hate this office.
I opened the knife. "His arm." Lee moved to take his arm.
"No." Srecko pulled his sleeve up and extended his left hand, palm up. "Is honor."
Just five little lines, Maisie. A monkey could do it.
I wish a monkey would.
The blood pulsed so hard at my temples, when I sliced the first stroke, I almost thought the blood was mine. Four more small slashes, and the letter *M* appeared on his forearm, just above his wrist. It was beyond awful.
Lee didn't look at me. *Thank God.*
Keck, whom I hadn't realized had left the room, returned with one of Stannis's white terry bar towels. He wrapped it around Srecko's wrist, the snow-white plush turning to crimson before my eyes.
The symmetry of the event was unspeakable. But worst of all was the sick, starry-eyed look of adoration in Srecko's eyes.
"Unfortunately, I have business this evening at The Storkling," I said. "But I would have you dine as my guests."
Lee took the three men into the kitchen, leaving Keck alone with me.
"You did very well, Mrs. Renko." He gave a sad bark of laughter. "Soon they will all want one."
Oh, hell no.
I was exhausted. I had no idea how I made it the fifteen steps to the door. He waited for me to step through. "Do you know the name of Stannislav's sister?"
"Senka." The corners of his slanted eyes crinkled. "It means 'shadow.'"
"Christo?" I said softly. "Let's get one thing perfectly clear. While I will appreciate your counsel, I will not be governed by it."
"But of course, Mrs. Renko."

Chapter 44

Lee was driving my Dodge Challenger Hellcat SRT, Amy Winehouse's "You Know I'm No Good" playing in the background.

Gee, thanks for the theme song suggestion.

"Where were they?" Lee said.

"Who?"

"The bones, Maisie. Where the fuck were you keeping the bones?"

"Under the bed," I said and caught myself just before I went into the whole aquarium-sand extravaganza.

"Jesus Christ. You're supposed to be a cop. Do you have any goddamn idea how much forensic evidence is in there?"

I tipped my head from side to side. "Definitely a lot, but it's not all from the U.S., so . . ."

"Do you even fucking hear yourself?"

"Yeah, Lee, I'm pretty much losing it right now, and I need to pull it together before we beard the lion in its den."

Lee tightened his hands on the steering wheel, seething with the need for speed, but not wanting to shake Keck and the boys behind us.

I couldn't bear it for another minute. "Turn off that stupid song and say what you need to say."

He snapped off the music. "You have to turn the bones in."

"What?" I shook my head. *Seriously?* "Okay, no. Not gonna happen."

We pulled up to the club and went inside.

The Storkling was, as always, sexy, swanky, and suave all rolled into one. I got my new crew situated in the bar; the dining room was members only.

Lee, naturally, wasn't drinking nor sitting with us.

A little FIFA talk and a couple rounds of rakija with dire toasts like, "Do evil and look for like," and "One man's death is another man's breath," and they were sitting in the palm of my hand.

Lee came over and pressed my arm. "Mrs. Renko? Your appointment."

"Have fun," I said, rising. "Just not too much." The men nodded, smiling. "Except you." I pointed at Srecko. "No fun at all for you." Which left them all laughing.

Taking my arm, Lee led me through the sea of golden draperies. Two shots in and I still flinched at the fabric's every undulation. "With great power comes great responsibility," he said.

"I'm more of a Captain America girl myself."

The red-haired siren Bobby Blaze kept it sultry with "Angel Eyes." The maître d' led us to a tiny private table in a dark corner.

"This is some place," Lee said, scanning the room.

"Can we please just cut to the chase?"

He flashed me a crooked smile. "You said you didn't want to talk about the bones."

"I don't!" I said, a little too loudly. Lee put his hand on mine, and I blew out a breath. "Just say what you want to say about the kid and get it over with."

"Srecko's going to be a handful. Hair-trigger temper. His looks have spoiled him. And now he's mooning over you like a lovesick calf."

"That's not what I meant."

"I'm not following."

"Geez," I hissed. "Isn't this where you climb down my throat about cutting Srecko?"

"The way you handled him?" He cupped my cheek in his hand. "Maisie." He ran his thumb across my lower lip. "I'd follow you into hell after that."

Wow.

"Don't we look cozy?" Jimmy the Wolf's voice was as hard and unforgiving as his eyes. "I'm gonna bring Vi over." He disappeared and resurfaced with the mob princess on his arm. Tonight she was wearing a beige Hervé Léger bandage dress, an armful of gold bangles, gold stilettos, and an ankle bracelet with dangling gold charms.

Lee and I stood up to meet her.

"Vi, you look amazing," I said as we exchanged air-kisses.

"And this is?"

"Lee Sharpe. I work for Mrs. Renko." He took her proffered fingers in his. "A pleasure to meet you, Ms. Veratti."

She took her time, getting her money's worth before removing her hand. "I was surprised by your . . . reservation."

"We'll be ready to move forward by the end of the month."

"That's news worth celebrating." A canary-eating smile creased her catlike face. "You work fast, kid. Are those your boys in the bar?"

"Some of them."

"Make sure they're happy, Wolf."

With a nod he left us.

"Thank you," I said.

"You need anything, anything at all, it'll be taken care of." With a last appraising look over her shoulder at Lee, she sauntered away.

The white-coated waiter was well aware of Veratti's presence and what that meant. I ordered two champagne cocktails.

"Maisie," Lee said. "Don't."

"C'mon. Only one, because it's just like what the real Stork Club used to make—Krug champagne and Martell Cordon Bleu cognac."

He shrugged. "Whatever you say, boss."

The cocktails arrived in Tom Collins glasses with ice and lemon peels.

I picked up my glass.

"Uh-uh." Lee wagged a finger at me. "Those were the worst toasts I've ever heard in my life. I got this." He raised his glass. "Here's to having your back . . . And your front."

"And that's better?" I laughed.

He stared at me over the rim of his glass. "I think so."

I wasn't sure if it was the champagne, the music, or the fact that I'd just narrowly escaped amputating another finger, but I felt as light and iridescent as a dragonfly on an updraft.

"Dance with me."

I bit my lip and glanced away, trying to think of a clever way to say I was a terrible dancer. Coles leered at me from across the room. My hand flew to my neck.

Hank's Law Number Twenty-Two: When among wolves, you must act the wolf.

"Bae?"

"Sorry?" I pressed the center of my forehead.

Screw it. Man up and face that sonuvabitch.

Coles rolled a stub cigar between his fingers, lip curling in contempt. He put it in his mouth and sucked.

Immobilized, I stared, transfixed by the cherry-red ember of his cigar.

"Maisie." Lee snapped his fingers. "Hey?"

My cheeks trembled. I untucked my hair from behind my ear, finger-combing it over the scar. "If you wouldn't mind keeping an eye on Coles—I really, really need some air."

His eyes went flat. "No sweat."

I snuck out past the bar, where my new crew were having a grand time. I stepped out into the Chicago night, the cold air chilling me from the lungs out.

"Yo', bluebird. Where you been?"

Poppa Dozen, clad in his ridiculous chauffeur costume, leaned against Coles's limo, Camel in the corner of his mouth. "You running with that cop, ain'tcha? Now, I ain't one to tell you your business, but you're fuckin' stupid."

"Aig!" I stamped my feet in a little dance of pure irritation. "Dozen. For the last time. That's the bodyguard Stannis hired for me. A former Marine, he just can't seem to shake that military edge, but he's pretty handy. Almost killed a guy tonight."

"Then you best keep him around, bluebird. All kinds of crazy mutherfuckers cattin' off 'round here nowadays."

"Tell me about it." I popped my chin. "So how goes it with Coles?"

"I been tellin' him he's puttin' too many eggs in his south o' the border basket. But will that sumbitch listen? Pfft." He scratched the underside of his chin.

"And Dafinest?"

"Still jonesin' for some of them FN 5.7 MK2 pistols." Dozen shook his head. "Like a short bus rider cryin' and caterwaulin' for a goddamn Wii when every other kid has an Xbox."

"I don't have a line on the 5.7s. But I might on some more Sugar Skull."

He shifted his weight back and forth between his feet. "Didn't Dafinest tell you to see him direct?"

"Mr. Peanut can want what he wants, but you're with me or I'm out."

"How much?"

"Half of last run. Same quality. Every other week. Eight weeks guaranteed."

Dozen took a tiny Ziploc bag from inside his jacket and held it between two of his fingers. Four white rectangular tablets with bars stamped on them. "Just in case."

In case what?

I took the bag, building trust, and took a closer look. Xanax.

"Give one o' them to Soldier Boy if he get a lil' too intense. Chill him the hell out."

Which was incredibly sweet in a sick and twisted way. "Thanks, Dozen. I better get back."

"Peace out, bluebird."

Chapter 45

My phone rang at 7:00 a.m. The ring was the generic Unknown Caller aka Autodialer-trying-to-sell-me-something. I thought about ignoring it.

Too late. Already up. "Hello?"

A deep male voice said, "Is this Maisie?"

"Yes." I shot up in bed. "Who am I speaking with?"

"Jimmy the Wolf."

Ughhhh. I flopped back down again. "Hey, guy. What's up?"

"Miz Veteratti requests the pleasure of your presence at The Storkling in an hour. You got a problem with that?"

"Nope. I'll be there."

"See you then." He disconnected.

I ran a brush through my hair while using a Rembrandt-loaded Sonicare. Skintight black jeans, knee-high boots, snug black Ranger Up tee, makeup, and a spritz of Oribe's Silver Pearl perfume and I was off to the races.

I grabbed the motorcycle jacket off the hanger in the hall closet and hit the elevator.

Jimmy the Wolf and Vi were waiting for me in her office.

"You're on time," she said. "I like that. Let's go."

I followed the Wolf and Vi to a door with a keypad for a handle. She typed in a code and the door swung open. The security room.

A bank of LCD screens made up the entire wall. Violetta leaned against the main control console and crossed her legs, while the Wolf took a seat at the computer. "Do we have a problem?" she asked.

I shook my head. "I don't think so."

"Roll tape," she said to the Wolf, who complied.

I recognized myself. From behind. Leaving the dining room.

Saliva ran down the back of my throat as I watched Coles step between the golden draperies, grab my ponytail, and jam his lit cigar against my neck.

"Jaysus," I said, turning away but not before I caught an eyeful of myself stumbling blindly through the endless swaths of fabric.

"See? Now that . . . That's what Wolf and I call a problem," Vi said. "You tell Wolf not to worry about it. A classy move, you getting your own back. Recognizing my club isn't to blame, yeah?"

I nodded, not sure where this was going.

"Unlike Eddie, I prefer to reinvest the capital in the club rather than up my nose. We've revamped security at The Storkling. Every angle full-color captured, every conversation miked." Her arched brows shot even higher. "Intel is currency in the Information Age. Play the next clip, Wolf."

Last night's time and date stamp ran in the upper left corner of the screen. A myriad of camera angles showed the men's room.

Eeeew.

The era of privacy forever past.

Talbott Cottle Coles was at the sink, washing his hands, checking his hair. His man inside, on the hinge side of the door.

Lee walked in, subtly pulling the door closed behind him.

He took one step past the mayor's bodyguard, then spun, striking the man with a downward chop to the base of his neck. The guard's head came forward. Lee hit him again, crushing his temples between the heel of his left hand and his right fist.

The bodyguard hit the floor like a load of pig iron.

"Your boy has fast hands. Nice soft tissue work, nothing permanent, no marks." Jimmy the Wolf shot me a sideways look of approval.

On-screen, Coles dove into the stall, locking the door.

Lee rifled through the downed bodyguard's clothes, pulling the guy's gun from the shoulder holster and the backup piece at his ankle. In less than thirty seconds he'd unloaded the guns, removed the slides, tossed the pieces in the trash and the magazines out the small open bathroom window.

"Hit the sound, Wolf," Vi said.

He tapped the keyboard.

On-screen, Lee kicked open the stall door. Wedged into the corner between the wall and the toilet tank, Coles raised a small pistol. "Stay back."

Faster than an old magician, Lee jerked the pistol out of Coles's hand and dropped it into the toilet. He stepped aside, hand extended, for the mayor to leave the stall.

"What do you want from me?"

Lee said nothing, just waited.

Coles left the stall, his gait short and rigid. His head darted, looking for escape. "What do you want?"

"You put your cigar out on my girl's neck."

Blood drained from Coles's face. "That was an accident, I—"

"Now, I could get her plastic surgery. . . ."

"I know some of the best in the business." Coles leapt on the opening. "I'll take care of it."

Lee shook his head. "But surgery doesn't make up for me looking at that mess you made of her throat." He put his hands on his hips, suit coat sliding open, flashing his Sig Sauer. "Listening to her cry."

Coles glanced at his bodyguard, unconscious on the floor.

Lee took a pack of Marlboro Reds from his pocket and tossed them on the counter. "Have one."

With surprisingly steady hands, Coles picked up the pack and put a cigarette in his mouth. Lee lit a match. Coles leaned in and sucked in a lungful of nicotine. He blew it out in a long, thin plume. "How does ten thousand sound for your inconvenience?"

"Men don't settle with money."

"Twenty. Twenty thousand. Cash."

Lee shook his head.

"How much?" Coles demanded.

"Man up." Lee looked at the cigarette. "Get the end nice and red."

No escape.

Nostrils flaring, Coles faced the mirror and took two heavy drags. The decision to brazen it out set in his face.

Lip curled, he pressed the glowing end to his throat for a two count. Breath whistling between his teeth. "Ergh!" He jerked it away and flicked the cigarette into the sink.

He glared down his nose at Lee. "It's over."

Lee squinted at the blistering pink burn on Coles's neck. "Looks a lot smaller than my girl's." He rubbed the back of his jaw. "Two more oughta even the score."

"Fuck." Coles gagged and swallowed. "Thirty thousand."

Hank's Law Number Nineteen: Show no mercy. Ask for none.

Lee took another Marlboro from the pack and lit it. He took a deep drag, then another and handed it to Coles.

I could taste the stink of Coles's burning flesh. "Christ." I clapped my hand over my eyes, listening as Coles did it twice more, sweating and shaking and swearing.

Jaysus.

We watched Lee leave the bathroom.

Jimmy the Wolf hit Pause and smiled at me. "Wanna watch Coles fish his gun out of the toilet?" he asked, in all seriousness.

"No." I wrinkled my nose. "That was plenty, thank you."

"I don't like Coles," Vi said. "But I do like everything he brings with him."

"I'm sorry. Sharpe did that without my knowledge or permission."

"I figured as much." She sifted her scarlet talons through Jimmy the Wolf's dark hair. "That's the trouble with the best ones. They have difficulty understanding where the lines are."

The Wolf grunted.

She smacked him in the shoulder. "Print her a DVD." He started the procedure. Vi bared her teeth. "Us working girls gotta stick together."

I raised a truth-to-power fist in the air, not feeling it. At all. "You know it."

But the only thing I knew for sure was that if she found out I was a cop, she'd scoop my heart out with a rusty demitasse spoon.

The Wolf scrawled a date and time on the disc and handed it to me.

At least he didn't put his number across the bottom.

I walked the streets for a solid hour trying to get my head straight.

It didn't help.

My heart beat like a drumroll on a snare. I felt numb and charmed at the same time. For everything—the flirting, the kisses, hell, the bald-faced admission that Lee wanted me, wanted to be with me.

None of it touched me like what I'd just seen him do.

Serious, stepping-over-the-line kind of retribution.

For me.

Hank's stock-in-trade. Only Lee's didn't have the same sort of heady buzz.

Because Lee wasn't that kind of man. Was he?

My stomach whined like a college kid for a safe space. Eleven thirty-two. *Holy cat. Lunchtime.*

I circled back to the Hellcat and cruised by Publican Quality Meats to pick up a couple *Big E*s—wagyu brisket, horseradish cheddar, smoked onions, mustard, and green leaf lettuce on rye—before heading home.

Lee was hunkered down in Stannis's office pounding the phones, tracing every move Ditch Broady had made in the last three years. I held up the bags. "Lunch."

Tucking the phone under his chin, he held up both hands. Ten minutes.

Lee inhaled his sandwich, chips, and two bottles of water before I'd made it through a quarter of mine. "Now, that was fucking awesome." He stood up and cracked his neck. "God, you 'get' me, Maisie."

You're a man. I could pretty much feed you kibble from a Frisbee and you'd be okay with it.

"You all right? You don't look so good," he said.

My sandwich had somehow morphed from insanely delicious to completely unappetizing. "I'm . . . uh, great."

He smoothed my hair back and pressed his lips to my forehead. "Feel a little warm to me. Why don't you take a nap?"

"Because I'm fine?"

"I wasn't asking. I can't have you run outta gas on me this week." He jerked his head toward the bedroom. "Beat it."

Why argue what you can't win?

I slunk off to my room and lay down on the bed, the cool Matouk pillowcase beneath my cheek. I traced my finger along the double-pleated edging, thinking of Stannis. It was more relaxing to focus on the best friend who'd been ready to put a bullet in my brain, than on Hank and Lee or anything I'd done over the past week.

Somehow I actually slept for a couple of hours. When I awoke, I slipped out of my bedroom, Lee's muffled voice echoing through the silent penthouse. He'd left the door to the office open.

I got out the laptop, inserted the tiny drive from the bone jar, and typed "*SENKA*" into the flashing password bar.

It opened.

The 256G drive was almost full.

Neat-o. Just to make it easy, everything was in Serbian—Cyrillic alphabet, naturally. Ugh.

Traversing through the folders, eventually I got a video to open. Loud music, naked women, gambling, drugs, and far too many close-ups of male organs sproinging out all over the place. "Whoa."

Cripes.

And I thought orgies and key parties were dead.

I tried to scroll through the video, but the drive wasn't having it. It was hard identifying people through my fingers.

My eyes need a shower. With bleach.

"Why, Maisie," Lee said in my ear, scaring me out of my chair. "I had no idea you were so . . . voyeuristic."

My cheeks flamed. "Part of Stannis's legacy. How about you watch, and I'll run to the store for some ice cream?"

"You're terrific, you know that?" Lee chuckled. "You save—what, forty people from a kill house and earn Special Ops status in a Mexican drug cartel, but you get squeamish in front of a lil' homemade porn?"

"Not making it any better," I said through gritted teeth.

"I bet you'd rather die than let someone see you pee." He stopped short. "Oh, hell. That's why you lost the locator, isn't it?" He howled with laughter.

"Gee," I said. "Thanks ever so much for reveling in my humiliation."

"Aww, Bae. Don't go away mad. But go. Now. I'm hungry."

"Just for that, you're getting Rum Raisin."

I returned with milk, bread, eggs, and pints of Häagen-Dazs—Vanilla Swiss Almond, Rocky Road, Mint Chip, and one Rum Raisin just to rattle his cage.

Lee had moved his laptop and the printer out of the office. Sweet of him, but he was still getting the Rum Raisin.

He took a bite. "Ughhh!" His face screwed up like a little kid's. "Yuck. Dried fruit in ice cream? It's the curse of the fruitcake. Almost as bad as Raisinets." He stabbed his spoon for a bite of mine, but I was too quick for him. "C'mon, please?"

"No." I mock-pouted. "I'm sorry you don't care for your treat." I took the Rum Raisin from his hand and threw it out.

"Wait! It's not that bad. I can spit out the raisins. . . ."

I opened the freezer and held up the two reserve tubs. After a happy and inordinately long waffle, he settled on Mint Chip and dragged a chair close. He patted the seat. "Check it. Screenshots we need to show to Walt ASAP."

I sat down. There were a few of Stannis and Coles. But the ones Walt would want to see were of Coles with his favorite Mexican diplomat, Cesar Garza. And ATF special agent Ditch Broady.

"Like that?" Lee laid out several more prints. "Here he is again. El Eje kingpin Álvaro Garza's son, Cesar. And again."

A familiar piranha-mouthed face peeped out among the debauchery. "Holy cat! Is that . . . *Raúl?*"

"Sergeant Reptile Torturer at your service." Lee turned in his chair, knee bumping mine. "There's something we're missing."

I stepped through what we had. "El Eje wants Tampico and the eradication of the Grieco cartel. The strikers were supplied to El Eje via the ATF. The two bombs?"

"The cooler bomb was either a test and/or an obvious link to the bullet factory." Lee smacked his fist on the table. "Either way, I was Broady's bitch. Goddammit."

"Let's keep going," I said. "The drug raids. They've all been confidential informant tips. And only for Grieco stash houses. That's had to hurt."

"So, how do the guns fit?"

"I think they fit exactly the way El Cid said they did. El Eje is trying to set them up. The ballistic reports should back us up. We need to talk to Sawyer. ASAP."

"We're meeting with him tomorrow. It'll keep."

I slipped my phone into my pocket and gathered the ice cream detritus. My half-eaten pint went into the freezer, while his empty one hit the trash.

"Maisie . . ." he warned. "Don't."

I rinsed the spoons and put them in the dishwasher. "Don't what?"

"Call."

"Who?"

Lee dug his wallet out of his back pocket, fished out a hundred-dollar bill, and smacked it on the table. "A hundred bucks says you were slinking off to call El Cid."

"Oh . . . shut up. I'm going back to bed." I went and got into bed, waiting forever for Lee to walk past my room before grabbing my phone and dialing.

"Señora Renko," El Cid said. "Carlos and I were just talking about you."

"All good, I hope." But my flirting fell flat. El Cid wasn't someone I knew anymore. "Would you mind if I spoke with Carlos directly?"

"Why?"

"Please." The hitch in my voice must have swayed him, because Carlos came on the line.

"Hello?"

"Carlos, I've come across some information that could be . . . misconstrued. I'm concerned that El Cid's objectivity may not be as it was."

"Yes. An astute observation. What is it?"

"Photos of Raúl. With Mayor Coles. An ATF agent. And Cesar Garza."

"Situation?"

"Drug and sex parties mostly." I hesitated, not sure whether I was up for signing Raúl's death warrant. Although I was becoming more certain by the second that he was behind our hijack and kidnap. "Two parties prior to the assassination attempt. One post."

"And you have seen these pictures with your own eyes?"

"Yessir. It will be difficult for me to get copies, but not impossible."

"I would appreciate that."

"I'll do my best."

"Thank you." He disconnected.

I switched off the light and tiptoed into the kitchen. Lee had cleaned up.

On the table lay ten full-color prints of Raúl *in flagrante delicto,* paper-clipped with a Post-it:

You owe me $100.

Chapter 46

The following day at the *Chicago Sentinel,* we went to present our evidence to Sawyer. But he had questions he wanted answered first.

"Gunther Nyx seems quite bullish on you entering the narcotics market." Sawyer handed us each a folder. "Feeling the pressure from the U.S. Department of Justice, no doubt."

"You think?" Lee paged through the report. "Chicago's the only U.S. city to rank in the top five for all four major drug categories. First for heroin, second for marijuana and cocaine, and fifth for methamphetamine." He looked at me. "Nyx isn't going to let her go without a fight."

Sawyer cocked his vulpine visage. "Any thoughts on this last assignment, Maisie?"

I didn't have enough left to play it cool. "To be honest, sir, I feel pretty damn lucky to be alive. My connections with Grieco and El Cid are as tight as they can be with known cocaine abusers, but they won't be the ones doing the deals." My hands twisted in my lap. "And I don't want to be, either."

"Yes." Sawyer tapped a pen against his lip.

"However, I have no problem continuing Nyx's heroin distribution with Dafinest Johnson, aka Mr. Peanut, as long as Poppa Dozen is operating as go-between."

"Interesting, wouldn't you agree, Lee?"

Lee shrugged.

"The man she feels safest dealing narcotics with is the same gentleman felon who blew the back of Juan Echeverría's head off with a Taurus 85 revolver to 'save' our illustrious mayor."

"Wait," I said. "Lee, remember the other day? You were standing in the kitchen and Coles was on TV. What did you say?"

"Uh . . ." His face screwed up in thought. "He's such a self-righteous fuck he won't wear a vest after a goddamn assassination attempt?"

"That's it." I hammered my finger on the tabletop. "That's the answer, right there."

"What?"

"Where it started." I grabbed my laptop from my messenger bag, booted it up, and typed *Coles Assassination Attempt* into the YouTube search bar. I played the video, then played it again.

"Watch. There!" I pointed at the screen. "Coles raises his arms just before the gunman raises his gun. He knew. He knew it was coming."

"Explains why his private security team demanded full control," Lee said. "And why he hasn't worn a vest prior or since."

"Easily illustrated, difficult to prove," Sawyer said. "Flip to the ballistics report, please."

The FN Herstal 5.7MK2 used in the assassination attempt matched the 5.7 lot and rounds that Carlos Grieco had presented to me. It also had the name of the patron saint of drug dealers, Jesús Malverde engraved inside the back strap.

The 5.7 used to shoot Cash, as well as other pistols recovered at other sites, had neither the back strap engraving nor were from the same stolen shipment.

Just as damning were the ballistic markers. The Grieco cartel's hand-loaded cartridges were a match to the assassination attempt, but the other shootings had used mass-produced 5.7 armor-piercing rounds acquired from Honduras.

"Excellent work." A small, self-satisfied smile tipped Sawyer's lips. "Broady's in the vise. Theft and sale of explosive components to the El Eje cartel. Multiple federal offenses, falsified police reports, breaking ATF department policy."

That didn't sound little.

"He'll never go to trial. Even with the *Fast and Furious* white-

wash in the rearview mirror, it's virtually impossible for the
ATF to survive the scandal of a special agent selling classified
striker detonators for criminal enterprises abroad that could be
used in Mexico, the United States, or God knows where." Walt
gave a cavalier flip of his wrist. "We'll sweat him for Coles."

He stood up. "Time for the big guns. A third party not connected to the city of Chicago. A special federal prosecutor. Go
get some lunch and be back here in two hours."

Special Prosecutor Jon Gabriel was five-foot-nine, 165
pounds, with sandy brown hair, piercing eyes, and a short, tidy
beard. He sat down, pulled out a legal pad and pen, and said,
"Tell me everything you just told Walt."

When we'd finished, he turned to Walt. "I'll take it from
here. Baby steps and bread crumbs. I don't want these two anywhere near me until the trial."

Guess that's our cue. Lee and I looked at each other and got
up. As we hit the door, we heard Gabriel say, "Broady may be a
dirty cop, but he still knows how this goes down. And he's an
independent witness."

"You're going to start a probe?" Lee asked.

"Of course. Gonna see what we can shake free from the ba-
nana tree."

Two days later, Lee and I sat at a Formica table in a tiny room
ready to watch Special Prosecutor Gabriel sweat ATF Special
Agent Ditch Broady via video feed.

Lee pulled a small Styrofoam cooler from beneath his chair.
Inside it, an icy six-pack of Budweiser. He popped one and handed
it to me.

"Jaysus, you're a prince of a guy," I said.

"Don't you forget it."

On-screen, Walt Sawyer and Special Prosecutor Jon Gabriel
sat at a conference table talking quietly. Gabriel's massive goon,
aka "Investigator Snyder," waited inside the door, while a camera-
man and stenographer had set up in the corner.

Ditch Broady entered the room knowing something was afoot.

"How 'do, Walt?" He was a pretty cool customer, until he took in, per Gabriel's request, the long wall covered in the El Eje cartel's organizational chart and photos of their horrific handiwork.

Gabriel nodded at Investigator Snyder, who stepped forward and cuffed Broady behind his back with unexpected speed.

"Easy now, no need to—" Broady fell silent as the investigator patted him down, taking his piece and backup.

"Special Agent Broady, I'm Special Prosecutor Jon Gabriel with the Federal District Court. Take a seat, please."

He did. Uncomfortably.

"You have two options. One, immediately lawyer up, forfeit pension, and proceed directly to prison." Gabriel opened a folder and laid out the physical evidence of Broady's signature on the striker detonator requisitions, the Elmhurst destruction forms, and the capper—photos of the strikers from the cabin in Juárez and Carlos's Lincoln Navigator.

Ditch Broady turned to stone.

"Or two," Gabriel said, "you give a full confession and signed affidavit, and we put you in Witness Protection. But to do that, you roll on someone influential." Blank-faced, the special prosecutor folded his hands and waited.

Broady sighed. "Door number two."

"Read him his rights," Gabriel said.

Investigator Snyder did, carefully enunciating every word. He unlocked one cuff, so Broady could move his arms forward, and relatched the cuff. Gabriel pushed a Miranda form and pen in front of Broady, who signed awkwardly, steel handcuffs clinking.

"Well?" Gabriel said.

Broady pretended to think. "I can give you Cesar Garza."

The special prosecutor's mouth set in a firm line. "Strike one."

"I don't know," Broady hedged, eyes darting around the room. "Raúl Grieco."

"Strike two," Gabriel said.

Unmoved by Broady's distress, Sawyer leaned a casual arm

over the back of his chair. "Coles, Ditch. We want Talbott Cottle Coles. I suggest you start talking."

And Broady did.

Lee turned the monitor down. "What's that all over your face?"

I touched my cheeks. "What?"

"That chipmunk grin."

I shook my head, bashful. "It's stupid."

"C'mon."

"I finally feel like a cop. For, like, the first time."

"You're killing me." Lee groaned and ran a hand over his eyes. "Slowly."

I pointed at the screen.

Broady finally picked up a pen and signed the confession and affidavit. Investigator Snyder pulled him to his feet and spun him toward the door before Broady's signature had dried.

"Hey!" Broady said. "What gives? We cut a deal."

"That's right," said the special prosecutor. "We did. You no longer have any ties to the state of Illinois. You belong to the U.S. Department of Justice. And as such, we need you accessible at all times while we build our case." Gabriel turned to Investigator Snyder. "Get him out of here."

We watched as Investigator Snyder led Broady off to parts unknown forever. Sitting there, we finished our beers, laughing at the sheer inanity and desperation of Broady and the half-assed state of the world.

A rap sounded on the door.

Special Prosecutor Gabriel stepped inside, closing the door behind him. He glanced at the video feed, then to us. "Satisfied?"

We nodded, instantly solemn.

"Then get the hell out of here. You two have plenty of paperwork to fill out." He shut the door smartly behind him.

"Ready, State's Witness Number Seventeen-ten?" I asked.

"Roger that, State's Witness Number Twenty-one-twenty-four," Lee answered.

We rode the cavernous freight elevator down to the loading dock, then hiked the block and a half to his Mustang. Lee popped the doors and we got in, eyes locking as we slammed our seat belts home at the same time.

"Gee . . . Is that . . . all there is?" I said.

"We got a solid week of connect-the-dots paperwork, but . . . yeah." He rubbed the back of his jaw. "Isn't it enough?"

"Sure." I tried to play it straight, but my giggle-cough ruined the effect. "It's plenty."

We laughed all the way back to Stannis's penthouse.

Chapter 47

Lee knocked on the bedroom door and opened it without waiting for an answer. "Hockey game tonight, Bae, and I'm feeling hat-tricky." He leaned against the jamb. "Come watch me. I'll buy you all the beer you can drink."

"Aww. And I was feeling so thirsty." I zipped up the garment bag over my Monday work outfit. "Can't. Busy."

"Doing what?" Lee folded his arms across his chest, looking like a recipe for disaster. One I would not be cooking tonight. "Where are you going?"

"Home, Lee. I'm going home to Hank's."

"Why?"

How exactly do I explain that living with you like this is as easy as rubbing alcohol on a rug burn? That your casual hands on me all the time are making it hard for me to see straight?

"I need a weekend off." I jammed my underwear into the gym bag. "And so do you. Have a party. Go crazy. I'll help you clean up when I get back."

"You haven't heard from the guy in two months."

Three, but who's counting?

Lee's voice went flinty. "Is Bannon back?"

"No."

"So you're going there to do, what? Sit in the dark, eat ice cream, and bawl your head off?"

He looked brawny and angry and . . . sad.

I didn't trust him, didn't trust myself.

"Lee . . ." I said, careful to keep the bed between us. "I'm wildly attracted to you. You're funny and handsome and smart and sexy. But . . ." I had to force the words out. "I'm in love with Hank."

A cold light glinted in Lee's eyes. "Sure you are."

"Even if I wasn't, which I am, I respect him too much to sleep with someone else before our relationship is over."

"Hard to break up when he's not around."

"Please, don't . . ."

Frowning, Lee rubbed the back of his neck and leaned against the doorjamb. "You really are a good girl," he said softly.

"Yeah." My vocal cords knotted together. "I am."

He pushed off the jamb and came toward me, not stopping until our chests were touching. "I'm a good guy."

My lips curled in a sad smile. "Lee—"

He put his mouth to my ear. His breath made me shiver. "Right now you need to think that Bannon's not a bad guy. But he is. And that's okay. You're a smart girl. You'll figure it out."

Lee's mouth, hot and soft, edged with the faint rasp of scruff, slid down my jaw from my ear to my chin.

My lips parted.

His mouth hovered above mine. "Because I've got all the time in the world." He flicked his tongue across my upper lip, then turned and went down the hall without a second look.

I licked my lip.

Cinnamon.

I drove home to Hank's with a headache and a heartache. Just because Lee was coming in hard and fast and uninvited, hurting him was never something I signed on for.

Ragnar's janky blue pickup truck waited in Hank's driveway. I turned in, heart dancing.

For once I wasn't in trouble.

While it was possible Hank had heard from Vi that I was trying to get Stannis's band back together, it was far more likely he'd ticked somebody off. And he wanted me safe.

He's coming home.

I pulled the Hellcat into the garage stall, took my Kimber out of the holster, and slipped it into my purse. Grinning bigger than I knew my mouth could go, I swiped on a coat of lip gloss. I got out of the car and trotted to the front of the house.

Ragnar swung open the door of the pickup and stepped out. His beefy, six-foot-seven frame and shaggy, shoulder-length hair was pure Viking.

"Hiya, Ragnar!" I threw him a chipper salute.

He raised a palm, face blank. Not happy, not sad. I somehow had the strange sensation he was furious. It seemed to superheat the air between us.

I couldn't think of anything that would make him angry, except for having to babysit me again. Which absurdly pleased me to no end.

My little black heart skipped a beat.

Hank.

Ragnar stared at me for a long while, his stormy blue eyes boring into mine. He gave a slight bob of his head, and his hair fell in front of one side of his face. From behind his back, he brought out a thick, brown expanding legal folder with a red cloth tie.

We stood there, locked in a silent, motionless moment. My hands hung at my sides, Ragnar's arm extended, statue-still.

It's just a legal file. Chill.

I stepped forward and took the folder. "Thank you, Randolph." My use of his Christian name surprised us both.

He pressed a massive hand against my cheek, then turned and walked stiffly to his truck. He got in and the truck growled to life. I watched him drive away, irrationally expecting him to turn around and ask to come in for a beer.

The folder was smooth and heavy in my hands. Awash with the feeling that I didn't want to bring whatever was inside into the house, I undid the tie and slipped my hand inside. A card read:

M—

If

H

The corner of my mouth quirked up. *Rudyard Kipling.* Always Kipling. Because Hank believed what moved you should be remembered.

And I remembered.

Light-headed and fuzzy from missing him, my knees went soft. I dropped down onto the slate landing. Setting the card aside, I reached into the folder and pulled out a binder-clipped stack of credit cards.

On top of the stack was an Illinois driver's license with my picture, Hank's address, and the name *Maisie Bannon.*

The six debit/credit cards each bore the foil name stamp: *Maisie Bannon.*

I slid out the thick sheaf of papers. The cover sheet was a notarized legal document. Breath coming in short pants, I skimmed the text until I read:

> . . . *failure to make contact within any specified continuous 90-day period, Hank Kimball Bannon's estate reverts in its entirety to his wife, Maisie Bannon . . .*

I turned the page.

Hank Kimball Bannon and Maisie Moira McGrane's marriage license.

Backdated to the first night we spent together.

Blood pulsed in my ears. I rifled through the stack of documents. The deed to the house, titles to the cars, bank accounts, financials. Everything in my name.

Doesn't mean a thing.

I shook my head hard and returned the entire contents to the file. Smoothly, neatly tying up the cloth tapes.

Nope.

Not Hank.

I got up and turned to go inside. The cardboard file flew from my nerveless fingers and skittered across the sidewalk.

I stood staring at it.

Ought to pick that up.

But I couldn't seem to make myself.

I'd know if something had happened to Hank.

If.

If.

I covered my eyes. And heard him. Impossibly.

His deep bass reverberating in my chest, his voice inside my head. *"If you can fill the unforgiving minute. With sixty seconds' worth of distance run—"*

I felt so full of him I was sure my heart would burst.

I dropped my hands.

And ran.

Connect with Us

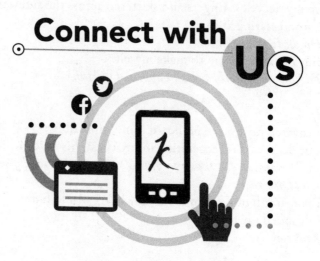

Visit us online at
KensingtonBooks.com
to read more from your favorite authors, see books
by series, view reading group guides, and more.

for sneak peeks, chances to win books and prize packs,
and to share your thoughts with other readers.

facebook.com/kensingtonpublishing
twitter.com/kensingtonbooks

Tell us what you think!

To share your thoughts, submit a review,
or sign up for our eNewsletters, please visit:
KensingtonBooks.com/TellUs.